Broken Rose

Review

Stefan Vučak offers a strong dramatic sense in this novel with its bold and emotive dialogue, yet there's a subtle confidence to the narration in between these moments that grounds the story and never allows it to feel too over the top. This results in a layered, emotionally intelligent exploration of family pressures and personal freedom that readers from all walks of life will be able to relate to, especially Mason Adamov, looking for peace after such a turbulent relationship with the male role model in his life. It takes true talent to capture the tension between love and autonomy in such realistic terms, and also deliver a well-penned plot with lots of interest, and a capable, strong central hero who can be vulnerable and open but still be a man we admire and root for. *Broken Rose* is a relatable and mature drama about carving a path through complicated relationships. Highly recommended to fans of well-penned dramas.

Readers' Favorite

Books by Stefan Vučak

General Fiction:
Cry of Eagles
All the Evils
Towers of Darkness
Strike for Honor
Proportional Response
Legitimate Power
Autumn Leaves
F/X-26
28th Amendment
Night Sirens
Broken Rose

Science Fiction:
Fulfillment
Lifeliners
All My Sunsets

Shadow Gods Saga:
In the Shadow of Death
Against the Gods of Shadow
A Whisper from Shadow
Shadow Masters
Immortal in Shadow
With Shadow and Thunder
Through the Valley of Shadow
Guardians of Shadow

Non-Fiction:
Writing Tips for Authors

Contact at:
www.stefanvucak.com

Broken Rose

By

Stefan Vučak

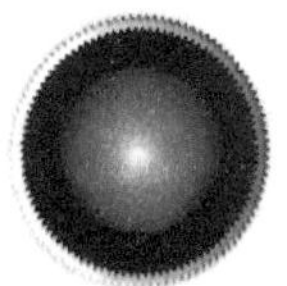

Dedication

To those who think writing is an end in itself

Acknowledgments

To Kelly Smith for additional proofreading and insightful suggestions.
Partners in Crime Book Services
https://partnersincrimebooks.wixsite.com/authorservices

Note: National Post is a fictional organization and not a real body.

Cover art by Laura Shinn.
http://laurashinn.yolasite.com

Chapter One

Mason laid down his knife and fork on the heavy green tablecloth, the crumbed veal and fries before him forgotten. The glare he gave the imposing figure of his father across the table would shrivel anyone else, but not the granite personality of his old man who stared at him with open disdain.

"One word of encouragement, that's all I ever wanted, but you couldn't bring yourself to give me even that little bit! Did I ask for too much? In your eyes, did I even have the right to expect anything from you? Instead of giving me that one word, you always found fault with everything I did." Throat suddenly tight, he slowly wagged his head as shards of regret and disappointment crumbled around him to vanish as though they never existed. As though he never existed.

"I never understood what it took to please you," Mason added bitterly, hating to spoil what started as a great evening to engender some closeness with his parents. At least pretend it was there; a façade everybody felt comfortable with, reluctant to face reality. Well, he faced it now. "What does it take, Dad?"

He did not want to have it dished out to him anymore in silence, nor maintain a hollow presence of congeniality every time they met that belied genuine discomfort and tension. It took too much out of him and he had precious little left to give. He needed what remained to maintain some scrap of dignity and self-respect. The possibility of an eventual confrontation with his father always cast a dark shadow over what should otherwise be bright days. To maintain a semblance of family peace, he always pushed back facing the inevitable moment. He could no longer pay the price, or wanted to.

His mom blanched, green eyes large with astonishment, brushed a blond streak along the right side of her flowing hazel hair, and cleared her throat.

"Now, Manny—"

"Don't 'Now, Manny' me, Mom!" Mason shot back with a withering glance, tired of the whole thing. "Every time you think I'm wrong, and it's mostly always, you side with Dad! Did you ever really love me, Mom?"

Brianna turned white and gaped.

He shoved the chair back and threw the maroon cloth napkin on the table. "I've had it with both of you. If you can't accept me for what I am, then don't accept me at all. You've been doing it long enough already. I need some fresh air."

"Sit down!" Nikola Adamov grated in a stern Navy voice. Twenty-seven years since he resigned as a lieutenant commander in the Navy, he still retained command presence. A terrible shadow that hung over both of them. Not a shadow perhaps, but an insurmountable wall.

Even as a kid, Mason found his father's uncompromising personality difficult to cope with. When his father came into a room, he dominated by mere presence, and his words were law, precluding argument or dissent, something Mason silently rebelled against. He should have stood up to him years ago. It would have made his life easier. Or at least drawn behavioral boundaries in an armed truce. After all, he inherited *some* of his old man's genes, but the raw power his dad projected always held him in check, all for the sake to maintain a fictitious peace.

Mouth tight, fists clenched to hold back a torrent of emotions he kept bottled far too long, wanting to let them vent in unbridled rage, he lowered himself onto the edge of the chair, back straight, openly hostile, not in a mood for another personality dissection, which he had many already. He should walk out to regain some personal perspective, unencumbered by his parents' patronizing blanket of condescension, unstated superiority, and self-right-eousness.

Nikola dabbed his full lips, neatly folded the napkin beside the plate in a habitual gesture, and settled back his muscled 174cm frame. Black eyes probed Mason beneath dark eyebrows not touched with frost. His short-cropped hair still a lustrous brown. A powerful man with a daunting stance even when sitting relaxed, his look now bore thunder clouds. Mason waited, determined not to be unnerved, regardless of what happened.

"You claim I never gave you a word of encouragement?" his dad rasped in a dangerously soft voice.

Mom laid a soothing palm on her husband's forearm. "This isn't the time, dear. Let's not ruin—"

Nikola shook her off. "It must be said, damn it!" He focused his gaze on Mason. "Who pushed you through high school? You were ready to enter university at fourteen if not for our tight-assed academics and their rigid curriculum. Nevertheless, at eighteen, you managed to get a BSc and a master's in a three-year accelerated course, which landed you a choice job with the ANZ bank. Bully for you. However, none of it would have happened if I hadn't kicked your lazy butt out of the comfort zone you hid yourself because you figured you were too damn smart and arrogant to study. You'd be a deluded bum now if I hadn't been on your case, blaming everybody for your problems except yourself."

"Lucky me," Mason muttered.

"That's right. Lucky you. You *are* smart, I'll admit, but even in grade school, you became dazzled by your genius and set yourself up to fail. You didn't need encouragement. You needed a spike up your ass to get you moving, which I gave you in spades."

"So you pushed me through school, but you did it with a whip, not the support and care I wanted!"

His dad scowled. "Support and care? I supported you in the only way you'd take it, you ungrateful, conceited shit! You started work and sponged off us for more than a year before you bought yourself that seedy St. Kilda bedsitter dump and move out."

"And you never let me forget it!"

"A dump, like I said. Before you left, you didn't pay us a single cent in rent while your mother washed and ironed your clothes and fed you. You never appreciated how we worried and cared for you, and you haven't changed one bit. Still a self-centered, churlish asshole."

"So she washed my clothes," Mason retorted in a clipped voice, face hot with indignation at the unfairness of it all. They never cared to listen to his side of things. The evening ruined, he prepared to give it to them now, his relationship already a crumbled ruin. "That's been her job from the day I was born, and everything else you could do for me! I didn't owe either of you any rent. You owed me all you had when you brought me into this crappy world. You now expect me to pay for that as some sort of gratitude debt? A salve for your conscience?" He leaned forward and stared into his father's hard eyes. "I only wanted a hint of approval for things I did, a modicum of affection, an occasional hug, but you only had words of derision and displeasure. Your version of care, I suppose."

"Manny!" Brianna gaped in horror. "That's so cruel and untrue."

"Is it, Mom?" Mason pointed a finger at his dad. "At five, I remember him in his Navy blues when not boating somewhere in the Arabian Gulf or wherever. When he came home on leave, I saw a stranger in a pretty uniform, not a father. I wanted so much to be close to him and do things with him. A few moments of closeness and attention would have been enough, but even then, he showed me scant consideration. When he left on another cruise, I listened to you cry at night and wondered why he didn't care for us. Why didn't he care, Mom?"

Nikola shot his wife a startled look.

"Then he left the Navy. To make it up to us? Nothing

changed, though. During his years at Thompson Engineering, he only had time for work. On weekends when I wanted to do fun things with him like other boys, he couldn't be bothered. You don't know how much that hurt. After your miscarriage in '93, I became an irritant to him—to both of you. Someone to be tolerated, ordered around, one of his underlings, not a son to be loved."

His dad pursed his mouth, placed both hands on the table, and pushed himself up.

"You thankless wretch! I should bash your head in for that! You have no idea what you're talking about."

"Then do it!" Mason shot back, not giving a damn anymore, his past collapsing to ashes around him. It had to happen eventually. "Throw me in the brig. It's your style. Your way or no way."

"One day, you'll come to value what your mother and I did for you. Sadly, tonight isn't that night. You better leave before we both say something we'll regret, you most of all, but get this. What's more, you have a wrong slant on almost everything."

"With you, I always had a wrong slant on everything."

"Your mother and I raised you to be what you are today, but despite your brains, you're too thick and full of yourself to see it." Nikola pointed at the door. "Get your ass out of here before I throw you out. Get out! Get out!"

Mason's grandmother strode into the dining room and beamed. "That cleared my head," she declared cheerfully, referring to a hasty bathroom visit. Her smile faded, replaced by a puzzled frown at the tense tableau before her, and glanced at her son. "What's going on? What's all the shouting about?"

Rigid with anger, Nikola merely glared.

"Thanks for the dinner, Mom," Mason choked, voice thick with emotion, intensely disliking what transpired, and gave Grandma a nod. "Talk to you later."

On a weekend visit from the nursing home, when he came tonight, he looked forward to spending some quality time with her. Regrettably, life dished out one of its disappointments instead. That's all he'd been getting from his family. He promised himself to visit her next weekend and explain everything. Provided he first explained everything to himself, he mused sardonically, too churned up inside to think straight. Or wanted to think at all.

"Manny! Don't do this!" his mother cried out, her sobs cut when he slammed the door shut.

He looked for a confrontation, but did not expect it to be so acerbic and acrimonious. Worse still, many things he sought to unload remained unsaid. Perhaps just as well. He may have pushed things beyond any possibility of reconciliation. Could there be a reconciliation? The look of contempt his father gave him as he left made him doubt.

A glittering half-moon shone bright against a backdrop of a few stars he could see not overwhelmed by city lights. He winced as a brisk southerly cut through his thin wool turtleneck. July in Melbourne strictly for the penguins. He hurried to his new Subaru Forester, climbed in, his thoughts in churning disarray, and slammed his fist against the steering wheel.

"Skits!"

A deep breath later, wanting to rage and lash out at anything and everything, he eased down Powell Street.

To hell with them all!

That's what started it, talking about the damned car. Instead of being pleased that Mason finally got rid of his old, but still reliable, Holden Apollo, his dad admonished him for not getting something like a BMW that holds its market and resale value. Once again, Nikola twisted things and left Mason with a foul taste in his mouth, feeling inadequate, incapable of decision, a failure, always at fault. Nothing he did was ever good enough for the man.

Not fair! Screw you, Dad!

He accelerated down Powell Street lined with old elms, winter branches bare, braked at the Toorak Road intersection, checked for oncoming traffic, and turned onto the broad boulevard. The house he left now only a shell of cold memories. Some bitter, some sweet, mostly faded dreams. Heart heavy, he swallowed something that stuck in his throat and it went down hard.

Not fair!

A short run along the always busy Kings Way, city skyscrapers a dazzling background, he turned left onto Cobden Street and made his way down the quiet, narrow, dimly lit tree-lined lane filled with residents-only cars. On occasion, an enterprising individual parked illegally in someone's spot to the irate reaction from the house owner, which more often than not resulted in the offending vehicle getting towed away. To stop illegal parking in his two invaluable spots, he allowed neighbors on either side of the street to use them. Both reciprocated with a bottle of wine or slab of beer at times. Good for a hello, Mason did not socialize much with either of them, content to live in his own private world. He simply did not fit the mold of an over-the-fence gregarious talker. An ingrained habit from his often lonely childhood days? A lot of truth in that, he admitted.

Not inclined to gnaw on it right then, Mason drove into the small garage of his double-story place, paused as the evening's events replayed in his mind, and got out. A sharp breeze coming off the Bay tugged at his sweater and he hurried toward the laundry entrance, the garage door rumbling as it slithered down. A welcome wave of warmth greeted him as he stepped into the open-plan kitchen/lounge, the spaces kept warm by the central heating system.

He dug out his cell and placed it on the glass-topped coffee table. Glowing blue numbers said 8:15pm, July 23, 2022. Too early for bed, not in the mood to watch TV or a DVD, he loaded the player with Mozart's *Eine kleine Nachtmusic*, fixed himself a double bourbon, sprawled onto a dark brown leather incliner, and closed his eyes. It did not blot out the images in his mind. They merely became sharper.

After a moment, he raised the tumbler in a salute. "He's to you, Dad, for all the transgressions I made, even though I never knew what they were. Not that I really give a shit anymore."

Despite the moving music playing with his heartstrings and emotions, by any measure, not his best evening. The weight he felt lay heavy on his chest.

"I need you right now, Gramps," Mason muttered forlornly, took a sip of bourbon, and allowed his mind to freewheel, determined to get a little tight. The words he and Dad exchanged kept replaying and put a serious dampener on Mozart's serenade. The price he paid for having an eidetic memory.

He wasn't a failure. At thirty-one, a modern-looking double terrace in South Melbourne an easy walk to the city center, nice investment portfolio, satisfying new job—he hoped it would be satisfying—he had everything others may envy and the world for him should be in lights. The one thing missing in his otherwise perfect life—parental love. Something he craved since childhood and never really had, not even from his mother. A bleak realization he harbored for a long time, but hesitated to acknowledge and face fully. He could rationalize it by admitting his dad spent all his time in the Navy, unable to provide the kind of companionship other fathers lavished on their kids when he did show up on infrequent leave. His mother held a demanding teaching job at RMIT University, which left little time to frolic with Mason when she came home, busy making dinner and taking care of necessary household chores. When a free moment did come, she wanted to unwind a little, not chase a football in the park. He understood it all now, armed with years of knowledge, but not as a pre-teen kid. All he knew then, there were many lonely days in grade school, and lonelier evenings at home afterward. To compensate, he lost himself in games of his own making, craving a smile every now and then from Mom, an endearing peck on the cheek, and a hearty slap of bonding on the back from Dad. Unable to phrase it in those terms at the time, he wanted his parents to fill a yearning for closeness inside him they left empty for some reason. What always bothered him, they never explained why. He needed from them what they rarely gave and he resented them for it.

Experts at psychological warfare, they never lost an opportunity to remind him what they did for him, the sacrifices they made so he could make something of himself in life. A crushing burden they bore with suffering stoicism for him, they said. They now expected him to kiss their feet in gratitude, be a good little boy, and don't question. Forget the hurt they inflicted on him, all for his own good. Classic guilt transference, perhaps done unconsciously, he allowed. Consciously or not, they kept doing it, and were clearly still at it.

His analytical mind tossed over his father's words. Did he have a wrong slant on things? His eidetic memory recorded everything in excruciating detail, but did not scrutinize or give him unbiased introspection. Whatever that meant. He learned those things later through research and life's hard knocks, which gave him a modicum of wisdom and an ability to cope. Too bad no manual existed on how to handle parents. Popular books and academic papers aplenty, but all offered hollow platitudes or highbrow philosophizing of little practical value he could use.

Why did things have to be so damn hard? With all his smarts, he still could not figure it out. Well, he could…now, sort of. It did not help, though.

Tonight's spat failed to resolve anything fundamental, he admitted, except widen the deep schism with his father that's been there for years. His old man wasn't an old-fashioned dummy incapable of dealing with modern issues and lifestyle challenges. Far from it. Mason accepted that most of his smarts came from him. Mom supplied his more artistic, emotional attributes. When much younger, he recalled many vigorous discussions with his dad on geopolitics, social extremism, religious polarization, cosmology, and other things. Both shared a passion for the universe and its unfathomable wonders. Sadly, those moments happened all too infrequently, and over the last few years, none after Mason graduated, refusing to pursue a PhD urged by his course advisor. The narrow academic world view held little appeal. He wanted to do things, make something happen, not study, and embarked on a business career.

Eighteen months later, he moved into his St. Kilda apartment, relieved not to have his parents underfoot, or live under a prevailing cloud of gloom that hung over their house. He immersed himself in work, thinking he no longer needed what they never gave him anyway. He did not cut himself off totally, and saw his parents and grandparents over dinner sometimes, celebrated Easter and Christmas as a social custom rather than from any genuine religious conviction none of them really felt, and chatted with Mom on the phone when not lecturing…and he did all the calling. A tenuous web that over the years became more tenuous. Mason realized early if he did not do something and soon, that web would not be strong enough to hold them together. Despite all the problems, he wanted to be close to his parents. Nothing else left in his life by way of family. What happened tonight did not help.

Perhaps he should swallow his wounded pride and chuck all the emotional baggage he carried most of his life and accept the fact that his parents were not perfect. The rational part of him agreed. He probably harbored a few cracks himself, he mused, the admission not difficult to make. Find common ground and go from there? Be the first to extend a hand and move on? Why should *he* be the one to always knuckle under? They never showed any inclination to meet him halfway. Life on their terms or nothing. He did not want it on their terms, though. No longer.

Pride…what a bitch!

A man needed *some* pride. Otherwise, he'd be a submissive mat for everybody to trample, and he'd been one long enough. Did he equate pride with self-respect?

Decide who you are and what you really want.

Right then, feelings warring with each other, he did not care to examine them too deeply. He desperately wanted to unburden himself to Gramps. Tragically, Milan died five years ago from a ruptured brain aneurysm nobody knew he had. At least it happened quickly and he didn't suffer. One moment, he laughed with Grandma over breakfast, then dropped dead at the table. Gramps understood how to handle his son. Too bad he hadn't passed that knowledge to Mason. Or had he?

He felt his mouth twitch as he fondly reflected on the fun times he had with his grandfather. Happy times, happy memories.

Snug in their Mt. Macedon cottage some seventy-five kilometers north-west from Melbourne, summer or winter—well, not always in summer—Milan usually stoked up the wood burner in the evening and watched the dancing, flickering flames with Grandma at his side, sip fine Shiraz, and suck on an old briar pipe stuffed with cherry or rum-flavored tobacco. Nada would be all over his case if he tried to smoke indoors, he told Mason more than once. Grumpy and resentful at the injustice of it all—he deserved his little pleasures, he always snapped—he contented himself by chewing the stem. Mason once bought him an expensive meerschaum pipe as a Christmas gift, but the old geezer preferred his worn briar. No accounting for taste.

On winter weekends, the landscape covered with a blanket of fresh snow or glittering frost, Gramps cooked *gluhwein* using Grandma's favorite recipe she picked up from her own mom back in Zagreb. A different, now forgotten world. A nostalgic, and on reflection, perhaps happier world, she would say in a pensive moment, not actually meaning it. They had it tough in old Yugoslavia and never considered returning, having made a new life for themselves in Australia. Gramps often groused that behind the appearance of freedom after the fall of the old regime, the new Croatia turned out to be equally corrupt and repressive. Those in power were the same old communist clique parading themselves under a veneer of democracy. Business as usual and screw the people.

At other times, politics forgotten, he and Mason drank warm *slivovitz*. The plum brandy radiated inner fire that reflected the flames in the burner and laid the foundation for deeper discussions, both skirting subjects damaging to inner peace. An educated, worldly man, Gramps had a driving thirst for knowledge, questioned everything with a cynical slant, and laughed heartily at local and international political shenanigans. Either that or worry himself to death, he said. They had fun times, all right.

Milan liked to sit back in his favorite black leather recliner positioned in front of the burner, nod as random thoughts cascaded through the corridors of his mind, and talked about days long gone. He'd reminisce on his wild youth in Varazdin, the turbulent war years as a partisan, how he met Nada, the struggle to create a new life when they emigrated to Australia, and of many other things. The old man possessed a rich past packed with unusual experiences and an uncompromising, down-to-earth attitude to life.

'Keep things simple and in perspective, moj mali stroj,' he'd say. *'Don't get sidetracked with irrelevancy.'*

"Not always easy to do, Gramps," Mason reflected pensively.

Mali stroj—little gadget in Croatian. He remembered Gramps calling him that forever.

After exhausting himself running wild around the small Mt. Macedon village during a weekend visit, then scolded by Mom for getting himself dirty, he welcomed a mug of hot cocoa and fresh blueberry cookies Grandma made. On sunny, warm afternoons, he'd sit on the back veranda; listen to Gramps and Dad talk, sometimes heatedly on a point of contention, and watch two resident magpies peck around the backyard. If Cricket, Grandma's black tomcat saw them, he immediately pounced on the birds, which resulted in squawks of indignation as they flew to perch on a nearby gumtree branch. He often wondered if his grandfather made up those stories, as they sounded too outlandish to be believable. During a drive home once, he asked Dad about it. His father smiled indulgently and assured him that Milan lived in colorful times, with a little hyperbole thrown in perhaps for drama and color, he'd add.

Mozart faded and silence took over the room. He sipped his bourbon as random thoughts tumbled in his mind. Alone in the thick silence, the emptiness he now felt threatened to overwhelm him. He lost Gramps, and now, it looked like he lost his father.

Unaccountably, Simon and Garfunkel's *The Sound of Silence* bubbled up from the chaos within and he hummed the tune.

Right then, it seemed kind of fitting.

He got up and poured himself more whiskey.

* * *

The tires whispered to themselves, a sound of hissing rain.

Beads on a string, cars moved along the highway. Although early, the hard white sun valiantly tried to warm the frozen, rolling landscape and burn away stringy remnants of clinging mist. With shrill squawks, a gaggle of yellow-crested cockatoos flew overhead and settled on massive eucalypt trees beside the carriageway.

Mason adjusted his shades, switched stations to ABC FM Classic, and nodded solemnly to the hypnotic rhythm of Ravel's *Bolero.* Not into heavy symphonies, he liked his music light and cheerful. *Bolero's* enchanting tempo sent his mind along meandering memory paths. Opera made him wince, but in a quirky way, his heart sang to some of its music. His mom always tuned into

60s and 70s popular stuff, and he inherited her tastes for the old-ies. Modern, sharp, acid compositions made him switch stations. When nothing came up on the radio, he replayed favorites stored in his mind.

A silver hatchback roared past him. The decibels of its speak-ers rivaled an A380 taking off, guaranteed to blow out the driver's eardrums. He shook his head, not understanding any of it.

A green signboard on the shoulder said Mt. Macedon exit, one kilometer. *Bolero* finished in a crescendo and the familiar ABC news break broke his reflective reverie.

Virginia Trioli came on to present Saturday's *News Breakfast* in her cheerful, bubbly voice that nonetheless failed to soften what she said. He paid scant attention, noting the main points.

The Greens Party pushing Labor to shut down coal and gas-powered electricity generators. The rub, no renewables existed to take up the load deficit. Mason shook his head at the stupidity of it all. People across Australia protesting against rampant price gouging by Woolworths and Coles supermarket chains. House and rental costs soaring across the country. The draconian Covid restrictions almost gone, with dictator Dan Andrews at the helm of the Victorian Labor government, no one could say what that man would do next to ruin the state. On the other side of the globe, Russian forces were mauling Ukraine's cities and eastern positions as US and EU sanctions began to bite. Israel launched missile strikes against Hamas strongholds in Gaza. Mason sighed and shook his head.

His dose of doom and gloom done, he pushed a stiff finger at the display screen and switched off the radio. Peaceful silence descended, broken only by the soft engine hum.

He kept a close eye on local and international politics, world trade, environmental issues, and scientific developments. Like a junky, he had to have a regular news fix. Sometimes, he felt as though everything crowded him, stifling his ability to think, smothering him with the worst the world had to offer. He often wondered why nobody reported nice, cheerful things, already knowing the answer. People simply loved to wallow in someone else's misery, convincing themselves their misery wasn't as bad. It helped them cope with their days.

Last night, two double bourbons warm in his belly, still unsettled, he wanted to jump into the car and rush off to his grandparents' place. The Mt. Macedon property now his, but from earliest childhood, he always considered it a fixture with them in it, and he a welcomed visitor, although a rumbustious neighborhood terror let loose from an otherwise strict home discipline. They were a permanency he relied on. He missed that connection.

If he could not talk to Gramps, Mason needed his ghost to help him sort out conflicting feelings stirring inside him. Last night, tempted to find refuge and solace in the clean, unspoiled Macedon hills, he resisted giving into the impulse. Cops usually prowled the roads, especially on Fridays, and he did not fancy getting nabbed for being over the alcohol limit, which he probably pushed after the drinks he had.

Past Gisborne, he took the off-ramp onto Mt. Macedon Road and motored down the peaceful arterial. Sheets of mist hung low over paddocks and the sun glinted between white-barked eucalypt branches. Frost painted the grass with crystal on both sides of the road, and the airconditioner whined a little louder to maintain the set temperature.

Before the hill that led into the small township, the local golf course clubhouse stood deserted, although he figured it would fill rapidly with weekend warriors who sought to test their skill against the devilish white ball. Mason liked the small nine-hole course and played when he could tear himself away from the city. Preferably early in the morning during the week when he often had the place to himself, everybody else otherwise at work.

He slowed to sixty, drove past a cluster of old-fashioned houses and stores, and turned right onto the narrow, sleepy Cheniston Road lined with bushy trees and tall gums, providing shade and tranquility. Cottages and larger, more modern houses nestled on mostly half-hectare lots occupied by old-time residents and newly arrived retirees who sought to escape the city pressure cooker. Some owners used larger plots as do-it-yourself hobby farms or held them as investments. Looking at it all, his mood improved as the prevailing sense of peace descended on him. The place did it to him every time.

Mason pulled up before a two-meter steel gate hung on local bluestone columns and gazed with nostalgia at the single-story sandstone dwelling. A chicken wire fence ran around the entire property and gave an uninterrupted view of gently rolling hills falling away behind the house to merge into flatland. On either side, tall pines provided shelter from the neighbors. At nights, lying in bed, window wide open, he always listened as the pines softly whispered to him until everything faded and he slept. During a storm, the sounds were more agitated—hissing surf running up a beach—but they too soothed away the day's cares.

He opened the gate expecting Cricket to come bounding toward him in welcome, tail held high. His dad disliked cats and never kept pets, a characteristic Mason shared. In a quirky way, Cricket nonetheless warmed to them and often rubbed himself against their legs as they sat on the veranda, purring loudly with satisfaction, knowing he left a bunch of hairs on their trousers. The black tomcat only a fond memory now among other memories tucked away in his memory drawers.

Then, on May 5, 2017, over breakfast, Milan Adamovié died at ninety-four from a massive stroke. A loss Mason felt keenly, as Gramps' death ripped out one of his life anchors. Grandma had him cremated at Altona Memorial Park and buried the brass urn in a back corner of the property. Nikola planted a miniature pencil cypress sapling to commemorate the spot.

Understandably enough, Grandma took the loss hard. Dad immediately offered to move her to their place in South Yarra in town, not wanting Mom to live alone. A feisty, independent woman, Nada put up a fight, saying she didn't want to live in a crowded, smelly city. She had local friends for company, kept busy doing community work, and looking after the property. At eighty-nine, a burdensome task, Nikola pointed out reasonably. Having friends did not make up for some lonely days and empty nights. What if something happened to her and nobody around to help? If she didn't move, he insisted she wear an emergency bracelet, not a solution he liked and an idea she detested. Dad gave her an ultimatum: bracelet or the city. In the end, she accepted the inevitable and wore a bracelet.

Mason walked around in denial for a week, hoping to wake from a terrible nightmare, and Gramps would still be there, puffing away on his briar, cracking stories. Impossible that he was gone. No more chats, no more stories, no companionship. Mason somehow took it that Gramps would be there forever. All he had left were treasured memories he could replay over and over. It would have to suffice.

Three weeks later, Cricket vanished.

The double loss took a heavy emotional toll on Grandma, and a better part of a year passed before she became her more normal self. Mason officially took over the place and came up often to help with the chores. Either by himself to enjoy a weekend, or with one or more of his three closest buddies. He knew beforehand he'd own the property one day, but had not figured to inherit so quickly.

By then, it became obvious that Grandma could no longer look after herself or the property, and Dad took her to South Yarra. He and Brianna made a valiant effort to care for her, but twelve months later, everybody admitted it would not work, and they moved her into a nursing home, as Mom did not want to quit her job and become a permanent caretaker. Initially grumpy at another move, Nada gradually accepted the necessity and soon made new friends. Mason and his parents visited often and had her at their South Yarra place on most weekends to keep a connection everybody wanted. His parents sought to have Nada with them always, Mason had to give them that, but Grandma needed professional care, something Mom could not provide. They all made it up to her by taking her to Mt. Macedon whenever she wanted to reconnect with Milan and old friends.

Mason parked the car in front of the double garage and strode up broad sandstone steps to the solid wood doorway. He winced at the chill inside as he disabled the alarm, then busied himself to fire up the wood burner. Chore done, he went to the bathroom to wash up. He put aside the towel and stared at the 176cm slim figure in the mirror. Muddy green eyes inherited from Mom gazed back at him above a square jawline and nicely tapered nose. He passed a hand through charcoal hair and a lighter streak that ran along the top of his head and pursed his lips. The streak came in for lots of jibes in primary and secondary school, which forced him to fend off a bully or two. In the kitchen, coffee percolator going, he checked the fridge. Apart from bread and milk, no need for a major shopping outing.

Buttery sunshine streamed through tall back veranda windows and made a bright pool on the polished redgum floor. A gaggle of white cockatoos in the yard pecked around the small vegetable garden. He always planted potatoes, onions, carrots, tomatoes, cabbages, and some herbs, preferring genuine flavor in vegetables he ate. Over the last four years, the garden shrank as his interest to maintain it diminished, and overseas work commitments prevented him from coming up. His parents looked after the place while he worked in the Middle East, something he reluctantly agreed they had to do, but a chore he did not want to burden them with. An idyllic weekend retreat, the property still required regular maintenance. He always cleaned during a visit, and a local man took care of mowing and trimming. It all mounted up, though, when he added council rates and utility charges, and none of it tax deductible. More than once, he thought of selling, but could not bring himself to do it while Grandma lived, and he did not want to rent it out. She may consider it betrayal, seeing how much of her life she and Gramps spent here.

A mug of hot coffee in hand, Mason slid back the lounge ceiling-high glass panel and stepped into the enclosed veranda now warm from the sun. He dragged over a chair, back and seat made comfortable with tied-on cushions Grandma made, and placed the mug on the heavy table. He pulled out a mild King Edward cigar from his breast pocket and lit up. A couple of satisfying puffs later, he gazed absently into nothing in particular. He never smoked cigarettes, although as a kid, he and his friends tried them for taste. Not for him. He did not like the stink, but enjoyed the aromatic whiff of a cigar.

The cockatoos looked up from their chore when he emerged and went back to teasing the ground. His eyes drifted past the back fence toward patches of old-growth forest and rested on a distant horizon where the air turned fuzzy. Melbourne lay somewhere over there. He could not see it, too far away, but easily pictured its cluster of skyscrapers clawing upward. Another life, another existence.

As his thoughts tumbled, he imagined Gramps sitting on the other side of the table as he often did, old briar clenched between his teeth, bushy eyebrows drawn together in a frown. Mason lifted his mug in acknowledgment.

"We need to talk, Gramps," he murmured, then grinned. If someone saw him right then, they'd be right to consider him ready for the funny wagon. No one could see him, of course, and he did not give a damn if somebody did.

"I screwed things up properly last night, haven't I?"

A rhetorical question, as Gramps couldn't answer anyhow. Still, he did drive here to get some answers. Lay it all on the table, pick through the family pieces, and see what picture they made? Instead of losing himself in nostalgia, feeling sorry for himself, he should go back to South Melbourne and attend to real chores.

They would not get done by themselves, and he started work on Monday. A new start with Global Systems after five years with Deloitte.

A magpie swooped over the cockatoo gaggle and they took flight, screeching in protest as they wheeled toward a stand of trees down the hill.

Perhaps he should latch on the trailer and drive off into the bush to look for fallen logs to top up his supply of firewood. Most easy to get at stuff already taken years ago, but lots still remained along lonely forest tracks. Physical work may clear his head and make him forget reality for a while. He took a sip of coffee and decided not to get sweaty. The back shed held enough chopped dry wood to last the winter, and two five-meter-long shoulder-high stacks would see him through at least eight more years. *Keep today's visit focused and intellectual*, he told himself.

As a teenager, he liked going into the forest with Gramps to cut timber and haul the plunder home. He enjoyed the earthy forest smells—something different from the usual city odors— listen to the whisper of rustling leaves and the cradling comfort the woods engendered. When he first started work and got a car, an old secondhand Honda hatch, he'd drive up in casual gear and got friendly ribbing from Gramps for looking like a bum. Mason shrugged off the japes.

"I'm in a white shirt, a strangulation tie, and suit five days a week," he'd retort, not taking umbrage. "On weekends, I don't care if I look like a bum." And he did not, although he did not *actually* look like a bum.

Warm air drifted in from the lounge as the burner got into its stride. He relaxed and allowed himself to drift into retrospection, home chores be damned. Mt. Macedon's outback retreat promulgated an atmosphere of tranquility and peace. A far cry from the hectic city lifestyle he lived during the week. The city and work provided the means through which he secured his ongoing financial and retirement needs, but did not fill his soul in the way

Gramp's place did. A job simply fulfilled his economic needs. Well, it did far more than that, he acknowledged grudgingly. People who lived here had their share of problems, everybody did everywhere, and Grandma loved to share local gossip about someone's misfortune, social or financial, but they seemed to take life's knocks with a more phlegmatic, philosophical attitude, and smiled readily. If he could somehow instill such an outlook in the city, he'd make a fortune, and along the way push a lot of psychiatrists on the street. Not a bad thing, perhaps, he mused.

Still in grade school, his mom or dad often dropped him off on a Friday evening or Saturday morning to leave him with his grandparents for the weekend. Under loose discipline, Mason ran wild, free from constraints life in suburban South Yarra imposed. He had the nearby Fawkner Park to romp around in, but it wasn't the same thing as real countryside.

Alone or with several local youngsters he came to know, they roamed through open fields and patches of forest pretending to be explorers in African deeps, played war, or chased Indians. Cowboy games were always fun. They all liked to meander through tall corn unseen and pick wild red poppies in their play. When ripe, Grandma boiled or barbecued corn cobs, then smeared them with golden butter. They ate with relish, washed down with hot tea and cookies for dessert.

He disappeared in the morning, showed up for lunch to stoke up with fuel, and be gone the rest of the day until weariness and hunger forced him back. Grandma tended to his scratches and scolded him when he got his clothes dirty or torn, but the words held no sting, unlike what his mother said when she came to pick him up. Mason preferred to forget those moments and the smacks on the rear end for his misdeeds. Small penance for the fun he had.

Mason recalled an emotionally bumpy and often lonely childhood. Early on, he discovered his eidetic memory. At first, he thought everybody had it, but as he listened to his parents and other people, the realization he might be different came as a shock, mixed with wonder at possibilities the ability opened for him. As he began to understand words and articulate, comprehend what he saw on TV, his intellectual horizons expanded exponentially. Shortly, it became clear to everybody that he picked up things far more rapidly than a normal ten-month toddler did. The transition from crawling to walking stimulated his insatiable curiosity, which undoubtedly added to his parents' growing collection of gray hairs.

The picture books they got for him opened a window to more marvels, but he found their simplistic formats boring. Around three, at the RMIT faculty Childhood Center, he became fascinated with the printed word and demanded real books designed for far older children. A lecturer in English at the University, having him there relieved his mom from many worries where to put him, not wanting to damage her career by taking extended leave. The Center teachers recognized his budding intellect and slotted him into an accelerated learning class.

Way above average smart had its good points, but also created a social barrier with less gifted classmates and children in general. He often found himself alone, by choice when he refused to join in their boisterous play, or shunned because they saw him as someone odd, then teased him for being a bookworm. He found early that children were very cruel. Perhaps straightforward and unpretentious would be a better way of putting it. Either way, he did not like those bullying episodes. His teachers protected him from the worst of it, but rejection forced him to build a defensive shield against barbs that came his way much earlier in life than normally happened.

His dad still in the Navy then, was not around to help him and be someone Mason could lean on for emotional support. Busy lecturing and taking care of the house, Mom's fleeting words of encouragement never filled the loneliness in what should otherwise have been a relatively happy life. When Dad came home on leave, they did some fun things together, went to places and wandered the city, but Mason found those activities superficial. Then his dad would be off again on a cruise and he would retreat into his shell.

He knew things were missing in his life other kids his age appeared to take for granted, unable to clearly define what he wanted. The few times he haltingly tried to sound out his parents, particularly Mom as she represented a constant presence, she told him not to worry about it, and he'd soon have friends like everybody else. A normal phase he was going through, she assured him dismissively, and would go back to making dinner or whatever. He never developed close friendships, though, and worked to strengthen his shield against the world.

Mason started primary school at five, skipped prep and went straight into grade one. He devoured the curriculum and also bypassed grade three. Only ten, he entered University High School in Parkville, a short hop by tram from RMIT. Both his parents had little time for expensive private schools and claimed a good public school adequately prepared students for tertiary life.

His teachers knew him to be exceptionally bright, but were amazed when he completed Year 7 and 8 in his first year. He could easily have skipped another year, but the school stood firm, insisting he follow their rigid program. Fascinated with computers, he decided to make it his career. He persuaded Mom to get him the RMIT IT degree curriculum and books, taught himself COBOL and FORTRAN, and submitted programs to the computer center prepared initially on punched cards until screens and keyboards did away with that. With a Higher School Certificate pass of ninety-eight percent, he enrolled at RMIT University to study information technology. Released from relative high school discipline, for the first time in his life, he experienced genuine freedom.

Although he had a course advisor, nobody cared if he attended lectures, tutorials, did his assignments, passed or failed.

Some of his classmates embraced this unexpected release and forgot why they entered university, which invariably effected their studies. Still a teenager struggling to be a young adult, Mason also fell into that trap, which almost derailed his degree if not for a few figurative wake-up kicks in the butt from his dad.

At one Student Union gathering, he met three cheerful guys who turned into firm friends. Arthur Landry, the bookworm as the others affectionately called him, enrolled to study electrical engineering, while Liam Anderson, thin and gangly, a little awkward, specialized in electronics. Logan Bernard, chubby and always cheerful, pursued a degree in geology. Although they were all three years his senior, put together, the four of them were definitely a weird mob, Mason admitted.

Independence also meant a chance to devote some dedicated time pursuing girls—a fascinating new subject for Mason—and the campus provided a broad selection of local and international targets. He maintained a friendly relationship with two girls in his class and sometimes went out to lunch with them, but never asked any on a date. This attitude naturally generated some ribbing from his friends for being a cube, which he ignored.

Early in their second year, Arthur said that Mandy in his circuit design class was a ready lay and Mason should ask her out. They met a few times as a group over lunch and Mason admitted he liked the willowy brunette. His hormones sizzled at the prospect of having her alone with him. All the while, struggling to avert his straying eyes from her firm cleavage. A gangly, engaging, 176cm-tall, sixteen-year-old youngster, totally innocent with girls, and she three years older, he plucked up enough courage to ask her out. He remembered her mischievous smile as she said yes. That afternoon between lectures, she waylaid him, dragged him into an empty classroom, and Mason had his first encounter with sex. The startling episode left him excited, but also frightened at the prospect of someone barging in while they were at it.

In the evening, he replayed the episode in vivid detail, relishing the tantalizing prospect of another memorable encounter. Not to be, though. They remained friendly and went out a few times, but without further intimate escapades. Arthur later told him Mandy went out with him only to find out what it would be like with the college nerd. Over time, not interested in a serious relationship, Mason lost track of her and often wondered what became of the enchanting brunette, not curious enough to ask Arthur.

He smiled indulgently at the pleasant memories.

The sun higher in the sky, his thoughts jolted when a lone magpie swooped in front of him. Wings lifted, it flared for a landing, and began to inspect the lawn for available tidbits. Coffee mug in hand, Mason took a sip, back in the real world. The ache in his soul inflicted on him last night still throbbed. He badly needed Gramps to make it all better. The irony of that wish clear to him, he chided himself for avoiding a repeat confrontation with his old man. Instead of dealing with the problem, he sought a soft way out from a ghost, of all things. An emotionally convenient solution perhaps, he admitted, but he could not confide in anyone else. Any of his three friends would be prepared to console him and offer sage advice, but right now, he felt reluctant to reveal deep personal wounds to them. Some things, he simply could not share. Instead, he talked to his spectral grandfather, knowing his trust would not be abused when he opened the dark corridors of his mind. To maintain his sanity, he sometimes needed to firmly lock stuff in his memory that prevented him from forgetting. Lots of things he wanted to forget, though. As with everybody, his life contained a deed or two best left buried, and why he put an 'open at own peril' lock on them.

Enveloped in warm sunshine, Mason realized he must open some of those creaky memory drawers, shake out the contents, and see what they revealed in the light of objective honesty untainted by emotional bias. His father made a point perhaps, when he said Mason harbored a wrong slant on everything. Definitely not everything, he pulled himself up sternly, but perhaps on one or two things, he allowed. Despite the impulse to come to this country retreat and cut himself off from his parents to find solace, he acknowledged judiciously that he did not want to cut himself off from them completely. Apart from Grandma, they were all he had, and children were imprinted from day one to love their parents no matter what, which inflicted a lot of misery and conflicting feelings on some kids later in life.

He had a bunch of cousins who lived in Croatia, Slovenia, Austria, and Germany from both sides of his grandparents, but they were distant acquaintances at most, good for a few laughs and sharing a drink when he came to visit, not done in a while…since 2019 to be exact while on leave from his UAE job. Then the Covid thing struck and no one traveled anywhere much. Time to water his family tree with another visit? However, none of his relatives meant enough to him to draw him back there. One day, maybe…

That which is 'I' is a tangible, quantifiable self that exists, feels, and is aware of the infinite. The 'I', which encompasses everything, is the image of myself and eternity. I am the all.

Why in hell did those words suddenly come to him?

Whether his father wanted to acknowledge it or not, Mason by his very presence impacted everything and everyone around him, in the same way they impacted him. He deserved a measure of respect and approval for his life's accomplishments. He wanted it! He never roamed the streets as a bum. Not necessarily done in a way Dad would have approached things, but his father grew up in a different world with different values and expectations not necessarily compatible with those Mason grew up with. Was that acknowledgment too much to ask for from his dad? He chewed his lower lip and pondered a more profound question. Did he deserve it?

Skits! He did deserve it. Just one word…

Did he secretly hate his father for not receiving any word of encouragement or approval? A potential can of crawling demons, but Mason decided he could not push it that far. He wasn't so emotionally unstable. Still…one word.

He imagined Gramps nod from across the table, puff out a cloud of aromatic smoke from his worn pipe, and smile in agreement.

'*Ti banac,*' he often said to emphasize a point, and habitually scratched the right side of his head. '*Kako boa, boa,*' he'd add philosophically, meaning 'what will be will be'.

A somewhat phlegmatic and fatalistic attitude, but Gramps survived many turbulent years and experienced things Mason hardly found credible. When still alive, the old man never gave a crap what others said or thought about him or about anything, removed from the need to seek approval or acceptance from others, totally confident in himself. Mason admired that outlook and sought to emulate it, but the raw rub, he still wanted acceptance and approval from his parents, especially Dad, and that sucks, he admitted with chagrin. Why couldn't the dick say once, 'Well done, son'? Perhaps he did and Mason locked away the memory as it disturbed the preferred mosaic how he regarded his domineering father.

He so much wanted Dad to be like Gramps. One of life's imponderables, he decided with a forlorn sigh, knowing it to be impossible, the two coming from totally different environments and social matrix.

Since he bared everything, it did not take much smarts to figure out what soured his relationship. Although lack of approval for things he did played a prominent part. When looked at objectively, mainly small things caused fractures that over time developed into a deep rift he had now. As a kid, Mason felt an emptiness he wanted filled with laughter, fun, games, and someone to share things with. He made casual friends at the Childhood Center, and they filled his days, but did little to fill time at home.

Other kids had brothers and sisters, and he wanted one too. In September 1993—he recalled everything like it happened yesterday—Mom announced he would soon have a little sister. Mason couldn't wait, his spirits buoyed. In March 1994, she miscarried and a blanket of gloom descended on the house. His parents became withdrawn and somber. He did not understand it and voiced an obvious solution.

"Why don't you have another baby, Mom?" he asked with innocent naivety, Dad off boating somewhere with the Navy.

She fought back tears and hugged him. "I can't, honey."

"Why not?"

"When I had your sister, something happened inside me and I can't have any more children."

Later, when he came to comprehend these things, Dad told him, after the miscarriage, Mom had a hysterectomy. Mason disliked that strongly and felt cheated.

With the prospect of having another son or daughter snatched from them, his parents came to treat their house as somewhere only to stay and sleep, with Mason an unwanted nuisance. At least that is how it appeared to him. Sometimes, alone in his room, he could hear them arguing, and he pretended it never happened. At times, they sat in the lounge, stiff, silent figures, the TV providing the only movement and sound. His mom and dad had a barrier between them he could not breach, and it kept him from them. Faced with smothering emptiness, he often went to his room to watch a program or read a book, not knowing how to reach them or stifle the pain that gnawed at his chest their silence created.

Sometimes, he would retreat into his own special world and paint.

Early on at the Childhood Center, with other kids in the class, he tried his hand at painting simple settings, but quickly became dissatisfied and frustrated with the amateur results of his unskilled hands. So many vivid images crowded his mind he wanted to express, but could not make the brushes translate them to paper. One day, his elderly art teacher gave him a book on drawing techniques, composition, how to use watercolors and oils, brushes and different painting knives. Under her patient tutelage, Mason's hands eventually became extensions of his mind and the images were at last mirrored on paper and canvas. Childhood renditions that lacked sophistication, but that did not matter. He had another avenue of expression.

Many gaps remained to completely understand his parents, and they refused to open up to him, which left him to form his own conclusions, perhaps erroneous ones. Critical of almost everything Mason did, a time came when he no longer sought outward approval, although deep down, he secretly still wanted it. He needed his parents to pay for his education, but promised himself he would leave as soon as he could and rid himself off their influence.

A year later, Dad resigned his commission as a lieutenant commander and took a job with Thompson Engineering at Laverton as a senior designer. He said the company made specialty stainless steel containers for breweries, milk tankers, chemical processors, and the like. Mason recalled noise, clanging machinery, sparks, and confusion when he visited. His dad could have picked an executive job in the city, but for some reason, Nikola preferred to be a hands-on engineer. Mason did not care why his dad took the job, excited at the prospect of a full-time father at home, anticipating days of fun and games. Instead, the Adamov house remained a place of silence and dark moodiness, somewhere he came when not at the Childhood Center.

Mason felt betrayed by his parents. Both appeared to devote all their time and energy to work, and the outings they enjoyed before increasingly far apart. He liked weekend visits to his grandparents' house in Footscray, and later to their retreat at Mt. Macedon when they relocated in 1998, he only seven at the time. They gave him love and acceptance Mom and Dad failed to do.

Isolated at home, Mason learned to rely on no one. It took a number of years and a degree of maturity for him to appreciate the psychological toll his lonely home environment exacted from him and how it shaped his personality. Coupled with a sharp IQ, his teen years fueled a burning determination to leave and have a place of his own and become completely independent as soon as he started work. If his parents wanted to stew in mutual misery, they were welcome to it. He would write more satisfying pages for his life. That is exactly what he did eighteen months after he graduated. As a junior computer programmer, the ANZ bank gave him a low-interest loan and he bought a bedsitter apartment in St. Kilda not far from the beach. The day he moved in turned into pure exultation and a sense of unbounded liberty.

In many ways, he wanted to be like his father: tall, a Navy officer, athletic, a somebody. When Nikola came home on leave, Mason could not get enough of him, constantly underfoot, following him around like a puppy, looking for crumbs of affection. His dad appeared not to mind, and often shared stories about life aboard a frigate, adventures in the Arabian Gulf fighting off Iranian gunboats who sought to disrupt the flow of endless tankers exiting through the Strait of Hormuz chokepoint. This set Mason's imagination on fire, picturing himself on the bridge of a destroyer, his gaze lost somewhere on the ocean waters.

As a youngster, he often perused Dad's books stacked in the lounge's ceiling-high bookshelf, and worked through them, surprised at his father's ranging interests. For some reason, he never pictured Nikola as a bookworm. As a teen, he noted his dad rarely seemed to buy a new book, and Mason often wondered why. For him, the bookshelf opened whole new worlds, and he learned about politics, various religions, history, engineering, and sciences. He devoured texts on astronomy and enjoyed fiction on English/French naval warfare, modern warfare, techno-thrillers, science fiction, sprinkled with unusual fantasies. He adored Mary Stewart's *The Crystal Cave* and *The Hollow Hills*, amazed that Dad read such stuff. An avid reader himself, Mason often bugged Mom for money to buy books for his own growing collection. She'd shake her head and give him a handful of dollars.

Nobody's dummy, his dad entered the Australian Defense Force Academy in Canberra at eighteen, much to Milan's disapproval, considering a naval career a waste of his son's talents, and graduated with an honors degree in marine engineering. In one mellow mood, his dad said he met Brianna in 1987 at a Melbourne café, she at her lunch hour. His pretty Navy uniform helped capture her heart, he added with a nostalgic grin. They married in June 1988, her parents not enamored with their daughter spending many lonely months alone while Nikola went off cruising. A budding career as a lecturer at RMIT helped offset some of the loneliness, but Mason recalled times when his mom looked sad and despondent, and wondered why. Understanding came later. Soon after the wedding, Nikola received a subsidized loan from the Navy and the couple bought a comfortable house in South Yarra, some half-hour by tram from downtown.

As far back as he could remember, Mason's image of his father comprised of kaleidoscopic fragments. He recalled a stern figure in uniform, some outings, talks when Dad happened to be in the mood, and infrequent companionship. He loved it when Nikola came home, but they were always brief stays.

He never heard Dad argue with his parents. At least not when he was around. During one visit in 1988, Nikola announced that he submitted papers to change his name from Adamovič to Adamov. When he married Brianna, both would bear the new name. It triggered a heated row with Milan and left Mason confused. Gramps accused Nikola of forsaking his heritage, whereas Dad said he only wanted to blend into Australian society. Grandma shrugged it off, which caused Gramps to be sore at her for a time. Nonetheless, the new name stuck. Mason never cared one way or another, but admitted that Adamov came out easier.

His dad told the truth when he said Mason never paid any rent when he started work. To them and most parents, it seemed the expected thing from their children, the practice not questioned by anybody. Like taxes, one simply paid up. Questioned perhaps, but not acted on. Payback time for everything they did to raise them? It seemed the unspoken reason. Right or wrong, he rejected what he considered an outmoded philosophy and refused to pay rent. Mom tiptoed around the subject a couple of times and Dad frowned at his son's intransigence, but Mason remained unmoved, perhaps out of spite.

Subconscious revenge for what they did to him? He readily acknowledged the possibility. He may be intellectually superior to most people, but raw intellect did not protect him from reacting passionately or impulsively. Hindsight provided a very stark mirror on past reality, he reflected wryly. As he sifted through his yesterdays, Mason felt a twinge of guilt for some things he did. Because of that and reasons never fully understood or wanted to acknowledge, he sought to maintain an amicable relationship with his parents, even if a façade. A rocky road as it turned out with a deep pothole at its end.

He took a sip of coffee and grinned in acknowledgment Dad's forceful prompting to study. Without that pushing, he would probably have flunked high school and ended up as a factory worker somewhere, blaming his parents and the world for his problems. He had to give the bastard his due. Nikola instilled discipline into his life that despite the stumble in his first year, served him well at RMIT and resulting career, but he resented the way Dad went about it. Instead of dishing out constant criticism with harsh, dogmatic edicts, which generated instinctive resistance, Mason figured a softer approach might have achieved the same result. Would it have, though? Would smiles and gentle coaching move Mason from his smug complacency and sense of infallibility? Perhaps his dad knew him better than he thought. In the end, he submitted to the pressure, studied, and passed, not from any personal desire to succeed, but prove his old man wrong and show him he wasn't a failure.

Mug cold between his hands, Mason gazed at the rolling fields lost in blue haze as they merged with the horizon, and came to an unpalatable conclusion he'd shied away from admitting for a long time. All his life, he clearly lived under a blanket of pride and conceit in his abilities that blinded him to many things about his parents. Last night, he stormed out because he reached a cusp his father triggered over the damned Forester. The car meant nothing, but it did serve to bring his load of emotional baggage to the fore. Overreaction on his part? With all his achievements, did he consider himself so psychologically insecure that he still sought his dad's approval? It certainly looked like it.

He respected his parents and appreciated what they did for him, but without love. Why should he love them, when parents did some of the worst things to kids that almost irreversibly affected the child's psychology and outlook on life? Yet, society drummed into children the command to adore their parents, no matter what. This set up internal conflicts that often resulted in trauma for the child, with disastrous consequences for everybody concerned. In his case, apart from an occasional warming of the bottom for a minor misdeed, they never physically abused him. He considered what they did to be far worse. They punished him verbally without understanding the devastating effect of their words. His inability to forget made him replay incidents in his mind and he constantly stewed over the unfairness of it all.

You're an adult now, Mason. Look at your problem as an adult and stop raking over the past.

Know thyself, someone said, he reflected.

He pictured Gramps sitting on the other side of the table, puffing on his pipe.

"What now?"

'Apologize, moj mali stroj,' came the unbidden thought. *What do you know about your parents anyway? You ought to know by now what life is about. So you had one of those 'sucks' moments. There'll be others. Don't*

let one event color everything you do next that may deprive you of the good times.'

"What's the use, Gramps? I can't hope to change any of them."

'Perhaps, but you can change yourself, which in turn may be the catalyst that changes them. So far, it's all been about you. Did you consider their side?'

Mason bit his lip, admitting that Gramps could have said those words when alive, but they were not his words now. They came from Mason's psyche. He pondered the conflicting emotions they generated and wondered if they could be right. He did know a lot about his parents! After all, he lived for years with them. Pride and selective memories may have clouded his judgment, but why should he be the one to say, 'Sorry'? When he walked out last night, his subconscious told him he acted from wounded pride. He came here for answers and apparently got it. Why couldn't he accept it?

Skits!

He pursed his mouth and sighed deeply, accepting with great reluctance what he had to do, and pride be damned. The decision also brought with it a sense of relief and possible closure. He needs a man-to-man with Dad and come to a workable arrangement acceptable to both that promoted a live-and-let-live relationship or a state of permanent war. Grandma now in a nursing home with Lord knows how much time left to her, and Gramps gone, Mason did not want to alienate his parents totally, which would really leave him alone.

You wanted to be alone, didn't you?

Perhaps, but living alone did not turn out exactly fun as anticipated, he mused with a sardonic grin. He would swallow his pride and try to make things right. Better, if nothing else.

Chapter Two

Mason remembered one fine weekend—he just turned eight—sitting with Gramps on the back veranda, everybody else amusing themselves in the lounge, when his grandfather chuckled and began a story. Milan had a bagful and found in his young grandson an avid listener. Mason remembered every word, of course, but still loved to be a sounding board and simply be with Gramps. Each telling came with a slight variation, but in essence true. Mason never tried to correct Gramps on a point of inconsistency as changes or additions often provided spice and new detail.

The old man took a puff and started one of his favorite after-war yarns, still picking up the pieces after discharge from the Partisan resistance.

He and a friend, he said with a fond snicker, hid in a cornfield once and watched a crabby, stingy man without a kind bone in his scrawny body guard a small peach tree. He wore a permanent scowl as he walked the Varazdin streets and glared at anyone who greeted him. Children gave him a wide birth and tittered as he stomped by. They threw pebbles at him and scampered away with glee as he raged after them, fist held high.

Hidden by tall corn, the smell of ripe peaches made Milan's mouth water. The awful man guarded the tree all night, shotgun in lap, sometimes nodding off. Too mean to offer any peaches to his neighbors, he feared they might steal the precious fruit before he could harvest it.

Milan and his friend sneaked into the corn before dawn broke and watched the old sod guard his tree. As the sun came up, golden light filled the open, rolling meadow and the world became a bright, cheerful place, perfect for some devilment.

The old coot stood, looked around warily, and hurried off for a quick breakfast, a familiar routine by now. With no idea when he might return, not wanting to be on the receiving end of a shotgun, Milan and his friend rushed to the peach tree and quickly sawed off two limbs heavy with fruit. The plunder slung over their shoulder, they disappeared into the corn and made for their hiding place.

Minutes later, they heard a frantic bellow of rage and a torrent of profanity. The old buzzard had returned and vented outrage when he spied the damaged tree. Later in the morning, a mighty uproar swept through the town as the scandalized man sought to find who took his peaches. The incident generated a lot of local hilarity, everybody figuring the old sod deserved what he got. Nobody admitted anything, of course.

The two culprits gorged on delicious peaches, sharing some with neighbors who never cared where they came from. They merely nodded their thanks with a faint smile of understanding.

The tale finished, Mason laughed softly and shook his head at this wicked deed, clearly picturing the outraged man rampaging around in search of the miscreants. The story always generated a warm glow of deserved justice. From what Gramps said, nobody went to the old man's funeral.

"I tell you, *moj mali stroj*, although we never regretted what we did, I sometimes felt a little remorseful," Milan reflected pensively. "The mean devil had it rough during the war. First, he lost a son to the Ustaše, then a wife when the Partisans bombed his house because they thought he was a collaborator." He took a puff. After a while, he shrugged. "Anyway, the bastard still had the rest of the damned tree."

The peach episode not the only tale in Gramp's store of adventures. Like the one when he and two friends caught a stray cat. They halved two walnuts, cleaned them, and proceeded to fill the shells with tar. They stuck the shells to the cat's paws and let it go. The poor thing tried to gnaw off the annoying shells as it clanged its way along the sidewalk to disappear under a fence. Mason snickered when Milan finished, although he felt a little sorry for the poor cat, vividly picturing its plight. The things young men do…

One of Gramps' favorites was how, fresh after the grape harvest, he and three friends managed to break into a barrel of new wine.

Several streets from Milan's house, a neighbor stored four large barrels of newly fermented wine in a backyard barn. Not predisposed to share any of the old stock, he sold the stuff to local bars and supplied parties and wedding functions.

Milan and his buddies often contemplated how to get at the wine. Come late fall, the man would decant the barrels and move the wine to his cellar beyond reach. They huddled behind the barn and sniffed at the enticing aroma of fresh wine longing for a taste. After much debate and rejection of several nutty ideas, they came up with what everybody agreed to be a devilishly cunning plan. They drove a nail into a long pole, filed the end to a point, and tied a rubber hose to the pole that left a meter or so to hang from the end to serve as their instrument of dark deed.

The barn, clad with old boards, had enough gaps to push the pole through to the closest barrel. With patience and determination, they drove the nail into a large cork that plugged the barrel and gently worked it loose. The barrel open, they lowered the rubber hose and sucked until the young wine began to pour out. With no time to waste, they sampled their prize, nudging each other to be next. Head swimming, Milan suggested it would be far too dangerous to linger behind the barn where the old coot could catch them. Everybody clearly pictured the disastrous consequences that may ensue. A hurried retreat to their homes produced several bottles and jugs to be filled and enjoyed at leisure. Plunder safely stored, they replaced the cork and tapped it down.

For some two weeks until the rubber hose could not reach farther into the barrel, Milan and his pals enjoyed a happy time.

When the man eventually came to inspect his barrels, he found one only half full. This naturally set off a cascade of accusations and arguments, everybody denying knowledge of the stolen wine. Some suggested the codger drank it himself and forgot he did it, which generated nasty amusement. If the neighbors saw four youths wandering the streets looking slightly inebriated, no one said anything, figuring the stingy man deserved it.

"He never suspected you and your friends?" Mason ventured.

"Sure did, *ti banac*. Even came to our house demanding to see our wine bottles. My father sent him packing in short order, of course." Milan winked at Mason. "You see, even though still young, my dad also liked the old coot's wine."

Both burst into hearty laughter.

Other stories Gramps told were more serious.

"Like kids everywhere," he reflected once, "I liked to listen to my own paternal grandfather regale me with tales of witches and strange goings on. True or not, I found them entertaining. Kolarovec only twenty kilometers from Varazdin where we lived, my parents often visited on a weekend to scrounge a free Sunday lunch from my grandparents. We'd take an old, creaking bus and stop at Jamnik's Tavern on the road to Maribor, and walk the rest of the way. Allowed to run wild with other kids, I roamed the open fields, played games in the forest, and swam in the nearby Drava. Tired from all the action, I'd sit with Grandpa on the front veranda and bug him to tell me a tale. The way you bug me," Milan added with a disarming grin. "Anyhow, more often than not, the old man obliged. I remember one particular story…"

A beautiful maiden, his grandpa began as he puffed on his cherry wood pipe, rocking in a favorite rickety chair, often frequented a nearby forest filled with all sorts of wildlife. Long, corn-colored hair fell to her slim waist. Large blue eyes sparkled with laughter and the joy of being alive. Youths from nearby villages came to court her, but the tall, willowy maid repulsed them all, much to the lament of the youths. Of course, this raised all sorts of gossip, and mothers wanting their son marry the maid speculated what may be wrong with her. Some even considered her a witch. When the women demanded to know why the maid never wed, her mother paid them no never mind, which only fueled further speculation. The maid ignored the gossip, the barbed innuendos, and lived a carefree life, preferring the company of her forest friends.

No one knew where the maid went when she disappeared into the forest or what she did there, and those who followed her often got lost. She sometimes came home with scratches on her long, supple legs and slim arms, and her parents scolded her. How can she hope to attract a boy looking like that, they said. The scratches came from branches and shrubs, she explained cheerfully, eyes dancing with inner fire.

Milan's grandfather said he loved to hunt, an old, battered rifle cradled in his arms. He regularly brought home a hare, wild boar, or a deer, always welcomed at the farmhouse by his wife.

One sunny autumn afternoon, his worn Jager percussion rifle slung across the shoulder, a large leather rucksack to hold any game he may catch, he pecked his plump wife on the cheek and declared he would be back in time for dinner. His wife did not mind her husband's wanderings, knowing he never left chores undone.

He took a familiar worn trail into the forest, and after some time, the warm sun flickering between old birch, oak, and poplar, he took a meandering track that led to a meadow with a small lake tucked against a hillside. He liked the place, one of his favorites, as animals often came to graze on the lush grass and drink, and generally managed to shoot something. Even when he did not, he enjoyed sitting at the forest edge, take an occasional swig of wine from a flask, and listen contentedly to the soft buzz of insects as swallows swooped low over the sleepy meadow.

Suddenly, a graceful doe emerged from the trees some forty meters on his right. She paused, lifted her slender neck, sniffed the air, and slowly made her way toward the lake. Every now and then, she stopped and turned her head on lookout for possible danger. Satisfied, she walked through the tall grass with small, mincing steps.

Grandpa never saw such a beautiful deer, and watched the doe in rapt fascination as she approached the lake. At possibly fifty kilos, she would provide welcomed fresh venison for the table. He picked up the rifle and aimed at the doe's chest. A quick kill, the animal would not suffer. As he took up the trigger slack, the doe turned and looked directly at him. Even from some 150 meters, he saw her large blue eyes, something most unusual. He took a deep breath, held it, and squeezed the trigger.

The sharp crack caused startled birds into flight, and two hares bounded into thickets across the meadow. Without a sound, the doe dropped to the ground. Milan's grandfather raced through the grass to inspect his kill.

Chest heaving, he slowed and gaped in shock at what he saw as color drained from his face. He dropped the rifle and stared in startled wonder as the graceful doe turned into a naked young woman, golden hair spilled across full breasts. Bright blood oozed from a wound in the center of her chest. He thought she looked at him then, not with accusation, but resigned acceptance. Then the light faded from her eyes. As he stared at the village maid, her form shimmered, became transparent, and faded. Gradually, the flattened grass rose where she had lain.

Milan's grandfather said he felt his eyes sting and hot tears warmed his cheeks from deep loss and regret. He knelt beside the spot where the woman laid and sobbed, his heart tearing with pain. He begged forgiveness, knowing the forest had claimed the strange maid. Whether she heard him or not, he thought he saw her enchanting young face, eyes alive with laughter, rosy lips open in a broad smile. Perhaps she did forgive him, because he felt the load of guilt roll off his chest and he stood up with a lighter heart. He took a deep breath and let it out with a soft hiss as he wiped his face with a calloused hand.

He cradled the worn rifle and wearily made his way toward the forest and home, the years heavy on his shoulders. For a long time afterward, the villagers often talked about the strange young maid and wondered what happened to her. A search through the forest revealed an ankle-long green dress the maid used to wear neatly draped across a low branch. Some said she ran away with a youth from another village, but nobody knew for certain.

Mouth clamped on a pipe, Milan's grandfather declared roughly that he never went hunting again, and his old rifle remained mounted above the fireplace. On long winter afternoons, he sat before the flickering flames and stared at the gun. His wife often asked why he never hunted, sensing something unusual happened on that fateful autumn day, but he refused to say.

Finished, Milan sat in his chair and quietly puffed on his pipe.

"Believe it or not, the way my grandfather told it, I never doubted its truth, *ti banac*. Strange things happened in his day."

After a time, he'd clear his throat and start again.

"My grandmother also used to spin yarns about witches and odd happenings in Kolarovec and nearby villages around Zagorje. I often sat beside her as she rocked back and forth in her own squeaky rocking chair, eyes dreamy, lost in a time that no longer existed. I can tell you, *moj mali stroj*, she told me some whoppers."

Milan admitted to Mason that he often wondered if Grandma invented those fanciful fairytales for his entertainment or if the events actually happened. She left that for him to decide, he said.

"Real or not, I listened as she opened a magical world from an enchanted past. Take it from me, something wonderful left the world when people stopped believing in magic," he remarked solemnly and puffed.

"On one visit, I sat beside my grandmother munching a slice of cornbread smothered with homemade blackberry jam and listened to her tales of bygone days. I enjoyed it more as I used to pick the blackberries, and I got scratches to provide it," he added with a grin.

During a hot, humid summer night, Grandma began, a powerful, handsome youth from nearby Lovrečan, unable to sleep, went down to the Drava for a refreshing swim. As he broke through the thicket along the bank, he spotted four naked maidens dancing around a cairn of stones. The full moon made it seem like day. The youth froze in his tracks and stared mesmerized at the beautiful women, unable to move.

Suddenly, they stopped dancing and turned as one to look at him. Something in their dark eyes broke the youth's stare. He turned and ran back toward the village. Behind him, he heard soft footfalls and knew the girls were after him. Gasping for breath, lungs burning, he ran faster, knowing something bad would happen if they caught him. Before he reached his house, they did catch him. One by one, they rode him and left him senseless by the roadside. In the morning, an old woman going to the local store found him and demanded he tell her what happened. Reluctantly, intensely embarrassed, he told her. Instead of laughing at him or dismissing the story as a product of a drunken imagination, she revealed in a rasping voice that the four maids were sisters who lived in nearby Babinec, and everybody suspected them to be witches. She also said he should never go to the Drava after midnight or they would possess him.

That night, despite the warning, afraid but excited, the youth went to the river and spied on the dancing girls. This time, he stayed put when they dashed toward him. They rode him, smiling all the time, whispering soothing words, and left him at the water's edge when they finished.

The next day, something screamed inside him never go to the Drava again, feeling the women somehow drained him of something, but he could not help himself. They clearly enchanted him, captivating him with their beauty and bodies.

For seven nights, he went to the river where the maidens rode him. Each morning, he felt older, depleted of energy, hair graying, muscles wasting. On the eighth morning, wandering children found an old, shriveled man by the river. No one knew him or how he came to be there. The youth's distraught mother claimed him to be her son, recognizing the clothing he wore, but the villagers did not believe her and scoffed. They said her son was a vigorous youth of twenty-two years.

Two days later, someone said the four sisters left Babinec and moved to Cestica. The mother always insisted they bewitched her son, but no one could prove anything against the sisters. The villagers laughed at her, saying her son probably ran off with some maid and never returned. One year to the day after her son's disappearance, a neighbor found her dead in her bedroom, a wooden stake driven through her heart.

"Make of that what you will," Gramps mused. "I'm a believer. There is more to this world than physics and engineering," he added sagely with a grave nod.

Mason also wondered, although the tales went against every scientific principle he knew, but as Gramps said, not everything revolved around known physics. After all, magic merely describes a phenomena not understood. It definitely gave Mason material to gnaw on.

"One story my grandma liked to tell that always stuck with me was about a wandering old woman and a rich miser. A small detail here and there changed with the telling, but the story remained true in essence, and she always started the tale in the same way."

One blustery evening with cold drizzle coming down, an old woman, a crooked cane held in a gnarled hand, stooped after carrying a lifetime of burdens, hobbled wearily toward an iron-wrought gate. Dressed in black, a dark scarf covered a surprisingly youthful face. She opened the creaking gate and made her way along the gravel roadway toward a stately mansion. Bright light came from tall windows. Gray smoke drifted up from two red brick chimneys, instantly whipped away by a frigid wind. The woman clutched her meager garments tight around her chest and shuddered from a sudden chill spasm that raced through her. She ambled to the grand entrance guarded by four white columns that held up the portico. Enticing aroma of roasting meat and hot broth drifted toward her and her stomach rumbled in anticipation.

No one knew her in the village, her age, where she came from, or where she went. She appeared, and as mysteriously, vanished. Kindly people fed her and sometimes gave her a bed. She did not mind where she slept. Before a warm hearth or barn beside cows who sent their warm breath on her and nuzzled her. The old woman appreciated the kindness extended her and always thanked everyone profusely. Some said, and it might be simple idle village gossip, those who helped her enjoyed a change of fortune in their lives. They were either happier, their luck turned, or found lost love. Just talk, Grandma rumbled thoughtfully as she rocked, pipe stuck between stained teeth.

Anyhow, the woman stopped in front of the elaborately carved door and twice banged the iron clacker shaped like a lion's head. Footsteps sounded inside and the door soundlessly opened. She saw an elderly man wearing a butler's regalia and warm air wafted around her from inside. Yellow light danced from candles mounted on a crystal chandelier hung from a dark wooden ceiling crossed with heavy black beams.

In a labored breath, she asked for shelter from the inclement weather outside. A rough voice demanded who stood at the door. The butler winced and declared that some poor woman wanted refuge for the night.

A middle-aged man in maroon trousers and evening jacket appeared and glowered at her. The butler politely stepped back. Everyone in the area knew the miserly, mean, self-centered coot who lived in the stately home. The selfish thing never gave anybody the time of day or a moldy crust of bread, preferring to throw it to the hogs. Nobody loved him, and he regarded the villagers with equal scorn.

One look at the woman and the man's mouth curved up in a sneer.

"Begone, you old hag. I have no time for you. Find work and you'll have shelter. I'm tired of all your kind, wanting everything for nothing. Begone, I say!"

The woman studied him, then straightened. "I hope you found everything in your life and are enjoying the rewards of your labors, sour sir," she declared in a surprisingly strong voice. "May lightning strike your grave if you don't mend your ways."

Back bent, she slowly walked toward the gate as the heavy door slammed shut behind her.

Nobody knew what happened to the old woman or where she went. Tales filtered from nearby villages who said they saw her and benefited by showing her kindness.

The miserable rich man never changed, became even meaner, and turned into a recluse. Shaking their heads, people often prayed for some misfortune to overtake him.

"Grandma always paused then, gray aromatic smoke rising from her pipe as she rocked back and forth. A darker cloud of smoke shot from her mouth as she puffed," Milan said, reflecting on the memory. "Although I knew what happened next, I always asked. Three years later, she said with a soft growl, the miserly rich man took ill and suddenly died to the delight of nearby villagers. The funeral procession had only a handful of mourners, mainly household staff. They came because they genuinely cared, or more likely, Grandma added with a dry cackle, they celebrated the miserable man's demise.

"As the procession neared the cemetery, dark clouds gathered overhead. The priest looked up and scowled, urging the procession to hurry. When they reached the gravesite, two men waited to lower the polished, carved casket into the ground. By then, it became quite dark and a rumble of ominous thunder marched across the sky.

"The priest grew frantic, demanding the casket be lowered right away, not bothering with the usual prayers. Hardly in the ground, the priest shouted to everyone to stand back. Seconds later, a bolt of light crashed into the open grave and the air trembled from the sharp crack that followed. Everybody looked at each other in wonder, then approached the smoking grave. They peered into the hole and gaped at the shattered, empty casket inside. The devil claimed his own, they whispered soberly and nodded wisely. As rapidly as the clouds gathered, they scattered and warm sunshine bathed the countryside, dispelling the air of evil in the air."

Milan went on: "I once asked Grandma if she ever met the old woman. After some time, lost in contemplation, she denied ever seeing her. The way she said it, though, prompted me to think otherwise, certain that more lay behind the story than she said, and I chose to believe their paths did cross, as she and her family always enjoyed a good life, health, and a modicum of prosperity."

A puff of aromatic smoke later, he waved a hand. "Fetch us that bottle of *rakija*, boy."

Tall tales for an impressionable youth, or something from a different reality. Mason could not decide. In the end, he simply enjoyed the tales without injecting metaphysical mush into them.

Sun warm on his face, he allowed himself to drift through youthful yesterdays.

Grandma never had such stories to tell. Raised in Zagreb, a large city, she grew up in a comparatively modern, mechanical environment, a car here and there, electricity, plumbing, and sterile cleanliness. Removed from nature, people forgot magic. That's how Gramps explained it.

Mom and Nada talked incessantly when his parents brought him to Mt. Macedon. Women talk, which never interested him. He preferred to sit quietly with Dad and Gramps on the back veranda and listen as they exchanged stories, mulled over an odd domestic problem, or pontificated sagely on world issues, always with a smirk at political antics everywhere. Without realizing, he absorbed a lot of information, not all true, of course, their discourse colored by personal bias.

Gramps…

Born in 1923, Varazdin, Croatia, in the old Kingdom of Yugoslavia, life handed Milan Adamovič his share of curves. Not very tall, only 166cm, but physically surprisingly strong. A man with a coarse temper, he tended to be impatient with people he saw as obtuse, but could still be sensitive and tender, particularly with Grandma, his first and only love for whom he burned a flame only death managed to quench. If Milan's soul still existed somewhere, Mason knew that flame still burned. Whenever he visited, he never heard Gramps raise his voice to Nada. A disapproving sigh or shake of his head conveyed admonition or dissatisfaction. It is almost as though they communicated telepathically.

Gramps said he was the youngest, with two older sisters who considered him a late nuisance in their comfortable, three-bedroom, solid brick house. He learned early to fight for his rightful share of any cake or dessert his mom made. He particularly loved *palačinke*, light crepes filled with cheese or marmalade—jam a rare luxury even when home-made—and baked until crisp.

During his high school years, he loved economics and accounting, and often told his dad he wanted to study for a *fakultet*—degree—and the family could afford it, he'd say. With a degree behind him, he would manage the family farm and wine business, something his parents looked on favorably, as their daughters showed no interest in running any enterprise, considering it beneath them. His dad's oldest sister lived in Zagreb and he'd move in with her until he finished his studies, Milan pointed out with unshakeable logic. It never occurred to him that his dad's sister might not want him around. They were family, no? In summer of 1939, at sixteen, he graduated high school with honors, applied to the University of Zagreb, and took English as an elective. On Friday, September 1, he attended orientation day, keen to start the academic year and explore the city's attractions. On the same day, Hitler invaded Poland. Despite understandable unrest and insecurity that spread through the country, the University remained open.

The Ustaše, *Hrvatski revolucionarni pokret*, the Croatian Revolutionary Movement that promoted independence from Serb rule, forcibly recruited most male University students, pressing the older ones into uniform. The organization aligned itself with Germany who promised them statehood if they won the war. With Hitler's army marching through Europe, they figured statehood to be a sure bet. Milan said he detested the movement's fascist policies, ultra-nationalism, and atrocities committed against fellow Croats, Serbs, the Romani gypsies, and political dissidents in general. He had little choice, though. Remain a card member or be branded a traitor with negative consequences for his family, and probably get thrown out of the University.

In April 1941, Germany invaded Croatia and renamed it the *Nezavisna Država Hrvatska*, a puppet state ruled by the Ustaše. In July, the school year ended and the University shut its doors for the duration. Two years into his degree, Milan saw an opportunity to escape the Ustaše and joined the Partisan resistance. A fate he soon realized left him in a perhaps worse predicament. Guerilla warfare hardly something he envisaged or enjoyed. He saw nothing romantic or glamorous about it the after-war stories and films made out. Nevertheless, the decision turned out to be immensely beneficial at war's end. Discharged in August 1945, Sergeant Adamovič ended the war with four medals awarded for bravery under fire—that's what the citations said, and Milan did not want to spoil things with truth—which later helped him secure a job at the new Ministry of Finance and a free apartment in Zagreb, a prize beyond measure for the newlywed veteran.

He never warmed to the Communist Party or its socialist manifesto, but his former Partisan commander, a Serb, but otherwise a nice enough guy, quietly told him to join or he'd find it difficult to obtain decent work, and the Party would always be on his case, considering him a counterrevolutionary. Joining did not mean he must become a communist, and a membership card enhanced his social standing. So he joined, a matter of pragmatism rather than political conviction. He attended twice-yearly indoctrination classes to maintain a facade of loyalty, but everybody slept through them as the Party mouthpiece droned on, not believing any of the propaganda himself. Milan also worked at a local collective farm a few times a year, regarded as a huge joke. When equipment broke down or tools disappeared, nobody came to replace them or fix a broken tractor. No one benefited from the harvests except a few Party manipulators, and much remained to rot in untended fields when not plundered by the locals.

The way Gramps told it, he met Nada in July 1945 at a Zagreb hospital suffering from a painful infection on both feet he got in the last months of the war. Good boots hard to come by at any time, everybody made do with what they could scrounge, seeing how a dead German had no further use for them. Milan immediately fell under the spell of the 168cm-tall, raven-haired student theater nurse, and they began to date, much to her parents' fervent disapproval. Only eighteen, still too young for a mature relationship, they told her. If she really wanted someone, pick a prominent Party luminary. Pragmatism, though, never had a chance when faced off against crazy love.

Telling the story, Milan always paused and puffed contentedly on his pipe. Mason could only imagine what went on in the old man's mind.

"You know, *moj mali stroj*, you heard every soldier's eyeball click when your grandmother walked into the ward. Black eyes large enough to drown in, perfect milky features, cheerful disposition, stunning figure, she laughed easily as she fended off endearing propositions from amorous patients. Mine too." Milan chuckled and winked at Mason.

"You'll know all this soon enough yourself. Her mere presence more than any medicine helped me get better. You've never seen a more gorgeous *puca*. I loved her sunny smile and the way she absently brushed a little black mole on her right cheek. When a lock of hair fell across her left eye, she'd absently tuck it behind her ear and tilt her head, eyes bright with amusement, and kept talking. The day I left the hospital, I plucked more courage than I thought I had and asked her out. When she said yes, I danced in heaven and never questioned my luck.

"With only a year to finish my degree, I did not want Nada to marry a common laborer. In 1946, the country still a mess, the University of Zagreb opened its doors again and I enrolled. My four medals and a recommendation from my former Partisan commander, now a big wheel in the Party, helped get me accepted. In August 1947, I married my sweet twenty-year-old bride, a double celebration as I also got my *fakultet*. Her parents accepted the inevitable with good grace and turned out to be very nice folks. We both wanted kids, but without a measure of financial security, life would be tough and we held off for a while. Elena came along in 1952 and life became sweet. Unfortunately, she died in 1960 from a Rotavirus infection the hospital couldn't treat. Her death hit Nada hard and probably contributed to a miscarriage in 1961. In 1962, Nikola came along and life settled down." He paused and scratched his head.

"Everybody had it rough after the war as people scrambled to salvage what remained of their shattered lives, *Bog ti mazne oči*," Gramps used to say, teeth clamped on his pipe. "Many saw it as an opportunity to settle old grudges through anonymous denunciation. That's how my father got himself into trouble. A jealous neighbor, resentful of my dad's land holdings and business success, dobed him to the Udba, claiming he collaborated with the Germans. A load of cow poop, but the action saw Dad thrown into jail and all our properties confiscated. They left us the house, though. I pleaded with the Zagreb Commissar, my former Partisan commander, that he had a case of sour grapes, and begged him to release my father. They eventually let him go, but we never got our lands back. If not for my medals, my dad would probably have ended his days on Goli Otok, *ti banac*. Yep, things were rough for a while and never got better."

"How do you mean?" Mason wanted to know.

"The Serbs moved in and occupied most government and civil service positions, and installed themselves into major businesses," Gramps remarked ruefully and shrugged. "The victors claim the spoils, I guess. What grated on my nerves and with people generally, although nobody dared raise a voice in protest and risk getting nabbed, was rampant corruption, nepotism, and plain incompetence running the country. In late 50s, I often talked to Nada about escaping to Austria and settle in Canada or Australia. Stubborn like all Zagrebčani, she didn't like the idea of moving to some strange country on the other side of the world and abandon her family. We had a nice two-bedroom government apartment in the center of Zagreb, good jobs, a relatively comfortable life, and friends. Why leave? If we stay, I told her, Nikola would end up a true communist, something I didn't want. Nada's no dummy and understood perfectly how the system would turn her son. Despite everything, we never moved, and you can understand why."

"If you got caught, you'd probably end up in jail," Mason ventured.

"No probably about it, *jebem ti brž vuru*. If I wasn't married, I'd probably go for it, but I had Nada and Nikola to think of. Funny how fates work, because in the fall of 1963, Yugoslavia allowed people to leave freely and many did. So, in December 1964, after some tearful family goodbyes, we took a train to Vienna and applied to the Red Cross to emigrate to Australia. The authorities held us for two months in Traiskirchen, a camp some twenty kilometers from Vienna while Australian authorities processed our application. I felt certain they'd accept us, as Australia at the time badly needed skilled and unskilled labor to support a growing post-war economy. When the red tape unwound, they took us to Genoa with other immigrants and we were shipped to Melbourne."

Mason knew what happened then. Gramps told it often enough. The Australian authorities moved them to the Maribyrnong Immigration Detention Center, made from corrugated iron military 'Nissen' huts used during WWII. They lived there for ten months until Milan managed to put a deposit on a house in Footscray. While in Maribyrnong, his friends told him about the Croatian House—*Hrvatski Dom*—and helped him get a job at Rio Tinto in the city as an accountant. For two years, he attended the Footscray Institute of Technology part-time for an upgraded accounting degree, as Australia did not accept all his Croatian qualifications.

"Bureaucratic cow poop, but that's how things were," Gramps grumbled between puffs.

The *Dom* also helped find Grandma a job at Olex Cables in Tottenham. A six-minute train trip from Footscray, something she appreciated. Not able to speak English then, it made things difficult for her. She tried to get a job as an attending nurse at several Melbourne hospitals, but her dated skills were a downer. Unable to take time off to study with young Nikola to look after, she took what she could get. By 1974, life became easier and they owed the bank very little on their Footscray house.

Past tales and images crowding him, Mason tossed back the last of his now tepid coffee. Although amusing, he did not come to Mt. Macedon to be diverted from solemn soul-searching. Distracted temporarily perhaps, but only to fill out the mosaic he wanted to assemble. He still needed to put several large pieces into their proper place.

Enough daydreaming and focus!

He disliked confronting his parents, especially Dad, but accepted the stark need if he wanted closure and a measure of inner peace. His mouth twitched. He may get closure of sorts, but not necessarily peace. Everything depended on how his father would react. What if he refused to see him? Last night, Mason said some cutting things—his dad lashed out as well, he reminded himself—that may have widened the chasm between them beyond bridging. No way to know until he faced his old man, and mulling over 'what if' scenarios a waste of energy.

A loud exhale, he padded into the kitchen to wash the mug. He'd see his parents tomorrow, Saturdays always busy for them.

'Do it now, moj mali stroj! Don't procrastinate.'

His grandfather's words loud in his mind, Mason pursed his lips, accepting that putting things off would not solve anything, and probably make doing something later harder. *This afternoon, then*, he told himself with resolve, not looking forward to the encounter at all. While here, may as well do some cleaning…

Chores done, he walked down the grassy slope to where the cypress stood almost three meters tall. It would not get any taller. Hands clasped before him, he looked down and pictured the craggy face, old briar stuck between the teeth.

"Rest, Gramps. I miss you."

Chapter Three

Mason eased the Forester into the driveway, bit his lower lip, and switched off the engine, wishing the butterflies in his stomach would bugger off. He never liked confrontations, which often tended to degenerate into something physical. He never backed down or knuckled under to a bully, though, having learned early that submission only encouraged more bad days.

An episode in grade four served as a turning point.

Bonzo, two years older, always picked on younger kids and found the withdrawn Mason with his streak of pale hair an easy target to torment. One day, surrounded by three hangers-on, they began to push him around as he stood in the canteen queue for lunch. Bonzo knocked him to the floor and his cronies jeered. Mason got up and they tripped him again. One teacher saw everything and hauled Bonzo and his buddies before the principal. It apparently made the thug more determined to make Mason's life miserable.

He came home once with a bruised cheek and Mom naturally wanted to know what happened. On leave at the time, Dad walked into the lounge and waited for an explanation. Mason often sidelined his mother, but his father's imposing figure and stern expression demanded a straight answer. So he spilled everything. With a surprising show of understanding and support, his dad said he must learn to handle himself and enrolled him at a local karate club, adding a harsh warning not to become a bully himself once he gained some skill.

Five weeks later, Mason learned enough to face Bonzo with resolve. The bully began to shove him, helped by his sidekicks. When Bonzo attempted to punch him, Mason blocked the move and sent his fist into the kid's solar plexus. His nemesis doubled over and panted for breath. Mason kicked him in the stomach, which sent Bonzo flailing to the ground. He looked at the other three, ready to deal with them. If they rushed him, he'd be in trouble, but such thugs relied on a leader to start something. With kids crowding them, waiting to see what would happen, the three walked off with threatening glares at Mason.

It took another altercation with Bonzo to convince the bully to leave him alone. He never had that kind of trouble again. Confidence boosted, he continued his karate lessons through high school until he earned a brown belt, not interested pursuing the more intellectual side of the art.

To face a bully takes resolution, a measure of skill, and preparedness to get hurt, not always possible. Confronting his dad only required resolution. Any hurt would be psychological, not physical, perhaps a worse outcome. He stood at the double door entrance and extended a stiff finger toward the doorbell button, not wanting to admit he felt intimidated at the prospect of facing his father, feelings still mixed after last night, Gramp's imaginary words notwithstanding. He clenched his teeth and pressed the brass button. Tubular bells chimed and, after several seconds, he recognized the heavy footfalls. Mouth tight, he waited. The door opened and Nikola's face froze into an expressionless mask.

"We need to talk, Dad," Mason declared evenly, not flinching from his father's hard gaze. After a moment of palpable tension, Nikola stepped to one side.

"Come in," he said gruffly.

Somewhat relieved—he could've had the door banged in his face—and more than a little apprehensive, Mason strode into the lounge. His mother looked up from watching TV and her eyes grew big.

"Mason…"

Without saying anything, he walked to her and planted a kiss on her cheek. Surprised, she stood and hugged him.

"I'm so glad you're here," she whispered, leaned back, and brushed his cheek with a soft finger. "We parted—"

"Mom—" He stopped when Nikola cleared his throat.

"After last night, I didn't expect to see you," his dad declared truculently.

Mason swallowed a rush of resentment and squared his shoulders. If he did not do this now, he may never want to again. Afterward, neither may want to make the first reconciliation gesture, which would permanently cement the rift between them.

"I've been doing some thinking," he replied evenly.

"With what?" Nikola retorted imperiously.

A hot wave of indignation swept through Mason, mixed with acute disappointment at having wasted his time coming. It appeared his old man had no interest in mending fences. About to make a snappy remark, he let it go, not looking for an open fight. It wasn't worth it. It cost him a lot to make this gesture by coming. If his dad failed to meet him halfway, he would not wear the blame because he did not try to patch things up, and he needed to have his say.

"Stop it!" his mother barked. "You're being an ass, Niki. Your son said some hurtful things last night, some of it justified—"

"Brianna!"

"—and you said some hurtful things too. I don't want to see you two fighting. Forget your resentment and hear him out."

Nikola glared at her. "Resentment? It's years of taking shit from him and pretending everything's peachy. He walked away from us to be on his own. Well, if he wants to be alone, fine. I don't need him either."

"You're such a jerk! He left because we drove him away! If we don't make an effort to settle things now, we *will* lose him. Do you really want that?"

Mason regarded his mother in new light, startled that she stood up to Dad. A hard woman at times, she tended to avoid making a scene in an effort to maintain family harmony, which only shelved the issue, allowing it to fester and grow. He seldom heard them quarrel, at least not in his presence, although he did hear them sometimes when in his room. Children actually did not understand their parents, he admitted. Of course, it went both ways.

Nikola pursed his mouth. "Okay, boy, spill it."

Still smarting from his father's rebuke, Mason wasn't sure he wanted to settle things. He swallowed his pride, realizing he faced a tipping point. Did he want to be totally alone, his parents only a bad memory? Alone sucks sometimes. It hadn't been all bad, though, and why he came here. He wished his parents were like Liam Anderson's. Every time he visited, they seemed to mesh so well, he sensed it, and Liam never said they gave him a hard time or argued. So he said. One of life's imponderables.

He held his breath and let it out slowly.

"Let's get something straight, Dad. I'm not a boy and don't treat me as one. That's been your problem. You cannot admit that I'm a grown man with my own ideas, plans, and ambitions. I made some mistakes, I admit, and I'll probably make more, but they're my mistakes. You don't run my life. I don't mind constructive input from you. You have a lifetime of experiences I never did, and I'd welcome your advice, but not constant criticism for everything I do."

Nikola scowled. "No shit."

"No shit. I didn't like the way we parted last night, and I'm not here to unload a litany of grievances that drove us apart. Perhaps I do have a wrong slant on some things as you said. Well, I know I do. On the other hand, you never bothered to understand my point of view either, automatically judging that I'm wrong, forcing your rigid dictates on me."

"Now, just a damn minute—"

Mason raised his hand. "Let me finish. You know how much I always wanted your approval and acceptance, but on the way here this afternoon, I realized you're incapable of showing it and

I don't need or want it anymore."

His mother gasped. "Manny!" she cried out, then blushed crimson.

Mason gave a tight smile. "It's all right, Mom. I've gotten over it."

She blinked, taken aback by his reaction.

"Like I started to say, Dad, what happened last night forced me to do a lot of hard thinking."

"You went to Mt. Macedon?" Nikola prompted.

"I wanted to clear my head."

"Running away, eh? You're good at that. Always skulking to your grandfather when you couldn't take it."

Mason stiffened and his insides melted. "You don't know the half of it. You never did. I came to try and patch things up, but it seems I'm wasting my time with you as always. I tried to deny it, but I'm forced to accept that you're a total flake, Dad. I give up. I give up trying to find a way to please you. Go to hell," he declared and headed for the door.

"Wait, Manny!" Brianna grabbed his arm.

Mason stopped and slowly turned.

Cheeks flushed, she looked like she wanted to slap her husband. "For heaven's sake, Niki! Don't be so churlish."

He shot her a dark look. "That's how you treat a child!"

"Bye, Mom."

Bitter, disillusioned, Mason pursed his lips and departed, heart heavy, burdened by a lifetime of regrets. His part done, not his problem if Dad refused to meet him halfway. He closed the door after him and hurried to his car, annoyed to feel the sharp sting in his eyes. Brianna's cutting voice came through the lounge window, but he couldn't make out the words. He didn't care, resigned to the realization he might never step through that door again. Buckled up, the Forester purred at the touch of the starter button and he engaged reverse. His dad appeared in the doorway, hesitated, and strode toward him.

"Come inside, Mason." No longer commanding, his father looked tired and worn out.

About to tell him to screw himself, he stared at his old man for what seemed an eternity, then switched off the engine and climbed out.

Skits!

Nikola exhaled loudly, reached out and tugged Mason's arm.

"Come, son. You're right. We need to talk."

"Dad—"

"I won't be an asshole, if that's worrying you."

Mouth tight, Mason nodded, not trusting himself to speak. It would be easy to say the wrong thing.

Nikola tugged harder and Mason allowed himself to be led inside. His mom held clenched fists on hips, cheeks flushed as she glared at her husband.

"Niki—"

He waved her to silence and faced Mason. "I'm the one who must atone. You really pissed me off last night, boy, but in my clumsy way, I appreciate that you had the courage to face me and try to sort things out. You talk and I'll listen. How about it?"

It clearly cost his dad a lot to say those words, not usually prepared to back down to anyone for anything. Although still angry, Mason pushed back his bitterness. If he walked out now, it may be forever, and he did not want that, not really. He took a few seconds to settle himself.

"Jeez, Dad. You never do things the easy way. What happened last night had to come sometime and left me badly shaken. I so much wanted the evening to talk openly, have a few laughs with Grandma, and enjoy each other's company. We didn't have many such evenings. Then you assumed your navy commander persona that allowed no quarter and I resented you treating me like a kid. I have my dignity, something you never recognized or weren't prepared to accept, and I couldn't take anymore from you. Despite what you may think, I did not run away when I went to Gramp's place."

"Mason—"

"My turn. Being there helped me sort out a few things I didn't want to acknowledge. You of all people should understand why I did it. You liked to see your father for the same reason I did. Well, sitting on the back veranda, I faced my demons. Believe it or not, I came to apologize for what I said last night."

His mom paled and placed a palm across her mouth.

The orderly speech he prepared in tatters, Mason hurried to unburden himself, his resolve crumbling under an assault of conflicting emotions and his dad's hard stare.

"I'm sorry for what I said and the hurt I inflicted on both of you. I know saying it doesn't wash away the past, but I forced myself to understand and accept many things better, and I hope you'll forgive me, or at least not hold things against me too much. I admit my faults, which shaped how I behaved all the years I lived in this house. I don't care to dissect my life or yours, except to say this. Because I didn't get acceptance from you, when I started work, I sought to leave as soon as I could and free myself from your stifling influence. I haven't said it before, but I'm saying it now. I appreciate the sacrifices you two made to send me through school, and," Mason's mouth twitched, "the kicks you dished out to make me knuckle down because you're a flake, Dad. You can't help it."

Nikola clamped his mouth and stood there, appearing to take it.

Mason turned to face his mother. "About the rent. I didn't pay you anything because I felt you didn't deserve it. Rebellion on my part, nothing more."

"Manny—"

"As for you, Dad, I don't know why you never gave me a single gesture of acknowledgment. Like I said, I gave up trying to understand. Regardless of my psychological baggage, you're my only family and I want to feel welcomed when I walk into this house. Not that I feel welcomed now," Mason added bitterly. "We can't paper over the past, and we shouldn't, but I came in the hope that perhaps we can be more tolerant of our failings and go from there. A fresh start," he ended, emotionally exhausted. He searched his father's inscrutable eyes. "Just one word of approval, Dad. That's all I ever wanted. One lousy word."

"Mason, the rent, it was never about the money, dear," his mom said. "It represented a symbolic gesture we expected from you for everything we did to raise you."

"Yeah, I got it," Mason said, weary of the whole thing. Chagrined, he realized he sounded as stubborn as his old man.

"You finished?" Nikola demanded.

Mason noted the heavy scowl and waited for his father's judgment with indifference, not caring what his old man thought.

"You certainly unloaded a lot of baggage...son. Something I didn't expect, and I respect you for it. This is kind of hard for me, but since we're airing dirty laundry, a lot of it mine, I guess, it makes it my turn. Life would have been much easier for everybody if you were only a normal boy instead of a damn genius, but you are, and that's been *your* problem! Never mind.

"You're right when you said we owed you everything we could do for you. I never wanted or demanded servile gratitude from you. I did expect a measure of understanding and respect. Despite all your smarts, you showed that you didn't understand and wrapped yourself in a smug cocoon of superiority, blaming everything that went wrong for you on us. It puzzled and disappointed me. My fault. I should have been around more and talked to you to make you understand."

"Dad—"

Nikola raised a hand. "This must be said. I spent a lot of time in the Navy absorbed in my career, which I realized made life very hard for your mother. I didn't realize how hard it actually had been...and on you. Last night, she and I talked about many things. You weren't the only subject of discussion. When I came home on leave, we all pretended that everything was fine and I never looked beyond the superficial façade. I admit my life went off the rails a little when she miscarried. I so much wanted another child. I resigned my commission to be with her and make it up to her, and be with you. That's what I told myself. For a long time afterward, I hid the pain of her loss by taking it out on her, and indirectly on you, and buried myself in work."

Brianna stared at her husband in shock.

Mason also stared, never expecting his dad to make such an admission, painful memories etched deep on his face. An apology of sorts as far as Nikola could bring himself to make. Mason wondered why everybody kept things bottled up that allowed issues to simmer until the whole thing became too sour to resolve. He included himself in that multifaceted equation, he acknowledged ruefully. Had he confronted his father years ago, everybody would have avoided the subsequent angst. At least he liked to think so.

"It took a while before I came to my senses," Nikola went on looking bemused at the realization. "By then, the damage was done. When I decided to reach out, you were already at RMIT, a willful teenager set in your ways determined to do it alone. I resented your standoffishness and I punished you by withdrawing my approval, which, I admit, only made things worse between us. Believe it or not, I wanted to change things, but I didn't know how. Proud and willful like you, I guess, not prepared to admit my faults. Then you started work and moved out. When we did see each other, both of us had a protective wall neither wanted to breach. I didn't say it before, but I'm saying it now. I've always been proud of you and admired your accomplishments. I'm also sorry about last night, but you made me so angry." He snorted. "Shit. I never thought I'd hear myself say these things."

Brianna embraced him and he cupped her face between his hands. "You're a lug. Did you know that?"

His mouth twitched. "I never blamed you for the miscarriage, my noble soul," he growled, "and in my clumsy way, I tried to make it up to you. I did, didn't I? If just a little?"

"Since we're being honest, you're an asshole," she murmured tenderly. "But I took you for better or worse, and I swallowed the hurt, although there were times I wanted to leave you. I resented that you drove Mason away, and I resented the lonely months I endured while you were off boating, but it hasn't been all your doing. I wasn't exactly an exemplary mother either. We both made him into what he is now." She turned to face her son. "Your father allowed the Navy to take over his life. Without realizing it, I allowed my career at RMIT to do the same thing and misunderstood your tendency to be alone as self-reliance instead of what it was…need for a real mother."

Mason did not trust himself to speak. After a moment of echoing silence, he brushed her arm. "And I pretended I didn't need you in an attempt to compensate. A tender smile and an occasional hug would have been enough."

"I'm so sorry about that, Manny," she replied in contrition, eyes ready to spill tears.

Nikola wrapped her in his arms and stared at her. "It looks like we were a couple of jerks."

Her face shone with inner light. "One of us certainly was," she replied huskily and kissed him.

Nikola pulled back and looked at Mason. "Son…" He swallowed and took a deep breath. "I know I'm not a good father, and it's my fault how things turned out. Your apology caught me by surprise." He exhaled loudly and shook his head. "It's something I never expected from you and showed great maturity. It also reinforced your accusation that I don't really know you. All this time, I thought I did, colored by my preconceptions." Nikola gave a bitter laugh. Brianna pursed her lips and reached up to touch his arm, then thought better of it.

"Milan sure as hell didn't know me, but I sort of understood why. We grew up in two different worlds and he used his last years living in a nostalgic past. A past I never paid much attention to. I was glad, though, that you two got along. I'm sorry as hell, son, that we never managed to do the same. If not too late, I'd like to change that and get to know the Mason you're now," he growled and stuck out his hand. "A grown man I can treat as an equal. I won't say this will wipe the slate clean, but I'm prepared to make a fresh start if you are. You're my son and I don't want us to part in anger, perhaps forever. How about it?"

Mason stared at the preferred hand. What the hell went on here?

A cascade of memories tripped over each other as his life unfolded before him in fast forward. They said time heals all wounds and dulls the pain. His problem, eidetic memory did not permit him to heal, or he chose not to, and the pain never went away, always sharp and poignant for him to recall. It is what he remembered most about his father…the pain, broken by rare moments of treasured closeness. Mason resented that pain, unable to forget or heal.

'Shove them into the open at own peril drawer, moj mali stroj.'

Grave, uncertain and tense, his father waited. Strong-willed, he rarely showed emotion, considering display of any feelings a weakness. For him to lay it bare now…

Mason took the proffered hand between both of his and squeezed hard. "I'd like that, Dad," he said gruffly. A surge of unexpected affection made him want to embrace his father, but he refrained. He wanted his dad to treat him as a man, not a fawning adolescent. Nikola appeared to recognize the change and pursed his mouth as he returned the grip. His mom felt no such inhibition, hugged him, and kissed him on the cheek.

"Welcome home, Manny. Your home always. This calls for a celebration of sorts. I'll get some coffee and cake. Walnut roll; your favorite. I made it this morning."

Mason winced, uncomfortable with all the raw revelations everybody had spilled, the air thick with them. "Thanks, Mom, but maybe I should leave. I'm still mixed up about many things—"

"Then we'll talk and sort 'em out," his father announced firmly. "It's been a while since we had a good heart-to-heart, and…" His face became blank as he stared at nothing.

Mason glanced at his mom about to make a comment, but she shook her head.

"…it seems the time for it," Nikola resumed as though nothing had happened. He caught Mason's concerned look and winced. "I did it again?"

"Uh huh." Dad's involuntary episodes of narcolepsy bothered him, especially lack of treatment. Nikola had the usual CAT and MRI scans, but the specialists found nothing. Not surprising, his mom would say, as he had nothing in his head to find.

Brianna patted Nikola's shoulder. "Don't worry about it, dear. You were saying?"

"That our son should set his ass down and let you fuss over him. Coffee for me too," he added and steered Mason to the beige leather couch. He grabbed the remote, switched off the TV, and glanced out the window. "Not a bad looking car."

Mason chuckled. "You're a piece of work, Dad."

"Yeah, so I'm told," Nikola responded cheerfully. "Not always in a kind way. How about a shot of bourbon, your poison."

"I could use one."

"So could I. Perhaps more than one."

Nikola went to the liquor cabinet and poured two tumblers. Neither took ice. He handed one to Mason and sprawled onto a chair opposite the elaborately carved wooden coffee table. A gift to his father from a friend at the Croatian House.

Mason brought up his and they touched glasses. "Cheers." He took a sip of smooth whiskey and looked around. "Where's Grandma?"

"Having a nap. After you left last night, we talked and she was understandably upset." Nikola slapped his knees, clicked the tumbler on the coffee table, and stood. "Stay here! Let me get her and we'll make this a real reunion."

Still somewhat unsettled and on an emotional high, concerned about Dad's condition, Mason took another sip, relieved the confrontation he dreaded appeared to end agreeably for everybody. Many things remained unsaid and unresolved, but the past cannot be rewritten. Better that way perhaps, as the past provided the paving stones on the road of life. Each event and experience made them into what they all were, hopefully more mature as they walked that road. Conflict can enrich or embitter an individual, and he admitted some of his family encounters embittered him, fueled by resentment of his father and, if he wanted to be truthful, his mother. His dad said he sought to make a fresh start, which suited Mason. Carrying grudges never did anybody any good and only served as a frosted window that blurred and distorted his outlook on everything. His dad made a gesture to wipe the window clean and Mason felt ready to reciprocate. It would take a while, he admitted, but both made that important first step.

His mom came in carrying a large bamboo tray laden with a steaming glass carafe, cups, and sundries. He stood and helped lay the stuff on the coffee table. Without waiting to be asked, he snatched a slice of walnut roll sprinkled with icing sugar and took a hefty bite. The rich filling set off a cascade of sensations in his mouth and he grinned.

"Nobody makes them like you, Mom," he declared warmly. "You should sell them at supermarkets. You'd make a fortune."

She slapped him playfully on the chest. "Go on, you. Save it for the girls. By the way, do you have—"

He winced. "Don't! No matchmaking!"

"It *is* high time you settled down. Your three friends are married and have kids. From what I've seen of them, they're all happy. It isn't healthy being alone. You had a good thing with Aliana, then went and ruined everything," she added with a disapproving frown. "She looked such a nice girl."

"Mom, it was never a good thing," he warned, the scabs of that turbulent relationship still somewhat raw. "Let's drop it."

"Fine, I won't mention it again."

"Don't!"

He downed the rest of the whiskey, poured himself a cup of coffee, added milk and sugar, and took a satisfying sip. His mom made it perfect, not too strong nor weak. His dad liked it almost muddy, abrasive enough to peel varnish. A carryover from his watchstanding days in the Navy, he always retorted when Mom got on his case.

Nada appeared and stopped in her tracks. "Mason!"

He got up and hugged her tight. "Grandma! Looking pretty as ever." A little thinner perhaps, still able to walk unassisted, all her mental faculties intact, at ninety-four, she did look good.

The parchment-thin skin around her eyes wrinkled with amusement. "Naughty boy," she cackled merrily and absently brushed a lock of snowy hair behind her left ear. "You don't look half-bad yourself. It's high time a handsome man like you took a wife."

"I just told him that!" Brianna added mischievously.

Mason groaned. "Not you too, Grandma!"

"Leave the poor man alone, will you?" his dad growled as he seated his mother on the couch. "Want some coffee, Mom?"

"You know I prefer tea, Niki."

"I'll get it!" Brianna declared and hurried into the kitchen.

"Sorry I ran out on you last night, Grandma," Mason told her.

"Nikola told me what happened, but I'm glad to see you settled what's bugging you."

"Turned a new leaf would be more accurate."

"Whatever. It's never good to carry grudges," she declared firmly.

"I learned that one the hard way," Mason quipped.

"I understand you're starting a new job on Monday," his dad put in, apparently not keen to rake over the past. Mason didn't care for it either, the encounter still a sore wound.

"That's right."

"I thought you liked Deloitte, dear," Nada said. "Weren't you in Arabia or some ghastly place for three years or something?"

"Abu Dhabi in the United Arab Emirates. Two years initially, but I accepted an extension."

She slapped her forehead in a characteristic gesture. "How could I forget! February 2018, wasn't it?"

"That's right."

In December 2017, Deloitte asked if he cared to take a two-year contract in UAE, starting in March. Etisalat wanted to replace their GSM cellular customer activation and billing system, to be operational within fourteen months. It sounded simple when he read the brief, but quite complex to execute in detail. He would write the tender, select the winning software, install the system, set up customer activation and SIM card uptake protocols, and devise necessary front line staff training.

Mason knew nothing about GSM and cellular communication, or how telcos operated, and he had to learn a lot quickly, his eidetic memory of enormous help. Etisalat provided everything for him: a fully appointed three-bedroom apartment five minutes' walk from the telco and all living expenses, except food. After eleven months, he would get five weeks' vacation. A good deal every way he looked at it. His head filled with films about Arabia, magic carpets and genies, he found the prospect of working in such an exotic country intriguing and irresistible, and went for it.

His parents did not understand why he wanted to work overseas, and in a hot Arab country of all places. He had it all in Melbourne, and he'd be alone for two years minimum. Alone never bothered him. He tried to explain that he had a great opportunity to broaden his professional skillset and work at a higher level had he stayed at the Deloitte Melbourne office, and for lots more money, he added. They listened, but clearly did not like it.

With time on his hands before starting the contract, he took five weeks leave and spent four of them in China, an eye-opening adventure. He'd seen documentaries, but reality came as a shock when he saw the level of services and infrastructure modernization. Despite five-star treatment, he and other tour members realized that behind the facade of achievements lay a repressive, authoritarian regime. The point driven home when they probed their guide for views on several sensitive subjects, like Taiwan, treatment of Uyghurs, and tofu dreg construction. In every respect friendly and cooperative, he refused to open up, fearful that some Party stooge might hear and he and his family would be in grave trouble.

"Three years in that horrid place," Grandma murmured and gave a shudder. "I don't know how you stood the heat."

Mason shrugged. "I got used to it. It wasn't really so bad," he added for her benefit, not really meaning it. He never actually got used to it, especially the oppressive humidity.

"Then you went to Thailand," she added with a hint of disapproval.

His UAE assignment completed, he expected to settle down and take on a project in Melbourne, but Deloitte had other ideas and offered him a one-year contract in Thailand to upgrade the local telco's GSM roaming procedures. Tempted to reject the offer, he weighed up the professional pros and cons, the potential financial windfall, and took it, subject matter experts of his caliber not running loose on the ground. This time, his parents made little fuss over his decision, except to warn him to take care not to catch Covid. Before he jetted off, his friends treated him to a sendoff blowout.

He found Bangkok a seething, buzzing cauldron of people frantically rushing everywhere seemingly without purpose. Like every tourist, he visited the Chatuchak Weekend Market, among others, and explored various temples, including the Wat Pho with its Reclining Buddha. A must Longtail boat ride and several dazzling night tours that included glimpses of more earthy attractions. He did not much care for that part of the city or seeing smiling little women openly flaunting their wares. It took a while to explore the vast metropolitan sprawl, and comfortable work commitments left him lots of free time to enjoy the sights.

Advanced Info Service—SET:ADVANC—the largest telco in the country, had its futuristic headquarters in the central Phaya Thai district, a five-minute walk from his extremely comfortable apartment block; the company made sure he wanted for nothing. His team were mostly locals eager to work, with a sprinkling of expats. Bitten once at ANZ, he maintained a tight, strictly professional relationship with everybody, although there were endless opportunities to indulge his desires. The corporate execs he came into contact with liked how he did things, and offered him a contract extension. Not interested, job done, he refused politely, hoping the company would consider using Deloitte on other projects.

"It paid well," he told her with a chuckle, "and Covid didn't affect me. Genes, I suppose." Nobody in his family ever had it.

"Deloitte then shafted you when you turned down their Sydney offer," Nikola remarked with a scowl. "Bastards! Big corps will do it to you every time."

Mason wondered a number of times if Mercer, his Melbourne boss, really tried to shaft him. Mercer said they wanted him to take a very senior position in their Sydney office, a permanent relocation, though. It meant promotion to executive rank, but Mason did not want to move. The man showed keen displeasure, saying Mason didn't have the right attitude. Unless he took the posting, his career options with the company would be negatively affected, which meant, 'Play ball or you'll get tossed'. Independently well off, Mason had the luxury to pick and choose what he wanted to do and tendered his resignation with immediate effect, bypassing the normal four weeks' notice, and left. At the tram stop, he felt relief as though some weight rolled off his shoulders. Deloitte gave him a lot, he had to give them that, but he also gave them a lot, working many long days never paid. It came with the territory. That evening, Perkins himself, head of Deloitte treasury systems Australia-wide, called and apologized for Mercer's abrasive attitude, then asked Mason to reconsider his resignation, happy for him to stay in Melbourne, as he hated to lose one of his star performers. Tempted for a fleeting moment, he declined, having already crossed that bridge. Once done, some things cannot be patched up. Had he stayed, Mercer would always have it in for him, and he intensely disliked the idea of playing ongoing office politics warfare. Afterward, he sat back in his favorite lounge chair, a tumbler of bourbon in hand, and listened to Beethoven's sixth symphony, a grin on his face.

Eat shit, Deloitte.

"It's possible, Dad, but I doubt it. Mercer got shitty and over-reached himself."

Nikola shook his head. "You're covering for them, son. I can see it in your face. Still, I'm glad you decided to stay in Melbourne. Your roots are here, and Global Systems will be a fresh start."

"I like to think so. We'll see."

"Funny how they snapped you up. You hardly had a week off."

"Market grapevine, Dad. My predecessor at GS had the bad taste to break his leg by falling off a ladder, decided to have an extended break, and resigned. A cruise with his wife and daughter around the Adriatic and the Aegean, I understand. GS has a hot project on its hands with National Post and needed somebody urgently to run with it."

"Well, one man's misfortune is another man's opportunity."

"You probably said it, dear, but I forgot. What kind of work do they do?" Grandma prompted.

"They're a strategic planning and consulting think tank. In many ways, they compete with the likes of Deloitte, PwC, and

KPMG, but they're not as diversified. They've only been in business nine years—"

"You mentioned it," his dad said.

"—but they have a good reputation in the US and here, especially after the big four consultancy firms got tarred with a stink brush for getting too cozy with Canberra."

"Our governments aren't squeaky clean either. They allowed the big four too much leeway to dictate policy. A classic conflict of interest case."

"You're right there, but once the glare of publicity stops shining, it will be business as usual."

Mason shrugged. "I like to think there'll be some industry changes, but you could be right. Everybody's been in bed with everybody else for too long. For big consultancy firms the government is a bottomless money bucket."

His mother came in with a mug of tea, handed it to Grandma, sat down, and crossed her legs, content to listen.

They talked late into the afternoon and Mom urged him to stay for dinner. He declined, but accepted a lunch invitation for tomorrow. There were still chores to do. After hugs all around and a firm handshake from Dad, Mason drove home more satisfied with life and the world, although concerned about his father's persistent narcolepsy. Nothing to be done about it. Callous of him perhaps, his old man would just have to suck it up and live with it.

One thing he never told his parents. In November, seeing the value at the top of its curve, he sold his Bitcoin holding for under one point-nine million. The move did not set him up financially for life, as the government would take out a hefty tax bite when he filed his return in July, but it did clear his debts. When he got back from Thailand, Arthur Landry initially resented his success, sore that Mason did not tell his friends to take a flyer in crypto. That one stung, as he *did* tell the three of them to invest—citing his conversations word for word thanks to his infallible memory—but they considered it a passing and risky fad. He disliked shouldering the blame for their inaction and hoped to patch things up with Arthur.

Tough skits.

Time to look at his shares portfolio perhaps and the Bitcoin market as the thing now hovered around $33,000.

Mason shared another potentially more serious secret Mom told him never to reveal, but something she felt he ought to know. Two years ago, he visited on one balmy October afternoon and enjoyed a slice of walnut roll, accompanied by a specially blended brew of Earl Grey tea. She opened up then. After difficulties passing urine and two episodes of letting blood, Brianna urged Nikola to get tested, a major achievement, as she had to drag Dad to a doctor for anything. Tests revealed an enlarged prostate and had it treated at The Alfred hospital. Not cancerous, but he had to take a blood test every six months. Mason regularly pestered Mom about Dad's condition, but no new developments so far. Should his father's situation deteriorate, he felt relieved that today's visit ended on an amicable note.

After a light tuna salad dinner, he relaxed to the sound of Tchaikovsky's *Capriccio Italien*. A cognac balloon in hand, he figured it may be time for his three friends to come over with their wives and kids and rake over old times. Been a while since they visited. The months marched inexorably even if he did not notice.

He smiled when he recalled how his friend Liam Anderson got snared by a striking blonde he met at the St. Kilda Beach—his rugged good looks and athletic body, having filled out a bit, may have played a part—which sharply curtailed weekend camping outings the four used to do. In May 2014, the two married, and in March 2016, the couple had baby girl. The four of them got together at his place for a baby shower.

Mason enjoyed the reunion and an opportunity to catch up

on latest gossip and events. Arthur and Liam kidded him for being the odd men out. In February of that year, Arthur fell for a brooding, unusually pale, brunette of Polish parents, the wedding celebration done in a style only Europeans can do. In July 2017, he welcomed birth of a baby girl. At the shower, surrounded by all the women, the four grabbed bottles and ice, retreated to a backyard gazebo, and reminisced on all the good times, their lusty conversation sprinkled with an odd exaggeration and outright lie.

Invariably, discussion turned to kids, family, relationship hiccups, and bills. Liam pushed up his rimless glasses in a habitual gesture and waved a stubby at him. "Not good living alone, pal. Look at me. Happy as a clam. Snag a woman and join in the fun."

"Hear, hear," Arthur echoed solemnly, a glass of Shiraz in hand. "Best thing I did getting married. Mind you, though, I kind of wondered at the time if I was doing the right thing."

Liam punched his arm. "You never had a chance, man! Once a woman sinks her anchors into you, there is no escape. Still, I never struggled all that hard," he said and everybody smiled.

"Mason's trouble, guys," Logan went on as he stroked his little goatee, "he's too busy raking in money. With no looks to speak of, it's is the only way he can hope to attract someone."

Mason flipped him the bird. "Hah! You should talk! Saving your energy, are you?" he shot back, patted his friend's ample belly, and laughed with the others, wrapped in the warmth of their company and friendship.

Seeing them enjoying life to the full, being complete, made him reflect on his solitary days. Getting involved had not occupied his mind much, although on some cold, wintry nights, he did contemplate the prospect of having his arms around someone to share himself with. Intellectually, he realized that focusing on a career might not be a life's goal in itself. Time to review his objectives?

He took a cab home, a satisfied glow in his soul.

A girl eventually did sink her anchors into Logan, and in September 2017, he married. Served him right, Mason mused. In January 2019, he took a hurried flight home from Abu Dhabi to celebrate the birth of Logan's little boy. Then in May 2020, his friend had a baby girl. It did seem that Mason was the odd man out in the group.

Funny how the tide of time tugged at life.

His friends and those around him may think him odd—in many respects, he knew himself to be odd—but the march of time and apparent urgency to procreate did not affect him as it did others. He figured he had plenty of time to form a stable relationship and push a pram along a footpath. Right now, his career meant more than chasing a woman for the questionable privilege of marriage, having seen the anguish marriage created for some.

In June 2014, between projects at the bank, Mason took his leave early and went on a twenty-one day tour through Western Europe, much to his mom's chagrin and displeasure. She saw it as an extravagant waste of money, saying he should pay off his bedsitter loan. She simply did not comprehend that travel filled something inside him that books and documentaries could not. When the subject came up again, he told her not to worry. The loan would get repaid in due course and he went on his eye-opening trip.

In April 2016, promoted to senior analyst, Mason put the bedsitter on the market, took out a bridging loan, and bought two dilapidated adjoining terrace houses in South Melbourne. He initially intended to gut the two residences and renovate, but after doing the math, he decided to tear down both buildings and built a modern house that included a small garage, something almost unheard of in the neighborhood, the land plots only some six meters or so wide. No matter how nice, a reno still retained old architecture look and feel.

He capped the gas mains that fed cookers in both old lots and went all electric: water, ducted heating, evaporative cooling, cooktop and oven. A five kilowatt solar system helped offset his power bill. Happy with the result, he finally had a place he could truly call his own.

Ten years…where did the time go?

Last May, everybody tired of the Liberal Party and its in-fighting, and voted in the Albanese Labor government. After sitting on their hands for ten years, the Liberals left the new administration without an environmental or energy policy. Mason recorded all expenses in a yearly spreadsheet and noted the sharp upward creep of gas in his bedsitter. He now congratulated himself for going electric, but wondered whether Labor would do anything to curb soaring cost of living and energy prices, with the Greens demanding an insane shutdown of all coal and gas generating stations to reduce the national carbon emission footprint and help save the world, as though Australia's negligible carbon emissions percentage would make any difference.

He shook his head, not understanding any of it. Definitely time to call his three friends for a get-together, hash over current events in their lives, and solve the world's problems.

His mom's mention of Aliana got his memory machine to unwind. Some memories pleasant, others not so.

In September 2014, Gerard, head of ANZ retail systems, asked him to restructure their credit card operation, a major step for someone only twenty-three. Five years with the bank, he started as a programmer straight out of RMIT. Eighteen in December, eager to taste life outside academic walls. He tasted it, all right, and learned a lot how grown-ups ran a major corporation, working with others, running small teams when promoted to systems analyst, and most importantly, he learned a lot about himself. Intellectually mature, but still an inexperienced youngster, he had to learn the hard way how to run a real business.

A high IQ turned out not to be a license for arrogance. A painful, but invaluable lesson he later admitted had to be lived.

Initially, his older coworkers puzzled how someone so young got such a plum job and talked about him behind his back. More so, after it became known he also had a master's degree. A know-it-all smart ass, some said. He did not particularly care what they thought and focused on doing his job, learning painfully that system design theory must bend to business needs. Apparently impressed with his efforts, his immediate boss and the IT division manager assured him he had a bright future with ANZ. It certainly looked bright at the time.

Excited to run a major project, Mason and his team of two analysts began to review the requirements specifications and delved into the existing credit card system. It helped that both were current-system subject matter experts. If they resented a twenty-three-year-old managing the project, they kept their reservations to themselves. He told himself to cultivate a friendly team atmosphere and never become buddies with them, or he could no longer be in charge. That's what he told himself. Reality had other ideas.

He replayed the first team meeting in his mind.

Aliana, lustrous copper hair tied in a bun or allowed to spill down her back, he later learned, smiled at him whenever he ventured to look at her. He tried to control his juvenile reaction to the beautiful older analyst and her captivating violet eyes, but his hormones betrayed him. She burned like a flame and he felt himself inexorably drawn to her. Intellectually, he understood the danger that flame represented if they became involved, but cared little about consequences. Young, impressionable, unsophisticated in the ways of women, his body doing some of the thinking for him, he forgot to be a manager, gave in to his basic instincts, and went a little crazy.

It started innocently enough with an occasional coffee and lunch to hash over the requirements and user change requests that always happened. He organized team lunches to engender cohesion, but having Aliana alone to himself made him think they enjoyed something special together. Three years older, friendly, approachable, she laughed easily, and ignored his awkwardness. A month into the project, Randal, his senior analyst, took him aside and warned that Aliana was a corporate climber and liked to string men along to get what she wanted.

"She'll play you like a trout, and when you're landed, she'll rip out your heart and stomp on it. Be careful around her."

Mason took it as jealousy; entirely taken in by her to the extent he believed she loved him.

One lunchtime, he hurried down to the cafeteria to grab a quick bite and saw her in what he considered intimate conversation with a project manager he knew in passing. Heads close together, she nodded, and laughed. A stab of cold fury and jealousy raced through him and he wanted to march up to her and demand an explanation, when a perfectly reasonable one presented itself. She obviously knew the man, probably from a previous project, and took an opportunity to rake over old times. He did not want to damage his relationship with her by doing something impulsive and tried to forget the incident, but it continued to gnaw at the back of his mind.

A month later, Gerard called him into his office and told him in a friendly, oblique way not to get involved with a team member. Focus on the job at hand. It appeared the whole floor knew about Mason's infatuation, something he thought a secret. A bucket of cold water thrown in his face, he realized he *had* been distracted and preoccupied with his fantasies, and felt a wave of shame. With all his smarts, he allowed personal considerations to override his professionalism.

His parents were delighted that he finally found someone and thought the relationship serious enough to possibly lead to something permanent. The incident in the cafeteria shoved into a back memory drawer, he continued his outings with Aliana, the warning from his boss pushed aside.

During one lunch break, he asked if she wanted to have dinner with him, their first, at an exclusive St. Kilda seafood restaurant. Afterward, he drove her home to Richmond where she seduced him, startling him with her directness. His second encounter with sex, his feelings for her blossomed and he confessed his love for her. When he and his three friends met, he told them about Aliana, but not the sexual encounter. They applauded, telling him time had come to settle down.

For two weeks afterward, they had several intimate encounters and he thought life had an up curve. His mom kept bugging him about this wonderful girl he'd been going out with and demanded he bring her over. Mason could read the signs. She wanted to check out Aliana for herself and add her stamp of approval. Despite his better judgment, he caved in and brought Aliana to his parent's place as a one-time dinner thing. His mom gushed over her, dropping not so subtle hints about an engagement, which left him embarrassed. Thankfully, his dad never made a fuss.

One Sunday at his place, they lay entwined talking about inconsequential things. Calm and satisfied, he reflected that perhaps his friends were right and he should consider something permanent with Aliana. Living alone did not satisfy everything in his life. Pondering, he absently stroked the silky smoothness of her back.

She regarded him with dreamy eyes, a hint of a smile on her lips, and brushed his nose with the tip of her finger.

"You know, I think it may be time I stepped up."

"What do you mean?"

"Work, dummy. I can take some of the load off you."

"You're handling enough as it is."

"I can run your Issues Register."

He looked at her closely. "That's not something I can delegate."

She frowned and her eyes lost some of their sparkle. "You don't think I can handle it?"

"It's a question of responsibility. Your job is analysis, not project management."

"So, I'm not responsible?"

He regarded her with genuine surprise. "What brought this on?"

Her finger traced his chin. "Nothing really. I simply meant that I'm ready to do more on the project. I can be your 2IC."

Mason chuckled. "With only you and Randal as my team, I don't need a 2IC."

"You're saying no?" she demanded softly, but he sensed her growing anger.

His face lost expression. "Aliana, I don't want to talk shop. Let's table this for tomorrow, okay?"

"Let's talk about it now, Mason."

"If you want. Finish your system specs and I'll review your position. I don't want you losing focus by taking on something for which you're not ready."

"You think I'm too junior? I've been an analyst longer than you've been with the bank!"

Whatever he said, he sensed a tipping point in their relationship. A crushing feeling of disappointment settled on his chest as he recalled Randal's words of warning. He refused to believe that all this time, Aliana played him merely to advance herself. He couldn't!

"Look—"

She flung back the comforter and climbed off the bed. Street lighting coming through the window outlined her naked form, clenched hands on hips, lips pressed in fury.

"You're a heel, Mason!"

"What the hell?"

"You're a user and a manipulator. It seems I'm merely a sex object for you. Well, buster, that's not how it works. I'll talk to HR and you'll find out how it works."

His cheeks flamed at the unfairness of it all and reached out for her hand, but she backed off. "That's unfair and untrue. You've done a great job so far and I value your expertise. I'm prepared to give you more responsibility, but not now. You're not ready. Let's not spoil what we have together by adding the work dimension."

She laughed. "My God. Listen to yourself. Work dimension? It's all been about work, you silly boy."

Stung, he stood beside her and scowled, the crumbs of what may have been thick at his feet. "It seems to me that you've been the user here."

"You're such a baby," she hissed, gathered her clothing, and stormed out.

He wanted to run after her, take her into his arms and promise everything she wanted, but his feet remained rooted on the cold carpet. He'd been a fool for not seeing it. A fool who'd been warned, which came harder to take.

The front door slammed shut and he bit his lower lip. Still stunned at how fast all this happened, his ego bruised, he realized he faced a professional shit storm tomorrow.

Skits!

Bridges burnt, Aliana could no longer remain on the project, which would seriously affect the schedule, budget, and rollout date by having to get a new analyst onto the team not necessarily versed with the credit card system, or not at the level he needed. He also faced a personal downer sorting out how he allowed Aliana to string him along.

And he didn't see any of it, blinded by physical desire for her.

Many factors contributed to his stumble, he reflected, the main being his naiveté. The protective shell he built around himself as a kid turned out to be a sieve when it came to handling female relationships.

Predictably, Gerard reamed him out with a severe reprimand for involving himself with a colleague and placing the project in jeopardy.

"My fault actually," Gerard groused. "I should have warned you about her, but I thought you could handle it. Forget the sexual harassment charge. You're a most promising asset, Mason, but no more distractions in any shape or form. Got it?"

"Yes, sir!"

"You're here to do a job. Don't get sidetracked."

Mason later learned that Gerard demanded her resignation. Understandably enough, everybody on the floor derived much amusement from the episode and his ensuing embarrassment.

His mother found nothing amusing about it, openly critical how he screwed up an opportunity to settle down. He wanted to explain what happened, but her attitude said she blamed him for everything, and he kept his counsel. Eager and trusting, he allowed sex to cloud his judgment. Over the previous few years, even his dad dropped oblique hints that he marry. Robbed of having more children, he wanted the Adamov name to continue. An item low on Mason's priority list. At that time anyway.

The unpleasant episode drove home a poignant lesson. He realized men were prepared to do almost anything for promise of sex. Women appeared to know that instinctively...and used it to get what they wanted.

Stung badly, he took the lesson to heart. He maintained friendly relationships with female colleagues, but shunned all workplace entanglements. It earned him a moniker for being standoffish and cold, but he would not be shamed or burned again.

Project and program management at ANZ filled out his skill-set portfolio, but he got tired playing office politics and clawing for power to climb the corporate ladder. Especially after the game became more important than the job. The realization left him jaded and soiled. It also forced him to face a brutal reality. Perhaps he should discard his childish idealism and see the world through adult eyes and accept what it really represented: unrelenting struggle for survival. The shield he developed as a kid to insulate himself? It probably needed a hole or two to see and intercept the arrows that came his way. A shitty way to do business, but nice guys simply weren't in demand. The name of the game? He had to be hard and ruthless or end up as a cutlet for all the circling wolves.

In June 2016, Deloitte Australia offered him a senior consultant posting in their treasury systems group, a major step for someone only twenty-five. Although still very young, Mason used his ANZ knocks to develop a mature bearing of someone older, and Deloitte liked to present an image of being a progressive company. Clients also liked to deal with young, smart executives. That's what he'd been told. Mason relished the change and an opportunity to start somewhere else with a clean slate, his skin of tender naivety shed for good.

Tchaikovsky's serenade finished, he selected Beethoven's *Piano Concerto Number Five*, and topped up his cognac.

United Arab Emirates, a ghastly pace, Grandma said. For some perhaps, but he did not consider it so. He took it as an unprecedented opportunity to expand professionally and personally and see something of the world.

On February 25, 2018, Mason took a business class Emirates flight to Dubai, something he appreciated for such a long haul, followed by a local hauler to Abu Dhabi, and opened a new chapter in his career.

He read up on it, but the major downside to living in the Middle East was the oppressive heat and humidity, which hit earnestly in April. His day would start at seven and end at two. Nobody ventured out until about six when the temperature started to ease from the day's 45C to a balmy 32 or so and allowed the city to wake up. For nine months, no cloud marred the pristine blue sky. After a while, he longed to see that sky torn by lightning and see pouring rain. It only rained every four or five years there. In the morning, he would step out of the apartment block and be physically assaulted by a wave of heat and heavy air, enough to make him wince. Interestingly, the walls of surrounding buildings ran wet from overnight condensation. A hell of a place.

In March, Bitcon fell from its January high and he bought twenty for under $190,000. Everything he read about the things told him the speculative investment would fly, but he faced a major downer if the stuff bottomed out. On the other hand, he would make a killing if crypto kept rising along the predicted market curve. He urged his father to buy and, for once, the cantankerous, stubborn man listened and made a major investment.

Another expat introduced him to the Kangaroo Club where Aussies and Kiwis, mainly engineers who worked for one of the numerous oil companies in the Gulf, got together once a week and shared events on life in Araby.

That is where he met Verena, a financial accountant who also happened to work at Etisalat. Worldly-wise, short hazel hair, twenty-eight, divorced from a two-timing husband, she demonstrated incisive understanding of local corporate cut and thrust. Already three years with the telco, she gave him pointers how to deal with Etisalat's internal politics and understand the power plays conducted at senior levels. His program of work specs said one thing, but to get the job done, he'll need to navigate through office politics and opposing departmental interests. He found her advice invaluable.

Still wary of emotional entanglements, Verena quickly put him at ease, telling him she only wanted to have a little fun with a fellow Aussie while doing her time in Abu Dhabi with no expectation of anything else. They met for dinner every now and then, went to the beach at end of Electra Street where all the international hotels crowded the shoreline—the strict Muslim norms forgotten at the front entrance—visited Dubai's Souk market a couple of times, and toured the vast, open desert once, the outings a welcomed break from project work.

Ever since he saw *Lawrence of Arabia* with Peter O'Toole, and its stirring music, the vista of rolling dunes, colored sands, and impenetrable silence captivated Mason. When the tour minibus disgorged eager sightseers, he walked off and climbed a steep dune. A hot breeze stirred his hair as he stood gazing at a clear horizon. The dunes looked like marching waves and went on forever. Enthralled, he drank it all in, allowing the desert to envelop and fill him. After a moment out of time beyond measuring, satiated, he slowly walked down. Verena gave him a probing look, took his hand, and without saying anything, they made their way back to the minibus where their driver laid out snacks and drinks.

Neither sought a deeper relationship. Mason liked her company and she confessed appreciation that his interest in her was other than a predatory desire to get into her pants. He did not want to entertain that component and risk spoiling what they had, although he indulged in an odd fantasy as any healthy man would when accompanied by a pretty woman. With her, he felt enriched.

They enjoyed some good times, all right.

In February 2019, he took his vacation, appreciating business class comfort on the long flight to Melbourne. It gave him a chance to have a break in a Western country, catch up with family and friends, and enjoy entertainment not available in Abu Dhabi.

In January 2020, with successful implementation and minimal teething hassles, Etisalat offered him an extension. Despite restricted social facilities, Mason enjoyed life in Abu Dhabi and used the time to develop into a hardnosed professional. He cared little what others said behind his back. He got the job done and Etisalat management liked it that way. Deloitte told him if he wanted to stay another year, he should accept the contract. The prospect of computerizing Etisalat's network maintenance and work orders procedures by installing a CAD planning, tracking, and execution system set his mind on fire. He had an opportunity to change work practices for a major corporation that spanned the entire country…and he accepted. A fortuitous decision, as it turned out. In February, Covid-19 broke out and the world shut down international travel.

Mason endured, as did all the other expats. He could have stayed longer with Etisalat, but after three years away from everything he knew, he wanted to reconnect with his old life, and came home.

He did miss Verena, though. They never exchanged emails and he often wondered what happened to her, writing it off as a pleasant encounter for both of them on the far side of the world.

Beethoven's piano concerto ended and he decided to retire. He picked Mary Stewart's *The Crystal Cave* off the bookshelf and slipped into bed to read.

Chapter Four

Misty drizzle drifted down from a dark sky and swallowed the tops of surrounding skyscrapers. Not the most cheerful start to his day. Cold, wet, miserable, the rain sabotaged Mason's morning exercise run through the Kings Domain Park, which forced him to extend his calisthenics session in the bedroom and left him in a grumpy mood over breakfast.

The tram jerked to a stop at the Collins Street intersection and he squeezed out with other commuters, while those outside impatiently pushed to get in. What was their damned hurry? He squinted at the massed clouds, buttoned his overcoat against a chill breeze, and merged into the sidewalk throng going who knows where. To check the Covid spread, the state government still urged everybody to work from home if possible, and many did. However, some jobs demanded a presence in the office. Mason did not mind the short commute from South Melbourne. Besides, it is hard to shake hands with a client through a computer screen or do on-site consulting.

Without an umbrella—he should have listened to the weatherman—he hurried past the familiar old façade where Deloitte reigned. On cruise control, he almost turned toward the entrance out of habit, then continued down the street.

The imposing Rialto twin towers' paved forecourt opened on his left and he strode toward the broad entrance steps. He hated to think what it cost Global Systems to rent two whole floors in the shorter North Tower, but an office in such a prestigious location promoted a reputation of stability, success, and competence. Apparently, New York corporate were prepared to pay the price to attract cream clientele.

Inside the enormous foyer, a small group waited at each of three elevators. A triangle lit above two of them, followed by a sharp *ting*. Mason shook water off his coat and waited. The polished steel double doors slid back and he got in. He pressed his access card against the sensor and tapped the thirty-fourth-floor button, not objecting to such layered access. If anyone could walk into the GS office, they might rummage through desks and possibly lay hands on sensitive corporate and customer material. Then again, with security on the prowl 24/7, they probably would not get to the first desk.

A wave of mounting excitement tingled through him as the elevator surged up.

The door halves opened and he stepped out. The floor held management offices, all Melbourne consultants, and an extensive research library. A lot of information came from Internet sources, but as he learned from his time at Deloitte, no one should rely exclusively on the Internet for accuracy. Hence, the need for legitimate publications as fact-checkers. The floor below housed Accounting, Legal, HR, and IT. High-speed data links connected the company's New York headquarters, Sydney, and Brisbane offices. That's what they told him.

He swept his eyes around open-plan workstations, some manned, sprinkled with an odd tall potted plant and gave an illusion of privacy. He approached the attractive platinum blonde Delora who sat behind her slightly curved reception desk and waited. She looked up and fixed on a warm grin.

"Mr. Adamov! Welcome to Global Systems. Still raining outside?"

"Still," Mason confirmed cheerfully. The first time he saw Delora, her bubbly personality and readiness to help endeared her to him.

"It must rain sometimes," she remarked phlegmatically and shrugged. "Please take a seat while I ring Mr. Renolds. He'll want to see you right away. Care for a coffee or something?"

"I'm fine, thanks."

Mason took off the bulky overcoat, then eased onto the soft gray cloth couch and placed a thin black Vuitton briefcase at his feet. He usually started work at eight or earlier, but figured eight-thirty would do for a first day.

The diminutive, portly, bald Walter Renolds wearing a black pinstripe with a dark blue tie strode briskly toward him.

"Glad to see you, Mason," Director for Infrastructure Projects said amicably and extended a hand.

"Pleased to be here, Walt," Mason replied as they shook.

After two induction interviews and an orientation session where Renolds outlined the assignment for his new principal consultant, both were on first name basis. Mason learned early not to underestimate the diminutive man. Behind the smiling façade lay an incisive mind that dissected everything with scalpel precision to lay bare the crux of any issue. He figured Walt would make a formidable debater.

When Mason showed up for his first interview, he remembered how the Director's eyes registered mild surprise, expecting someone much older to fill the position, as Mason did not include his date of birth on the resume, wanting his qualifications and list of accomplishments to speak for him. Renolds obviously studied his resume in detail, probably not believing everything, something he admitted with a deceptively innocent grin during the second interview. After he checked Mason's references, he accepted the fact that he had a unique applicant. A hard professional, he grilled Mason relentlessly, demanding details on past projects, theoretical understanding of program management and strategic consulting processes, general comprehension of major Australian corporations, state and federal client opportunities, views on business practices, and his long-term career objectives. Mason studied up and accepted the interrogation, knowing GS wanted to make sure he would fit the company's profile before offering a handsome $180,000 salary, plus benefits.

"Grab your gear and we'll talk," Renolds said briskly and walked down the carpeted aisle along the wall toward several offices. He paused before his door and waved a hand at the adjoining office. "Karter Kending is in Sydney. You can catch up tomorrow."

Mason met the Director for Strategic Projects during his second interview session and liked the tall, softly spoken man who seemed to exude an almost palpable aura of competence. Mason joined Global Systems to do strategic planning, but realized he would need to prove himself with Renolds first by doing some infrastructure projects first. He did not mind, and would use the trial period to familiarize himself with all GS projects and their clients.

"Your office is next to mine," Renolds added. "Lavinia Stroud is next to yours. Catch up with her at your convenience."

As the only other principal consultant, Mason definitely wanted to chat with Lavinia for a personal slant on how things really worked at GS. Four senior and eight investigative consultants occupied the floor in personal bullpens.

"Delora offered you coffee?" Renolds demanded as he opened the polished wooden door and waited for Mason to get in.

"I'm good."

"Right! You can tank up later." Renolds sat behind an executive desk made out of dark wood and waved at a leather chair. "Take the load off." Apart from a computer screen linked to downstairs network servers, keyboard, mouse, a desktop calendar, a profusion of papers threatened to spill to the floor.

A wilderness of associations, Renolds told him with a jovial laugh during the first interview. He said Delora straightened everything one evening, not pleased with the clutter, thinking she did him a favor. For a week afterward, he couldn't find anything, he remarked with a grin. He told her if she touched his desk again, she'd be out the door. She knew he was kidding, but left his stuff alone.

"You ready to start?" Renolds asked sharply. A wrong answer and Mason would be in the sin bin.

"I went over the business case and project requirements brief in detail," he replied, the material locked indelibly in his memory.

When the Director described the scope of work, Mason wondered why Global Systems put a principal consultant in charge of a seemingly simple analysis job any competent consultant could handle. Obviously, GS wanted to know if *he* could handle it. He didn't mind. At Deloitte, he witnessed an incident where the team carried their project manager because he gave them too much head and basically failed to understand the difference between leadership and control. Needless to say, he did not last long. An impressive resume and glowing references did not always reflect genuine ability.

Beyond the plain brief, he suspected something deeper lurked to snare him.

"National Post wants our recommendations by mid-August or sooner," Renolds added.

"Which means sooner," Mason drawled, which produced a chuckle from the Director.

"Of course. Easily doable, as they have an internal report commissioned nine months ago that pretty much covered every issue."

"Including several analyses from international think thanks that said the same thing," Mason pointed out.

Renolds nodded. "Frankly, they don't need us to tell them what they already know. It's common industry knowledge that over the last eight years, physical mail has shifted markedly to parcel handling as emails took over most correspondence. As you're aware, the rise of Covid has seen letter volumes plummet even further, with a correspondingly sharp increase in parcel volumes as people ordered goods online. If Post likes what you tell them, we can expect more business in that space. Take care how you tackle this one, Mason. Raymond Clarke, head of Parcel, Post and Products, wants to make parcel handling their main retail line. Terry Deakin, the guy in charge of all national letters processing, sees it as a direct threat and gradual shaving down of his power base."

"He's right," Mason added.

"Of course, he's right, but it's a no-win scenario for him. Nonetheless, he'll try to dissuade you from any attempt to reduce the number of letter and barcode sorting machines Post has in every major city center, and will cite the usual sob story about having to lay off employees with the resulting negative effect on families. Don't fall for that busted flush. Clarke wants objective recommendations for sound operating options to carry the business into the future, regardless of any affected individual empires."

"The internal report he commissioned told him what he needs to do, Walt," Mason told him seriously. "I suspect he wants to use us as a gun against Deakin."

"A gun with one shot, and I'm glad you picked that up, but it can't be the whole picture. I don't have to tell you then that Clarke has given us a hot political brick. Whatever we do, unless handled delicately, we could lose the Post account. I worked hard to get it for GS. See to it that we don't lose it. Do whatever it takes. Stornwell, your predecessor, worked on this for two weeks and didn't get anywhere."

"I get that part, but at the same time, we shouldn't make ourselves the fall guy in Post's internal power game," Mason added softly.

Renolds' eyes probed him. "Then don't fall on your own sword. Clearly, there is more to this job than meets the eye, but I'm leaving that to you. Talk to Turner. He worked on this with Stornwell and should already be up to speed with background stuff. Call Leola Lanaro at Post and let her know you're on board. She'll appreciate a face-to-face with you. While there, I suggest you intro yourself to Clarke and Deakin."

"I planned on doing that anyway," Mason said.

"On Friday, there's a group lunch to let everyone see your face. Meanwhile, network around and let people know you. If you have questions, my door is always open. Every Wednesday at five, we have a program of work status meeting with all senior staff. You'll need to attend."

"Of course."

"Glad to have you with us."

Mason walked out and strode to his office. Fall on his own sword? If he cocked up, Renolds would be there to drive it in. At the level he now operated, GS expected him to handle all client politics. If he could not, do something else for a living. He now played in the grownups sandpit and should act accordingly.

Inside, he found a similar executive desk with a ceiling-high window behind it that provided excellent natural lighting and a panoramic city view. He opened the slim white folder that lay in one corner. A welcome pack from Delora with his logon details, internal GS contacts list, and names and phone numbers of all Post people he'd likely interact with. A wry smile tugged his mouth when he saw the CommBank Neo Business card, appreciating the gesture. Global Systems clearly did not want him to use his own money for expenses. He opened a small box that came with the pack—business cards—and shook his head. He tucked several into his jacket breast pocket and extracted two disks from his briefcase: project specs and Turner's summary resume. He already had a prepared tasks outline and a Microsoft Project schedule; time and cost the most important parameters as always. With material already at hand, he figured to easily beat the mid-August deadline.

Logged into the GS system, he created a project directory with several sub-directories, then uploaded the specs, schedule, background documents, and an issues register template—there were *always* issues! The administrative bits done, he programmed several numbers into the desk phone station, did the same to his cellphone Contacts list, and pressed a glowing white button.

"Scott Turner," a strong, pleasant voice answered.

"Mason Adamov. Please come to my office when convenient."

"Not a problem. Be there in a minute."

A knock came shortly afterward and the door opened. Mason looked up and fought to suppress a startled reaction. The black pinstripe suit hung on the skeletal figure as though draped over a pole. Short black hair topped an unusually pale, gaunt face, highlighted by small, dark eyes tucked deep beneath thin eyebrows. Around 172 centimeters, perhaps in his late thirties, the man flashed a broad smile that made the eyes twinkle with amusement. He stepped into the office and closed the door with a backhand shove.

"Glad to meet you, Mason. We heard you were coming," he remarked in a surprisingly deep voice and stuck out a hand.

Mason stood and grasped the proffered hand, all skin and bone. "You must be Scott."

"The least of my sins." Without waiting for an invitation, he dragged a visitor's chair closer to the desk and eased himself down.

Turner's unusual appearance had Mason on the back foot for only a second. If he believed the resume, the man had an impressive list of achievements, and Global Systems appeared to pick only the best. The corollary did not escape him when he considered his own position.

"Welcome to the team."

"A team of two!" Turner quipped as he scanned the office. "One day…"

"You'll be sitting in my chair?"

"More comfortable than the bullpen I'm in now. I'm not complaining, though. Never mind. My time will come. Now, I presume you want to know where I am with the Post study?"

"We need to be on the same page."

"I reviewed the project brief and Post's analysis paper that told them what basically we'll also tell them. Namely, scrap a whole bunch of letter sorting and barcode machines in all major mail centers. Some are more than fifteen years old and present a serious maintenance cost drain. I also went over a number of independent think tank reports that regurgitated the same spiel. Perhaps you already got it, Mason, or Walt told you. Raymond Clarke doesn't want a new study. A sharp executive, he's well aware of all market trends. The letters business is dying, no surprise there. What he wants from us is a handy excuse to flush Terry Deakin's empire down the tube. A case of personal rivalry. Deakin tried once for the head of Division job, but Post appointed Clarke instead. He'll defuse any negative reaction from Deakin by waving our report in his face and blame the whole thing on us. At the same time, he'll gain brownie points with the Post Board. Whichever way you play it, this is a no-winner if you piss off one of them."

"Thanks for pointing out the obvious," Mason observed with a grin, "but is the situation that obvious?"

Turner shrugged. "I know how Post operates, and I've been over it with Stornwell. I wanted to make sure you're aware of the potholes."

"Oh, I know where the potholes are, Scott. Do you?"

"Come again?"

"Office politics aside, we cannot ignore the social aspect," Mason said quietly, carefully ignoring Turner's abrasive attitude. "Post isn't just a profit center. The amended National Post Corporation Act 2015 outlines their areas of responsibility."

Turner frowned. "So what?"

"One part of the Act states that Post has community service obligations. Namely, the requirement to ensure letter service is reasonably accessible to all Australians on an equitable basis, and performance standards must meet social, industrial, and commercial needs. Raymond Clarke undoubtedly knows all this, and so does Deakin, who'll probably milk it for all it's worth to stop Clarke from dismantling his facilities. Clarke may want to shift all retail business to ecommerce and parcel handling because that's where the money is, but the Act binds his hands how far he can push that strategy. As long as one person in Australia needs a physical letter, Post must deliver. It's the obvious conclusion, but I think there's more to this project than what's in the brief."

Turner leaned forward, his brow furrowed in concentration. "Are you suggesting we ignore Post's own study and other reports?"

"Not at all. I'm saying our recommendations must address Post's parcel and letter handling operations from every angle. If you read the fine print in the Post26 Strategy paper, it's part of our terms of reference."

Turner waved a hand. "A throwaway to cover their ass."

"Maybe, but it's there and we cannot ignore it. Even if it weren't there, we cannot ignore it. As an example, over the past six years, Post substantially raised stamp prices, which generated a negative public reaction. With parcel handling a growing profit center, I think Post should consider using some of those proceeds to keep stamp prices stable for the social good, or even reduce them."

Turner snorted and shook his head. "You're dreaming. Post doesn't give a damn about the social good. It's all about the bottom line and playing the corporate power game. If we piss off Clarke with some Utopian scenario, Global Systems can kiss Post goodbye as a client. Renolds will be sore, I can tell you that, and you'll be out the door. Post is his baby."

Mason leaned back and stared hard at the man. "I value your input and I'll keep your assessment under advisement."

"Just telling you how things are done at Post."

"Over the last two years, you worked on three Post projects, right?"

"You read my resume."

"You like being there?"

Turner's condescending demeanor changed and he sat up in alarm. "Hey, wait a minute! I never said—"

"If you're looking at a positional opportunity, hand in your resignation. In the meantime, stop trying to bulldoze me with your insider knowledge. I'm running this project, not you. Are we on the same page, Scott?"

Turner shifted and cleared his throat. "We're good," he mumbled.

"Fine. To get things rolling, I'll arrange a meeting with Clarke and Deakin to glad-hand."

"You'll probably want to talk to each of them separately."

"It's only an intro meeting and a chance for everybody to see me."

"You'll touch base with Leola Lanaro? She'll be handling any equipment decommissioning. At least I think she will. Watch yourself with her. She's one hot bird. Burns the ground under your feet."

Mason chuckled to ease the suddenly tense atmosphere. "Did you get burned?"

"Let's say I'm singed."

"Did she send you any project-related stuff we can use?"

"I got some files from her, including a preliminary schedule for new Siemens sorting machines, but I haven't had a chance to look at 'em in detail. I did read a summary of her final report. It tells Post everything they need to know how to decommission surplus inventory."

Mason frowned. "You didn't look at them? You're supposed to be on this full-time."

"I've been wrapping up something for Lavinia Stroud. You can check with her if you like. With Stornwell gone, I didn't know who'd be taking over or when."

"Never mind. Email me the files."

"I'll send you a link to his project directory. Anything else?"

"Take a stroll through Post's Sunshine West and Avalon Airport parcel processing centers and see how they do things. Then, I want you to see their Dandenong Letters Center."

Turner blanched. "Why bother? We have all the performance volume stats we need for the study."

"Those stats don't give us the human element. I want to know how people there work and the effect of possible layoffs."

"It's Post's problem and outside our terms of reference."

"No, it's our problem."

"Mason, Post HR will handle that stuff."

"We'll make their job easier by giving Clarke options. Not everything is about office politics, Scott, or greasing your ass. It's the value-add Global Systems provides. Get it done."

"It's your show."

"Scott, did you ever visit a mail or parcel center?"

"Well…no. Stornwell and I talked about it, but then he broke his leg…"

"In that case, I'd suspend judgment until you've gathered some first-hand information. That would be the way to go, don't you agree? Reports and dry stats, although valuable, form only part of the picture. Once you're done with the Melbourne centers, arrange a visit to Sydney West Letter Facility and the Western Sydney Sort Center. Get Delora to arrange a flight for you. I suggest you start with Sydney West. When you get your ticket, let me know the arrival time. I'll let the site managers know you're coming."

Turner frowned. "Aren't you overdoing it? Consider the cost. Renolds won't like it."

Mason ignored the implied impertinence, tired of having his decisions dissected by a junior. "Let me worry about that."

Tempted to tell Scott that anything he is told must be treated in strictest confidence, he refrained. The man had done this kind of stuff before and should know how to treat clients. Still, if Scott screwed up, Mason would wear the ensuing fallout, but not before he saw Scott burned. A shallow victory at best.

"That's all."

Turner jerked his head in a nod and made for the door.

Mason watched him leave, chewed his bottom lip, and swiveled the chair. Rain smeared the large plate window, blurring the world outside. He understood now why Scott hadn't advanced to senior consultant. A technician, not a planner or thinker. Mason acknowledged the possibility he misjudged the man. He probably made an enemy, but didn't give a crap.

A knock and he faced the door. Renolds pushed it open and stood there. "I see you met Turner. By the way, he didn't look happy. An hour on the job and you already ticked him off. More likely, he ticked you off."

Mason grinned. "Both. I should be annoyed, but I understand why you did it."

"Did what?"

"You deliberately stuck me with him."

Renolds lifted his palm. "Before you start throwing furniture at me, I didn't do it to test your people skills, although it naturally went into the mix. Turner can be irritating to a point of insolence, but he's a superb data harvester and dishes it out straight."

Mason grinned. "I know. He served me a plateful."

"He'll do what he's told," Renolds said, "which will free you to focus on the project's objectives and human factors. He may lack the holistic view, but that's your job, not his. Anything else?"

"I'm good," Mason said without reservation. He dealt with people like Turner before. Eager to display their insider knowledge in a gambit to take control away from a new man. He liked initiative, but not insubordination. Wherever he worked, there always had to be a hardcase, and Turner appeared to be one here.

Without a word, Renolds turned and closed the door after him.

Mason reached for the desk phone and pressed a direct line button.

"Raymond Clarke," a gruff voice answered after four rings.

Mason got an image of a middle-aged busy executive interrupted doing something important.

"Mason Adamov, Mr. Clarke. I'm running the Global Systems study you commissioned."

"Ah, Walt told me about you. What's going on?" he queried in a light American accent.

"I would like to see you and Mr. Deakin and get any slant not in the terms of reference. Separately if you prefer."

"A slant, eh? Well, Terry's at our Dandenong center, but I can see you at eleven this morning."

"I look forward to it, sir."

"Just Raymond, okay?"

"Suits me. At eleven then."

Another high-speed, low-drag operator, he reflected and pressed a different preset button. When Deakin answered, Mason agreed to see him at Post headquarters tomorrow at eleven-thirty. Satisfied, he touched another button.

"National Post. Leola Lanaro," a melodious voice replied and set off a cascade of pleasant images in his mind.

"Hi, Leola. This is Mason Adamov. I'm—"

"They said to expect you, Mr. Adamov. You have it all wrapped up already?"

Mason sensed amusement and wondered if all Post people were characters.

"With every T crossed. Can we meet at eleven-thirty today or thereabouts?"

"With Scott Turner in tow?"

"Just you and me this time. I gather you already met Scott."

"I did," Leola replied sardonically, which made him smile. It looked like Turner went out of his way to ruffle everybody's feathers. "Eleven-thirty is fine. East tower, ninth-floor."

"See you then." He hung up and let out a deep sigh. A hell of a way to start the day.

* * *

Pale sunshine burst through a torn sky and splashed the street with light devoid of warmth. It nonetheless made a pleasant break from constant drizzle. A crisp southerly off the Bay tugged at Mason's overcoat as he exited the Uber sedan. He watched it pull away from the curb into heavy Swan Street traffic. A city-bound tram hissed by, trailing a convoy of cars in its wake. Clad in winter gear, pedestrians hurried along the glistening sidewalk, probably wishing they were somewhere tropical. He would not mind it either.

He turned and gazed at the connected twin towers of Post's new headquarters. A new building and a new name. Large glass panels reflected the surrounding old-style structures. Opened in 2021, the ultra-modern edifice stood out among drab architecture around it. He strode toward the main entrance and shuffled in with two women as heavy double glass doors slid back. Both walked briskly toward the left bank of three elevators as he approached the security desk. A middle-aged guard in a gray uniform looked up from his computer screen, a toothpick stuck in his mouth.

"Can I help you?"

More characters…

"Mason Adamov to see Raymond Clarke."

Without changing expression in his cast features, the guard glanced down and held up a badge attached to an alligator clip.

"Your 24/7 ID, Mr. Adamov. Please wear it at all times."

Mason took the badge and pinned it to his jacket breast pocket.

"Mr. Clarke is on the eleventh floor, west tower."

"Thanks."

The spacious foyer gave the impression of stability and permanence, and Mason figured the public didn't got much change from $420 million it cost to build the complex as he walked briskly toward the right bank of elevators. One opened with a sharp *ting* and disgorged a woman and three men dressed in formal office wear. Mason walked in and pressed the eleventh floor button. A youngish individual hurried in as the doors were closing and stood beside him, touched his card to a glowing red sensor, grinned, and pressed the fifth-floor button. Mason got the hint and presented his pass.

The polished steel double door hissed open and he walked toward a chest-high reception point. A pretty redhead, hair flowing over shoulders framed a round face, flashed him a warm smile that lit her green eyes.

"Mason Adamov to see Mr. Clarke."

She checked something on her computer screen, rose, and waved her left hand. "This way, Mr. Adamov."

Ceiling-high window panels gave a nice view of the city and Treasury Gardens. Skyscrapers hid in low cloud the sun hadn't parted. Potted plants added diverting color among spacious bullpens. Four offices graced the northern wall painted utilitarian beige. His minder tapped the corner office door and grabbed the handle after a muffled 'Come!' from inside.

"Mr. Adamov," she announced politely and stood to one side.

Mason nodded and walked into a large office lit with dull sunshine. A brown executive desk strewn with papers, a computer screen, mouse, and keyboard occupied the corner. A tall bookshelf against one wall held a variety of manuals, magazines, and file folders. So much for a paperless office.

A surprisingly young-looking man sporting thick brown hair, thin mustache, a slightly crooked nose, rose from the black leather chair to his above average height, and held out a hand.

"Glad to see you, Mason," Clarke announced firmly and waved a hand at two visitor's chairs. "Pull up a rock."

"Thanks for seeing me on such short notice, Mr. Clarke," Mason replied evenly as they shook hands.

"Just Raymond, remember? Care for a coffee or something?" he offered and sat.

"I'm fine." Mason dragged a gray cloth chair closer to Clarke's desk and eased himself down.

Clarke glanced out the window and shook his head. "Ghastly Aussie weather, but that's Melbourne for you. Enjoy the sun while it lasts." His black eyes probed Mason with undisguised curiosity. "Renolds told me about you, but you'll pardon me when I say I expected someone older in a principal consultant."

"I get that all the time," Mason said, taking no offence.

"Mmm. Yes." Clarke leaned forward and crossed his arms over the desk. "So, you're here to tell me how I should run my business?" he quipped in his American accent.

"That's what you asked Global Systems to do, but if that were all, you wouldn't need us…Raymond," Mason said, giving the man equal scrutiny. He faced a hard professional, and it would be fatal to underestimate him. "Your internal report, backed by external studies, already outlined Post's action map. You don't need Global Systems to tell you what you already know, something I'm sure Walter Renolds already pointed out—"

"He did."

"You want a value-add factor to complement equipment decommissioning."

"Sum it up for me."

Mason expected the grilling. "The statistics are undeniable. Post's parcel volumes have grown steadily since 2014. Last year, they topped one-point three million items. In 2017, you had a thirty-two million loss in the letters delivery arm. In 2019, that rose to $192 million. This year, it's likely to top $256 million. Letter revenues fall steadily in every state, accelerated by the Covid-

19 pandemic as customers increasingly switched to emails and other electronic media. International letter handling has shown the same downward trend and reflects a global reaction not exclusive to Australia."

"Go on."

"Since 2014, the number of permanent employees has remained relatively stable at around 38,000, as has your extended workforce of 42,000. Your parcel arm absorbed some excess manpower caused by decline in letter volumes. Nevertheless, Post is overstaffed, the situation exacerbated by Amazon, DHL, FedEx and other carriers squeezing the parcels marketplace with cheaper pricing models and quicker deliveries. To counter them, you need to differentiate yourself to make parcel handling more profitable, your main revenue stream. Failure means declining volumes and profits, and Post will become an industry also-ran as your competition modernizes operations through automation.

"The letters handling side of your business is dying, but it's something you're still forced to provide. Many of your sorting machines are more than fifteen years old and why you want them removed. Hence, Lanaro's study. To modernize, you installed some BEUMER Group and Siemens Flats Sorter Machines and plan to install more as soon as you can decommission old inventory. The equipment is already in the pipeline. Although your surplus machines are fully depreciated, they represent an ongoing maintenance cost you need to plug.

"Post is not an independent corporation free to maximize market penetration into more profitable ventures that maximizes profits. Your activities are constrained by the Commonwealth government to which you're accountable for all postal services. Whether you like it or not, you must keep your letters processing business, even if done at a loss. That means expediting the modernization program or be forced to ask the government for financial relief, which might be difficult given the billions they wasted to prop up the economy during Covid-19." Mason paused, not wishing to overcook his position by rehashing the obvious. "Nothing I'm saying is new, which I'm sure you already know."

"You've done your homework, all right," Clarke growled with grudging approval. "Your predecessor didn't cut it so straight, but I appreciate it cut plain. Hardly fair that I should put you on the spot your first day here, but what's your take?"

Mason shrugged. "To ensure long term viability, you need to look at alternative revenue streams. Given your competition in the parcels handling space, that's going to be tough. However, your Post26 Strategy position paper has everything mapped out…on a theoretical level, and they're sound business objectives. My take? You want practical to-do tactical plans to achieve those objectives. Decommissioning surplus inventory nationwide as soon as possible will fulfill part of that objective, and why you approached Global Systems…among other things."

Clarke snorted and shook his head. "You're right about everything. You sure you're not an ASIO spy or something? Nobody so young should know all these things and have such a holistic perspective on Post business."

"Basic research, Raymond."

"Hah! Okay, wiseguy. You mentioned 'among other things'. I take it you're referring to Terry Deakin." Clarke made it a statement.

"Decline in letters business means a corresponding reduction of his position as a Post executive. I'm certain he knows that and may fight to stop you dismantling his facilities."

"Perhaps."

Mason tilted his head, sensing a shift from Clarke. He needed to be careful here not to alienate a powerful Post executive by being too blunt hashing over the obvious. At the same time, taking sides in Post's power politics may give GS immediate positive returns, but it would be a negative long-term strategy. He had to maintain impartiality.

Clarke waved a hand. "Don't worry, Mason. I don't intend to

use you or Global Systems as a weapon in Post's internal machinations. Terry is a friend and I don't want to undermine his position. At the same time, I must steer Post into viable future revenue streams. Terry will accept the inevitability of that future."

Mason stared at Clarke and a lightbulb went off. Scott Turner may be a good data harvester, but he clearly missed an important one.

"It just hit me. Terry Deakin is not fighting to maintain his letters processing facilities. He knows cuts must be made. He's positioning himself to head the Post26 Strategy implementation program in the same way you are."

"A sharp piece of analysis, Mason, and quite correct," Clarke mused, voice tinged with admiration.

"Something isn't clear to me, Raymond. You don't need Global Systems to tell you how to decommission letter and barcode sorting machines. I understand Leola Lanaro's report has that covered. Why the GS study?"

"My objective is to further Post's interests. That's all. Talk to Terry and get his view on things. When you connect the dots, we'll talk." Clarke stood and offered his hand. "It's refreshing to have someone cut through the fog without resorting to obfuscating rhetoric. We'll get along."

"Thanks for your time, Mr. Clarke."

Mason closed the door after him, paused, and shook his head. Clarke said he didn't want to use Global Systems as a weapon to further his agenda. Mason didn't believe a word. Power, that's what mattered; what always mattered. He had seen it done at ANZ, Deloitte, and Etisalat, and understood the rules. He had to tread carefully here to ensure he or GS weren't served as sacrificial lambs. A negative endorsement from National Post would spread through the consulting community in a flash and seriously affect future assignments…with him on that limb for Renolds to saw off.

As he strode toward the elevators, he glanced at his

smartphone: 11:20 am. Time for the next item on his list. He took out his cell and touched an icon in the Contacts list.

"Lanaro!" a crisp, impatient voice answered after two rings.

"Mason Adamov. Did I catch you at a bad time?"

Her merry laugh cast sunshine on his day. "No more than usual, Mr. Adamov."

"Just Mason. Are we still good to meet?"

"Where are you?"

"Outside Clarke's office."

"Go to the second floor cafeteria and I'll meet you there in five," she declared and cut contact.

"Fine, in five," Mason muttered into a dead phone and slowly walked toward the elevators.

The ride down made in silent contemplation, he went over his conversation with Clarke looking for trigger keywords. He considered the meeting a revealing interview, although somewhat intrigued why Renolds did not know about the tug of war over the Post26 Strategy position. Clarke may not have told him or Renolds never looked beyond the obvious. Perhaps he did know and wanted to see if Mason would figure it out. A test of sorts? No matter. What did matter, Clarke neglected to say, deliberately perhaps, why he commissioned the GS study.

A sharp *ting* and the door slid back to reveal a dining area that appeared to take up the whole floor. Still a little early for lunch, enough occupied tables and background conversation filled the vast space. He sniffed lasagna, spaghetti, parmesan cheese, and winced. Of all cheeses he liked, the odoriferous parmesan never made the list. He simply could not get past the awful smell.

An incident in childhood did it, and he scowled at the memory. One Saturday, his mom had him go to the supermarket for some groceries. Apart from dry goods, she insisted he pick up fresh cream cheese for *palačinke*, something she made from time to time when Dad happened to be on leave from the Navy.

On that particular morning, the supermarket had a tray of assorted cheeses on a glass counter for shoppers to sample. Among them, parmesan cubes, a yellow thing with blue-veined streaks, and something with red spots. As he walked past, the sharp odors hit him and he gagged. No more cheese shopping for him. Gouda, Edam, and Cheddar were things he could handle.

The elevator doors hissed behind him and he quickly stepped to one side. Two youngsters ambled out deep in conversation about HTML and hurried toward a long service counter on his right. Then he noticed the woman and had a visceral tug of instinctive desire.

Not tall, probably 165cm, slim in tailored gray slacks and jacket, short black hair framed a perfect face and long neck. Her small mouth set in a pretty frown, largest black eyes he had ever seen, highlighted with a touch of blue shadow framed by long lashes, focused on him. They seemed to expand and he found himself powerless to look away. Her pert nose crinkled as she broke into a warm smile that dimpled her left cheek. Apart from some lipstick, she wore no other makeup he could see. In late twenties perhaps, hard to say, though. A delicate perfume he could not place came his way.

"Mr. Adamov?"

The lyrical sound of her voice tugged at his emotional fabric with primal force he embraced with abandon. She absently brushed back a lock of hair behind her right ear.

What the hell happened? Ogling like an adolescent lout, Mason finally surfaced, blinked hard, and held out his hand. *Keep things professional, idiot!*

"Guilty, Miss Lanaro," he managed to croak and cleared his throat.

Ti banac!

Her hand warm and dry in his, and he held it a moment longer than strict protocol demanded. He let go and silently berated himself for a drooling fool.

"If I can call you Mason, you must call me Leola. Fair is fair," she returned with an amused twinkle in her eyes.

Did she notice the momentary look of raw lust on his face? He hoped not, clearly picturing what she must be thinking. Another lecher in a business suit, but he felt powerless to stop himself. She exuded some magnetism that compelled him to take her in his arms and crush her against him. The encounter with Aliana bubbled, went off with a sobering pop, and Mason recalled his commitment never to get involved with a colleague.

Impossible as it seemed, Leola's eyes grew larger and he felt himself drowning in their depths. Then the magic light in them faded, as did the imperceptible glow around her, and she became an ordinary woman. Well, she would never be ordinary to him, he told himself, sensing she also felt a connection. Then again, it could be his feverish imagination making more of the encounter to satisfy his craving.

His professional persona firmly back in place, he inclined his head. "A somewhat unusual setting for a formal discussion, wouldn't you say?"

Her carefree laugh made his skin tingle. "I skipped breakfast and my body is clanging alarms. I hope you don't mind. I could snag a meeting room if you prefer."

"No problemo," Mason said. "I could use a coffee myself."

Her eyes twinkled. "No problemo?"

He shrugged. "Ever since I saw the second Terminator movie…"

"I also liked it. Powerful story. A bit overdone with action, though. But then, with Schwarzenegger in it, there had to be bullets flying and bodies everywhere. Right?" she declared emphatically and started toward the serving counter that offered a large selection of cold and hot foods, sandwiches, desserts, fruit, and drinks.

"Interesting hairstyle," she remarked obliquely, referring to his white streak.

"Something I inherited from my mother."

"I like it. It gets you noticed."

"Believe it."

Tray loaded with chicken parma, orange juice, tea, and a tub of Yoplait yogurt, she steered him toward a window table. Although she protested, he insisted on paying, telling her it's a business expense. Clouds had rolled in and rain smeared the floor-to-ceiling windows. He placed his large mug of black coffee and a plate of blueberry Danish opposite her and sat down. A thirsty sip, he held the warm mug between his hands and focused on the astonishing woman as Leola tucked into her parma with gusto. Sensing his scrutiny, she looked up, fork held up.

"What?"

"I'm enjoying watching you demolish that plate with such determination."

She giggled, a musical tinkle that tugged at his heartstrings.

"Are you hitting on me, Mr. Adamov? All this time, I thought you were a gentleman."

Mason decided to chuck all pretense and the unstated courting rules. "I guess I'm hitting on you a little, Leola. Don't worry, though. I'm a perfect gentleman."

"Mmm. I wonder. All men are wolves, you know."

In his case, she had no idea how close she came to being right.

"And some women are tigers. It's a jungle out there."

Her face lost some light and her eyes became dark. "So I learned."

Mason gave himself a deserved mental kick. "My apologies, and excuse my inappropriate behavior. It won't happen again."

Her eyes cut into him and he felt himself weighed. She appeared to reach a decision and took a sip of juice.

"How did you make out with Clarke?" she ventured after several seconds of poignant silence, the change of subject like a jerking car turn.

Mason did not mind returning to reality, but wondered how

much to reveal what he considered confidential. She noted his hesitation and grinned.

"Don't worry, Mason. Everybody in National Post knows about the undeclared war between Clarke and Deakin. Except the Board perhaps. Their heads are so far up in the clouds, they're suffering from lack of oxygen."

Mason could not help himself and laughed with genuine mirth, vividly picturing the scene.

"I did hesitate to tell you," he replied.

"I know. I'm a lowly project manager and you're a principal consultant mired in high-stakes Post politics. I won't put you on the spot again." With that, she dug into her parma.

He wanted to be open with this wondrous woman, but reminded himself to keep things professional. Leola may know all about Clarke and Deakin, but he still could not divulge privileged conversation.

A large gulp of surprisingly good coffee, he took a hefty bite out of his Danish, absently pondering if the kitchen here made it. It tasted fabulous.

Perhaps he *could* sound off on something.

"You'll be in charge of decommissioning letter and barcode sorting inventory?"

"I hope so," she confirmed, dabbed her lips with a black tissue napkin, and sipped some tea. "After Global Systems tell us which ones to take out," she added impishly.

Mason raised his eyebrows. "Turner told me your report clearly spelled out how to go about it and which machines to scrap."

"It took me about a month to put together, and I thought I'd be good to go."

"And you're puzzled why Clarke sat on it, then asked Global Systems to do another report?"

"Oh, I know why, all right. He doesn't want me to be Deakin's scapegoat when I start carting off his machines. Clarke will wave your report in Deakin's face and declare in his American accent that GS is to blame for everything."

"Yeah. I got that part," Mason said dryly.

"It's all a farce, you know. Clarke doesn't really want to dismantle the mail centers, but his hands are tied. He can't buck market trends and Deakin knows it. He's no dummy." She took another sip of tea and peeled open the yogurt tub.

Around them, the buzz of conversation had risen as hungry staffers filled the cafeteria. Rain still smeared the windows and he fancied he could feel the cold from the thick glass.

"Did you know that Clarke and Deakin chaired the Post26 Strategy group?" she remarked.

"No, I didn't. It's a visionary paper."

"And Deakin is visioning himself as its chair."

Mason sighed, more than a little confused. Information overload and not enough time to process and catalog everything. "It must be the coffee, but something doesn't click."

She giggled. "No doubt. Your mind was on other things."

He could not refute the obvious and raised both hands in surrender.

"I am mortified that you penetrated my gentlemanly façade with such ease."

"A skill every woman develops after puberty, Mr. Adamov." From amused banter, her eyes turned dark. "Sometimes, the lesson must be relearned."

He wanted to delve deeper into this enchanting woman's past and soothe her evident pain, but refrained from scratching old scab. One day perhaps, she would feel comfortable talking about it. One day?

Their eyes locked and he felt an unmistakable connection. The possibility of emotional entanglement excited and frightened him. He felt fulfilled with his life and had everything he wanted. Why risk whiplash of the heart if Leola rejected him? Would she reject him?

Skits!

They just met! He recalled his mother's warning: 'It isn't healthy to be alone.'

Shed your raw desire and be sensible! For all he knew, Leola had a muscular boyfriend—no ring on finger—who would not be amused by his clumsy amorous advances on his territory. She's merely being friendly, he told himself.

He switched mental gears and focused on the job at hand. After a moment, he thought he had it.

"Deakin doesn't want his staff thrown out on the street if you gut his mail centers. He'll come after you if you try."

Leola nodded with satisfaction. "I knew you would get it, but he won't be coming after me."

"Why wasn't that in your report?" Another lightbulb went off. "You did have it there."

"I didn't overlook anything, Mason. Clarke made me take out that section."

"'Curiouser and curiouser', as Alice said. I'd like to read it."

She shook her head. "I'm sorry, no can do. I wouldn't mind, but if Clarke found out, it would mean my job. I *can* give you a verbal summary, though. It's a detailed state by state breakdown of every letters processing center: Number of and type of machines, letter volumes by category, permanent employees, casuals with seasonal variations, and lists my recommendations for who needs to go. If Clarke asks, I can tell him you figured it out, which you more or less did. I gave a lot of files to Scott Turner that covers most of this."

"I know. He sent them to me. I'll ask Clarke to give me your full report."

"Don't bother. I'll do it after I get his go-ahead." She glanced at her wristwatch. "I'd love to chat some more, Mason, but I must catch a meeting at one. By the way. Can you tell me what Turner up to?"

"No secret. I asked him to look in on Sunshine West and Avalon Airport parcel centers, and the Dandenong Letters Center facility. Tomorrow, he'll do Sydney West Letter and the Western Sydney Sort Center."

She tilted her head. "The human factors?"

"It's always the human factors, Leola. Apart from floor operators, Clarke's initiative will also cost many low-level and middle managers their job."

"I'm glad you're looking at it that way. I know Clarke and Deakin are concerned about the human cost, but I wonder sometimes. Always the big picture," she remarked comfortably and rose.

"I want to catch up again, Leola. If that's all right with you. Tomorrow? I'm seeing Deakin at eleven-thirty and we can have lunch."

She held out a hand. "I'd like that."

Did he sense something extra in her invitation that went beyond impersonal professionalism? Probably his feverish imagination working overtime.

He took her hand and squeezed gently. "Done."

He watched her walk off, totally captivated, professionalism be damned. He could not recall ever being taken in by a woman like that. Aliana did not count, considering it a juvenile hormonal reaction. He had become a lot wiser since then, but wondered if he really *had* become wiser.

He resisted temptation to grab a hot sandwich or salad and followed her to the elevators, hoping she wouldn't see him as merely another wolf on the prowl. She wouldn't be wrong, he mused with sardonic honesty. A quick cellphone request for an Uber, he felt he'd had enough of National Post for the day.

Broken clouds drifted eastward, pushed by a prevailing westerly his overcoat struggled to keep out. He scrunched his nose at the sharp sting of exhausts coming from cars trailing white vapor. More than one horn went off as irate drivers vented frustration at creeping traffic, the old street never designed to hold such loads. He felt mildly sorry for tenants here who endured this 24/7.

Mason took all this at a glance and threaded his way toward the curb between pedestrians going both ways. A navy blue sedan pulled up two minutes later. He recognized the Uber registration number and climbed into the back seat. The driver merged into the flow without a word. On the left, the Richmond rail yard extended all the way to the suburban Flinders Street hub. On his right, skyscrapers stood in sharp relief as the clouds lifted.

Leola occupied his thoughts as he replayed their meeting in lingering detail. He recalled every exquisite line of her cheek, jaw, nose, and lips he wanted to kiss. In the end, he decided she must have cast a spell on him. He could not possibly be infatuated after only one encounter. Could he? One day on the job and he found himself fantasizing over a woman. And what a woman! Turner warned him, but he took it as banter between men. He slowly released a deep breath and shifted mental gears to the substance of his meetings.

Clarke and Deakin playing each other for the same Post26 Strategy job? He'll have to be careful how he handled this part. Talk it over with Renolds, of course, and get his take. One thing stood out clearly. He could no longer execute his project by adhering strictly to the stated terms of reference, not that he ever expected things to be simple. Clarke wanted a to-do list, which Leola already prepared for him. What value-add could Mason give him?

He needed to gnaw on everything until he squeezed out all relevant data and information, the two not the same thing.

Before he realized, he found himself in the Collins Street canyon. The Uber did an illegal U-turn in the middle of the street and stopped beside the Rialto towers. He got out and strode quickly toward the main entrance.

Delora beamed as he exited the elevator.

"I trust you had a productive morning?"

He grinned and peeled off his overcoat. "Enlightening."

"Hah! What's it like outside? Looks miserable."

"Not too bad, actually. Cold, but the weather is breaking. Good for a brisk walk."

"I may do that."

Mason strode to his office, hung up the overcoat, and logged on. He clicked the Post Study directory, the Meetings sub-directory, and opened Word. In point form, he summarized his encounter with Clarke and Leola. He saved the file with a date tag and opened the issues register. With eidetic memory, he did not really have to write down anything, but Renolds would want to see records for everything to track progress in case Mason ended up under a tram or something. Keeping records also helped him focus on critical items and risk factors. As far as he could see, only one risk factor could threaten his project. Two, actually. Clarke's unstated expectations and Deakin's agenda, which he'll likely find out tomorrow.

Satisfied, he ambled out and headed toward the kitchenette for some liquid fuel. Many bullpens were occupied, their owners peering at computer screens or chewing lunch. He realized a meal might not be a bad idea.

Dressed in a black sweater and pants, long blonde hair that fell to her waist, taller than him by several centimeters, the trim woman finished pouring hot water into a large mug and glanced up.

"Hi, I'm Mason Adamov," he announced brightly and stuck out a hand. Her classic long face broke into a grin that lit her violet eyes and they shook hands.

"Lavinia Stroud. I heard you were coming. Ready to quit?" she added in a pleasantly deep contralto.

He reached for the glass coffee carafe. "After my meetings at Post, I'm tempted."

She flashed even teeth, eyes highlighted with a dark liner, and glanced at his pale streak of hair. "So, you drew the short straw. Renolds offered that one to me and I walked out on him. Good luck. It's a bear trap."

"I appreciate your support," he growled good-naturedly, and she laughed.

Her violet eyes probed him, measuring everything. In mid-thirties maybe—hard to tell once a woman sheds her twenties coltish years and matures—he intuitively recognized a fellow professional.

"Want to swap your job for my BHP study?" she ventured with a tilt of her head.

"That good, eh? Give me a couple of days and we'll see. Are they giving you a hard time over there?"

She pursed her lips. "Sometimes it's hard to differentiate between corporate politics and strategic direction. Everybody has an agenda. If I get it wrong, Kending will carve me up."

"That's why we get the big bucks." He scrutinized her more closely. "He wouldn't do that to you, would he? I got the impression Global Systems doesn't work that way."

"It doesn't," she added hastily. "And Kending is far too shrewd an operator to let things degenerate that far. Still, I must be careful," she said and raised a slim finger in warning. "Always satisfy the client. The golden rule." She sipped her tea and grinned. "We need to talk some more, Mason. I can't let a fresh fish like you get gobbled up by sharks before you build some armor."

A cascade of memories cascaded over him. "My armor is always up, Lavinia," he told her seriously.

"Still…Catch you later."

Renolds suddenly appeared and glanced after Lavinia. "Remarkable woman."

"I'm getting that impression," Mason replied and stirred sugar into his mug.

Renolds poured himself what remained of coffee, refilled the percolator with fresh grounds and water, and leaned against the bench.

"How'd you go with Clarke?"

Mason calibrated the words. "He didn't tell you?"

Renolds laughed with genuine amusement. "I see I'll have to watch myself with you. He rang me after you left his office. Let's go to my hole. That way, I can shout at you without causing a spectacle," he declared with a grin.

The Director for Infrastructure Projects sprawled into his seat and Mason relaxed in a visitor's chair.

"You made quite an impression on Clarke, and he doesn't impress easily. I knew from our first interview that you'd be a valuable asset for Global Systems. I won't apologize for throwing you a hot brick with Post. To be blunt, it's what you signed up for."

"I understand completely, Walt. Besides, I like a challenge."

"I thought you would. Anything juicy I ought to know from Clarke?"

"Did you know he and Deakin are after the Post26 Strategy job?"

"Actually, I did, but I wanted you to figure it out for yourself. Obvious, of course."

Deep in thought, Mason took a sip of coffee. "My talk with Leola Lanaro may have been even more interesting."

"Interesting how?"

"Threats and intentions. Her internal study told Clarke and Deakin what Post must do vis-a-vis the letters centers. Clarke's intention for our study? It can't be to wave our report in Deakin's face to absolve himself of blame while he guts every facility. The threat? He doesn't want anything to stand in his way to head the Post26 Strategy group, even if it means throwing Global Systems under a bus. What's more, I'd say neither does Deakin. See what I'm getting at?"

"Whatever we do, Mason, GS would wear the blame," Renolds remarked dryly. "Make sure we don't."

"Or I'll be the one under the bus?"

Renolds shrugged. "It's an unjust world, my boy." He sobered. "We want to make Post happy, but our primary objective is to safeguard GS interests. I shouldn't need to tell you that, as you already know it. With Post, see to it that everybody does walk away happy. Lots of future business for us there if we pull this one off. I'm always here if you need help, and so is Kending," he added. "I won't think any less of you if you ask. Just don't dig yourself or GS into a hole."

Mason stood. "I got it."

His stomach told him he ran on empty. Outside, the wind whistled down Collins Street, driving freezing rain. Despite the inclement weather, pedestrians filled the street. He hurried to the Saint Marc Rialto restaurant and had a chicken salad, Renolds' words vivid in his mind. Not altogether an amateur, Mason knew how to recognize and tick all the right boxes to keep himself afloat. He told Renolds he liked a challenge, but not necessarily one with an attached anchor ready to pull him down.

To hell with all of it.

His inner self satisfied, back in his spacious office, he checked the email Inbox and, among several, saw one from Turner; location of project folders he asked for.

Mason opened Turner's and clicked the first of four Word files and two Excel spreadsheets. Reading, he appreciated how Leola nicely summarized Post's threats and issues facing their letters processing business. His respect for her grew as he went over clear analyses devoid of personal bias. The gal had it all in one bag, all right, he mused. The other two files provided a summary of every letters and parcel processing center, supported by hard stats from the spreadsheets. The fourth file and the most interesting contained her recommendations, a decommissioning work schedule, and management summary. He easily saw the glaring gaps Clarke asked her to delete. Mason did not need the missing pieces to work out the human elements they contained, but would not mind seeing her full report.

Stornwell's directory contained project notes, interview summaries, and issues points, but nothing substantive of any use. He bailed out before getting that far.

Two hours staring at a computer screen. He snagged a coffee refill and updated the issues register. By Friday, he should be in a position to give Renolds a skeleton report and anticipated closing the assignment in another week.

Around four-thirty, he strode toward the kitchenette and glanced at Turner's empty cubicle. On impulse, he walked to Delora's desk.

"Ready to quit?" she demanded.

"Give me a few more days. Tell me. When is Turner flying out?"

"I made a booking for a four-fifty Virgin Air flight."

He bit his lip. Given the packed schedule he faced, Mason did not mind if Turner spent the night in Sydney.

"What's his return flight?"

"Tomorrow at six pm."

He nodded and made his way to the kitchenette.

In his office, mug held chest-high, he stood beside the tall window and gazed absently at the city's jagged sprawl not really seeing it, his mind chewing over Leola's documents. This is where his eidetic memory became a valuable tool. It spared him endless hours staring at a screen to take in and retain what he read.

He compartmentalized. He had everything he accumulated in life at instant recall, but an organized approach helped him ignore irrelevancies. His memory did not differentiate between clutter and important bits. So far, he had not suffered any memory loss, which ran counter to most textbooks and psychologists who claimed eidetic retention is not permanent. Perhaps he should write a paper about his condition in rebuttal. The thought made him smile, happy with how his brain worked.

At 6:05, he logged off, put on his overcoat, and strode out, Delora's space empty, as were most bullpen cubicles. Downstairs, a chill westerly made him wince and pull up the overcoat collar to cover his ears. Pedestrians hurried to get to wherever they were going, clutching umbrellas that did little to ward off a steady drizzle. A stream of traffic, headlights bright, moved both ways. The Clarendon Street tram squealed to a stop and he stepped in, thankful to be spared the rush hour crush. No empty seats, he did not mind standing for the short trip to South Melbourne.

A balloon of cognac and a mug of freshly percolated coffee complemented a warm tuna and salmon salad mixed with finely cut carrot and green capsicum strips. Mason sprawled into his favorite leather recliner and sipped. After a while, he got up, slid Neil Diamond's *Jonathan Livingston Seagull* CD into the player, and closed his eyes.

Chapter Five

The cell's six o'clock alarm went off with jarring clamor. Mason groaned and rolled over, wishing for a few more minutes of sleep. Five minutes later, pleasantly drowsy, the alarm went off again. This time much louder.

"The fates are against me," he mumbled belligerently.

With a heavy sigh, he threw back the comforter, shivered in the chill air, slid his feet into felt slippers, and padded toward the bathroom. Chores done, he dragged back the bedroom drapes.

Thick fog obscured everything. Streetlights created spheres of brightness and a surreal, magical atmosphere. He donned his running gear and went downstairs, relishing the warmth, the heating system kicking in at six. A biting chill made him wince when he opened the front door. Clammy air clung to him as he surveyed the empty street without enthusiasm. No rain, for which he thanked the guy upstairs. According to last night's forecast, Melbourne can look forward to a sunny, nine-degree day. He jammed on his baseball cap and started to lope toward Kings Way. Once he crossed St. Kilda Road, he would share Domain Park with other masochist joggers.

Five minutes short of eight o'clock, Mason stepped off the tram and sighed with satisfaction. For once, the weather people got it right. He figured they would get it right more often if somebody opened a window to see what really went on. They were good telling him to expect spring in September and summer in December, but not so good at what it would be like tomorrow. Melbournians loved to laugh at the Bureau.

Despite feeble sunshine, fog still shrouded the skyscrapers, but it would eventually burn away. The mushy yellow orb trying to push through the overcast made him look at life in a positive mood. When he walked to the tram stop earlier, frost covered exposed grass and his breath hung before him. His face tingled in the crisp air, hands warm in leather gloves. He probably would not need it today, but a small folding umbrella in his overcoat pocket provided emotional reassurance in case the weather turned. Yesterday reinforced a lesson he thought he knew: always be prepared.

The elevator doors hissed open and Delora looked up. It appeared she shared his early starting time. Several bullpen cubicles were already occupied.

"And how are you on this fine, invigorating morning?" he queried cheerfully.

"My, chipper today, aren't we?"

"Why not? We had our dose of gloom and misery yesterday. Time for a payback."

He walked briskly to his office, powered up the computer, and headed for the kitchenette to refill. A short Asian, not more than 155cm, squirted lemon juice into a fat mug, then added a dollop of honey. He grinned broadly and stuck out a hand.

"Horito Hashigawa. Call me Joe, and don't ask why. You must be Adamov. We were told you'd be coming."

Mason gripped the small hand and blinked when Joe squeezed hard.

"Pleased to meet you, Joe, and you can call me Mason. Don't ask why either."

Joe chortled. "Deal. I'm a senior consultant doing strategic stuff for Kending. They stuck me by the window at the far end," he added and indicated with his head. "All seniors rate a window cubicle. A lot of crap if you asked me, but that's how it is. I'm not complaining, mind you. I get a great city view, and since my desk faces out, nobody can see when I nod off." His infectious laugh made Mason like him immediately.

He could not tell Joe's age. All Japanese look young or middle-aged for a long time until they were suddenly old. Joe could have been in his forties. Walt told him all senior consultants were mature, experienced people who'd been around a while in more than one position and knew how things worked. Everybody else were all much younger.

Joe wore his jet-black hair cropped short. His ink eyes gave Mason a quick once over.

"I heard Walt stuck you with the Post study."

"What's with it? Lavinia also said it's a poisoned chalice."

Joe raised an eyebrow. "Don't tell me you haven't realized you've been given a hot poker. We all wondered who'd get it. When Walt announced you'll handle it, we breathed a sigh of relief." He took a sip of tea.

"So, it's political. Isn't everything?" Mason filled his mug and added half a teaspoon of sugar.

"Coffee man, eh?" Joe pointed at his mug. "You should try this stuff. It's a special green tea blend. This place doesn't serve it. I bring my own. What they have here is no better than dried lawn clippings."

Mason grinned. "Another time."

"Did Walt give you that shit Turner as an analyst?"

"He does seem to be a personality."

"Slap him down and don't let him get under your skin. He's good at what he does, or we would have canned him. Well, I gotta go. Come by anytime. I want to find out how you conned Walt and Karter into giving you your job."

"Over lunch someday."

"Deal!" Joe slapped him on the shoulder and walked off.

Mason wondered if all GS people were personalities.

A quick check of emails, mostly CC stuff from Renolds, Kending, and Stroud on status of pipeline projects. He made a mental note to check with Walt if he should send a general email on his project. A sharp knock on the door made him look up.

"Come."

Kending walked in and scanned the office with a quick glance. Tall, around 180cm, thick hair touched with frost around the temples added dignity. Deep blue eyes regarded Mason with friendly amusement. Trim, he exuded an air of purpose and determination.

"Morning, Mason. Got a minute?" Director for Strategic Projects remarked softly in a deep voice.

"Of course," Mason said as they shook hands. "Please, take a seat. Did you have a good trip in Sydney?"

"Going over a NSW government project with their counterpart. You'll hear more about it at tomorrow's senior staff meeting. All settled in?"

"Everybody's saying that Walter has thrown me to the wolves," Mason quipped, and Kending laughed.

"That's Walt, all right. Doesn't waste any time putting people to work. I know about the Post thing. An interesting case study in organizational organic dynamics."

"The human variable that transcends formalistic constructs?"

"Exactly! That's what we do here, Mason. We dig out the human factors in an otherwise totally coherent situation. Illogical, emotional drivers often motivate people, and that makes us irrational. In turn, it sometimes makes it difficult to discern motive, and explains why some perfectly structured corporate and government initiatives fail."

"Organizations are not living entities," Mason added after a moment.

"You got it. They're people subject to all ills and failings that afflict us. Keep this in mind when you're looking at Post. Anything you care to tell me about it?"

"I had a talk with Clarke yesterday, and I'm seeing Deakin this morning. Clarke seems to expect some value-add beyond the terms of reference. Right now, I don't see where we can do that, but I don't want to pre-judge anything until I collect all the information."

"Don't worry about it. You've only been on it a day. Did you met anybody else on the floor?"

"I had a brief chat with Joe and Lavinia. She offered to swap jobs."

Kending chuckled. "She's handling a delicate piece of strategic analysis for BHP. If we stuff up, I could lose the account. It won't get to that, though. She's a very competent consultant."

"So I gathered."

The Director for Strategic Projects slapped his thighs and rose. "Well, I've got to go. I'm pleased to have you on board, Mason, and I hope you'll like working for Global Systems."

"I'll let you know once I finish the Post job."

Kending shook his head and walked out. When the door closed, Mason shook his head, appreciating the visit. He intended to call on Kending, but it appeared most people here were self-starters. To do well, giving 100 percent may not cut it, but he knew that before applying. Global Systems never struck him as merely another also-ran body shop consultancy.

He recalled an old adage: 'Careful what you wish for, you might get it.'

Well, he got his wish to move into senior level consulting. No use bitching now.

Something else he looked forward to—lunch with Leola.

Last night, he tried not to dwell on her, but found it impossible. The woman had him captivated. What he felt for her transcended mere physical desire and he found himself in a new dimension. He felt unbridled longing and enjoyed the thrill of unchecked sex before, but with her, more than anything else, he wanted to cradle her in his arms, protect her from all hurt, and shelter her forever. With all his smarts and knowledge, he felt helpless. In the end, he gave up analyzing his feelings and replayed their conversation in lingering detail.

He faced a new day and another opportunity to meet her.

* * *

"Have a seat, Mason," Terry Deakin invited after they shook hands.

Portly, balding, Mason did not judge. The man regarded him with piercing brown eyes that seemed to photograph everything. In his early fifties perhaps, he enjoyed power after years of struggle to get it…and keep it. Another overachiever. Something Mason recognized immediately. His research told him Deakin took over national letter processing four years ago, probably knowing it to be a withering business arm. Why then take a dead-end career posting that would eventually be relegated to a junior manager?

Something else his research told him. Before Raymond Clarke showed up, Deakin helped Post set up parcel handling facilities in Melbourne and Sydney. Post then recruited Clarke from FedEx in the States to lead Parcel, Post and Products, which must have ticked Deakin off, getting bypassed like that. It's what the official blurbs read. Did Deakin rub somebody on high the wrong way?

"Thank you for seeing me, sir."

"Nonsense! And call me Terry, seeing how we'll be in bed together for the duration of your study." He paused. "How did you go with Raymond?"

"Better than I expected. He surprised me by being very frank, something I appreciated."

Deakin grinned. "He doesn't hold back, that's for sure. I suppose you clued him in on how Post faces a disaster with our letters processing business."

"I went over some stark stats with him. Stats I'm sure you're aware of."

"I know I'm sitting on a dry branch, Mason," Deakin growled, "but I'm not waiting for Raymond or anyone else to saw it off. Yankee bastard. We're friends, but what he knows about letter processing can be put into a plain envelope." He tilted his head. "Did he tell you he wants to head the Post26 Strategy transformation group?"

"He didn't. I told him. I also told him you were after the same job."

"You did your homework. No secret, though. However, my esteemed colleague may have outmaneuvered himself, with a bit of help from me," Deakin added with a conspiratorial grin. "Post hired him to head our front line operations, and he hasn't done a bad job," he observed grudgingly. "Because he has done reasonably well, the Board will not move him somewhere else. Get the picture?"

"He's the one on that dry limb?" Mason ventured, and Deakin laughed.

"Precisely! Mind you, the limb he's sitting on is fine and healthy, and the Board wants it to remain that way. Our parcel business is a major revenue earner, but it's not Post's entire future."

"Hence the Post26 Strategy paper," Mason said.

He felt surprise, amusement, and satisfaction that Deakin chose to be so open with him, an outsider, and wondered why. Then it hit him. Deakin respected his position as a principal consultant and felt free to be somewhat informal. Then again, the man simply might not give a damn, but Mason doubted it. People at his level always greased the rungs of their career ladder and watched what they said to everybody.

"I spoke to Raymond yesterday and he told me about you," Deakin mused. "I'm glad to see his opinion of you is warranted. Don't look surprised. I'm not revealing any confidences not already known to all senior Post management. Including Raymond."

Mason decided to take a mental leap. "Did you reject the Board's offer to head Parcel, Post and Products?"

"Perceptive, aren't you. I've been in operations my entire career. For a change, I wanted to shape Post policy, not just execute it."

"That's why you want the Post26 Strategy implementation job," Mason made it a statement.

"I helped write the definitive paper."

Mason got it. That paper made Deakin the front runner.

"Strictly speaking, none of this has any relevance to your terms of reference, but it always helps to focus on the bigger picture, I say. Tell me, Mason. Apart from the obvious, what do you see as the main issue facing the Global Systems study?"

"I might be off a little, but your concern isn't with mechanics involved to decommission surplus inventory. Leola Lanaro's report covers that in detail, and I can't see myself improving on it."

"Smart girl, that."

"Your concern is what happens to Post employees during the rationalization and is the missing bit in Lanaro's report Clarke asked her to take out."

"She told you?"

"Not the content, though. I don't believe you're overly worried about the casuals. You're probably planning to move some into permanent positions, but parcel centers can absorb only so many, and other business areas require more skilled staff. A whole Post26 Strategy paper section talks about supporting First Nation people, the disadvantaged, the disabled, looking after communities, and resisting closure of unprofitable Post offices. Your handiwork?"

"You're right. To me, people always matter. In any rational analysis, they're the ones who get things done and get impacted first by change. Machines are only there to facilitate processes. Raymond probably told you he gets it, but he is primarily a numbers man and doesn't look at people the way I do. Not a bad thing sometimes."

"And because he's been effective, Post will keep him where

he is," Mason added meditatively.

"Right again, and I want him to stay there." Deakin rubbed his chin. "Two days on the job and you wrapped it all up. You'll no doubt talk to Raymond again. Feel free to tell him anything, including that I think he's a Yankee bastard." He laughed, his ample belly heaving, then turned serious. "You've been wondering why he asked for another study when, as you said, he already has what he wants."

"I did wonder, and I'm still wondering."

"No, you're not anymore, are you? You figured it out."

Last night, he thought he *had* figured it out, but could not believe it would be that simple. He also recalled his discussion with Kending.

"I think so. Corporate blindness," he said slowly, and Deakin beamed.

"That's it. I like to deal with smart people, and you're smart. As with many large organizations, National Post suffers from a prevailing disease—disbelief in the competence of its staff. With your study, the Board wants reassurance that Leola Lanaro's decommissioning plan is the way to go. So, we're paying Global Systems a stack of money to tell us it is, which will make them happy. Stupid, I know, but that's how things are run."

"Will it make Clarke happy?"

"Ah, that's the rub, but not your concern. Stick to your terms of reference and you'll be fine."

Sensing dismissal, Mason stood. "Thank you for your time, Mr. Deakin."

"I'm here always," Terry said, heaved himself up, and stuck out a meaty hand.

Mason closed the door and glanced at his smartphone: 12:10. Running a little late for his lunchtime appointment with Leola, but given the circumstances, he felt she would understand. He pressed her contact icon.

"Hi, Mason. All done with Deakin?" she answered cheerfully.

"It's been a most revealing session," he countered carefully, and she laughed.

"I don't doubt it. Meet you at the cafeteria in five?"

"Suits."

The elevator disgorged its load and he stepped out. She stood near the wall, looking neat in a clinging navy blue sweater and black pants. A pearl necklace adorned a slim neck. For a thrilling moment, he allowed himself to sink into her black eyes that seemed to expand the longer he stared at them. He finally surfaced from a distracting fantasy, hoping his moment of raw desire went unnoticed.

"Looking smart today, Leola," he told her by way of greeting and lightly brushed her arm.

She flashed him a smile that showed off her endearing dimple. "Not bad yourself," she remarked jauntily and pointed at his suit. "We both picked black today."

He strangled the obvious rejoinder about great minds and extended an arm toward the serving counter, the cafeteria already noisy with bubbling customers enjoying a spell of bright sunshine.

"Shall we?"

In the queue waiting for service, he pushed his tray along the counter eyeing the offerings and decided on chicken curry with rice and apple juice. Leola went for beef stew with chunky potatoes and orange juice. He paid for both meals and they sauntered toward an empty table beside the unbroken panoramic window.

Mason spread a tissue napkin across his knees and tried the curry. Spicy, full of flavor, he like it.

"Not bad."

"Post serves good food," Leola remarked and spooned her stew. "Tell me about your encounter with Deakin."

"I must admit, he's not what I expected. Behind that jovial facade lurks a sharp mind."

She grinned. "Lots of people underestimate him."

"You held back yesterday because you wanted me to form my own impression?"

"I thought it important that you did." Her eyes cut into him. "And…"

"First impressions…tricky how that works. Yesterday, I walked away thinking Clarke made all the main moves here, but it's really Deakin who's pulling the strings," he said and waited to see if she really did know what went on, reluctant to divulge the substance of his conversations.

"I like it that you're careful, unwilling to spill everything."

"I must treat what Clarke and Deakin tell me as confidential, Leola."

"Don't worry. I understand. Deakin *did* tell you he's aiming to head the Post26 Strategy group?"

"He did, and it gave me a useful insight into my project."

"How?"

"I cannot take sides in any turf war."

"You shouldn't. Anyway, it won't be a turf war. Although Clarke wouldn't mind getting the posting, he knows he'll never get it. He's too useful where he is. It's the reason why Post hired him." She spooned more stew, clearly relishing the taste. He watched her mannerisms, precise and economical. A product of her training as a programmer and systems analyst, or natural behavior?

"I went through the files you sent Turner, and I'm genuinely impressed. You obviously wrote more than one report in your time."

A slight flush of pleasure colored her cheeks. "Thanks. I always make a special effort to be objective."

"Something Clarke and Deakin appreciated, I'm sure. Did Deakin ask you to give him the missing sections?"

"He didn't have to. He and Clarke sponsored the study and had the right to see the complete report. Clarke wanted a redacted version sent to other managers interested only in dry figures."

Two middle-aged men took a spare table in front of Mason and unloaded their trays. The buzz of background conversation rose in volume, and he wondered how many people worked here.

"This can't be the only cafeteria?"

She shook her head. "There's another one in the east tower. One couldn't service more than two thousand people who work here."

A satisfying time later, he sighed and patted his stomach. "I may come here for all my lunches."

Her merry laugh lit her face. "Greedy gut. Your meeting with Deakin. Has it made a difference how you're looking at your study?"

"Early days yet. I need to see what Turner comes up with."

Should he tell her that Clarke wanted him to value-add? One thing she mentioned yesterday appeared to be wrong. Deakin fully accepted the need to decommission surplus sorting machines. After all, he helped author the Post26 Strategy. Whatever Mason recommended in his report, Clarke would not make Leola a scapegoat or wave it in Deakin's face as a shield. The thing he needed to work out, what value-add did Clarke want.

"Tea?" he offered.

"Thanks," she replied with a nod.

Seated again, he added sugar to his coffee and took a sip.

"What's on for the rest of your day?" he queried, not in the mood to dwell on his study.

"I'm running a project that uses AI software to process data files Post accumulates in the course of doing business and come up with a way to present three-dee analysis imagery. The whole thing is supposed to be voice-driven."

Mason raised both eyebrows. "I wanted to do something like that when I worked at ANZ, but the technology wasn't available then."

"I don't understand everything my analysts tell me, but I'm excited to see what they'll come up with. I've seen a couple of prototypes and the stuff is awesome."

"It should keep you busy for a while."

"I need to show Clarke a fully working prototype by end of year."

"Can you?"

"Probably, even though I've been on the thing for only a month."

On impulse, he reached across the table and brushed her hand. "I'd like to talk more about your AI project, Leola…and just talk. Care for dinner sometime this week? I promise not to be a wolf," he added with a disarming grin.

Her large eyes regarded him above the rim of her cup. "I wouldn't mind."

His heart sang. "Great! Seven? Thursday?"

"Sounds good."

"Text me your address and I'll pick you up. By the way, where *do* you live?"

"North Melbourne, not far from the train station. It's handy, as it brings me directly to Burnely, which is around the corner. When I studied at RMIT—"

"You went to RMIT? Me too."

"Small world. After I got my graduate diploma, I joined Post as a programmer. I've been with them ever since."

"You were in their old Latrobe Street building?"

"Yes. During my break, I used to stroll through Carlton Gardens. I miss the greenery. No place to stretch your legs around here." She stood and patted down her pants. "Thanks for the lunch, Mason. I liked out talk." With a flutter of fingers, she threaded her way between tables toward the elevator alcove. He inhaled the remnants of her perfume and sipped coffee.

Somewhat bemused, he found himself in an inexplicable, wondrous state of confusion that he might actually be falling in love with Leola after only two encounters. Not some superficial juvenile physical desire, although a definite contributing factor, but something deeper and more profound. He tried to figure it out, but what he felt could not be reduced to coherent factors.

He thought he'd been in love with Aliana, but looking back on that unsettling episode, he saw it now as something shallow, driven by hormones and naiveté. With Leola, an entirely new set of emotions threatened to swamp his thinking. Emotions he wanted to indulge in, but realized he should also be careful in case Leola did not share his feelings. He may find out on Thursday, he told himself. After all, she accepted his dinner invitation, which suggested she had some regard for him.

Although cool, pleasant sunshine bathed the world outside with cheer. Pedestrians did not huddle into themselves, the cast of gloom left somewhere else. Even the streams of cars seemed to flow more easily, with only an occasional blare from a horn.

Mason read several reports from the learned establishment suggesting that sunshine, regardless of season, affected positive behavior and engendered cheerfulness—until the next electricity bill came. A shaky hypothesis at best, with no verifiable evidence to back it except several questionnaire studies, he nonetheless attested the efficacy of sunlight on mood and behavior from personal responses. Some papers concluded that higher air pressure during a fine day promoted an endorphin reaction in the brain. Perhaps, but he always felt better—most of the time—when the sun shined.

Delora also looked cheerful as he appeared, but then, she always looked cheerful. An official mask she placed on her face each morning?

"Mason, Mr. Renolds wants to see you."

He waved a hand and strode to his office. Overcoat unloaded, he stepped out and knocked on the Director's door.

"Come!"

"You wanted me?"

"Ah, you're my man. Grab a chair."

Renolds ran a hand across his bald head and leaned back in

the seat. Dark eyes seemed to scrutinize his latest acquisition with a lively twinkle. Mason sat down and returned the stare without feeling intimidated.

"Karter dropped in this morning. He thinks you're wasted doing infrastructure work and wants to steal you from me. You're not playing office politics already, are you?"

Mason laughed with genuine amusement. "If I were, I wouldn't be so obvious."

"Right! I know you eventually want to do strategic planning—"

"Walt, I'm happy where I am. What I'm doing now gives me an opportunity to learn how Global Systems does business, about your national portfolio of projects—infrastructure and strategic—and hopefully be a successful contributor. If you have something new in the pipeline, I'd like to look at it. I'll wrap up the Post study be end of next week."

Renolds raised both eyebrows. "Next week, eh? Before he broke his leg, Stornwell ran with it for two weeks without a clear end date. What makes you different?"

"He may be counting trees and forgot to look at the forest. I cut through the chase with Clarke and Deakin."

"Buried himself in processes, eh?" Renolds massaged his chin. "Mmm. Possibly. Deakin called me about half an hour ago, you know. He likes you, and he doesn't like many people."

Mason grinned. "I guess I'll have to be more annoying."

The Director for Infrastructure Projects gave a hearty chuckle. "Tell me, then. How will you get the Post thing wrapped up so soon? You don't know what Turner will dig up."

"Clarke looks at numbers and graphs, and that's a good thing in a senior manager. Deakin obviously does the same thing. He has to or he wouldn't be where he is. However, he goes beyond dry statistics and looks at the human aspect behind them. This forms the basis for his holistic outlook and applies it to strategic thinking. Did you read the Post26 Strategy paper?"

Renolds nodded.

"There's a platform there called, 'Workforce modernization and shifting for the future'. It has Deakin's stamp all over it."

"A glossy throwaway." Renolds waved a dismissive hand. "Every large organization transitioning itself would say something about its workforce to placate the Unions and tree huggers."

"Agreed, but there is another section that talks about supporting Australians with diverse needs. Another throwaway perhaps, but I don't believe it. There's too much Deakin in it."

"Let's say you're right. How does all that play into your study? Before you bring it up, I know Deakin wants to head the Post26 Strategy implementation group."

Mason wasn't surprised and pointed a finger at him. "Because of that, we cannot get involved in any power struggle between him and Clarke. We must play it straight and adhere to our terms of reference. Nothing more. The reason Clarke commissioned us is because he or the Post Board didn't want to accept Leola Lanaro's report at face value. They wanted independent verification. Deakin said as much. Clarke is after some value-add from us, but apart from focusing more on the human angle, I cannot see how I can deliver. Not from the information I have now. Maybe I'll get something from Turner tomorrow. You warned me this could be a hot brick. I don't believe it is."

"Mmm. You know, of course, Clarke and Deakin opened up because they want you on their side, hoping to influence your recommendations."

"I got that, all right, but not so much with Deakin. He doesn't really give a toss about the study. He chartered his course and nothing will divert him from it."

"Do you intend to visit one of Post's parcel and letters centers?"

"I thought about it, but I want to read Turner's report first."

Renolds gave a long sigh. "Right. Give me a draft on Thursday and I'll gnaw on it. Karter also has an interest in this. He's been sounding off Clarke and Deakin to get us a slice of the Post26 Strategy pie. If he gets it, he said he wants you to be part of it. What do you think?"

"I wouldn't mind, but it's up to you what I do here."

"A nice evade, and we shouldn't count our eggs before they're laid, right? If you wrap this up early, we'll talk about giving you something else to do."

Mason got himself a coffee refill and holed up in his office to cogitate.

What a tangled web we weave…

Everybody pulled strings to land the largest fish. He never expected anything else. And the fish he wanted to land? Cold and analytical, he decided not to give a damn…yet. He'd only been on the job less than two days. His immediate concern: avoid being someone else's bait to be gobbled up. A cynical outlook perhaps, but that's what it took to play at the grownups table.

He updated the issues register and jotted down dot points for a draft report, careful not to inject personal bias. The whole thing a scribble really, as he still needed Turner's input. Should he visit a parcel and letters facility and see how Post did business? After some pondering, he decided not to. He had to trust Leola's findings and Turner's data gathering competence. A risk, he admitted, but doing everything himself would not only undermine Turner's position, it would undermine his as well. Anyway, he had all the dry stats he wanted in Leola's report.

Chance meetings with two consultants in the kitchenette imbedded their faces in Mason's mind, and the two would no doubt fuel the gossip grinder about the youthful new principal consultant.

At 5:30, he called it a day, lots of things to mull over, not all of them business.

* * *

A sharp knock on the door and Mason looked up. "Come!"

Turner breezed in and eased himself into a chair. "You know, Sydney has better weather than Melbourne."

Mason grinned. "You want to relocate?"

"Hey! Just saying."

"I don't see a tan, so you must have done some other things."

"Nose to the grindstone. I hate to say it, but I'm glad you asked me to look at Post's parcel and letters centers. It opened a whole new world and dispelled some of my flawed preconceptions."

Mason leaned back. "Tell me."

"It's organizational bedlam on the floor. Parcels flying on conveyor belts, x-ray booths everywhere, and people rushing around. They even have sniffer dogs looking for drugs. The Dandenong Letters Center isn't any different. No conveyors, just rows of letter and barcode sorting machines. Some sitting idle, I noticed. I compared what I saw with Lanaro's spreadsheets. Her figures were right on. I imagine, though, come Easter and Christmas, most of those machines are busy."

"Probably."

"Sydney's centers pretty much reflected what's going on in Melbourne, but on a larger scale. NSW is a big state."

"Did you get to talk to anybody?"

"I had a word with all site managers, shift supervisors, and several floor grunts. Everybody told me the same thing. Parcel volumes are growing at the expense of declining letters. Not news, though. It all squared with Lanaro's findings."

"Did you consider the human elements? It's the reason I asked you to visit the sites."

Turner frowned. "As a matter of fact, I did. I know I can be a pain, Mason, but I'm good at what I do."

"I'm sure you are. Otherwise, Renolds wouldn't have assigned you to me." Mason peered closely at his analyst. "Give me the bottom line."

"Nothing new I can add to Lanaro's report and spreadsheet data. Not everybody at the letters centers I spoke to on the floor talked freely, but some did. About sixty percent are casuals, although many of them worked there for years. They're all worried about their jobs. That also goes for the permanents. The cost of living is going up, as are interest rates and rents. Add to this Post's restructuring plans, people don't know where they'll be tomorrow, but they accept the inevitability of change. This air of uncertainty has affected general morale and productivity. I know Post must restructure, but I feel sorry for the floor grunts. There must be a stack of low and middle-level managers who will be affected, and some are bound to be out the door. You asked me to look at what you call the human elements, but I still think it's Post's HR problem and nothing to do with us."

"When can I have your brief?" Mason asked, not prepared to discuss morale and productivity angles missing in Leola's report.

"On your desk by end of day."

"Good enough."

"Can I ask how you went with Clarke and Deakin?"

"You thought Clarke wants to use our study as a political weapon against Deakin. Perhaps he does in a way, but there is a much simpler explanation."

"Oh?"

"Clarke and the Post Board wanted an independent validation of Lanaro's findings."

"Damn! Another case where an external study holds sway over an internal report. I should have picked up on that. Instead, I focused on the political angle."

"That's why we do our own research. Whatever objective Clarke has in mind, I won't simply regurgitate Lanaro's report. I want to give him some value-add and your input has already given me an angle."

Turner heaved himself up. "I'm sorry if we got off on the wrong foot on Monday, Mason."

"Don't worry about it. I'll just have to develop a thicker skin when you're around."

Turner goggled, then laughed. "Touché!" he quipped and walked out.

* * *

The Uber driver turned the sedan into Elm Street and Mason let out a slow exhale, excited and a little nervous. A first date in quite a while and he wanted everything to go right. Be yourself, someone said. Fine, but that 'someone' did not have to front up to Leola.

Lit with yellow lamps, old-fashioned rustic houses along the street exuded an atmosphere of comfort and stability. Most were early last century weatherboards with a similar look and feel. The larger, stately, brick veneer dwellings added welcomed variety. Mature trees lined nature strips on both sides, to which owners planted their own in small front yards. In many respects, this reminded him of the street he lived on. He liked it.

The driver came to a stop beside a brick house fronted by a low stone fence. Two tall evergreens screened the frontage of the double-sized block. He climbed out, walked up the concrete driveway, and followed a paved path to a wide front door, guarded by frosted glass panels. He pressed a glowing blue doorbell button and heard a pleasant chime. Hurried footsteps came from inside and the door opened.

Dressed in cream pants and a heavy, dark brown turtleneck, Leola tilted her head and batted long lashes. Black studs highlighted her ears.

"Hi there, kind sir."

Her low voice rippled down his back. Getting into the game, he bowed and swept an arm at the driveway. "Looking good. Shall we?" he replied with mock gravity and offered his arm.

With only momentary hesitation, she wrapped her arm around

his, and they walked slowly toward the waiting car.

"Have fun, dear!" a woman's voice shouted from within the house.

A fresh westerly ruffled his hair. Street lighting killed all the stars, but he knew they were somewhere up there in what should be a clear sky. He opened the back door and Leola stepped in. He buckled up and the driver moved away from the curb.

"You've got a nice place," he remarked.

"It's not mine. I live with my parents. I had an apartment in Carlton, but after weekly rents went vertical last year, I swallowed my pride and desire to be an independent woman and slinked back home. A year already. I can't believe it." She shook her head. "My parents didn't mind at all, glad to have me, and I do pay them token rent," she added hastily, "which at first they didn't want. It helps with the groceries. Living with my parents helps a lot, but it also exacts a heavy emotional toll. It reminded me why I want to move out in the first place. Worse still, I didn't have Despina or Brian, my siblings, to back me up."

"It must have cost your parents a bundle to buy a house so close to the city center," Mason remarked, wanting to steer the conversation away from emotional thorns.

"Not much, actually. It used to be my grandparents' investment property. Mom and Dad rented a small unit in Essendon at the time. When I came along, they talked about buying somewhere, but my dad's parents insisted he take this house at a hugely reduced price. A wedding present, they said."

"Your dad's parents still alive?"

"They have a nice place in Pascoe Vale, and my mom's are in Strathmore."

"Everybody conveniently close when visiting."

"It's handy. These days, you can't get anything near the city without paying a fortune."

"So I know. Your parents got a good deal."

"I grew up in that house. For a while now, Dad wanted to do

a major reno. Rip out walls to get rid of a useless corridor and turn the place into something modern. He's in real estate and knows all about that stuff. It would be an expensive exercise, though, and after living there for such a long time, he's not sure if it would be worth it. Then Covid came along and everything went on the back burner, but he keeps talking about it. I'm sure he'll get around to it one day. He's very determined once he puts his mind on something.

"Another reason everything is delayed, he wants to see me settled in first. He owns three rental properties and offered to sell me one for about a third what it's worth after I refused it as an outright gift. Pride, I guess. That's how he helped my brother and sister get their houses. Even at the price he offered, I couldn't afford the mortgage. Not on my salary."

"Take it," Mason told her firmly. "Property prices are crazy and will only go higher. In a couple of years, it will be almost impossible to get into the market unless you win a lottery."

"So my dad told me. I don't know…"

"Do what he does. Rent the property to offset the mortgage, and negative gearing will help reduce costs. That's what he's doing with his houses. He must have mentioned it."

"He did, and I'm thinking about it, but it would mean living with my parents for some time and I'm not sure I want to do that. It's already a strain. I'm grateful to them, mind you, but…"

"Yeah, I know what that's like."

Her eyes regarded him with interest. "What about you? Living alone?"

"Years ago, I bought two adjoining dilapidated terrace units in South Melbourne, tore them down, and built myself a contemporary double-story."

"You were able to afford it?"

"I dabbled in Bitcoin. Still do. It turned out to be a good investment and helped retire my debts."

"Wow. I thought of getting into crypto, but I always considered it too risky. It has no intrinsic value at all."

"I can tell you how to invest a little every month. There is some risk, but all trends point to a good future return."

"Mmm. Anybody else in your family?"

"A paternal grandmother. She's in a retirement village. My parents looked after her for a while, but holding down jobs and being carers didn't work. My dad felt rotten having his mom in a home, but it had to be done, and Grandma didn't hold it against him. She actually looked forward to living somewhere where she would mingle with people her age." He leaned toward her. "In a way, she was relieved not to be under my mom's thumb."

Leola laughed. "That's mean."

"My dad's father died in 2017. I adored him and miss him a lot. My mom's parents are in Croatia. She offered to relocate them to Australia a number of times, but despite the promise of a more comfortable life here, they weren't interested."

"Roots," Leola put in immediately. "Coming from an Italian background, I know what that's like. Any brothers or sisters?"

"Just me, I'm afraid," Mason said, not willing to lay bare everything. One day perhaps.

"A pampered single child, eh?"

Mason grinned. "If you only knew."

"Not pampered?"

"Hardly. You said you have a brother and a sister?"

"Despina is younger and Brian is the oldest. Both are married. He's in the Navy, by the way. He had a terrible row with Dad about it." she added and noted his amused expression. "What?"

"My dad used to be in the Navy. It made life tough for me and my mother."

"Brian's wife told me the same thing."

The Uber turned onto Dynon Road and Leola frowned. "Where are we going?"

"An eatery I found in Footscray. Never been there, but from

what I read, it's supposed to be good."

"A voyage of discovery for both of us, eh?"

In a moment of silence, he watched the oncoming traffic heading into the city, very conscious of Leola's presence. He turned his head and her eyes locked on him. Whatever fragrance she wore, it enveloped him and they were one in a private co-coon.

"Any excitement in your day?" she ventured and the spell faded.

"Busy putting together a draft report for Post," he told her.

She tilted her head. "Care to tell me something about it?"

"Sorry. You know I can't do that. I know you wouldn't say anything to anybody—"

She placed a slim hand on his wrist. "Don't worry about it. I know how these things work."

He liked the feel of her touch and wanted to clasp her hand in his, but held back, careful not to appear possessive. A first date after all.

"I used elements of your report and added your spreadsheets as appendices after I got Clarke's permission, but I'm not merely repeating your findings. Not altogether. I'm giving him and Deakin something extra.

"Yesterday at the office after everybody went home, we had a staff meeting where I caught up with all senior consultants and hashed over pipeline works. Eventually, I want to do strategic consulting, but I need to prove myself to Global Systems first with infrastructure stuff. I don't mind. At the end of the day, all strategic projects turn into infrastructure and system implementation, and I want to know how GS handles both. What about you? Satisfied with what you're doing at Post?"

"I like the variety I had so far. They have me on a sort of fast career track toward senior project management, and the sorting machines study gave me a real down-to-earth look at floor operations. I learned a lot how mail and parcels are handled. It broadened my knowledge of Post business. All useful when I step up into a more senior role."

"It definitely helps a career when you run a variety of projects in different business spaces."

"Ticks on a resume?"

"That's it."

"Mmm. It's a calculating way to look at things. Almost cold."

"It is, but that's how the game's played if you want to get ahead. You don't wait for an opportunity to fall into your lap. You reach out and grab it. There are no awards for being a nice guy."

"Wow. Who stabbed *you* in the back?"

"Sorry. Didn't mean to be so serious."

The sedan crossed the Maribyrnong Bridge and traffic became heavy along Barkly Street. The driver pulled up at the brightly lit Rati Road restaurant and Mason hurried to open the door for Leola. A chill gust made him wince and they walked quickly into the spacious and noisy interior, welcoming its warmth. A beige brick wall took up the entire right side, and a well-stocked bar occupied part of the left wall. Square, black-topped tables randomly littered the floor. Mason inhaled exotic food scents and winked at Leola.

"Somebody's having fun," she observed cheerfully, eyes alive as she checked out the animated guests.

Their receptionist, wearing a white blouse and black pants, walked up, a tablet in hand.

"Mason Adamov for two," he told her.

"This way, please."

She led them to a window table and offered menus. They could only see traffic outside, but Mason did not mind. Better some view than stare at a brick wall.

Leola looked around and pursed her lips. "Nice," she remarked and opened the menu. "My God! What do I pick?"

"The idea this evening, my dear, is to subject your body to a gastronomic assault. No rules. Pick everything you see. Eliminates frustration having to choose."

She laughed and slapped his forearm. "Creep."

Their receptionist showed up and waited.

"Fried calamari to start, and a glass of chardonnay," Leola ordered.

"Nasi goring with chicken for me," Mason added, "and a Woodward bourbon."

"Very good." She tapped into her tablet, then headed for the entrance to wait on an elderly couple who came in.

"You know about my day. What have you been up to?" he prompted.

"Until Post decides what to do with their sorting machines, I'm fully into my AI thing."

"Turner told me you'll manage the decommissioning program."

"I'd like to, and it would be something different for me, but I'm not sure I'll get it."

Mason raised an eyebrow. "Why not? You know everything there is to know about every letters center."

"I do know a lot, but decommissioning is a huge project. Deakin and all state center managers must first decide which machines will go. I made recommendations, but Deakin has the final say. Once that's done, everything must be scheduled, technical people allocated, disposal organized, transitioning staff and casuals, deciding which ones will get fired, identify risk factors, and develop contingency plans."

"I'm sure state centers will handle a lot of the detail."

"You're right, but I'll have to be on top of everything. I never handled anything so big before. Frankly, I don't know if I'm up to it. You're talking about an Australia-wide program."

"It'll be a full-time job, all right," he agreed, "but if you break it down into individual mail center sub-projects, you won't be overwhelmed."

"It's the overall planning I'm worried about. If I stuff it up…"

"Post has done decommissioning projects before. Dig up the documentation."

Their drinks arrived and he held up his tumbler. "No more business talk, right?"

She beamed and they clicked glasses. "Deal." She took a sip and her eyebrows climbed. "This is good. Fruity and crisp."

Mason sipped his bourbon, warm in her company, surrounded by cheerful guests. "Not really business, but do you ever consider leaving Post?"

"A few times, but I'm doing okay. I never wanted to be a programmer, but I had to do my apprenticeship when I joined. I always preferred doing systems analysis stuff. Fortunately, a senior project manager took an interest in me, purely professional, mind you," she added hastily.

"Of course," he deadpanned, vastly amused.

"Creep! Anyway, I learned a lot under his mentoring. Nine months ago, he recommended me for promotion to project manager, and my first major job was to look at mail centers. It took me four weeks to get the thing done. I hand in my report and…nothing. Oh, I didn't mind, and they gave me other things to do. I guess the wheels of bureaucracy turn slowly everywhere. The next thing I know, Clarke commissions Global Systems to redo the whole thing."

"No justice in the world."

She slapped his wrist and sipped her wine, regarding him over the rim of her glass. "I'm curious about you, Mason Adamov. You're very young to be a principal consultant. Who did you kill and where is the body?"

He laughed, totally relaxed in her presence. "Comes from having good genes."

"And smarts, no doubt."

"My eidetic memory helped me skip grades and get a degree

and a master's at eighteen."

Her eyes grew large. "Eighteen? Wow. You *must* be smart."

"I started work at ANZ, and in 2016, tired of bank politics to get ahead, I joined Deloitte."

"From what I heard, they do some impressive consulting."

"They do. I worked three years in Abu Dhabi and a year in Thailand doing cellphone systems stuff. When I got back, not interested in more overseas contracts, I joined Global Systems, and here I am."

"I'm sure there's much more behind that condensed resume," she murmured, eyes lively.

Their minder showed up with a tray and unloaded the starters. "Ready to order?"

"I'll have the seafood tom yum hot pot," Leola said promptly.

"A barramundi for me," Mason declared.

"Anything to drink?"

Leola looked at Mason and shrugged. "You pick."

"A bottle of Marty's Rose," he said, deciding for both of them.

"Very good. Enjoy."

Leola eyed her calamari, added tartare sauce, cut a portion, and popped it into her mouth. "Super. How's yours?"

"Good." He reached for the whiskey tumbler and drained it. "Want some?"

They exchanged portions and took several minutes on serious food business, Mason glad to see Leola enjoying herself, relishing an enormously satisfying sensation being with her.

"You said you own a modern house in South Melbourne," she remarked. "Your first time away from home?"

"Actually, some eighteen months after I started work, I got myself a bedsitter in St. Kilda and lived there for a couple of years before I bought those two terrace houses. I wanted to be away from my parents in a space I could call my own to do what I wanted, when I wanted."

"Same with me," she replied with feeling. "Six months into

my job, I rented a one-bedroom apartment in Carlton." She cleared her throat. "Freedom at last, I thought, until reality hit me. I had to do all my cooking, cleaning, shopping, and pay bills. I didn't mind the cooking. Mom made sure her two girls could look after themselves and their husbands." Eyes twinkling, she grinned, showing the dimple. "Despina and I spent hours with mom, baking, playing 60s and 70s oldies, and talking girl talk. You wouldn't understand," she added impishly.

"Of course not," Mason replied with a straight face, fighting an impulse to laugh.

"Creep. Neil Diamond and ABBA would drive my mom wild. I guess I'm kind of fond of that music myself. What stuff turns you on?"

"I like classical—"

"Figures."

He gave her a mock stare. "You're making it difficult to like you right now."

"I'll get over it," she replied, betrayed by a conspiratorial twinkle in her eyes.

"Right. As I tried to say before being so rudely interrupted, my mom also liked that period music. Enya, Shania Twain, and Celine Dion had her in the zone and I'd get an earful during weekends when she handled chores. I didn't mind. I also do a bit of painting on the side."

Her eyebrows climbed. "You paint? Anything in particular?"

"Landscapes, seascapes, some portraits. Different things."

"A man of many talents. I suppose you also have a large book library at home."

"I've got some. Do you read a lot?"

"It comes in bursts. I sometimes go weeks without reading anything. Then, I'll walk into Dymocks and grab a load."

"What genre do you like?"

"Oh, lots of different things. My interests vary. Before you ask, I'm not into mushy romance much. Not all girls read such stuff, you know."

"I never doubted it," he quipped and laughed, captivated by Leola's openness and playful sense of humor. "You were telling me about your apartment."

"So I was. Until I moved out, none of those details entered my head. My parents took care of everything. Then I remembered why I wanted to move out and kept at it."

Mason cocked an eyebrow. "Problems with parents?"

"You could say that. My relationship with my parents is confusing. What?" she demanded after seeing his smile.

"We're on the same wavelength. My father and I were always at loggerheads, and was one of the reasons I moved out as soon as I could."

Leola gave a long sigh. "Parents…I respect mine and appreciate everything they did for me. Sometimes, though, I could strangle them. Mom is a darling, provided you don't cross her. She's very manipulative and wants to run everyone's life."

"Mother knows best, eh?" Mason added.

"Dad, on the other hand, didn't bother us girls much, but he gave Brian a hard time. All three of us were rebels in a way."

"I know how that feels," he mused.

"Stubborn and willful, that's my dad. Anyway, I moved out and thought life alone meant freedom. It did in a way, but on lonely days, and there were some, living alone lost its shine, and I wasn't much into discos and stuff." Her eyes probed into him. "You go out a lot?"

"An occasional concert or play, that's about it. Modern entertainment isn't my thing."

She demolished more calamari. Then…

"Apart from painting, what else do you do when not working?"

"I read a lot and I'm a book reviewer."

Her eyebrows climbed. "That's a twist. I never pictured you buried in someone's book. What kind of stuff do you review?"

"Most fiction—"

"But not romance or fantasy, eh?"

"You're mean. Did you know that?"

"Despina mentioned it once or twice. So…"

"I don't do much non-fiction and I stay clear of anything religious. Authors tend to be possessive about the subject and resent someone poking holes in their cherished ideas."

"I can imagine. You mentioned your eidetic memory. Does that mean you remember everything?"

"Everything."

"Wow. I can see how that can be useful. How do you handle it? The clutter and the bad parts, I mean."

"I put those memories into 'open at own peril' drawers," he remarked lightly. "The clutter is sitting there somewhere, but I'm not consciously aware of it unless I deliberately focus on a day or event."

The starters done, their minder brought fresh glasses, poured them rosy wine, left the bottle in an ice bucket, and cleared away the used plates.

Leola sampled the chilled wine. "Fresh without being dry."

He took a deep sniff. "Remands me of strawberries."

She held the glass between her hands and peered at him. "What's it like in Abu Dhabi? I'd love to travel, but never had a chance to do it."

"Seen any documentaries?"

She nodded.

"It's all that and more. Deserts were always a magnet for me. To stand on a dune and stare at the endless sands is something unfathomable and awe-inspiring. I found the Emirates to be a magical, enchanted place." Memories flashed through his mind and he took a moment to relive them. Time passed and he cleared his throat.

"What the films don't convey is the oppressive heat. Nine months in a year, you won't see a cloud in the sky, and it rains only every four or five years. Lately, though, so I've been told, they had more frequent downpours. Climate change, I guess. What eventually wore me down is not heat or endless sand, but humidity. If you can stand it, Abu Dhabi and Dubai are modern cities where you can go berserk shopping, and living there is cheap. The people are amazingly friendly and don't give expats a hard time. They consider Westerners People of the Book gone astray from the true faith. They despise Indian and Filipino workers and consider them infidels. I liked being there. Professionally, it's the best decision I made."

"If you didn't like the humidity, why did you go to Thailand? From what I know, it's also humid."

He shrugged. "I worked at a level beyond my reach had I stayed in Melbourne, and it also paid well. The telco I worked for provided everything except food, which meant I saved over eighty percent of my monthly salary. I lived well on almost nothing."

Leola sighed, eyes dreamy. "I'd love to see South America. Visit the Amazon, see Machu Picchu, walk with the llamas…"

"No reason why you can't. With four weeks annual leave every year, you can go anywhere."

"In theory, yes, but not if I want to buy a place of my own. Mom and Dad offered to subsidize a deposit for a modest house, and I may take them up on it. It would help me greatly getting a bank loan. Dad even suggested suburbs where prices were merely atrocious instead of astronomical."

"Take short trips somewhere. Go to Queensland, New Zealand, or one of the Asian countries. It won't cost you a fortune, and a break will recharge you. It did me a world of good."

Her eyebrows climbed. "Where did you go?"

"In 2014, I did a twenty-one-day Western Europe tour with Cosmos, a London-based travel company. I had quite a trip."

"Did you see Paris?"

"And London, Barcelona, Rome, Athens, Venice—"

"Ah, Venice. Gondolas…I'd kill to go there. Did you go anywhere else?"

"In January 2018, I went to China. A real eye-opener. Given the current political climate, I would never go there now, though."

Their mains arrived and both tucked in with an appetite. He offered Leola some barramundi. She declined, but suggested he try her hot pot, which he found delicious.

"I could get used to eating out like this," she observed between mouthfuls.

"So could I."

She tilted her head. "Do you cook or go out?"

"I go out sometimes, but mostly, I cook. There's no one else to do it for me. As you can see, my culinary experiments haven't poisoned me yet. Come around and I'll show you."

Her eyes glinted. "Said the spider."

He put down his cutlery and looked sorrowful. "I am deeply wounded by such an unwarranted slur on my sterling character."

"You'll get over it."

"Look, it's only dinner, not a marriage proposal."

Her face lit with mirth. "A nice line, Mason. After getting burned once, I learned to be careful."

"His fault or yours?"

"I met him during my last year at RMIT. He ran the campus computer room. Charming, dashing, and me young and inexperienced, I fell for him."

Mason said nothing, memories of Aliana vivid in his mind.

"After a two-month whirlwind romance, he wanted to marry me right away, but I insisted we do it after I got my graduate diploma. If I didn't finish it, I knew it would be difficult to do it later. Settled in his two-bedroom St. Kilda apartment, his true colors began to unfurl and he became domineering. He wanted a social ornament and a placid stay-at-home hausfrau. None of that showed when we dated. He even encouraged my desire to have a career. I tried to reason with him, but he wouldn't be swayed. The problem I had, Mom and Dad liked the creep. She told me once that a woman's role in life was to look after her husband and children. You can't believe the disappointment I felt when she said that. I thought she'd be the first to understand. Her Italian heritage, I guess.

"Anyway, after a year of rows and lots of shouting, I filed for divorce. Thankfully, no children to mess things up, although I eventually wanted some." She sighed and took a sip of wine. "I loved him, but I wanted my relationship to be a partnership, not a lifetime slavery sentence."

He reached out and touched her hand. "We all make mistakes," he told her softly, understanding completely.

Her eyes expanded in mock disbelief. "Even you?"

"Believe it. Events in our lives mold us, and in the process make us better people. Or they should."

"Into philosophy as well. My, my." She instantly looked contrite. "I'm sorry, Mason. That was way out of line. It looks like I still haven't purged that snot out of my mind."

"Forget it, but thanks for sharing."

Somewhat subdued, she concentrated on her hot pot, and he did not want to intrude into her thoughts.

Finally satiated, Leola leaned back and fingered her almost empty glass. He topped up for both of them.

"Great meal. I hope you enjoyed yours."

"I'm glad we came."

"Care for coffee or tea? Some dessert?"

She patted her stomach. "Nothing more will fit into these pants, I tell you, but a nice shot of espresso would go down well."

Their minder appeared unbidden and he made the order.

Rain slanted outside and cast a soft blur on everything. It did not dampen the cheerful atmosphere inside.

"What are you thinking?" Leola prompted.

He regarded her with undisguised warmth. "I'm thinking it

has been a long time since I enjoyed more pleasant company and stimulating conversation."

A faint blush infused her cheeks, and she dabbed her lips with a black cloth napkin.

"I like being with you too. You're easy to talk to and you don't judge. That's rare."

He brushed her hand. "I'm not going to hide it, Leola. You're something special and I want to see you again."

A whimsical smile tugged her mouth. "We can have lunch tomorrow," she suggested.

"I'd love to, but that's out, I'm afraid. GS is having a welcome thing for me. How about dinner on Saturday?"

"Your place, I suppose?"

"I wouldn't mind at all, but it doesn't have to be."

She frowned and bit her lower lip. "Well…your place at seven. If you don't live up to your self-proclaimed reputation as a cook, it's strike three."

He felt a broad grin split his face. "Deal! It could be a Domino's pizza, mind you."

She rolled her eyes. "Creep."

The coffee topped things nicely, and Mason escorted Leola out when his cell told him the Uber waited outside. Soft rain made the roadway shine under the streetlights.

Leola hugged herself and shivered. "Jeez! I expected full service on this date, Mason, but you flubbed out on the weather."

"The guy upstairs obviously lost my email," he replied comfortably and opened the door for her. He climbed in beside her, buckled up, and the driver headed into the night.

Content with her beside him, Mason felt little need for idle chatter. Hands clasped in her lap, Leola appeared to feel the same way. Traffic still flowed heavily along Dynon Road, and the rain eased to an occasional drop. Melbourne's brightly lit towers clawed upward in a spectacular vista. All too soon, the sedan turned into Elm Street. He touched her arm.

"Thank you for a memorable evening."

She grinned. "That's supposed to be my line."

The car eased to the curb and Mason opened the door for her. She stepped out and flowed into his embrace, arms tight around his neck. He held her and kissed her with unrestrained abandon, something he wanted to do since he first gazed at this wondrous woman. A lingering moment of tender sweetness made him want to stop time. She leaned back and gave him a quick peck on the cheek.

"Good night, Mason."

"'Night, Leola," he murmured, reluctantly let her go, and watched her hurry up the driveway. When the front door closed, he got into the sedan, very aware of her lingering fragrance.

As the Uber headed into the city, he lovingly replayed the evening in his mind, accompanied by the haunting strands of Jeremiah Clarke's version of *Trumpet Voluntary*. Pleased with himself and immensely satisfied with how the day ended, Mason conjured Leola's smiling face and slowly sank into the depths of her black eyes.

Until Saturday...

Chapter Six

Mason finished his limbering-up exercises and stepped out into a crisp, clear dawn. Hardier stars stared at him with brittle brightness. Along the deserted street, trees stood guard like silent sentinels.

No use putting it off, he slowly started to jog. Along Clarendon Street, most cars headed downtown to be swallowed by an indifferent metropolis. Every day the same thing. In the morning, people vanished into its canyons, and come evening, the city would disgorge them to battle clogged freeways to reach home in some suburb mentally and physically exhausted. Sometimes, he wondered at the purpose of it all. Did it have a purpose? Did it need one? Perhaps some university should look into it and produce a learned paper no one would give a damn about.

Warm, he picked up the pace, jogged to Albert Lake, and did the entire perimeter, waving to others on the track, occasionally seeing a familiar self-punisher. The fresh air stimulated his senses and power flowed through his legs. Done, he welcomed a cleansing shower.

Over breakfast, he watched ABC to catch the latest news presented by Michael Rowland in his signature blue suit, and the plump, bubbly, Lisa Millar. Not interested in car crashes, holdups, sports coverage, or Canberra's political antics, he switched to YouTube for international tidbits, the war in Ukraine center stage. China made more threats to invade Taiwan, and sore because many international companies started to pull out, finally realizing that dependence on a single supply chain had left them seriously vulnerable. The US 7th Fleet, supported by other

QUAD navies, paraded through the South China Sea, boldly proclaiming its right to freedom of navigation, daring China to do something about it.

He took it all in, not really paying attention, his thoughts not on the clips. Funny how a week can change everything. Last Friday, he almost abandoned his family. Somewhat reconciled, emotions still a little raw, he now found himself at a cusp of a major life change. Did he finally find the right girl? And what the hell meant the 'right' girl? A torrent of tantalizing images stampeded through his mind and he had his answer. Last night, she kissed him with unrestrained passion, not merely polite convention dictated by a date. It told him in no uncertain terms they were connected. At least that's how he took it. Wishful thinking? No! It felt real. Then again, it felt real with Aliana.

Skits!

Some say a person loves deeply, without reservation, only once in life. Others profess love is an intangible, gossamer thing, fleeting from person to person with gay abandon, alighting with dazzling, fluttering wings…and departs as quietly. It can touch many times, each wondrous as the first, so they say. It can morph from purely physical to ethereal that indelibly touches the soul, every one equally enchanting…and potentially devastating.

Mason could not say, never having experienced the ethereal. He knew its physical manifestation well, or thought he did, and mistook it for a shining light he hoped would be with him always. All too quickly, the light faded and left shadows and darkness and confusion behind. He welcomed the shadows, because cloaked within their veils, he did not have to feel the pain of rejection. Coping with life became easier…and lonelier.

With Leola, the veils did not merely lift. They were shredded by the primal force of her presence and personality, replaced with a luster of light and compelling beckoning. To step into that light meant losing himself, or perhaps become more than himself as she merged with him, one in everything. He refused to accept possible rejection, not after last night. Not after that kiss.

He could second-guess himself forever, never knowing real love. How to define 'real' love anyway? So much went into that mix. What now? He would move the next chess piece tomorrow and find out. Alternatively, she may be the one moving the pieces. As long as somebody moved them.

Resolute, he would walk out of darkness that sheltered him all these years, step into her light, and sample her shade of love. She also got burned, he reflected, and may be taking an equally hazardous risk by letting him get close. He made himself a promise that she must never regret the kiss.

He cleaned up and went out to greet a new day with an easy heart and a beatific smile.

Delora gave him her usual cheerful greeting, the floor now familiar and comfortable as he walked to his office. A fresh mug of coffee beside the keyboard, he powered up and opened Outlook. Renolds barged in and slapped papers on the desk. He sat down, crossed his legs, and scowled. Mason readied himself for the inevitable storm.

"When I read that thing last night, I thought you'd gone crackers. It made me reconsider my decision to hire you. Despite your sterling qualifications and experience, I should have trusted my initial impression of you. Nobody that young can be principal consultant material. A senior consultant perhaps, nothing more. After I calmed down, I read the thing again. Damn me, you rubbed my nose in it."

Mason expected a blast and felt a wave of relief when it didn't come. "I'm glad you liked it."

He agonized for hours over the draft's wording, then decided to dish it out plain. Clarke wanted the value-add and Mason gave it to him. Definitely more than he will expect, but to implement their own strategy, Post must acknowledge market reality or watch their competition take over the parcel segment, leaving Post with a budget-draining letters rump nobody wanted to touch.

"Liked it?" Renolds pointed at the report. "I think you nailed it. I would never have dared take your approach, though. Shows I've been shuffling paperwork and numbers too long and turned into another conservative corporate political animal. You covered all the mundane elements, no room for maneuver there. Then came the unexpected bits and I thought you *were* cracked!"

"Clarke wanted something different," Mason added with a grin.

"I'm not sure he'll swallow all the bilge you proposed, but Deakin will love you." The Director ticked off points on his fingers. "Reduce stamp prices across the board, domestic and international. That'll be a kicker. Absorb twenty-five percent of parcel handling costs. Clarke will have hives when he reads this."

"Lowering costs to promote turnover is not a new idea, Walt, but if he wants to compete with Amazon, FedEx, and DHL to name a few, he must do something to expand Post's customer base as a countermeasure."

"I agree with you there, and so will Karter. Some of your recommendations fly in the face of Post26 Strategy paper, but the general public will like it if Post goes through with it."

"The Post Board must be reminded they're not a pure profit center. Something the government ought to tell them more often."

Renolds sighed and shook his head. "Utopian dream, my boy. Your brazen vision to provide services in rural and suburban areas through local stores and supermarkets instead of dedicated postal offices isn't unique. Several countries in Europe did it, and done it well, but it's new to Australia."

"It may be new here, but Post should still look at this option closely," Mason countered.

"Agreed. That's why I'm happy for that section to remain in your report. You know, of course, you'll be making waves with

Clarke and the Board. He'll howl when it becomes clear his division will have to fund most of these initiatives."

"Not for long. Once he takes into account savings incurred by closing postal offices and profits generated from sale of buildings, he won't have a leg to stand on."

"So you said."

"The bottom line, Walt? I didn't want Global Systems to merely rubber stamp Leola Lanaro's findings."

"I got that, all right."

"Clarke may not like some of my recommendations, I accept that, but he won't be able to say we can't think outside the box. It should also help Karter get a slice of the Post26 Strategy program."

"We hope, but you've given him a foot in the door with your report."

"Anyway, the paper is only a draft. You and Karter can still chop and change before it goes to Clarke."

"He and I will chew on it." Renolds stood, shook his head, and grinned broadly. "Your idea to relocate permanent and some casual staff to partner stores as a tactic to minimize layoffs will make Deakin kiss your feet, as will the Unions."

Mason shrugged. "It's an obvious solution. Some people will have to go no matter what Post does, and he probably considered this already."

"Don't bet on it. Corporate blindness, remember? Sometimes, we only see the obvious when someone else points it out. He said it himself. Good job, Mason. By end of next week, maybe sooner, I think we'll have something for Clarke."

"Can I talk to him and Deakin about it?"

"In general terms only. Stornwell said it took Leola Lanaro four weeks to do the analysis and write her report."

"So she said."

"I want Post to see we're working equally hard to earn our princely fee." Renolds laughed and headed for the door.

"By the way, Walt. Turner's findings helped crystalize my recommendations. He needs to work on his people skills, but you were right when you said he's a good analyst."

"Do you still need him?"

"Put him to work."

"Don't forget lunch today," Renolds added and walked out.

Mason sat back and gave a satisfied exhale. He wanted to make a favorable impact on Walt with his report, and it looked like he succeeded.

Ti banac!

He opened the work directory and clicked on the report file. Time to put in some paid toil and flesh out the document. The words on the screen stared at him, his fingers poised above the keyboard.

What to cook for tomorrow?

* * *

The door chime went off with a pleasing tinkle. Mason cast a hurried glance at the dining table layout and nodded. Everything seemed in place, and he strode toward the entrance. Anything missing, he would fix it as the night wore on. Not a formal tux and evening gown deal, he nevertheless wanted to make a good impression.

A swirl of chill air failed to dampen the admiring look he gave Leola standing under the small portico. A whimsical smile dimpled her cheek. A red sedan moved away from the driveway and whispered into the night. Yesterday, he offered to pick her up, but she refused in a firm voice that left no room for discussion. She would take an Uber and save him two round trips. After all, North Melbourne wasn't a hundred kilometers away, she pointed out with unshakeable logic. Beaten, not prepared to make an issue of it, he gave in, accepting the hopelessness of arguing with a determined woman. Some fights were not worth fighting.

Dressed in black pants and olive sweater, she waited for him to stop gawking.

How the hell did she manage to make him feel all tingly and excited, his tongue dragging on the floor?

"Hi, stranger," she announced brightly.

"Hi there yourself."

With a flourish, he held out a single rose. The outside rich red petals merged into white, the whole coalescing toward a light yellow center. Her mouth made a small O as she took the flower and sniffed the delicate bouquet. It took him a while to find the thing, but her expression made it worth the effort.

"Wow. Thank you."

"Please…" He cleared his throat, waved an arm, and stepped to one side. She brushed past him, close enough to bring him into range of her perfume; a delicate, spring thing he felt suited her. He closed the door and beamed.

"Welcome to my palace—"

"Said the spider."

"—This way." A light touch on her arm steered her to the dining alcove beside the kitchen.

Her eyes sparkled as she surveyed everything. "This is nice, Mason. Somewhat sparse, but it suits you. Some flowers here and there would make it complete," she observed, and he winced inwardly at a typical feminine reaction wanting to rearrange everything.

Leola leaned toward two paintings: a seascape and a mountain scene. "These are good. Almost three-dimensional," she mused, then gaped when she saw the name, and faced him. "*You* did these?"

"All me."

"Wow. A man of depth. Have you always painted?"

"Actually, I was pretty good at it in high school, but I gave it up when I started Uni and I never had time for it later. When I moved into this place, I found my box of oils and watercolors and decided to give it a go again."

"What do you do with them? Sell them?"

"A guy at Vic Market sells them for me. My latest creations anyway." He pointed at the dining table. "Speaking of flowers and paintings…"

On the left stood a slim blue vase with two roses. One like he gave her, and the other a deep, rich red. On the right, the vase only had a single red rose. He hoped she would understand the symbolism—his passion and her multifaceted personality.

Leola studied the arrangement and slowly looked at him. A faint smile tugged her mouth. She did get it.

The spell broke and she sniffed the air. "Something smells good."

"It's not Domino's, so prepare yourself."

A carefree giggle and she slapped his shoulder. "Creep."

He mulled for a while before he decided what to prepare, keen to show off his culinary expertise without getting too elaborate. He hoped she would like what he came up with. If she didn't, he could always ring Domino's, he mused.

He seated her and she relaxed, eyes on the tall bookshelf in the lounge.

"Your ego wall," she said and inserted her flower into the vase.

"Ego wall?"

"Your books reflect your personality."

"You're right. They show what I like, which, I guess, tells you something about me."

"With an eidetic memory, why do you keep them? Just curious."

Mason grinned. "I don't *have* to, but I like to re-read some books. You see, when I read one again, the process generates new images and sensations, and links memories and experiences I accumulated since I first read it to create a separate, richer whole."

She pursed her lips. "I never thought about it that way, but you're right."

He rubbed his hands. "Care for an aperitif? I have liqueurs, spirits, wine, and a homemade Pina Colada I take particular pride in."

"In that case, I must try it. You'd be shattered if I didn't."

"In the dumps for sure."

He retrieved the glass pitcher from the fridge and poured them a milky mixture into large cocktail glasses. She studied the concoction with interest and picked up her glass.

"I'm glad you're here, Leola," he told her seriously and they clicked crystal.

She took a tentative sip and raised her eyebrows. "This is really good."

"How was the ride over?"

"Busy going through downtown, but easy once we crossed the Yarra River. I'm glad it's warm in here. A bit nippy outside."

"Can't have you catch cold and take days off from pressing Post responsibilities."

She laughed. "You're also mean, did you know that?"

"So I've been told more than once. Everybody okay at home?"

"Mom and Dad made sly remarks about me going out and added something about time I dated."

He gave an understanding grin. "My parents did it to me all the time. Look at your friends, all married, they'd say, and you're not getting any younger. A subtle hint I should continue the Adamov line."

"I don't get that, but Brian got an earful before he married."

"Kids?"

"A daughter and a boy. Little hell raisers. A bit tough on them, him in the Navy and all."

Mason reflected on his turbulent childhood, knowing exactly what she meant.

"With Dad away, I also took it hard. When he came home on

leave, I crawled all over him. I learned to handle it." He slapped his thighs before the conversation became too tender and stood. "Let's get this shindig going!"

He extracted a long roll wrapped in aluminum foil from the oven, placed it on a wooden plate, and carried it to the table. Leola sniffed with appreciative anticipation as he unwrapped the garlic bread. He added a tub of hummus dip on the side.

"Help yourself, because that's all there is."

"Stuffing me with only bread? I knew I should have brought a sandwich." Leola took a slice and ventured a bite, then a larger one. "My, this is tasty, and I like that there's lots of garlic in it. The supermarket things I tried have only a whiff of it. I can see you'd be useful around the kitchen."

"I also wash my own dishes," he retorted around a mouthful and took a sip of Pina Colada.

She reached for another slice and added hummus. A moment later, she dabbed her mouth with a maroon cloth napkin.

Next came one of his special chicken soup creations with lots of chunky pieces in thick broth made from pureed leftovers. She automatically added pepper and tried it, then sprinkled on some salt. He did the same to his, deliberately not salting the original mixture too much, not knowing her preference.

Another piece of garlic bread in hand, she dug in with gusto, which pleased Mason to see her enjoying it. Done, he cleared up and finished his cocktail, Leola declining a refill.

"That was good. You're a fair cook."

"Only fair? Tit for tat one day?" he ventured with a raised eyebrow.

"I guess. We'll see."

"Pizza will do if your experiment flops out."

She slapped his forearm. "I'm a very good cook, Mr. Adamov. Thank you very much."

"The proof is in the eating, so they say."

"If that's a challenge, you're on!"

"Deal!"

"It will have to be here, though. If I tried anything at home, Mom would be all over me and we'd never get any peace."

"Suits me. You won't mind if I'm all over you?"

"Ooh, I see I'll need to watch myself around you."

"Did anything exciting today?"

"Saturday is cleaning and washing at our place. With Mom retired, there isn't all that much to do. She's a fussy housekeeper and instilled neatness in us kids. What about you?"

"Same thing, with a bit of shopping on the side. I've lived alone for a while and learned to take care of myself."

"Professional men and women, I found, tend to be tidy housekeepers."

"If they live alone," he pointed out. "Once married…"

She grinned. "Leave everything to the wife. It happens, and it happened to me," she added, then waved a hand in dismissal. "Let's not chew old cud."

"Suits," Mason replied in total agreement. He wanted her to be cheerful and happy, not moody over a bad life episode. Burned himself, he preferred to leave those memories in the 'open at own peril' drawer. Although useful, valuable memories that taught him a lot about himself and life, but not to be dissected tonight.

He got up and pressed the Play button on the CD player. Stirring strands of *Knowing Me, Knowing You* from a collection of ABBA albums he put together permeated from the surround system. Leola gaped, face full of emotions. Without saying anything, he walked to her chair, took her hand, and gently coaxed her to her feet. Bemused, hand in hand, she walked with him to the center of the lounge. He faced her, took her in his arms, and they slowly rocked, eyes glued on one another. Her long lashes added a touch of mystery to her perfectly sculpted face.

"You have such gorgeous eyes," he whispered.

Arrival opened and he held her tight, lost in the compelling music. When *Chiquitita* finished, he let go and gently brushed her lips with his.

She sniffed, clearly moved. "My God. What are you doing to me?" Her arms went around his neck and her mouth sought him out.

He sank into her embrace and time stood still. A delicious moment later, he traced her cheek with a finger.

"I wanted you to enter my world and see for yourself a little of what I am. You're a wondrous person, Leola, and you be-witched me. If it's a spell, I don't want it lifted."

Her eyes gleamed. "I'm in your arms. It looks like I'm the one bewitched."

Mason put on Mozart's *Eine kleine Nachtmusic*. The magic bro-ken, he led her back to the table and took away the used plates and glasses.

"Now for the main event!" he announced with a raised finger and brought out a basket of small rolls, the vol-au-vent pastry cups, and served plates for both of them. He filled fresh glasses with a crisp Riesling and beamed. "Dig in."

She sipped the wine. "I like it," she said, tried the vol-au-vent, and went for more with relish. "Where do you get the rolls? They're terrific. Nice and chewy."

"A Chinese bakery up on Clarendon Street. They make all sorts of stuff and I'm a regular."

"You'd definitely be an asset at home. I haven't had vol-au-vent in centuries. It's delicious," she added and sipped wine.

Heart among the clouds, Mason felt content and at peace in Leola's company. She did not hold back her feelings and told him openly what she thought without pretense or demure modesty. Mature, sophisticated, she felt secure enough in herself not to pretend or play silly seduction games. He hoped she would see him the same way.

"Seconds?"

She sighed, patted her stomach, and leaned back. "No, thank

you. My body is full."

"In that case…" He cleaned up and refilled their glasses.

"Do you travel much?" she asked after a second of contemplation.

"Apart from my Europe tour, I'm yet to explore the world. Work has kept me busy."

"Remember what you told me?"

"With four weeks annual leave…"

"Right. So…"

"Actually, I booked a trip to Japan for mid-October. I've always been fascinated by that country, its tortured history, and tales of samurai. I've seen films and read a few books, and I want to see if reality will match my expectations. Not the samurai bit, of course. I don't fancy having my head sliced off." A sudden thought froze him. "Say! How about you come with me? It's only a fourteen-day tour and it won't cost you a cent. How about it?"

"Wow. You move fast."

"We must if I want to book you to the tour. October is a popular month."

"What about Post?"

"Tell Clarke you want to go jet-setting. There's plenty of time to schedule your leave, and decommissioning should be done by then."

"I'd love to. It's just…my project—"

"Look, I won't push you, but having you with me would be so much better. You'll love it."

"Can I think about it? After all, we hardly know each other, and many things can happen before November."

"You're right, Leola. They can, but I want us to look ahead without counting possible potholes. If something comes up, we'll deal with it."

"Let me think about it."

Mason knew better than to force the issue and got up. He extracted two glass bowls of nutty mousse from the fridge, his own recipe, and served her. Leola studied the thing with interest and spooned a mouthful.

"Mmm. Yum. Another one of your concoctions, I presume?"

"Believe it."

He brought out a bottle of Amaretto and poured for her, taking a cognac himself. Mozart's serenade ended and silence descended over the table.

"Coffee or tea?"

"I like tea, but right now, coffee would go down well," she replied after tasting the Amaretto. "My mom is into this stuff and Dad keeps a bottle just for her. This one has a slightly stronger almond taste and I like it."

He got the percolator going with freshly ground beans and laid out milk and brown sugar crystals. Wrapped in a warm glow of wellbeing, he held the cognac balloon between his hands and gazed at Leola. She noted his scrutiny and raised her chin.

"What?"

"Nothing. I like looking at you because you're the most enchanting woman I have ever seen," he said gruffly, meaning every word. "I like the way your hair done. I love your mysterious eyes that seem to go on forever, your perfectly molded face…Everything about you is fascinating."

A faint glow suffused her cheeks. "Creep, and wolf."

"Wait till you see my teeth," he retorted lightly and time flowed again. "Doing anything special tomorrow?"

She pursed her lips. "Nothing much. If the weather holds and it's a sunny morning, I may go to Vic Market and browse around for a handbag. Nothing expensive, mind you. I want to be in the open for a few hours. You?"

"I've got some laundry to do, but apart from that, it'll be an easy day. I may drive up to my Mt. Macedon place."

He made a note to himself, a reminder to visit Grandma as promised, and he never broke a promise.

Her eyes grew round. "You have a house up there?"

"Left to me by my paternal grandparents. I love the place, and it's somewhere I can forget my normal life and routine."

"An escape valve," she mused.

"I guess that's it exactly."

"I wish I had somewhere to go like that. What do you do there?"

"Oh, enjoy a relaxed country lifestyle. When I'm there, some things don't seem so important like they're here. Sometimes, my friends come over and we spend a weekend fooling around."

"Living with my parents is okay in a way and helps me a lot, but I wish I had a house of my own. Never mind…One day." She noted his concern and winced. "Sorry. I didn't mean to be so intense."

He brushed her cheek. "It's all right."

"And next week?" she remarked briskly and the somber mood broke.

"On Tuesday, I'm giving a summary of my report to Clarke and Deakin."

"Finished already?"

"Almost. The higher-ups at Global Systems want to chew on it. It's been a short project, seeing how you did all the work, for which I gave you richly deserved credit."

Leola laughed. "Buttering me up has a U-turn sign." She tilted her head. "Still can't talk about it?"

He shrugged. "Sorry."

"Never mind. I'll live with the disappointment." She reached across the table and took his hand. "Thank you for a lovely evening. It's been an unusual experience."

"In what way?"

"You…your cooking…music…everything. When ABBA started…"

She let go, stood, walked to him, and clamped her mouth to his. He got up, took her in his arms, and held her tight.

"I wanted to share…" he mumbled against her lips.

"And I want to share." Her eyes searched his. "Love me," she murmured huskily, firm with resolve. "I want you, and I know you want me, but not in the way other men do. I saw it in your eyes when we first met. It made me tingle all over. I haven't felt that in a long time, and I thought I never would again. The truth is, I didn't want to…until now."

Startled by her unexpected boldness, he cupped her face between his hands. "I do want you, Leola, but let's not do anything hasty. What I feel for you is deeper than a casual romp. I don't want to spoil that."

"You won't, and I appreciate what you said. I really do, but I'm a grown woman, Mason, and I know what I want. Don't hold back."

"What about coffee?"

"Creep."

He brushed his lips against hers, his skin on fire with yearning. Her hand in his, he led her upstairs. They tore clothing off each other before he could close the bedroom door. Her breasts hard against him, he wrapped his arms around her and kissed her deeply. She let out a stifled groan and tugged his hand toward the bed. He sensed her urgency and they merged with frenzied abandon. Her determination and unrestrained need left him stunned as her fingernails dug deep into his back. The almost painful sensation drove him to match her eagerness until the eventual explosive release consumed them both.

Momentarily satiated, she rested her head in the crook of his shoulder. Her fingers marched across his chest and set him on fire again. This time, slow and gentle, she purred from somewhere deep in her throat, then lay on her back and stretched.

"I needed that. It's been a long time. You?"

"Me too. Some years back, I had a bad encounter with a work colleague. I thought we were building something and I ignored warnings that she was a user and a predator. An emotionally painful lesson, one I swore never to break."

"You're breaking it with me," she murmured impishly and rolled over to face him.

A broad smile creased his face. "Not exactly. We're not work colleagues."

"Close enough. Never mind. I won't give you whiplash of the heart."

"And I won't do it to you either," he promised gravely and stroked her short, raven hair.

She bit his ear.

"Ow!"

"Just marking my territory," she remarked and kissed his forehead. "You're mine."

Her head on his chest, he wrapped his arms across her back and slowly stroked her velvety skin. What did Logan say about anchors?

"And I've staked mine."

She giggled. "I didn't mind." Her long finger traced his nose, paused at his lips—he kissed it—ran down his chin, throat, and slid it along the pale strip of hair that marked his head.

"I have never seen that in anyone."

"It gets me talked about."

"I love it," she added after a while.

He stared deep into her fathomless eyes. "Did you know that you have the most incredible eyes I ever saw? They bewitched me completely."

Her body snuggled closer against him and she threw one leg across his hips. "You did say, but thanks for saying it again."

"I've never known a woman like you."

Her eyes sparkled. "How many did you know?"

"Do you really care?"

"I want to know what I'm getting myself into."

"On your pretty head, be it. My first experience? Pure lust. She waylaid me in a classroom at RMIT. Frightened the crap out of me, thinking someone would barge in on us while we were busy."

Leola laughed. "I can imagine."

"I wanted more, but she wouldn't. Then an unfortunate affair at ANZ with one of my analysts."

"Mmm. You mentioned that."

"Then came Verena. I met her in Abu Dhabi at the Kangaroo Club. She happened to be an accountant who also worked at Etisalat, the telco I worked for."

"Ah, an affair under Arabian stars. Sounds romantic."

"It could have been, but we were strictly friends enjoying each other's company."

"You never wanted…"

"Of course I did. Any normal man would, but had I given into temptation, it would have betrayed her trust. I didn't want that. I valued her too much as a friend. Still, the first time I saw her in a bikini, it immediately cleared up my sinuses."

Leola gave a merry gurgle. "Randy old goat."

"There you are; the sum of my romantic entanglements."

"Sounds dull."

"That's me…dull."

"Oh, I wouldn't say that. There are one or two endearing qualities. My affairs, on the other hand, were less exciting."

"So, you had some?"

"Why is it always assumed that only men are allowed to have some fun?"

"Peace!"

Her fingers slid down his chest. "I told you how I fell from grace."

"And fully recovered, I see."

"Let's say it's a work in progress." She gazed into his eyes. "This could be complicated, you know."

"What's complicated?"

"You…me. My parents will demand I tell them all about you."

"They keep you on a tight leash?"

"Gave that up years ago, but they have a rulebook I'm supposed to follow and aren't shy pointing it out. They'll want to meet you and pass judgment. They're like that."

Mason shrugged. "I don't mind if you show me off."

"I do. For now, at least. I must break you in first."

"You mean, you want to domesticate me?"

"Totally. Iron out all the wrinkles."

"Typical woman," he remarked and grunted as she fisted him in the stomach. "Next Saturday. My place at six. This cooking deal works both ways, you understand."

"I know all about the road to a man's heart. Mom taught us girls well."

"I'm sure she did, my wondrous rose." He cupped her cheeks between his hands and kissed her.

"This rose has thorns, buster," she murmured, a twinkle in her eyes.

"They all do." He slowly stroked her cheek. "You've done something to me and I'm still trying to figure out what. When I'm with you, time seems to stop, and the world outside doesn't exist. You're my whole world and I want to be in it for all time. I cannot imagine living without you."

"Mmm. That's nice. Keep talking."

He whispered endearing things to her as they came to mind. Nothing ordered or planned, just what happened to pop into his head. To his frank surprise, he meant every word. Right then, with her snuggled against him, he never wanted to let her go as though some unfathomable force kept them joined. When he paused, she stirred, and he kept talking.

Eventually, she closed her eyes and her breathing slowed. He pulled the comforter over them, stroked her back, and stared at the ceiling. Then his eyes closed and Leola's smiling face filled his dreams.

He blinked at daylight outside. Beside him, the bed lay empty, and her clothes were gone. Mason locked fingers behind his head and turned his memory machine into replay mode. When the second ecstatic moment came, he shook his head, got up, and padded into the bathroom for a shower.

He dragged on black jeans and a surplus navy sweater, and headed downstairs to fuel up. Sunshine streamed through the windows, which buoyed his spirits, as did last night's memories.

A bowl of homemade muesli—the supermarket stuff mostly sugar despite labeled as healthy food—set him up for finely chopped fried onions mixed with speck cubes, topped with two eggs. The aroma of percolating coffee made his mouth water. A crunchy roll helped everything go down.

As he ate, he gazed at the clear sky, not in the mood to watch TV. It would only break his contented mood. He told Leola he might go to Mt. Macedon. The idea appealed to him the more he thought about it, and he could afford the time. The few minor chores to be done here could wait.

Bright sunlight beckoned irresistibly. Mason had no idea what the weather would be like tomorrow and decided to give into temptation. Later in the day, it could pour as much as it liked, although it did not look like it would. Then again, with Melbourne, hard to say.

This early, the downtown streets were almost deserted. Restaurants along Swanston and Elizabeth Street would undoubtedly have customers, but there were none along his route. An odd car he saw looked lost in the shadowy canyons. He hit Tullamarine Freeway and slipped on shades as the car whispered to him. A change of lanes took him to Calder Freeway, and once past the Keilor bottleneck, the drive toward Bendigo became almost automatic, his thoughts skipping through random memories.

Last Saturday—hard to believe it's been a week—despite an equally clear morning, the memories were darker and troubled. He tried to push them away, but they lingered, which highlighted how hard the schism with his dad affected him. The rift patched somewhat, but still very tender only time would heal. He hoped it would heal…if Dad did not revert to his old ways. What time could not erase were his memories, perhaps a good thing. The inevitable confrontation also served as a stark mirror to his own behavior. Once he accepted his failings and pushed back his ego, it allowed him to look at his father with a measure of new understanding and preparedness to forgive. Both should overlook each other's failings and concentrate on what really mattered between them.

One week…It could have been a lifetime.

Intellectually, he knew Global Systems would tax his abilities. That's what he signed up for, and the Post assignment did stretch him a little, forcing him to think laterally. Then came Leola, a totally unexpected variable in his otherwise orderly, predictable life. A variable he relished. Life ran without a script, he reminded himself.

Ti banac.

His smile grew broader.

Past the golf course, he drove up the hill into the Mt. Macedon township, the Post Office cum restaurant and small store already full of rugged up customers sipping tea, coffee, eating pastries, engaged in relaxed conversation. Golden beams slanted between tall gums as he turned onto Cheniston Road. A flock of pink-crested cockatoos made a wide turn overhead and disappeared among the trees. Gray smoke climbed in lazy columns from several houses.

He opened the steel gate and stopped the car in front of the garage. The air had a crisp, refreshing bite filled with the scent of eucalyptus and he inhaled deeply, expecting Cricket to come bounding in welcome. Thick silence lay over the property and he found himself alone in his private little kingdom. He never minded being alone. He'd gotten used to it over the years and welcomed the silence. Not really alone here as cheerful memories walked with him. Happy memories mostly…and a ghost who always made him welcome. The property now his, but in his mind, it would always belong to Gramps.

'Moj mali stroj.'

Gramp's words loud, Mason unlocked the front door and surveyed his small, comfortable abode. He slid back the rear veranda panel, the enclosed space already warm in sunshine. Two magpies strolled through the veggie patch pecking at tidbits. The wood burner stoked up, he made coffee and sat down with a sigh. He'll check out the garden and do some weeding—after his coffee fix. A note in his memory machine reminded him to load up with fresh vegetables. Not many things grew here during the harsh winter months, but he would use what did. He had no idea where supermarkets got their tasteless, odorless, sterile stuff, and had the gall to charge a fortune for it, Covid or not. For lunch, he would make himself a fresh salad and enjoy genuine flavor.

Coles and Woolies, you can shove it up your aisle.

He sipped and watched his resident magpies.

"A week full of fun, Gramps," he muttered and imagined his grandfather smile from across the table, old briar stuck between his teeth. "I apologized as you suggested, and you know something? All these years, I thought I knew my parents, but I don't. Not really. You were right about that."

'They don't know you either,' retorted a gruff voice. *'No parent does. We must strive to achieve a workable relationship and accept our differences regardless how irritating. Too often, though, it doesn't happen, and families are irrevocably torn, or endure a pretended truce that in the long run only embitters everyone.'*

Mason knew they were not actually Gramp's words—he still had a hard grip on reality—but Milan could have said them. The old man had wisdom acquired over a lifetime of hard knocks not always recognized or appreciated by those around him.

'What about your new puca, eh? A saucy one, isn't she?'

He grinned. Saucy indeed. His back tingled with renewed sensations.

Unexpectedly, he recalled a story Gramps told him once. Only once, he reflected. Something Milan's father regaled him when Gramps still had a roving eye.

A handsome, tall youth in their village went out a few times with a neighbor's daughter. Plain long, black hair fell to her waist, somewhat withdrawn, large dark eyes that seemed fathomless, she adored the youth. He, on the other hand, only had eyes for a flaxen-topped girl a few houses down the street. Gorgeous, a willowy figure, she pulled a train of admirers, flirting with them all, expecting little presents. Jealous of his competition, the youth confronted the flighty girl and demanded a commitment. She laughed gaily and told him to stand in line.

All the while, the plain girl next door vied for his attention, wanting nothing except a little affection. In a way, he knew her to be a good woman, and his parents urged him to marry her, telling him the girl he chased wasn't any good and would only break his heart. Hopelessly smitten, the youth refused to listen and kept after an unattainable love.

This went on for several weeks. One day, he learned his girl ran off with someone from a neighboring village. Shattered, the youth turned to the patient, understanding woman next door, only to find her gone as well. With a touch of scorn, her parents said she grew tired waiting for him to come to his senses and became engaged to a man from Varazdin.

Gramps paused then and puffed on his pipe, deep in thought.

The foolish youth, he went on, sought the unattainable, not realizing he had genuine love in his hand. In the end, he lost both.

Mason asked if the youth was Milan's father, but Gramps refused to say.

A true tale or something Gramps unloaded on an impressionable kid, Mason could not say, but wondered why the story came to him now. A warning, perhaps, about Leola? But he did not chase another woman.

"What are you trying to tell me, Gramps?"

In the seething cosmos of his mind, silence reigned. A totally expected thing. He would be understandably shocked had he actually heard a voice in his head apart from the imaginary ones he always did. Still…Why did this particular story pop into his mind? Random memory association brought about by familiar surroundings? Or some element deep in his subconscious tried to surface?

Just a story, he told himself, and sipped coffee, the sun warm on his face.

Coffee done, he ambled into the kitchen and washed up. Last Saturday, somewhat emotionally ragged, he had not done any housekeeping. He dragged out the vacuum cleaner and went through every room. Bedding ought to be washed, but decided to leave it until he came for a full weekend. A peek into the pantry resulted in a reminder of stuff to be brought up. He could drive down the street for the things, but he had enough for today's short stay. It's not as though he would be entertaining or anything.

That set him thinking. Perhaps he should call his friends and invite them over for a day. They had not had a stag blowout in a while, and he wanted to catch up on all the latest juicy gossip. Their kids would go nuts chasing each other around the backyard, free from normal house discipline. They always regarded Uncle Mason a soft touch.

Still winter, strictly speaking, the grass outside could be left, but he decided to give it a scrape. Besides, some fresh air and exercise would do him good. When he started the lawnmower, the racket invariably raised squawks of indignant protest from nearby birdlife as they rose from surrounding trees in search of somewhere quiet. Almost 12:30 by the time he had everything done, he walked to his garden and bagged mixed lettuce, radishes, onions, carrots, and herbs to take home.

Totally unconventional, he boiled two potatoes and shoved them into the freezer to cool, washed the lettuce for his salad, and grated a carrot into a steel bowl. A handful of salted cashews added crunchiness. He sliced in the potatoes and tomatoes, splashed on olive oil, vinegar, salt and pepper, and laced everything with a little pumpkin oil for added flavor. Lunch on the veranda table, followed by a fresh cup of coffee, topped by a King Edward cigar to pamper his weakness, made his stay complete.

Around two, he locked up and headed for Melbourne, satisfied with himself and the world, the drive to the city done in comforting silence. Once he hit Keilor, the traffic became heavier. Weekend warriors going into town in search of entertainment or heading home to prepare themselves for another day of labor tomorrow. Mason cared little who they were, why they were going to town, or what they did. They were merely vehicles he had to watch in case some fool did something silly that required taking avoiding action. Mainly young male drivers, but surprisingly, also some girls with lead feet who figured cutting him off to save a second represented a major victory over the system. He never got riled over driver antics and merely shook his head without bothering to understand it. Did they drive crazy as an expression of protest against modern high-pressure living and all the frustrations it generated? One of life's imponderables.

Once across downtown, most traffic headed in, and the drive to the Terniary Aged Care facility in Hawthorn became easy. He moved into the visitor's car park and gave the modern layout a cursory glance. Perhaps not top-notch, but very comfortable for Grandma, and close to his parent's place in South Yarra, as well as shopping and entertainment when she and her friends ventured out.

At the reception desk, the tall, plump, hazel-haired woman smiled brightly when he walked in.

"Good afternoon, Mason. Your grandmother is fine," she announced cheerfully. "A feisty lady as always."

"That's her, Evana. You doing penance this weekend?"

"Afraid so. Someone has to. Gives me a chance to get away

from my kids for a while. Let hubby look after them for a while, I say," she added and laughed gaily.

A cheerful woman who saw a bright side in everything. Given some of the grumpier and cantankerous residents here, Mason figured her positive attitude helped get her through the gloomier days. He waved to her as he strode past a spacious lounge occupied by several residents chatting, watching TV, or playing board games, and down a broad corridor that led to individual apartments clustered around a large courtyard. He knocked on the wood-veneered door and waited. Nada opened it and beamed.

"Mason! You didn't forget."

"I told you last Sunday I'd come," he replied gruffly and embraced the frail old woman.

A couple of weeks ago, Dad picked her up from Terniary's, took her home, and they celebrated his mom's ninety-fourth birthday. Happy to cheat death for another year, she became teary, saying she missed her old family in Zagreb, most of them now long dead, including her beloved brother. She used to get birthday and Christmas cards from nephews and nieces and their children, but these gradually petered out as memory of a relative in a faraway country faded. She longed to be with Milan again, she confided.

Nada held him tight, cleared her throat, and leaned back. A swipe of her hand pushed back a lock of white hair behind the left ear, tinted with a few remaining black strands.

"It's good to see you, Manny," she declared and waved him in. "Care for some tea? I made a fresh batch," she declared and slowly padded slowly into the kitchenette, her legs feeling the years. At least, she still managed to get around without a walker.

"I don't mind. Honey and lemon juice for me," he added and eased himself into a beige cloth lounge seat. Unlike a standard hotel room box, Nada had a small lounge, a large bedroom, kitchen—all fully serviced—and an entrance to a community backyard where residents could gather, talk, hold a barbecue, or simply enjoy peaceful ambiance among the trees.

Nada placed his tea mug on a plain wooden coffee table and sat opposite him.

"Did you have a good week?" he asked after a sip of the strong brew. A touch sharper than he liked, but he would never say so.

"Oh, the same old thing. Day to day. Can't complain. Even if I did, nobody would care," she remarked philosophically.

"Come on, Grandma! I care."

"I know you do, you naughty boy. Always causing mischief with neighborhood kids whenever you came to Mt. Macedon, but I didn't mind, glad to have you there."

Mason grinned. "I wasn't *that* naughty, was I?"

"You know you were. Anyway, don't be concerned about me. They look after us here. Thankfully, no major squeaks or rattles…yet."

"Good to hear," he replied softly, her appearance telling him otherwise.

Her relaxed attitude to life prompted an equal response from him and he sat back, content in her loving company. She came to terms with the march of years and the looming end, and did not put up a fuss.

She turned serious and her face became a mass of fine wrinkles. A little black spot on her right cheek added character to her gaunt features.

"I'm glad you and Niki sorted things out. It pained me to see you two constantly fight. I talked to him—"

"I know, Grandma. It's behind us now and I hope things will get better."

"He can be difficult at times, like Milan, but he always meant well," she added and habitually pushed back a lock of hair.

"Sometimes, Grandma, that's not enough."

"So I know, dear. At times, that's all we have and must make the most of it." She took a sip of tea, tilted her head, and regarded him with a quizzical smile. "Who is she?" She laughed merrily at his expression. "Don't pretend, Mason. You're positively glowing. So, tell me about her."

"It shows?"

"When you get to be my age, you see these things."

"She's someone I met at National Post," he said, astonished at her perceptiveness.

"And you obviously like her. It's high time you settled down, Mason." She raised a hand. "Don't worry. I won't tell Niki or Brianna."

"I do like her. She's totally different from anyone I've been with before."

"How old is she?"

"Not sure. Late twenties, I'd guess." He sipped and held the warm mug between his hands. "Grandma, how do I tell if she's the right one?"

"Ah, my boy. You can't. Nobody can. The first thing you feel is physical attraction, but that's hormones and youthful desire. We all go through it. For a woman, physical beauty can sometimes be a barrier, as some men will feel she's beyond their reach. A handsome boy, on the other hand, can become self-important. A problem you're not afflicted with."

He snorted good-naturedly. "You're saying I'm ugly?"

"A doorstop," she retorted with a grin. "Seriously, you're a handsome man and know it, but you've never been vain about it, and that's good."

"How do I tell, then?"

She shrugged. "You get to know each other. After a while, character becomes far more important than beauty."

Gramps' tale of the foolish youth sprang to mind.

"Even then, it can be hard, as there are many things that go into a lasting relationship, as you discovered for yourself. You make a leap of faith and see what happens."

"Is that how you and Gramps got together? A leap of faith?"

A mischievous smile lit her eyes and made her thirty years

younger. A gorgeous woman in her day…he'd seen pictures.

"When I first saw him lying there in the hospital, I knew he might be the right one. Oh, his eyes were all over me and every man in the ward wanted me. A girl can tell. We accept it as part of male base nature. With Milan, his look told me much more. Only eighteen at the time, I hardly knew anything about love beyond superficial attraction. When I told my parents about him, they were against any thought of something permanent. Young, quick to make a decision, their wise words meant nothing to me. What did those old fuds know anyway. Milan hypnotized me and drew me like a magnet. Luck may have played a part that I found a good man and I never regretted marrying him. Not for a minute. In many ways a rogue, but a loveable one. He'd give a person the shirt off his back."

Her eyes became dreamy. "He danced divinely. What youngsters do these days, gyrating and arm waving is not dancing. There is nothing like a waltz to sweep a girl off her feet, and I loved to dance. Back home, we had no discos, but there was always some wedding or party going on somewhere in the neighborhood. When we came to Melbourne and got to know people through *Hrvatski Dom*, we regularly attended functions." She gave a forlorn sigh. "I miss those days. Mad days. To be twenty again…Oh, we had our spats. Everybody does, but they were little storms that cleared the air and we didn't let them fester. We talked things out. I learned to accept his small foibles and compromised, and he did the same. One thing I *can* tell you. With your girl, be honest and never try to deceive her. If you do, she'll find out eventually, and that's instant death."

Mason listened and took her advice seriously. She had given him a lifetime of condensed experiences, lessons beyond price.

"Don't rush into things either, is that it?" he asked after a moment.

"You're not a flighty teenager, Mason, and neither is your girl. You treat life with respect and that's good. Let her get to know you. In turn, she'll open herself to you."

Leola already had, he mused.

"After a while, you'll be able to tell if she's serious or not," Nada added.

"I couldn't tell with Aliana, and it seemed real at the time."

"Pooh! You were young and silly. People will do crazy things for love which they would never normally contemplate."

"I learned that one the hard way," Mason growled.

"Be thankful the affair didn't cost you much. You're a grown man now and more careful. Your girl—"

"Leola."

"—isn't a teenager either, and is better equipped to handle a mature relationship. Was she married?"

"Divorced, and it left her scarred."

"Don't add to them."

"What if she gives *me* scars?"

"Comes with the territory. Anyway, aren't men supposed to be tough and take it?"

"If you only knew, Grandma."

"Have fun you two and don't dissect everything she says. We all blurt things sometimes without meaning it. Don't take it to heart. That's the problem with kids these days. Too impatient, not prepared to work a relationship, quick to break up when things don't go their way. Don't rush things with Leola. Let her get comfortable having you around."

Considering what happened last night, Mason had to smile. They were about as comfortable as could be.

"When are you going to tell Brianna?"

"We just met, Grandma!"

She nodded knowingly. "Don't worry. I won't meddle, and I'm happy for you. Come and talk to me if you want to chew the cud."

Mason felt a rush of affection for this wise woman who

walked over many thorns in her life without becoming embittered or crabby. He reached across the coffee table and held her hand.

"Thanks, Grandma. You always know the right thing to say."

"Did you go to our place at Mt. Macedon today?"

"Just came from there. Why?"

"You talked to your grandfather? Don't look at me like that, dear. I know you were close to him."

"I did, a little. I miss him, you know," he said softly.

"I miss him too. Every day. In a while, we'll be together, and everything will be all right."

"Don't talk that way! You still have years ahead of you."

"Kind of you to say so, but this old body is telling me otherwise. Oh, I'm not giving up on life, Mason, and people here are swell, but I must face reality. No regrets. I had more in my life than most and I won't mind going when the moment comes."

Mason sipped tea and regarded the frail old woman with wonder. She lived through a horrible war, suffered under communism, abandoned everything she knew and loved to find a new life in Australia. Through it all, she found a measure of contentment with Milan, and he felt happy for her.

All bills paid, all debts settled, she counted the days until she could be with Gramps again. He understood it all intellectually, but it eluded him emotionally, death still an imponderable. He guessed he had to live her years before understanding came.

Nada put down her mug and held her hands in her lap. He noted the change in her demeanor and immediately became concerned.

"What is it, Grandma? You didn't come down with something, did you?"

"No, no. Nothing like that. Before I tell you, you must promise not to say anything to Niki or Brianna. Promise?"

He hated secrets, but knew they were sometimes part of life. "I promise."

"You know about your father's prostate problem?"

Something cold gripped his chest. "He had an operation in 2016 and another in 2018. We talked about it at the time, and he said I shouldn't worry, and I didn't, too preoccupied with my own life."

"The operations cleared his immediate physical problems, but not the underlying cause, which may resurface. Over time, his bones may become progressively weaker, and the realization invariably affected his mood, behavior, and outlook on life."

"Mom told me about Dad's problem, but nothing about possible bone deterioration."

Memories flashed before him and Mason connected seemingly small incidents that now fell into place. It helped explain some of his dad's manner, but only some. His dad's behavior molded long before he developed a prostate problem.

"Niki never said anything?"

"Nothing," Mason murmured, concerned and angry at the same time. "Why the hell didn't he say something?"

"My Niki is a strong and proud man, Mason. Much like his father, and having this happen to him bruised his ego. He also didn't want to burden you unnecessarily, especially since he appeared to be in remission."

"Burden me? Did he believe I would think less of him?"

"Wouldn't you? You two always had a rocky relationship, and anything that made him look weak would reinforce your negative impression of him. Am I right?"

Mason bit his lip and sighed, hating to admit the truth. "Yeah, you're right, Grandma. It would have driven us even further apart and bolstered *my* ego!"

"I'm glad you're honest with yourself."

He looked hard at her. "There's more, isn't it?"

"In May, he had another procedure. A laparoscopic prostatectomy, they called it, to remove the gland. They said he can expect a full recovery with no noticeable dysfunction, and he seems to be his normal self. On the outside at least. However, if the disease reappears, he'll need another procedure." She wrung her hands, clearly upset. "I'm sorry to unload this on you, but I felt you had the right to know."

"Thanks for telling me, Grandma. I appreciate it. And don't worry. I won't say anything unless I see a visible symptom he can't deny."

"Thank you, dear. This takes a heavy load off my mind. I would never forgive myself if something happened to me and I didn't tell you."

On the way home, the revelation added a load to *his* mind.

Steady traffic along Toorak Road wound its way toward the city. Tempted to visit his parents before he hit Punt Road, he kept going until he entered Kings Way, not in the mood for a causal chat, unprepared to dance around Dad's problem until he obliquely wormed some information from him. He promised Grandma he would not.

She had Dad pegged out straight. Her son, she knew him better than anyone. Proud, all right, his old man would resent the affliction and consider it unfair. A diminishment of his manhood. Never mind that caught early, as with him, there should be no lasting effects. Bone degeneration? From what he knew, that only happened in extreme cases when the disease metastasized, not something Mom said would happen.

Still a little angry that his parents kept the full details from him, he shifted perspective and looked at it from their point of view. If they told him, what then? Nothing he could do about it except express fawning sympathy. Without visible symptoms, they figured best to leave it alone and not worry him. A joint decision or Dad's? Probably his, Mason decided.

No visible symptoms perhaps, but subconsciously, it had to be eating his father inside. In hindsight, the internal rebellion manifested itself in changed behavior to those around him, particularly to Mason. Less tolerant—although his dad never had much of that—more critical, moody, and self-centered. Earlier in the year, Mason recalled two altercations with his father, which neatly dovetailed with the operation in May. Dad clearly took it hard. Given all the emotional baggage he carried, it made last weekend's reconciliation more remarkable.

Gramps had it right. Mason never understood his parents.

Now, he had a secret to keep, in a way wishing Grandma never told him, but she did.

'So, deal with it, moj mali stroj. Keep your mouth shut and be more accepting of your parents. Ti banac.'

Still at university, Mason read Ivan Turgenev's *Fathers and Sons*. Printed in early sixties and far removed from today's world, in some ways the book accurately portrayed difficulties between father and son, and poignantly defined what later came to be known as the generation gap.

He gave a tight smile, having been on the receiving end of that gap the hard way.

Chapter Seven

"Come in, Mason." Clarke waved at a visitor's chair. "Drag up a rock."

"Thanks." Mason eased himself onto the comfortable seat and crossed his legs.

The head of Parcel, Post and Products regarded him with undisguised amusement. "Care for a coffee or something?" Clarke invited in his pleasant American accent.

"I'm fine."

Clarke pursed his lips and tapped the bound folder on his desk. "You caused quite a stir with your report. My colleague here," he added and stuck a stiff finger at Deakin, "has a few bones to pick with you, and so do I."

Mason grinned. "Are you going to shoot the messenger?"

Both men laughed.

"Not quite." Clarke leaned back into his chair. "We'd like you to go over some of your recommendations and justify why you made them."

Yesterday morning, Renolds walked into Mason's office and stopped before the desk.

"Karter and I made a few changes. Nothing dramatic. I emailed you the updated version. Polish the wording and send it off to Post. We don't see any reason to drag this out until Friday. Karter thinks you're nuts telling Post to sell off underperforming sites and slash stamp prices, but we're prepared to handle any adverse reaction if they chew you out."

Mason grinned. "You'll tell them I was too immature to do the study?"

"I won't, and I'll stand by you. Handle them and make them

happy," Renolds replied seriously and left.

Mason gave a mental shrug. Easy for his boss to say. Still, they paid him to make decisions and recommend options he thought were in the client's best short, medium, and long-term interest, however unpalatable. Global Systems expected him to keep clients smiling, but he would not varnish his recommendations to grease them. GS received hefty fees for information internal company studies sometimes omitted, employees always wary of potential career backlash if they told undistorted truth to senior management. Telling the truth always carried a degree of personal risk. Renolds did not say it, expecting him to understand that in their game, he should always play the politics game. It came with the job.

By early afternoon, he finished the thing and emailed it to Post. Politics be damned.

Mason uncrossed his legs, leaned forward, and gave Clarke a hard stare. He had to be careful what he said, but he must also appear resolute and on top of the subject. Sometimes senior execs required a nudge to make a decision they avoided, but knew to be right. They too were mindful of their careers.

"My report doesn't give Post anything not already addressed by external papers, your own internal study, and the Post26 Strategy paper. What's more, there are Leola Lanaro's findings."

Clarke scowled. "So, we're paying Global Systems for something we already know?"

"To confirm what you already know. More accurately, to reassure your Board you're doing the right thing, with some value-add from GS."

"Your value-add...You want us to cut postage and handling charges, and offer concession card holders half-price postal boxes? Do you have any idea of the revenue shortfall if we entertained such a notion?"

"I outlined the pros and cons," Mason replied evenly.

"Yes, I read them. The millions we'd earn if we sold off some of our office buildings would adequately compensate the initiative. You left out an important caveat, though. We'd need those millions to open service centers in stores and malls. Another initiative you recommended."

"Your Post26 Strategy paper talks about community involvement and social responsibility. Show the public that you're genuine and apply that rhetoric into real action. Appendix E in my report shows you'd be in a substantial surplus after you relocated your retail services. More than enough to cover reduction in pricing for the next nine years and fund other initiatives. You would also generate a lot of public good will, which should translate into increased transaction volumes."

"Unsubstantiated speculation," Clarke snapped.

"Not so unsubstantiated, Raymond," Deakin put in. "Mason provided references to similar successful practices in Europe, the US, and the Middle East."

Clarke waved a dismissive hand. "The Arabs are floating on oil and gas. They can afford to be generous to customers. The Australian enormous geographical base and comparatively small population requires a different model."

"With respect, Raymond, you don't have any choice," Mason pointed out with quiet force. "But you know that already or I wouldn't be sitting here today. My report gives Post sound options how to move forward that will keep your overall operations profitable to grow your business and keep the Board onside. Post is not a listed company driven by shareholder dividends. However unpleasant, everybody needs to accept the stark reality that letters processing will always be a drain on your resources. A drain you cannot plug as you're constrained by legislation and the march of technology. You can only mitigate the problem by automation and excelling in your parcels handling space."

Clarke and Deakin exchanged glances.

"You have a holistic approach, something I like," Clarke

mused at length. "We're not going to shoot the messenger, Mason. However, some of your more outlandish suggestions require further study, something I'll take up with Karter Kending. He's hardnosed like you, but he understands Post business and the marketplace. Moreover, he also understands the delicate relationship we have with Canberra."

Deakin cleared his throat. "Raymond and I think you did far more than our terms of reference demanded. You showed a great deal of maturity in how you handled the study and demonstrated an ability to think outside the box. Post wants to use that ability. We want you to manage decommissioning of surplus letter sorting and barcode inventory Australia-wide. If you agree, I'll ask Walter Renolds to quote for the work."

Somewhat taken aback by the announcement, Mason quickly gathered his thoughts. Did he want to embroil himself in internal letters centers politics and inevitable negative reaction from the Communication Workers Union? On the flip side, the offer presented a huge professional challenge, one that would also raise Global Systems' marketplace image—and his—if he pulled off a seamless transition.

"Did you consider Leola Lanaro? She's the subject matter expert."

"She is, and she'll manage the nuts and bolts as a senior project manager and act as your 2IC in parallel with her AI project. We can't spare her from that work. However, we need someone who can plan, organize, coordinate, and control the national effort. We considered using an internal executive, but those with the right fit are doing other things."

"Before Global Systems can provide a quote, we'll need a complete list of all machines Post wants to retire," Mason declared.

"You already have it," Deakin said. "It's in Lanaro's report."

"What do you intend to do with the retired equipment?"

"Scrap them," Deakin replied immediately. "Some of the

things are ancient and nobody in Australia would buy them. If a third-world country wanted them, the shipping cost is too prohibitive. We'd also have to give away the spare parts bins, and some of the items are custom-made. Then there's on-site installation and warranty service. It is not something we want to be encumbered with."

"And an overseas client would be better off buying new machines from someone like Siemens and the BEUMER Group," Mason added.

"Exactly. We'll use Cannard Engineering. They've done this stuff for us before. Mind you, your schedule must take into account replacement inventory. We don't want to be in a situation where a new sorting machine arrives and old equipment is still on the floor. Get the details from Leola Lanaro."

Clarke raised finger. "One thing. Your report contains suggestions how to handle redundancies and relocations, but Post HR will coordinate that part with letters center managers."

"Fine," Mason said. "I'll do it."

"I like people who can think quickly on their feet."

"Mind you, this will not be a full-time job. After a few weeks, Lanaro will be able to run most things. I'll reduce my involvement to two or three days a week at most. However, I'll still monitor everything from my GS office and involve myself when necessary."

Clarke waved an impatient hand. "I don't care how you run the program as long as it's done."

"I also cannot give you a fixed price quote for the work."

Deakin frowned. "Why not?"

"You know why. Too many variables that cannot be quantified, Terry. No letters center can provide an exact schedule to decommission each piece of equipment. The best I can do is an indicative timeframe, which Leola already covered. I'll ask for updated timeframes, but…"

"You want an open-ended check?"

"Hardly. I'll submit a weekly timesheet for hours I spend on the program. Each letters center will need to come up with budgets for work they do onsite, which I'll route to you."

Deakin gave a long exhale. "I suppose it's hardly fair to hold you to a fixed contract on a fluid timeframe. We'll pay you on time spent, and I'll hold every letters center to their budget. After all, they are part of Post," he added with a grin.

Mason allowed himself to relax a little. This could have been a major sticking point if Post had chosen to be difficult, but he'd be crackers to commit Global Systems to anything else.

"Thanks, Terry. I appreciate this."

"We'll want you to start as soon as we wrap up business negotiations with Global Systems, and Terry here will provide all the manpower you need." Clarke stood and stuck out his hand. "Welcome aboard."

"One thing," Mason started, uncertain how they may react. "I'm taking a two-week holiday in Japan in mid-October."

Clarke waved a hand. "Not a problem. The program should be more or less completed by then, and you have a cellphone to keep in touch."

On the way to the elevators, Mason shook his head. Post did not want to use one of their own because all were doing something else? *Balls!* Clarke never said it, but Mason could read between the lines. If the program stumbled, he wanted a head to chop, then put into place one of his bright-eyed boys to clean up the mess. Mason also faced early retirement from GS, but Clarke didn't give a toss about that. Protecting his own people came first. It is the reason why corporations use external consultants as sacrificial offerings to handle something delicate.

Manage a national program of work? It made his skin tingle. *Ti banac.*

The electronic wall clock said 11:40, and he dragged out his cell.

"Hi Mason. Clarke and Deakin didn't eat you alive?" Leola

answered merrily, and he pictured her cheerful face.

"Still some flesh hanging on the bones. Want to share a coffee?"

"See you downstairs in five."

Mason fixed on a broad grin and strode toward the elevators.

Leola emerged out of the opposite bank as he stepped out. Her presence lit up his world and he hurried to give her a quick hug and a peck on the cheek, not giving a toss at curious looks thrown their way.

She dimpled and her eyes sparkled. "More than a few pieces left, I'd say. What happened? You're positively radiant."

"Let's grab something and I'll tell you all about it."

Loaded, he found a window table and mixed milk and sugar into his coffee, an apple Danish at his side. He felt too keyed up to eat anything substantial.

Leola satisfied herself with tea, orange juice, and a plate of mixed sandwiches. She demolished one, took a sip of tea, and her eyes probed him.

"Spill it."

"You're looking at Post's program manager for the national equipment decommissioning project."

Her dark eyes grew round. "Wow. That happened fast."

"Clarke and Deakin want to kick over several issues in my report—"

"Not a draft, then?"

"I finished the thing yesterday and my boss told me to send it off. The contentious bits deal with the Post26 Strategy initiative and Clarke wants GS on it. It'll be a large plum for us. He then offered me the job."

"Congratulations."

He sensed reserve in her reply and reached for her hand. "You're thinking you were in line?"

"I always knew it won't happen. Although I know how to

manage, I never ran a large infrastructure project, and I'm realistic enough to realize it."

"Not as a program manager perhaps, but you'll be my 2IC as a senior PM," he added gleefully, relishing her startled expression.

Her mouth opened and color drained from her face. "Me? A senior PM?"

"Come on, Leola. Who else? You know everything there is to know about the equipment in every letters center."

"What about my AI work?"

"You'll manage both. Clarke and Deakin will give you all the resources you need."

She gave a loud exhale and sat back. "Not what I expected when I got up this morning. You sure know how to lay it out for a girl."

Mason took a bite off his Danish. "It'll take Post and GS a day or so to finalize the business agreement before we can start anything. Your report included a decommissioning schedule and costs, but if you have additional background documentation, send it to me."

"Such as?"

"Procedures to actually unplug a machine and how Cannard Engineering carts them away. If some are still in use, they'll need decoupling from other equipment."

"Of course."

"Post engineers will do everything, but I want to know what's involved. Ask every letters center to give us updated costs and schedules."

Leola tilted her head. "Will Scott Turner be on this? I don't like him much, you know."

"He can be a pain and I don't mind having him, but Deakin said he'll supply all the manpower."

"Makes sense," she pointed out. "We have very good technical support teams in every letters center."

He patted her hand. "We'll make a great team, Leola. Now, how about dinner to celebrate?"

She winced and looked contrite. "No can do, not tonight. Lunch tomorrow?"

Disappointed, he accepted that she also had a life. "Deal. I'll pick you up at twelve at the front entrance."

"Make it twelve-thirty. I have a meeting at eleven and it may run late."

"No problemo."

She slapped his wrist. "Creep."

Mason wore a beatific smile all the way back to Rialto. If the Uber driver noticed, she kept her own counsel.

Delora jumped up when he strode in.

"Mr. Renolds wants to see you."

"I'm sure he does," he replied with a grin.

"Are you in some sort of trouble?" she called after him as he made his way toward the offices.

"Nothing more than usual!" he retorted without turning.

He knocked on the door, heard a muffled 'Come in' and pushed it open.

"Ah, Mason. The man I want to see. Take a seat." Renolds swept a hand across his bald head. "Congratulations on the Post deal. Clarke called about a half-hour ago and told me all about it. Good work. There won't be a large profit margin for us on this, but we're getting a big foot into Post business, and that's just as good. Karter is in Singapore and hasn't heard the news. He'll no doubt be offering his congratulations when he learns he'll be part of the Post26 Strategy implementation. Post is yet to appoint the group's head?"

"Nobody told me anything, Walt."

"Well, it's not important, but I think Deakin will get it. Right! You know what's coming. I need you to write a proposal for Post. Since we're not in a competitive bid, we can skip the company blurbs and promo stuff. I'm glad you committed us to a pay-as-you-go contract. You had no choice, of course, as letters centers will bear most of the costs. However, try to be realistic as you can and include all the usual contingency factors. Give me a draft as soon as you put together some numbers. Look at our past bids to see how we do those things."

"Is it too late to resign?" Mason quipped, and Renolds chuckled.

"Handle it. Turner can do grunt work if you want him. He knows his way around bids."

"Thanks. I can use him."

"Who'll be running things at Post?"

"Leola Lanaro. She'll be a very positive asset."

"Are you going out with her?"

"None of your business."

Renolds waved a hand. "Go away."

Mason snagged a cup of coffee from the kitchenette and retired to his office. He leaned back in the chair, slowly sipped, and sorted through the morning's events. After some indeterminate time, he gave a sigh and planted the mug on the desk.

"They're not paying me by the hour," he muttered and went to work. He checked the email Inbox, saw nothing important, picked up the phone, and pressed a glowing white button.

"Scott Turner."

"It's Mason. My office if you're not doing anything urgent."

"Be there in a minute."

He hardly opened the Global Systems bids directory when a knock broke his train of thought.

"Come!"

Navy blue suit loose on the skeletal frame, Turner walked in and sprawled onto a chair.

"Rescue me from boring paper shuffling and I'm your slave," he announced in a deep voice, small dark eyes lively with interest.

"Post gave us the job to decommission old letter and barcode sorting inventory across the country."

Turner raised both eyebrows. "Good deal; and you want me on the project?"

"Sorry, Scott. Post will provide all the people."

"Makes sense. Well, I lived with disappointment before," Turner remarked with a philosophic shrug. "I presume Leola Lanaro is on the team?"

"She'll project manage the day-to-day stuff, but each site will do its own technical work."

Turner smiled knowingly. "Did she burn you yet?"

Mason bridled at this unwarranted impertinence. Turner saw the thunderclouds and immediately raised both hands.

"I apologize. That was uncalled for."

About to ream him, Mason slowly exhaled. "A word of advice, Scott. If you want to be a senior consultant, work on your people skills."

"So I've been told."

"Then act on it! I'm tired of your shit. Change your attitude or you'll be out the door."

"Got it."

"GS needs to prepare a time and cost proposal for Clarke, and Walt said you worked on these things before."

Turner nodded.

"I need the Global Systems time and manpower costs table."

"I'll send you a URL where you can find everything."

"Fair enough." Mason gave Turned a hard look, still sore at the man's casual attitude. "Get moving."

Turner got up, gave a mock salute, and walked out. Mason stared at the closed door and shook his head. Some people cannot be managed.

* * *

Feeble sunshine devoid of warmth struggled to break through

high, stringy clouds. Perhaps better that way. To embrace something too radiant invariably led to a fatal encounter, Mason reflected somewhat pensively. Unaccountably moody for no particular reason—he felt a little out of sorts ever since he got up this morning—but excited to see Leola again. Like having hot and cold flushes. A contradictory conundrum he simply let slide. One of those things.

Not exactly. Leola introduced an unexpected element into his life—genuine love. Or what he perceived to be genuine love. He thought he loved Aliana, which turned out to be simple juvenile hormonal reaction. With Leola, he felt something deeper, something more spiritual and soul-fulfilling. He did feel undeniable physical desire, as any man did for a beautiful, compelling woman. When he stripped away that veneer of raw lust, what remained went beyond the visceral. The sensations she created left him bemused, confused, and apprehensive, wary to tread this new road in his life, but also determined to find out where it led.

Heavy traffic crawled along Swan Street, each car contributing to the prevailing exhaust stink that clung to the roadside. He watched it all phlegmatically and gave a mental shrug. Life on the move, he decided. Nothing to get aggravated about. He absently wondered how the city's sky would look like once genuine air cars started to appear. What equivalent to traffic lights they'd use to control all the flight levels and corridors? Probably automate everything to take steering away from idiot drivers. Tell the onboard computer where you want to go, sit back, and sip your wine? A brave new world with brave new problems.

Both Post towers disgorged occupants in a steady stream, some looking for a quiet place to lunch, a break from regular canteen feed. Others possibly glad to be away from the place for whatever reason. He rubbed his hands to remove the chill, then broke into a wide smile when Leola emerged in a throng of fellow workers. She saw him, waved, and made her way down the steps to the sidewalk.

"Sorry for running late," she declared breathlessly. "I couldn't get away."

He gave her a peck on a cold cheek. "Not to worry. I liked feeling as an icicle."

She shoved an elbow into his ribs. "You're weird."

"I know. Shall we?" He offered his arm and she wrapped hers around it.

"Where are we going?"

"Mikanos B&J. It's around the corner."

"I've been there with my team and some girls. It's a nice place, but it'll be a crush right now, though."

He patted her hand. "No fear. I booked us an upstairs table."

Her eyes sparkled. "I like a man who plans."

A flood of exuberant conversation, mixed with enticing smells of food and beer, assaulted Mason as he held the door open for Leola. An attendant in a black blouse and trousers checked her tablet and pointed at the side stairs. He glanced at Leola and they went up dark wooden steps. The relatively subdued atmosphere on the upper floor made it easier to think.

Another attendant beamed and led them to a corner table covered with white cloth. Thick white paper napkins stuck out from a stainless steel holder, with salt and pepper shakers on the side. Guests already enjoying their meal hardly gave them a cursory glance. Seated, Mason looked around the compact room, white-washed walls sprinkled with Mediterranean prints. The attendant handed them a large plastic-covered menu card and sauntered off.

Leola bit her bottom lip in pretty concentration as she studied the limited selections. A minute later, their attendant appeared with two glasses of water and waited, fingers poised above her tablet. Mason suppressed a smile. The place obviously designed for fast lunchtime turnover.

"A Greek salad for me," Leola announced. "And a mineral water."

"A moussaka and a light beer," he added.

The attendant typed quickly and went off to take care of three executive types waiting at the staircase.

Mason sipped his water and sat back. "How's your day?"

"A rush," Leola replied promptly. "I never ran two projects. Although the decommissioning thing hasn't officially started, I'm finding it a handful. I delegated some of the AI stuff to my senior team analyst and went over all the material I gathered for the decommissioning study. I didn't realize I had that much stuff. Frankly, I'm a little daunted, but also keen to get into it. It'll be the largest thing I ever handled."

"I felt the same way when I went to the UAE. I knew practically nothing about telecommunication, and the prospect of screwing up a major cellular rollout, which an entire country will depend on, gave me some sober nights. Once I broke everything down and looked at each component as a project in its own right, everything settled into place. Do the same thing."

"Oh, I know what to do. It's the scale of the thing that worries me." She cocked an eye at him. "And what will you be doing all this time, Mr. Program Manager?"

"I'll sit back, puff a cigar, sip a tumbler of whiskey, and take credit for all your hard work," Mason told her with a grin.

"That'll be right." She laughed and slapped his wrist.

His took her hand. "Don't worry about anything, Leola. The proposal I'm putting together will list everything: manpower requirements, a broad schedule for every center, including costs. Thanks largely to material you provided. I'll make sure everything runs smoothly."

"While I do the grunt work," she mused.

"That's why you're getting the big bucks. Seriously, I cannot get involved in details unless you run into a problem."

Before she could reply, their minder came to serve them. Mason eyed his steaming moussaka and lifted the glass of beer to Leola. Her mouth twitched and she dug into her salad.

After a preoccupied moment, she looked up. "You're staring."

"I cannot get enough of you," he told her simply.

"You're weird, did you know that?"

"It happens when I'm with you."

"Finished your proposal for Clarke?"

Her change of subject came as a jarring U-turn. She clearly did not feel like getting personal and he left the matter rest. There would be other moments.

"Not quite, but I should get the thing done by today. There's a lot of material and detail to cover."

"You doing a fixed price quote?"

"For my time only. Global Systems won't be responsible for internal Post costs."

"Mmm. I suppose. Still, I'm glad I'm not playing at that level." She took a sip of mineral water, then pursed her lips. "About Saturday night…"

"What about it?" he ventured, neatly sidestepping a complex situation.

"Would you mind terribly if we had dinner at my parent's house? I'll do the cooking at your place on some other night."

"They're giving you a hard time?"

"I shouldn't have mentioned you, and now they're on my case. I'll never get any peace otherwise. Sorry." She really looked contrite.

Mason felt a stab of disappointment, anticipating another evening of intimacy. He took a pull of beer. "I don't mind if it'll plug the grapevine."

"Thanks for understanding," she gushed, openly relieved.

"I do understand. My mom did the same thing to me."

"Who was the girl? The heart-ripper?" Leola added with a mischievous grin.

"Aliana."

"Don't worry. I won't do any ripping."

"I hope not." Glass half-way to his mouth, his eyes widened. "Say! How about we drive up to Mt. Macedon on Sunday morning? You can make lunch and we'll relax on the back veranda. You'll like it there."

"Sounds wonderful. Deal." She frowned and raised a finger. "Not too early. A girl needs time to put a face on."

"And what a face!"

She rolled her eyes. "Creep. Around ten?"

"Done. You play golf?"

"My brother had a bash every now and then and I tried it once or twice. When he joined the Navy, that ended it."

"There's a nice golf course at Mt. Macedon. If you like, we can go for a hit."

"We'll see." She sat back and sighed. "Thanks for the lunch, Mason. You're a good provider."

"Not a problem. Care for lunch or dinner tomorrow?"

She winced. "Tomorrow is busy, I'm afraid, and I'll be too wrung out for a Friday night out. It's about the only time I can relax properly."

"I know what you mean." He patted her hand. "Call if you change your mind."

The rest of the afternoon drifted in a pleasant haze replaying his lunch with Leola and putting bones on the Post proposal. When he got home, the day left him very satisfied. He felt he slotted himself well into GS, and Post seemed to like him…provided he continued to deliver, he reminded himself.

A tumbler of whiskey in hand, he browsed through his CD collection, pulled out a medley of favorites, and slipped it into the player. He sprawled into his leather seat and reached for the remote. His cell trilled and his eyebrows rose when he saw the caller name.

"Hi, Mom. What's up?"

"Nothing, dear. Simply calling to see how you were. It's been a while since we talked, and I thought you might like to lunch with us this weekend. You can fill us in about your new job. By the way, how's that going?"

"Going great. As for lunch, I'd love to, but I have plans."

"Going to Mt. Macedon?"

"I might be."

"Who is she?"

"Mom! Why do you automatically assume I'm involved with a girl?"

"Aren't you? It's the only reason that'll keep you away from my walnut roll."

He laughed, genuinely amused, and decided to spill it. "Actually, I *do* have a friend I met at Post."

"Manny has a girl!" his mom shouted into background TV noise.

"About time," came Dad's muffled reply.

"So, tell me all about her."

"She's Italian, lives with her parents in North Melbourne—"

"How old is she?"

"I'm not sure. Late twenties, I'd guess."

"She'll be a sensible woman, then. Go on."

"Divorced for some time—"

"Children?"

"No."

"That makes life easier for everybody. Is it serious?"

"I think it might be."

"I'm happy for you. Look, if you're not going to Mt. Macedon, bring her over for lunch."

"I'll see how things work out and call you. If not this weekend, definitely the next."

"I'll make sure Grandma is with us."

"I'd like that. Bye, Mom."

He placed the cell on the coffee table, stared at it for a moment, and shook his head. Not exactly the way he planned to break the news about Leola, but in a way, glad that it came out.

If nothing else, the news would give his parents something novel to talk about and speculate.

Then, his WhatsApp gave a ping. It appeared fates were determined to interrupt his evening, but smiled when Liam Anderson's name appeared as the sender, picturing him pushing up his rimless glasses.

Greetings and salutations, old buddy.

His friend had a penchant for flowery texts.

Long time between tête-à-tête, *revered pal. You are cordially invited to a boys-only night out at* The Oriental Pearl *restaurant in Chinatown off the Swanston Street entrance for August 12 at 7 pm. Your esteemed presence will grace our humble table if you can tear yourself away from running the world.*

Nice of his friend to give him a weeks' notice. He smiled and typed, *See you there, you old bugger, and thanks. Looking forward to it.*

Peace at last, he pressed the Play button. The music came through in full surround system power and he closed his eyes to allow random images to cycle through his mind. Petula Clarke's rendition of ABBA's *Arrival* in French came on and he savored the magic of her voice reverberating through his heartstrings. *Tar and Cement* by Verdelle Smith resonated at some elemental level he found particularly poignant. The song even more relevant in today's world than in its comparatively serene 1966 release, happy that he kept his grandparents' Mt. Macedon house as a connection to a different, perhaps saner reality. He often wondered whether that song represented a pivotal reason why he never sold the place. A reminder that life indeed held more than tar and cement? Some mind bender would enjoy dissecting him.

When the last song ended, he sipped his whiskey, enveloped in serene satisfaction.

Not such a failure, eh. Dad?

Now where in hell did that come from?

Clearly, he needed more than one moment of reconciliation to banish the dark ghosts of his past. Not quite banish as he could never forget, but at least wall them off.

Skits!

* * *

Mason steered the Subaru Forester toward the curb and parked. Nothing moved on the lonely dark street lit with pools of white light from overhead poles that scattered the shadows. Like beads on a string, cars hugged the nature strips on both sides, garages rare on the narrow plots. He stepped out and winced, his thin llama sweater never designed to cope with the assaulting chill.

He hurried up the paved path to the front door and pressed the glowing doorbell button. The pleasant chime and anticipation to see Leola took his mind off the cold.

Footsteps came from inside and he brought himself back to the present. The door opened, followed by a welcomed wave of warm air. Leola flashed him a smile that showed off perfect teeth and dimpled left cheek. A tight white shirt spilled over black slacks highlighted a fine figure, feet in rabbit fur slippers.

Without saying anything, she flowed against him, arms around his neck, and kissed him. Enveloped in faintly citreous fragrance, he held her close and forgot everything for several enchanting seconds. Eventually, he pulled back and cupped her face between his hands.

"If this is the entrée, I can't wait for the main course."

She slapped his forearm and giggled gaily. "Is that all you can think about, you randy old thing?"

"I can't help it, sweetie. You bring out the beast in me."

"Wolf!" She tugged his arm. "Come in before we both get pneumonia."

She closed the door with a backward shove and led him down

a carpeted corridor lined with striped silver and gold wallpaper.

"I never liked that pattern," Leola remarked, noting his scrutiny. "Brian and I urged Dad to tear it down, but he never did, saying he'll do it when he rips out the wall."

Two ceiling lights lit the space with a pearly glow.

"Bedrooms on the right," she added. "Straight ahead is the second bathroom. My parents have an en suite. The corridor turns and leads to the kitchen and laundry." She stopped and slid back a clear glass panel. "The living room."

A large flat TV occupied a prominent center space in a wall cabinet that held a DVD player, a vinyl record player, amplifier, and rows of DVDs and CDs, surrounded by slim speakers, books, and two decorative blue glass vases. Two beige cloth recliners on the polished floor and a matching three-person sofa encircled a wooden coffee table. Landscape prints and family photos decorated the walls.

"This is where we hang out," Leola declared, then pointed at a frosted glass door on the right from which pleasant cooking smells seeped through. "The lounge. Come on." She slid back the panel and walked into a bright little room occupied by a formal dining table laid out with black plates, cutlery, and crystal glasses. Eight high-backed chairs ringed the table. A bar cabinet stood tucked against the far corner.

"Mom, Dad, he's here!"

"We can hear you," a strong woman's voice came from the kitchen. "There is no need to shout, dear."

The door slid back and a tall, trim man walked in. Black hair untouched by frost, thin Roman nose, dark eyes instantly measured him. Thin lips broke into a wide grin as he stuck out a hand.

"Glad to meet you, Mason," he declared in a deep voice. "Call me Renzo."

Mason took the proffered hand, squeezed hard, and let go, Renzo's grip equally strong. Mason sensed genuine friendliness and liked him on sight. Some people put on a phony face that masked reserve or dislike, but not this man. No pretense. Something else lurked in those eyes. A touch of dislike? What could have brought that on? His overheated imagination working? Although wary of first impressions, he always stored them in his memory.

Leola beamed, obviously pleased.

A slim woman in a navy blue T-shirt and dark brown pleated knee-length skirt walked in. Shorter by some fifteen centimeters than her husband, her maturity did not hide the underlying beauty age never erased. Mason figured she must have been a stunning young girl.

"So, this is the man Leola's been bending our ears about," she said cheerfully and held out a delicate hand.

"Mom!" Leola protested and flushed. Her mother merely laughed.

"I hope nothing derogatory," Mason replied. "Pleased to meet you, ma'am,"

"Martina," the woman told him sternly. "Renzo, you oaf. Don't stand there. Give the man a drink. Make yourself comfortable, Mason," she said and disappeared into the kitchen.

Renzo strode to the bar and turned. "What'll you have?"

"Bourbon if you got it."

"Right! I'm a scotch man myself. Some rosé for you, Leola?"

"Thanks, Dad," she said and sat opposite Mason.

"A rosé for you, Martina?"

"Yes!" came a muffled reply from the kitchen.

"Much roomier now that Brian and Despina are gone," Renzo stated as he handed Mason a tumbler and placed a crystal glass before Leola. He returned with another, laid it where Martina would sit, and waited for his wife to come in.

"A toast to our very welcome guest."

Everybody clicked glasses and Mason took a sip of fine whiskey that went down smooth as oil.

"Excellent," he remarked.

"I keep a bottle when Brian comes around," Renzo said and sat down with a grunt next to Mason. "So, you're working with Leola on a Post infrastructure project?"

"That's right. It hasn't started, but it should soon."

"I don't know if she told you, I'm in real estate."

"She did. How's that going?"

"Not too good at the moment. With this Covid thing, money is tight and nobody's buying." Renzo shrugged. "These things come and go. I'm with the Dominion Group. We're mostly into commercial property management. I don't suppose you heard of us?"

"I'm afraid not."

"No matter. If you have any spare cash, I can offer you a great deal."

"Dad! Stop trying to sell him a dead horse," Leola protested.

"I'm letting the man know I've got a good thing for him." Renzo gave Mason a speculative look. "She told us you've done well for yourself. Good to see a man looking out for his future."

"Actually, I'm looking to marry into money," Mason replied evenly, and Leola spluttered into her wine.

He thought he had the man figured out. Push until something gave way, then pounce. No surprise that Leola found it difficult living in this house. Parents…They do a lot for their children, but they also exact a heavy emotional price for doing it…and never let the kids forget it.

Renzo guffawed and slapped Mason on the back. "That was good. I like a man with spunk. It takes people a day or two before they dislike me."

"Give me time. We only met."

"We'll get along, my boy."

Martina set down her glass and glanced at Leola. "Help me with the soup, dear. Don't mind my husband, Mason," she added from the doorway. "He can't help his mouth do his thinking."

"Hey! That's unfair," Renzo shot back. "I only wanted to

help."

Mason liked the man's straight shooter attitude, the markings of a good high-pressure salesman. He watched the two women disappear into the kitchen and turned to face his host.

"Were you always in real estate?"

"Pretty much. I started with Ray White as a junior accountant. It didn't take me long to figure out the big money is made in property management sales. You don't scramble as hard for your commission agents do with houses."

The kitchen door opened and Leola came in carrying two steel sauce containers and placed them in the center of the table.

"Cream and pumpkin oil," she announced brightly and sat down.

Martina appeared with a black ceramic tureen and laid it down. "Pumpkin soup. I hope it's to your liking, Mason."

"I make it myself now and then."

Renzo went to the bar fridge and extracted a dark bottle. He undid the screw top and glanced at Mason.

"Some Shiraz? It's old enough and should be palatable."

"Thanks."

He ladled creamy soup into his bowl and added pepper, poured on a few drops of oil, and stirred. The oil left green smears and a pleasant aroma. He declined the cream, accepting that some people liked it. He tried the lightly spiced mixture and nodded.

"This is very good, Martina."

Pleased, she flashed him a smile. "I like to keep my men fed. Leola tells me you're not a bad cook yourself."

"I can grill a sandwich," he retorted, and she chuckled.

"It is my firm belief that every child should be taught how to cook, be it a boy or girl. A handy skill to have in life."

"What does your old man do, if you don't mind me asking," Renzo put in.

"He's a senior design manager at Thompson Engineering.

They've got a plant in Laverton."

"A technical man, eh? My Brian's in the Navy."

"So Leola said."

"He's executive officer on a frigate. A romantic fantasy for the young, if you asked me. Not a life for someone serious."

"Leave it alone, Daddy!" Leola declared firmly.

"We need the military," Mason said.

Renzo scowled at him. "For what? Is Indonesia going to invade us? Or Papua New Guinea perhaps? The billions we spend could be better used on badly needed social programs."

"The military is more than boots on the ground," Mason remarked with quiet force. "They patrol our northern borders against people smugglers and illegal fishing. They're also an important strategic deterrent in a coalition of allies."

"Against whom?"

"Our presence in the South China Sea, for example, shows the Chinese they cannot unilaterally occupy international waters to further their political and economic agenda. If the West does nothing, China will move into the Pacific and aggressively intimidate island nations and western South America, plundering their fishing grounds more than they're already doing."

"That's propaganda talking, my boy," Renzo retorted with a dismissive wave of his hand.

"Please excuse him, Mason," Martina added. "He's still sore that Brian went into the Navy instead of real estate."

"Silly fool," Renzo grumbled and dug into his soup. "He should be thinking about his future and family. They'll be eating thin bread if he stays in. Property, Mason! That's how you get ahead. I keep telling him, but he won't listen, spouting patriotic nonsense. Doing it to spite me."

Mason laid down his spoon. "Did you listen to his side and taken time to understand what drives him?"

"Hear! Hear!" Leola added vigorously.

"Enough of this talk," Martina declared firmly. "Stubborn like his father, Brian sometimes does things he knows are wrong."

"Takes after his mother," Renzo grated, then grinned. "I can tell you're another rebel who probably gave his old man a hard time."

"It worked both ways," Mason replied evenly and sipped his wine. "Leola said you want to knock down all these walls and make it into one big space."

"I wanted to do it for some time now. Everybody used the small spaces design in the sixties and seventies, but it's dated, and I prefer something that looks roomier. Say, a well-to-do guy like you could help me finance the reno. I would make it worth your while."

"Daddy! How can you ask him something like that?" Leola looked embarrassed and outraged.

"Hush up. This is between the two of us."

"I'm not sure, Renzo," Mason replied carefully. "It may be a good first step not to like you."

Renzo chortled and slapped the table. "You're something else. Damn me if you're not. Just kidding, my boy."

Ravioli in thick meat sauce followed the soup, Martina steered the conversation to more neutral topics, something Mason appreciated, not relishing the prospect of a heated political exchange with Renzo and ruin an otherwise pleasant evening.

"I haven't had ravioli in a long time. Not like this."

"Leola made it," Martina said and Leola blushed behind her glass.

"She tells me you're going to your property at Mt. Macedon tomorrow," Renzo said. "Did you buy it?"

"Left to me by my grandparents."

"Hang onto it, my boy. You'll never lose out on land. Seriously, though. Think over what I said about getting something in the city."

Over coffee and cheesecake, relaxed and at ease, he had mixed feelings about Leola's parents. He liked Martina's easygoing attitude that nonetheless hid a strong, forceful personality of someone who liked to take charge. Renzo had the same qualities, which Mason suspected led to occasional clashes of will. Since they were still together and not at each other's throat, they probably developed a workable way to live. He imagined a fiery encounter between Renzo and his own dad and smiled inwardly.

His host noted the bemused expression and raised an eyebrow. "Something amusing?"

"I'm wondering how life must have been here with three kids under one roof."

Renzo laughed. "A diplomatic way of saying we had twenty-four-hour bedlam. Especially when they became teenagers."

"Hey! I resent that!" Leola retorted. "Despina and I never gave you any trouble."

"Hah!" Renzo winked at Mason. "Girls are the worst. All of them took after their mother."

Martina glared. "A good thing too, you oaf. They'd be Mafia hooligans if you had your way."

"A slight exaggeration, Mason," Renzo added good-naturedly. "We didn't spare the rod and they all turned out okay." He sipped his wine. "Leola told us you paint. A somewhat unusual hobby for a professional man."

"It's a diversion. What's yours?"

"Hobby? I don't have one," Renzo remarked gruffly. "A man's responsibility is to his family and job. Everything else is a waste of time."

"Daddy! How can you say that!" Leola burst out.

"Perhaps you should play Monopoly," Mason ventured. "That way, you can pretend you own five hotels."

Renzo gaped, then roared with laughter. "Love it! *Touché*, my boy."

After more pleasantries and sparring, Mason said his goodbyes and Leola walked him to the car.

Thick fog blanketed everything and clung to him, cold and clammy. Streetlights were fuzzy orbs that seemed to float, free at last.

He brushed her face. "Around ten?"

She nodded and melted into his arms. The lingering kiss made the evening complete. "I hope you didn't mind Dad," she said after a breathless moment. "He can come on strong sometimes, but I learned to ignore him."

"An interesting character, I admit. Is that why you moved out?"

Some sparkle went out of her eyes. "It's complicated. Something you should know from personal experience."

"I'm sorry. I didn't mean to tease. Your mom is a doll, though."

"You made a good impression, but you're still to see her dark side."

"The other side of the force, eh?"

"Believe it."

"'Night, Leola." He touched her cheek and walked quickly to his car. She fluttered her fingers at him when he pulled away from the curb and he waved back.

A wall of white threw the beams back at him, visibility reduced to some ten meters. Along King Street, everybody drove slowly. He did not mind, preoccupied with the evening's reflections. Renzo's hard attitude rankled somewhat, but he filed the characteristic as a behavioral trait. After all, he dated Leola, not her father.

As he crossed Kings Bridge, he broke through the wall of fog into a clear night, and the city rose around him in a blaze of color as though the river represented some boundary. Relieved, he picked up speed and entered Kings Way boulevard, his spirits buoyed at the prospect of an easy run home.

Too early to retire, percolator bubbling in the kitchen, he filled a cognac balloon, put on a CD of Baroque music, and sprawled into his leather recliner, a wolfish grin on his face.

Tomorrow, she would be his for the whole day.

* * *

Neil Diamond filled the empty spaces as the kilometers faded behind them. Hardly anybody on the freeway, Mason easily imagined he owned the bright morning and the world. Beside him, hands clasped in her lap, Leola watched the rolling landscape under its blanket of tall eucalypt. It surprised him when she admitted never visiting this side of Melbourne.

He suddenly felt a rush of unaccountable contentment. The moment did not require conversation as the silence provided a bridge that made words redundant. Her presence, here, now, told him how she felt. She shared herself by being with him and he would share himself with her, unreservedly. On impulse, he took his hand off the steering wheel and touched her thigh, the black denim of her jeans warm on his palm. Her dark eyes regarded him with solemn attention before a faint smile of understanding tugged her lips. Right then, he would not mind to simply drive on and on with her beside him, no destination in mind, just share this moment with her forever.

The Mt. Macedon turnoff broke the magic and reality crowded them again. Past the golf course, he slowed to 50 and Leola craned her neck to see everything as he drove through the small township and its quaint cottages. Several plum trees were in flower and added charm to the picturesque setting.

"God, it's like stepping into history," she murmured in wonder.

"That's why I like coming here. It readjusts my sense of balance and somehow makes things simple again."

A right at Cheniston Road and they were there. Mason pulled up in front of the gate and glanced at Leola. "Here we are. My secret retreat from city madness."

Barely above the gums, the sun created sharp shadows from a brilliant blue sky. A gaggle of squawking cockatoos flew overhead and disappeared among the trees frozen in time with no breath of wind. Down the hill, patches of mist hugged the valley to create a fairyland scene.

Leola bit her lip as she gazed at the vista before her. "This is magical," she breathed and her eyes sparkled.

He nodded with satisfaction, glad that she understood a little of what he felt.

"Come," he prompted and climbed out.

She followed him out and shivered. "Wow." White vapor hung before her as she exhaled. "This air is unbelievable. And the scents…"

"Not bad, is it. If we could bottle and sell it to all the office slaves, we'd make a fortune."

Nothing stirred along the sleepy street as he opened the gate. Tendrils of gray smoke rose straight from several neighboring houses, which added a pleasant wood aroma to the crisp atmosphere.

"This is a wonderland."

"Not so jazzy in a storm, but we picked a good day. They say it'll rain tomorrow, but that's tomorrow. Today, this world is ours."

He parked in front of the garage and paused.

"Something the matter?" Leola wondered.

He turned and gave her a wan smile. "I expected Cricket, my grandparents' black tomcat, to come bounding toward me, tail held high in greeting."

She tilted her head and gave him a quizzical look. "You liked coming here, didn't you?"

"I loved it. It's where I came to escape," he said simply and walked up the sandstone steps to the main door. Inside, he disabled the alarm and winced at the permeating chill. Leola stood in the doorway and rubbed her hands, eyes roaming over the sparse interior.

"Wait till I get the burner going," he told her.

"You're not much into decoration."

"I like to keep things uncluttered."

"I noticed that at your house."

"Go to the veranda. It'll be nicer there."

She slid back the ceiling-high glass panel and beamed. "This is so much better," she agreed, the sun having warmed the enclosed space. Hands clasped behind her back, she gazed at the landscape as it fell away and merged into open flatland swathed in clinging mist.

The burner stoked up, Mason boiled water and prepared two mugs of Earl Grey tea with a dollop of honey and a squirt of lemon juice. Done, he carried them to the veranda and placed them on the heavy wood table.

"Sit."

She sank onto a chair, took a sip, and held the mug between her hands. "Nice garden, and fruit trees, I see."

"Grandma liked to make plum jam and dried apples and pears. They had to keep the drying tables covered or the birds took the lot. See those two large chestnuts at the back? I loved to roast or boil them. There's nothing like fresh chestnuts."

"The birds didn't get them?"

"Sure did. Cockatoos mainly. They weren't after the nuts to eat. The buggers pecked at them to make them fall to the ground. Sadistic destruction, that's all. Grandad wanted to shoot them, but the things are protected and were not uncontrollable enough to warrant such drastic treatment. So, he covered the fruiting trees when they were smaller, but gave up when they became too large. Anyway, the birds didn't get everything and left enough for us. Besides," he added with a broad grin, "shooting them would deprive him of the pleasure he got by chasing the pesky buggers. I didn't mind rampaging after them myself as a kid."

She smiled and sipped her tea. "What's that thin tree in the left corner?"

"The cypress? My grandfather's ashes are buried there."

The aroma of burning wood permeated the veranda and Leola sighed. "I could get used to this. A retreat…a place of my own…"

"My parents brought me here often for a weekend, regardless of season. In summer, I ran wild with other kids, and got spanked for my trouble when I tore my clothing."

Leola gave a merry laugh. "You were undoubtedly a terror."

"That's what the neighbors said. I wasn't that bad, though. Dad and Gramps used to sit here, sip wine or *slivovitz*, and talk, and I'd curl up on a stool and listen, happy to be with them. When Dad wasn't around, I'd listen to Gramps reminisce about his adventurous life, munching on Grandma's cookies or cake. I loved his stories about witches and strange things that went on where his parents lived. Another world, all right."

He sensed a tipping point and made a decision. Not a juvenile impulse driven by her enchanting presence, but a firm realization of what felt right based on everything he experienced. He reached for her hands and held them.

"Leola, move in with me."

"What? Are you serious?"

"I wouldn't have said it if I wasn't."

She scowled. "What brought this on? We barely know each other."

"Well, once you get to know me better, you may not want to. So, I'm preempting," he told her with a straight face.

She lowered the mug to the table. "Part of me likes the idea, but another part urges caution. It's complicated."

"It's not complicated. You're building artificial barriers for yourself. Is it because of what your parents may think?"

"That and what their friends would say. What my friends did say."

"Are those things more important than what you want for

yourself? Easy for others to be judgmental, but they're not living your life or deal with your problems. I'm not saying your parents will take this lightly, but if they really want what's best for you, they won't stand in your way. I also like to think your friends will support you, if they're genuine friends. If they're simply someone you know, what they say shouldn't matter or bother you."

"Everything you say makes sense, but it's not that easy, and you know it."

He squeezed her hand. "What do *you* want, Leola?"

She sniffed and wiped her eye. "Why did you bring all this up just when I started to enjoy myself? Is this a come-on gambit? I cannot forget that behind every smooth line, men want only one thing from a woman. Mom warned me when I became old enough for that to matter, but I didn't listen and had to find out for myself the hard way."

"I'm not like other men and this isn't a come-on. I told you, I'd never give you whiplash of the heart."

"You did and I came to appreciate that you're different. That's what makes this complicated."

"You want a place of your own and I know why. This is not only about your parents or wanting to be independent. A whole lot of things go into the mix, not the least of it is a desire to control and shape your own life. I know this because I went through it myself. Different circumstances, granted, but the basic reasons were the same."

"The thing is, if I moved in with you, I'd lose control."

"And living with your parents gives you control?"

"It doesn't and that's what's tearing me up. I'm grateful to them for a roof over my head, but part of me resents that I had to crawl to them to take me back. If I moved in with you, it wouldn't be my roof, but yours. I'd be your kept woman."

A sigh of exasperation escaped him. "My darling sweet. Don't you get it? It would be *our* roof! Equal in everything." Something else occurred to him, but he had to tread carefully here, lest she misunderstood his motive, then decided to chance it.

"Let's table the move. How about this. Your dad offered you a house. Take it. You'll never get a cheaper opportunity. I'll give you fifty thousand to help with the bank loan. You'll have a place you always wanted and be completely independent. We can meet and do things when *you* want to."

She gasped. "I don't need to move in with you?"

He shook his head. "No strings attached."

"Remember what I said men wanted?" she pointed out.

"Sorry. Just pulling your chain."

"That's how you could get spanked."

Her eyes sparkled. "You wouldn't, would you?" Before he could answer, she raised a hand. "What if things don't work out between us?"

He shrugged. "Nobody can tell what'll happen tomorrow, but that shouldn't stop us from making plans. Look…Regardless how things turn out, you'll have your house. I'm not trying to bribe you—"

"Like hell you're not!"

Mason let go her hand. "I didn't mean to rush you, we only met, but it doesn't seem like it to me. All I know is that I love you and you like me a little as well. I want to skip over the prolonged and expected dancing around and deal with what's important for both of us. Right now, having you with me is important."

"To you," she added.

"You're right. It is important to me and I admit to a little selfishness. I'm not demanding that you move in with me, or the 50K is an inducement to our relationship…if we're going to have one. I'm asking that you think about options and decide what you want. I won't bug you no matter what you do."

He never found it easy to know what went on in a woman's mind. They seemed to operate on a totally different level to men, driven as they were by unique life's drivers and priorities. Understandable in a way, given their biological makeup.

She sighed. "I think I'm falling for you, Mason Adamov, and it's scary. I'm scared to commit. I know I shouldn't dwell on the past and forget the jerk I married, but it's hard. The experience is always at the back of my mind and invariably colors my outlook on men. I know it's my problem and I must deal with it, but I cannot help how I feel. If I give into what you mean to me and you betrayed my trust, it would destroy me."

Mason leaned toward her, took her hands in his, and brought them to his lips. "I'm not much for making polished, romantic speeches with only one objective. In my clumsy way, I'm offering you choices. Nothing else. No need to say anything now. Think about it, okay?"

Time marched in slow agony as he waited.

Eventually, she nodded. "I thought about it...and...I'm crazy to say this, I hardly know you, but I'll move in with you."

He straightened at this totally unexpected reply, stood, and gathered her in his arms. Her hands went around his neck and he kissed her hard. Eventually, she pulled back and smiled into his eyes.

"Mind you, this is not a 'yes' to that other question," she murmured huskily. "You're on probation, nothing else."

"Deal." He crushed his lips against hers.

A delicious, timeless moment later, he kissed the tip of her nose. "You bewitched me, Leola Lanaro."

"And you bewitched me, my warlock, and why all this is so insane. You're insane. We both are."

"Since we seem to be under some primordial spell, let's drag in the groceries. You promised to cook lunch, remember?"

On the way to the front door, she stopped and tugged his arm. "You know, Dad will have kittens when I tell him I'm moving out."

"He'll trot out the guilt stuff about living in sin?"

"Believe it. Traditional Italian morality baggage."

"Will he deny you the house?"

She scrunched her nose. "I don't know."

"One hurdle at a time, my sweet. Don't sweat it. Let's get the stuff."

"A bit early for lunch, isn't it?"

"I only want to bring everything in, that's all. We can go for a short walk to Gabby's to build up your appetite, then cook."

"Gabby's?"

"A little convenience and souvenir store. It's a fixture around here."

The chore done, her arm wrapped around his, green beanie over her head, they made their way up the gentle incline toward the main road. Leola took a deep breath, exhaled loudly, and smiled sheepishly when he glanced at her.

"I can't get enough of this air," she explained with a shrug.

The chill taken out by the climbing sun, it warmed where it touched. Gravel crunched under their feet as they walked. A left turn at the main road and Leola pointed excitedly at a cottage across the street, probably built a hundred years ago.

"Look at that! It's awesome," she gushed. "I don't expect too many young people live here."

"You'd be surprised. Most aren't here permanently—"

"Like you."

"—and keep a place as an investment or weekend getaway. The retirees love it here. It's a pretty close community and everybody pretty much knows everybody else."

"I don't see many active farms around here."

"You won't. Old farmers are mostly gone and the young have little interest working small plots not commercially viable."

He stopped at the Post office cum small store and restaurant, and inclined his head at the entrance. Elderly couples occupied two of four outside round tables braving the cold, chatting and sipping a brew. Nobody looked at them as Mason and Leola strode past.

"Come, check this out," he said and held the door open for her.

A comforting wave of warmth made him nod with appreciation. On the left, scattered square tables filled the space, some taken. Wall shelving held assorted bottles, jars, and various compotes. The back wall had more of the same, including a selection of local wines. On his right, an attractive middle-aged lady served two local men. Beside her, a teenager worked the hissing coffee machine.

The woman pushed back a lock of auburn hair, looked up, and her face lit up. "Mason! My favorite customer. You still don't want to marry me?"

"You're top of the list."

"Teaser."

He turned to Leola, an amused expression on her face. "Meet Gabrielle. She's a fixture around here and wants to snag anyone in pants."

"Call me Gabby, dear," the woman replied warmly and sighed. "Looking at you, I suspect I'm off the list."

"There's no justice, Gabby," Mason told her.

The woman shrugged. "I lived with disappointment before. You two want to order something?"

Leola shook her head. "Thanks, but I'm fine. You've got a fantastic place here. It's like stepping into the past."

"I'm not *that* ancient!" Gabby protested with a twinkle in her eyes.

"I didn't mean—"

Gabby laughed. "It's all right, dear."

"Nothing for me either," Mason added. "I only wanted Leola to see your place."

"Come any time," Gabby replied and turned to a waiting customer.

Leola browsed the shelves and decided to buy a jar of fig jam.

Outside, she gave him a speculative look.

"Gabby wants to marry you?"

Mason snorted. "She's a doll and flirts with everybody. She also has a muscular husband who doesn't mind."

"So, that teenager is her daughter?"

"Nope. Hired help."

Well past twelve when they got back to his house, Mason slipped a compilation of 60s and 70s music into the player and started work on the salad while Leola got busy on the apple strudel. The main course—stuffed chicken breasts wrapped in a bacon rasher—took only minutes to prepare. Cubed potatoes boiling on the hotplate, she hummed to the music, totally relaxed. When *I'm a believer* by The Monkeys came on, he took her hands and held her close, cheek to cheek.

"I haven't heard that piece in centuries," Leola murmured against him.

"One of my favorites."

The song ended and broke the moment, and both resumed their chores.

Salad done, he used the coffee grinder to crunch some walnuts. Not exactly the proper tool, but it did the job well enough. Leola merely stared.

"I've never seen anyone use a coffee grinder to do that."

"It's a grinder, isn't it?"

She sighed and shook her head.

Apples peeled and grated, he squeezed out the juice as Leola spread a puff pastry sheet onto the bench. It did not take long to finish the strudel, glaze the top with a beaten egg, and pop the tray into the oven.

Potatoes ready, she put them into another tray, sprinkled on olive oil, salt and pepper, and the tray joined the strudel. Chicken breasts stuffed with duck *foie gras* wrapped in bacon went into a large frying pan. Browned, Leola slipped the pan into the oven to bake clear through.

Bottle of Riesling in hand, Mason paused and watched her precise, economic movements, totally absorbed in her work. She caught him at it and straightened.

"What?"

"Nothing. I like to look at you."

Her cheek dimpled. "You're weird, did you know that?"

"It's been mentioned."

He poured them a glass of Riesling and the crystal sang as they toasted each other. After a sip, she pointed a forefinger over her shoulder at a slim rectangular package wrapped in brown paper he laid beside the fridge when they lugged in the groceries.

"What's that?"

"A surprise, my sweet," he declared and heaved the package onto the bench. "Open it."

Lips pressed in a pretty frown, she used a knife to slice open the paper and began to tear it off. She saw the painting and gasped. Clear of its wrapping, she placed it on the bench, leaned it against the wall, and stared.

"For you," Mason told her with satisfaction and studied her reaction.

It took him a whole week of evenings to do the portrait in oils, scraping away parts he disliked and redoing them, her image indelibly carved into his mind. Nothing fancy; a simple dark background, her large black eyes bright with secret amusement. More an impressionist rendition than a photo-like representation. Still, he felt it captured her finely sculpted face and impish smile.

Leola sniffed and dabbed her left eye with a knuckle. "I can't believe you did this." She took a step and stood before him. Neil Diamond's *I am, I said* in the background, she gently rested her head against his chest.

"You're a remarkable man, Mason Adamov," she remarked softly, "and I'm still to figure you out."

He kissed her forehead. "It's how I see you, and how I'll always see you."

"You painted a dream, not me."

"You're a dream from which I hope never to wake."

She mouthed a 'Thank you', pulled away, and they were back in the real world. A check of the oven, she rubbed her hands.

"Almost done. Where are the dishes?"

He helped lay out the veranda table and put on a new CD.

Leola heaped more salad into the brown glass bowl, gave him a playful grin, and resumed to demolish her chicken. The scrape of cutlery teased moments of silence when she had to catch her breath to launch another verbal cascade. With barriers down, like a bee skipping among flowers, she regaled him with humorous snippets of childhood in a household with two siblings, rebellious teenage years, raging hormones, and unpredictable emotions as she grew into young womanhood. Glimpses into encounters with boys, university life, and sobering reality starting a professional job. Easy to be rebellious when she did not have to worry where the next meal came from or where she slept, she added wryly. Mason related to it all as he reflected on his often turbulent up-bringing. She avoided talk about her failed marriage and he did not pry.

He went through the mechanical process of eating, caught up in an ethereal haze of desire and something more he struggled to rationalize. Struggled because words were pale reflections of ram-pant feelings in an ocean of calm and unfathomable puzzlement that surrounded Leola in a halo of mystery he desperately wanted to unravel. To his logical mind, he disliked the feeling of not un-derstanding everything. He understood the biological drivers that attracted him to this striking woman, but he could not reduce what he felt to something merely physical because he felt so much more. She burned bright and he gladly stepped into its sear-ing embrace.

Skits!

She absently brushed back a lock of hair and he found himself sinking into impenetrable darkness of its strands devoid of light.

Endless midnight he wanted to touch and stroke to feel its silky luster. Her black eyes shone with an inner light that beckoned with an irresistible pull he felt powerless to fight. They were doorways he wanted to enter, and she would be waiting for him on the other side, arms open in invitation.

He mentally traced the subtle curve of her eyebrows, the way they tapered to frame her eyes to form a perfect bridge. He imagined running a soft finger down her nose to rest on full lips he longed to kiss. The way her dimple filled and moved as she talked created perfection. To hold her face between his hands meant fulfillment, forever holding it.

His gaze drifted to her long, delicate neck that somehow enhanced the overall devastating effect she had on him. Few women had a long neck and hers held him captivated. He wanted to stroke that yielding smoothness, lick it tenderly until she whimpered with flaming craving, then seek out her soft mouth and allow the primordial need to consume them both.

Leola caught him staring and abruptly fell silent. He had no idea what she said, but knew he could replay it all later at leisure.

"What? Something wrong?"

His mouth twitched in a tender smile. "Nothing. I'm enthralled, that's all, and time doesn't exist. There is only you. You're my world and I hope you'll let me into yours so we can be one. I never met anyone like you or felt even remotely with someone else what I feel for you. It scares me, something I guess a macho man should never admit. It also excites me and makes me reflect on what I want, which is you at my side forever. I want to hold you and never let go. I want to protect you from hurt life dishes out because your pain is my pain, but I don't want you to feel pain. I want to see you laugh, be happy, and I will always be there for you." He paused, cleared his throat, and shrugged with a sheepish grin. "I'm not making any sense, am I? Sorry. I didn't mean to spoil our lunch by being mushy."

Eyes grave, she regarded him in a silence that gathered around them like a comforting blanket. She stood, walked around the table, sat on his lap, and her yielding lips brushed his. Then she pressed hard and her mouth opened. He wrapped her in his arms, held her firmly against him, and allowed time to stop.

Eventually, time did resume. She pulled back, ran fingers through his hair, and her eyes shone.

"You're making it awfully difficult not to jump you, Mason Adamov," she murmured huskily. "Too bad we're not at your place right now."

"Give into temptation, I say. You never know if it will come your way again," he replied gruffly.

She giggled and slapped his arm. "A typical randy man after all."

"There is more to me than that, though."

"So I know. This move, when can I do it?" she asked and the cloud of fantasy dissipated.

"Anytime you want. You own a car?"

"A Honda Civic. It's parked on the street in front of my parent's place."

"I'll get you a resident's parking sticker and you can bring it over. My neighbor across the street won't be pleased when I tell him I'm taking back my spot, but he always knew it could happen."

Leola looked concerned. "I don't want to cause any fuss."

"Not a problem. His wife is using my spot. They're both elderly and don't need two cars. Anyway, it's my spot and I can do whatever I like with it."

"Thanks."

He stroked her hair. "You know, once you're with me, we can go to work together."

"And do lots of other things together too," she murmured, ruffled his hair again, climbed off him, went back to her seat, and resumed eating.

Images of what those other things might be set his imagination on fire. A randy man, all right.

He cut a piece of chicken and popped it into his mouth, firmly in reality again. He took a sip of refreshing wine, his thoughts pleasant, promising himself to relive every delicious moment with her in the privacy of his den. He wanted her now and knew she would give herself willingly, but the window he opened for her to peer into him felt satisfying enough. In a startling realization, although he understood it intellectually, he accepted there were things that transcended the physical, and he relished this revelation. No need to rush anything now.

A pair of magpies swooped into the garden patch and comfortably began to peck at the ground.

Lunch finished almost in silence, broken by 'pass the salad' and stuff like that, nobody needed to intrude into each other's thoughts. Mason still to come to terms with his, happy to simply enjoy Leola's company. She appeared to feel the same way, glanced at him once, and immediately dropped her eyes. Not uncomfortable or tense, her presence satisfied him.

To top things off, he served crispy, delicious strudel smothered with local blackberry compote. Leola gave into desire and had two pieces.

Afterward, they washed up, put away everything, and Mason made tea for her and coffee for himself. At the veranda table, he lit a cigar and puffed contentedly, his eyes lost in the sky's blue depths.

Leola sighed and shifted in her seat. "I could get to like it here. There is an atmosphere of peace and friendliness that's very attractive. I noticed it when we visited the restaurant and your not-so-secret admirer," she added with an impish grin.

"It's a special place, all right," he agreed readily, ignoring the little barb. "I found most small country towns have it. I guess it's the intimate knowledge everybody has about each other that brings out the good will."

"And gossip, no doubt."

"No doubt. People got to talk about something." He exhaled a rolling smoke ring and a thought popped into his head. "Do you want to take a drive to Hanging Rock? It's only a few kilometers from here and there's a terrific view of the surrounding countryside."

"Isn't that where some high school girls vanished early last century?"

"In 1917—"

"You'd know that, of course," she teased.

"—three girls followed their teacher through a crack in a rock face and vanished, never to be found. Some say they entered a time portal. In 1975, they made a film about it based on Joan Lindsay's 1967 book."

"Sounds creepy."

"Maybe we'll find the portal and vanish. Another mystery."

"You wouldn't push me in and leave me, would you?"

He gave a mock scowl. "That's an ignoble and unworthy thought, especially as I entertained the same thought about you."

Both laughed at the idea.

"Well…"

"Come on. We got nothing else to do. Unless you want to stroll up the street and Gabby can serve us cake."

"No. The strudel filled me. Let's do it."

It took some eight minutes to reach the touristy place, park, and get tickets from the vending machine. Enough people wandered about visiting the curio shop and restaurant without creating a crowd. They toured the museum that explained the local geology, and of course, provided lots of information and pictures about the lost girls and the film.

A gravel path wound its way to the top and Leola gasped at the huge boulders everywhere. Mothers shouted at children not to wonder about, a hopeless wish. Naturally enough, girls in pair or threes twittered excitedly as they searched the rocks for the elusive time portal. Two worn trails led to the hill's edge and open vista of rolling plains dotted by an occasional lone eucalypt. Although crisp with hardly any breeze, it made for a spectacular view.

Leola gazed in rapt attention at the barren landscape. "I've never seen anything like it," she mused in wonder.

"Not bad is it," he said beside her.

"Oh, I've seen open countryside, but it's always been from inside a car. This is a totally different perspective. We definitely live in a unique country. Too bad they never found the portal," she added wistfully, and Mason wondered what went on in her mind.

They jostled among other visitors and made their way down to the parking lot, Leola unusually quiet on the way back to Mt. Macedon. Thinking about the lost girls?

Almost five, dusk falling quickly, they headed back to Melbourne. Along the freeway, the Forester purred as it ate the kilometers in two lanes of other cars, their headlights cutting through darkness. At one point, Leola turned, touched his thigh, and looked solemn.

"Thank you for an enchanting day."

"You made it enchanting."

"Next time we're there, let's have a game of golf."

"It'll have to be during the week. The course is usually packed on weekends."

The tires whispered.

When the lit skyscrapers loomed tall before them, she gave a long sigh. "Seeing the city like this, perhaps we did step through a portal."

"Having to get up for work tomorrow will seem like it. Care for a working lunch?"

"Call me."

Night firmly settled in, Mason stopped in front of her house. She leaned toward him and kissed him on the cheek.

"Tomorrow," she whispered and hastily got out.

He watched her hurry to the front door and disappear inside. The car in 'Drive', he pulled away from the curb.

Chapter Eight

A brisk run around the well-lit Albert Park Lake got Mason primed for the day. Stars winked bright from a frigid August sky, dawn yet to break. He did not mind the cold. It acted as a stimulant.

Feeling restored to his numb face and hands, the hot shower made his skin tingle. Percolator going, he switched on the TV for his mandatory ABC and YouTube news fix. He wondered more than once why he bothered to follow the never-ending stream of doom and gloom everybody dished out all the time. Couldn't somebody say something nice for a change? People liked to wallow in someone else's misery, he told himself. It made them forget their own miseries, if for a while.

Always bubbly, Virginia Trioli and Michael Rowland in his signature blue suit announced that Canberra passed a comprehensive climate change bill. Meanwhile, Ukraine accused Russia of bombing the Zaporizhzia nuclear plant, the second of two such strikes. The Russians, of course, blamed the Ukrainian forces for the attack. Pfizer ramped up production of the vital Covid-19 antiviral drug to meet growing world demand. Israel and Hamas implemented a cease-fire, something Mason welcomed, pitying the poor innocents in Gaza who had to pay the price for a strained peace with their lives. China expanded naval drills in the Taiwan Strait and sent jet fighters into Taiwan's controlled airspace.

Disgusted with it all, he switched off, preferring soothing silence. Coffee done, he poured himself a cup and concentrated on breakfast. He stirred already fried tomato and speck cubes with beaten eggs and poured the mixture into a hot pan. The omelet finished, he slid the thing onto a dish and carried it to the table. A second cup of coffee settled everything and he prepared himself for work, yesterday's events coursing pleasantly through his mind.

Leola said she would move in with him!

His offer of $50K may have seen impulsive to her, but wasn't, his liquid assets and shares portfolio easily able to service it. It did not mean he could splurge, but in this case, he considered it a futures investment rather than a bribe, the difference a technicality, he admitted wryly. He looked forward to having her with him, hoping her parents did not give her a hard time over it.

Ti banac.

Packed as always, the tram—thirty tonnes of sudden green death—clattered over points and sighed to a stop. He got off in a crush of other commuters and pushed through a gaggle of people waiting to board. Why the damned rush? They'll get stressed out soon enough or bored out of their skull in a meaningless job. Not understanding any of it, he sauntered down Collins Street toward the Rialto Towers.

Delora looked up from her workstation and beamed. Only eight o'clock, she already had the place under control. One day, he promised himself he'd beat her in.

"Hi, Mason! Gorgeous morning, isn't it? Did you have a good weekend?"

"Great, thanks. You?"

"It could have been worse," she confided in a conspiratorial whisper.

From the subtle glow around her, he figured she had more than a great time. And why the hell not?

He gave her a thumbs up. "Go for it."

In his office, he powered up the computer, grabbed the mug off his desk, and strolled toward the kitchenette. Several workstations were already manned, the occupants bent over paperwork and keyboards. Global Systems definitely not a nine-to-five shop, something he found early, but did not mind doing the extra hours to get a job done. It came with the big bucks they gave him.

Lavinia Stroud, dressed in her usual black sweater and pants, blonde hair twisted in a bun, waved a stiff finger at Horito Hashigawa—Joe. The smaller man wore his tailored dark woolen suit with elegance, not at all intimidated by the tall woman.

"Hi, guys. Starting World War Three?"

Lavinia grinned, which lit her violet eyes. "This stuck-up jerk presumes to tell me how to do my job. When I offered to swap, he scuttled into his comfortable hole. Coward!"

Joe grinned at the friendly attack. "Once snared by BHP, there is no hope for salvation. You made your bed, as they say, Lavinia. By the way, Mason, we heard about your deal with Post. How'd you do it?"

"Nothing to it. Both of you told me it's a poisoned chalice, but it seems to me you were afraid to tackle something really big."

Lavinia cocked an eyebrow at Joe. "Did you ever hear a bigger load of poop? Fresh caught, he feels he can rubbish us. Plain cheek."

"It's sad," Joe agreed sorrowfully. "You know what they say, my dear. The bigger they are…"

Mason laughed and filled his mug. He never saw anyone prime the percolator, but it always seemed full. Delora's magic?

"Seriously, great job, Mason," Lavinia added.

"Thanks. Now comes the hard part." He peered into her clear eyes. "You know what you offered when we first met?"

She chortled and waved him away. "No way. I'll keep my BHP job, thanks. You had your chance."

Back in his office, buoyed bantering with colleagues, he checked the stack of emails in his Inbox and culled most of them. He did not run a team that demanded constant communication. Routine administration he could do without. However, once the Post program took off, he expected to be buried in emails from every mail center Australia-wide. He'll have to set parameters and ask everybody to send operational stuff to Leola. A little unfair perhaps, and she'll find it tough at first, but he would help her organize everything. He'd been through it all himself at Etisalat and Bangkok.

A knock and Karter Kending walked in. "Morning, Mason. Got a minute?"

"Of course. Please, take a seat."

"I won't be long. I popped in to congratulate you on the Post decommissioning program. Great work. Been in Singapore the last three days and no chance to see you. Frankly, I never expected you'd wrap things up so quickly. Deakin told me about getting GS involved in the Post26 Strategy program. Largely thanks to you."

Mason looked at him in surprise. "Me?"

"You made a deep impression on Clarke and Deakin, which greatly helped improve their image of GS. They'll be a very profitable long-term account."

"I appreciate what you said, Karter, but I fear my role in all this is overstated. You and Walter laid the groundwork before I came on board."

"Whatever." The Director for Strategic Projects said and walked out, to Mason's vast amusement.

Deserved or not, he'll take the credit and bank it.

He took a long sip of coffee and leaned back into his chair. Should he visit the Dandenong Center and the Sydney West Letter Facility and see for himself what went on there? It would only be polite to show himself to the site managers. Video conference other state centers? He bit his lower lip. No, better to see them in person as well. They should see he cared about everybody, not only the two major city players. After all, he needed their cooperation much more than they needed his. Foremost, projects were about people, not technology, he reminded himself. Too many managers got dazzled by technology and their projects tanked.

He had to make sure Leola understood that. She did a great job putting together the decommissioning study, but that only required interviews, onsite inspections, and gathering data. A far cry from actually handling people, even though local center engineers would do almost all the work. She needed to be the oil that made the whole operation hum. And that, he figured, is where he came in. Leola may be his love, but professionally, she had to carry her part of the load. Part of his load was to make sure the project did not overwhelm her.

Mason spent the next two hours creating Outlook email folders for every Post letters center, did the same thing in his computer directory, added a national Issues Register, and one for each state. He then tweaked the overall Microsoft Project schedule to help him monitor everything, and reminded himself to tell Leola, if she hadn't already done so, to create schedules for each letters center, a reflection of the centers' own schedules. He could not afford to bury himself in low-level detail.

Done, he backed everything to a USB stick and shoved the thing into his pocket to upload onto his computer at Post, which he figured they would give him. He could remotely log into the GS network to run things, but under the contract, everything he did for Post belonged to them.

Around ten, ready for a refill, a knock on the door and Walter Renolds showed up.

"We're in! I got an email from Raymond Clarke with a signed contract. He'd like to see you at 11:30 to formally kick off the program. Good deal, Mason! I always knew you'd come through for us." He gave a hearty smirk and marched out, which left Mason nonplussed.

Pleased, he sat back and allowed himself a smile. *Right, things were humming.*

He reached for the phone and pressed a glowing button.

"Leola Lanaro."

"Hi there. It's Mason. In case you haven't heard, Clarke signed the decommissioning contract. Get yourself ready for some heavy-duty action, my sweet."

"I know. He told me. We need to talk, Mason."

"You don't sound happy."

"It's not about the program—"

"About you moving in with me?"

He waited for her to say something, but only heard silence.

"I'm seeing Clarke at 11:30. I'll call you when I'm done. We'll grab lunch and talk. How's that?"

"Fine."

She hung up and Mason stared at the phone. Something cold unwound in his belly and worst-case scenarios flooded his mind. Did her parents toss her out? No, she would have called if something so drastic happened. Her father won't sell her the house?

He realized stirring this around did not get him anywhere and shelved everything. She would explain it all when they met. Nevertheless, he could not dispel the feeling of impending dread, which tainted an otherwise great morning. He grabbed his mug and strode out for a top-up.

At 11:10, he walked into a brilliant crisp day and hurried toward the Uber rank a few meters up the street.

The driver pulled up at the National Post headquarters steps and Mason took them two at a time. A couple of minutes late—unexpected traffic—he hurried toward the elevators. A knock on Clarke's door, a muffled 'Come!', and he walked in, relieved to see he made it on time.

"Ah, Mason. I like people who're punctual. Grab a seat."

Mason did not want to disabuse the senior executive and sank into the comfortable gray cloth chair.

"Walter obviously gave you the news. Are you ready to start?"

A lot of finicky details still needed working out and finalized, but that would be Leola's job. Clarke only wanted the big picture view, as did Mason.

"Ready to roll."

"Good! I approved the budget and notified every letters center that we're go. HR will handle relocations and redundancies."

"Glad to hear it, Raymond. It's one headache I don't need. Will there be any trouble from the Union?"

"Terry Deakin has them sorted out. Kara, that's the girl at reception, will show you your office, get you logged in, and walk you through our timesheet system. Keep all program-related material on your computer."

"I intended to do that anyway."

"It isn't a question of confidentiality, Mason. It simply makes it easier if everything is stored on our system, able to be accessed by anyone with a need to know."

"You don't have to explain, Raymond. I'm good."

"I'll want weekly status reports. Positive stuff only. I'm not interested in any problems you might run into. Solve them. That's why you got the job."

"And the gray hairs to go with it," Mason added wryly.

Clarke laughed. "One goes with the other. Seriously, though. If you run into a showstopper at any letters center, I'll want to know."

"Of course."

"Now, some different news. The Board appointed Terry as Director for the Post26 Strategy implementation. Bastard. I expect he'll be in touch with Karter Kending. It leaves a temporary hole in my team until I slot in a replacement Head of National Letter Processing who'll oversee the decommissioning program. Whoever I appoint will not interfere in what you're doing, but you must keep him in the loop."

"I understand."

Mason *did* understand. He and Leola may be doing all the top-level work, but Post management had overall responsibility. He would not have wanted it any other way either.

Clarke stood and stuck out a hand. "Good luck and knock

'em dead."

Mason closed the door after him with a soft click and shook his head. Clarke definitely a character outside the box. He wondered if Post deliberately picked them. It did not matter. Although mindful of what went on, he could not allow Clarke's internal office politics to sidetrack him. Still, interesting that Deakin got the Post26 Strategy job, although not entirely unexpected. Mason figured they were probably not going to see much of each other anymore.

At the reception desk, Kara saw him, flashed him a smile that lit her green eyes, and hurried over. "Congratulations on your appointment, Mr. Adamov. Let me show you to your office."

"Just Mason, okay?"

She led him past occupied workstations toward the far wall with four small offices, opened the right central one, and waited for him to get in. A large floor-to-ceiling window showed the South Melbourne sprawl and the blue of Port Phillip Bay. Apart from a standard gray executive desk, computer and monitor, a telephone station, bookshelf, and adjoining garment cabinet, the sterile cubicle exuded little charm. Mason did not mind. He worked here, not moving in to stay.

"There is an info folder in the desk that explains everything about our systems you're likely to use. Let me know if you strike a problem."

"Thanks, Kara. One question. Where is the kitchenette if I want coffee?"

She grinned. "Definitely an important item. All facilities are on the other side of the floor. Is there anything else?"

"I'm good."

She closed the door and he surveyed his new kingdom. Not in the mood for serious work, he dug out his cell and pressed a Contacts icon.

"Hi, Mason," Leola answered immediately sounding a little breathless. "Where are you?"

"My little office on the eleventh floor."

"Don't complain. At least you have an office."

"Can we meet?"

"See you in the canteen in five," she replied and signed off.

He pocketed the cell and strode out.

Leola turned her head as he stepped out of the elevator and hurried toward him, visibly upset. Immediately concerned, he waited. She gave him a quick hug, grabbed his hand, and pulled him toward the canteen entrance.

"Don't say anything or I'll lose it," she choked and almost dragged him to an empty window table. She sat down, yanked a paper napkin from the dispenser, and twisted it into a knot. Eyes bright, swimming in glistening tears ready to spill, she sniffed.

He squeezed her hand. "What's going on?"

A quick dab at the eyes, she gave a sharp exhale. "It's Dad. We had a horrid fight last night."

"About moving in with me?"

"That, and the house he wants to sell me. Mom didn't like the idea of me moving out and both went off their block. He called me a whore and worse, and Mom told me I was ungrateful for all the sacrifices they made for me. They don't like you much right now. I thought I'd get kicked out on the spot. Truth be told, I wanted to leave then and there. I never saw them react so spitefully." Another sniff and dab at the eyes.

"Go home, pack, and come to my place," Mason told her firmly, her words resonating uncomfortably with his own experiences. It didn't *have* to be that hard!

Her mouth twitched. "Believe me, I'm tempted, but I want another talk with them before I do something final. Especially Dad. Things aren't that desperate yet. I hope."

"Tonight, if things do get desperate, call and I'll be right over."

Her black eyes turned opaque and she looked at him with a puzzled expression. "Why are you doing all this, Mason?"

He looked at her in genuine surprise. "You still don't know? I love you, Leola. It hurts me to see you suffering. Forget your parents. Forget the house. There is only us."

"In some ideal world perhaps, but things aren't that simple, and you know it."

He let out a long sigh and stroked her hand. "Yeah, but no matter what happens, you know there is one person who cares for you and can rely on."

"Thanks. That means a lot. I cried a lot last night. Confused, angry, disillusioned, I couldn't understand why Mom and Dad turned on me like that. I love them, but last night, they gave me lots of reasons to hate them. That's so screwed up, isn't it?"

"It's complicated. We love and respect our parents because we've always been told that's how it is, even when they hurt us, and they do. They brought us up, looked after us, and guided us through life. Naturally, we should be thankful for what they did, right? I felt grateful to my parents despite the thorns strewn along the way, but love? At most, they only deserve to be friends. In a way, we're fortunate if they're only friends."

Her eyebrows arched. "Is that Mason Adamov's troubled childhood talking?"

"A little, I guess, and I shouldn't generalize. I didn't have a very happy childhood."

"I did, mostly," she countered. "A madhouse as Dad said, and Mom loved us. So did Dad in his way. He had a lot of time for the three of us and always listened to our problems. What we all liked, neither judged too much. That's why Dad's violent reaction last night surprised me and hurt so much." Another sniff and dab.

Mason vividly recalled the encounter with his father. "Did you consider his side?" he remarked gently.

"His side? There is no side except his."

"No matter what, he deserves a little understanding."

She glared at him, eyes flashing. "Understanding? I thought

you were on my side."

"I am. Your brother Brian married and left. Then you and Despina left, and your parents were suddenly alone. Probably happy that all of you were settled, but for the first time since they married, they were alone. Even if they never said so, it hit them hard. Then you asked to come back. I'll bet your mom gushed with joy to see you."

"You know, she did. She couldn't do enough for me."

"Last night, you told them you're leaving, which shattered their fantasy having one of their kids home again where they can baby you, and it probably fueled their exaggerated reaction."

A deep furrow creased her forehead. "You're too kind to them, Mason, but you don't know them. Ever since I moved back, they've been grinding me down."

"Grinding you down how?"

"Not so subtle hints from Dad that I cannot stand on my two feet. That I'm wasteful, which I'm not. I still owe the Commonwealth on HECS loan for my bachelor's and graduate diploma, and a Post salary doesn't exactly make anyone rich. My dad paid half of it up-front, but I'm still left with a lot." She tilted her head. "Did you take out a HECS loan?"

"My parents paid for my degrees."

"They must be well off."

"Not really. They didn't want to saddle me with a hefty debt when I started to work. I took it for granted and never appreciated their sacrifice until much later. Afterward, I helped them with some investments."

"I thanked my dad for what he did, not meaning it. I suppose I just accepted the fact that he would help. Now, where was I?"

"Your dad unloading on you for everything."

"Mom is worse. She blamed me for my marriage breakup and that I didn't have children. Oh, they can be charming and witty as you saw the other night, but living with them is death by a thousand cuts. I sometimes feel they want me with them so they can chip away at me. Kind of a hobby."

Mason understood perfectly and grinned.

"The things I said about having a happy childhood? There were many good parts, especially when the three of us were little. Things changed when we became teenagers. Partly our fault as we were a little wild and rebelled against parental authority. Brian and Dad had some terrific fights, and Mom and Dad took it out on us girls. I guess that's why Brian joined the Navy to get away. He simply couldn't take it anymore. I thought my life became perfect when I married, but that turned into a disaster." Leola sniffed, dabbed at her eyes, and looked miserable. "I don't know what to do."

In a rush of warm generosity, tempted to offer to pay off her HECS loan, he refrained. She had her life organized, had a plan for her future, and if he came on too strong, she may be initially grateful, but subconsciously may see it as a threat to her independence and resent him for it, thinking she must pay him back somehow…physically. If their relationship developed toward something permanent, time to make the offer then. They would be partners, right?

He reached for her hands and squeezed. "Listen to me. Move in with me now and make a fresh start."

"You're sweet, and part of me wants to, but the other part is hoping things aren't as bad with my parents as I think they are. Despite everything, it would hurt them badly if I moved out. At the same time, I don't want to live under their constant shadow." She gave a snort. "Now I'm making excuses for them. Crazy, isn't it?"

"Not at all. Living with parents is complicated. I know. Seriously, when you get home tonight, don't be surprised if things are much calmer. They'll have a whole day to think things through and talk, and will likely accept the inevitable that you must live your own life no matter how it turns out. You shouldn't allow them to manipulate you regardless of any sentimental feelings you may have because they're your parents."

"I hope you're right. I'll simply die if I had to go through another session of acrimony. It would tip me over, but I like the idea of moving in with you."

"I'd like that too."

"When can I come over?"

"Whenever you want, but remember what I said. If your parents make life miserable—"

"I'll come running," she added with a grin.

Glad to see her perked up a little, he withdrew his hands. "Do you want to tell me about the house?"

"Dad still wants to sell me one of his places. I've seen it, and it doesn't need any fixing up. He keeps all his properties well maintained. The last tenants are out and it's ready for occupancy. The only drawback is lack of any public transport. Perhaps I shouldn't have told him, but when I said you'd give me 50K to help with the bank loan, he looked surprised, then laughed. If you could afford to give me fifty thousand, he said, you can give him twenty for his reno, and he'll sell me the house for 200K."

"A great deal, but that's blackmail, Leola," Mason told her firmly, not liking extortion in any shape.

"That's what I said. He just shrugged."

"Where's the house?"

"Keilor. It's a very nice brick veneer four-bedroom place on a small hill with a great view of the local area and city. He said he could easily get 900K for it if I didn't want it."

"He's right, but don't you see? If he can give it to you for 200K, he can afford the renovation." After a thoughtful moment, he exhaled. "Leola, I won't subsidize your father's reno. If your parents want to help you get a house, it's their business. I don't want to be dragged into it."

She looked contrite. "It's all my fault for mentioning that fifty thousand. Sorry."

"Never mind. Let's get your move done first and we'll worry about the house later."

"I can live with that."

He reached into his jacket pocket, pulled out a sealed envelope, and placed it on the table before her.

She pointed at it with a slim finger. "What's that?"

"The fifty thousand."

Her eyes went round. "You mean it?"

"I told you I'd do it."

She picked up the envelope, held it to her chest, and looked at him, eyes misty. "I don't know what to say," she choked. "I thought you were only kidding."

"For the house. Now, do you want to order something?"

Leola slipped the envelope into her purse and cleared her throat. "No, thanks. I'm too keyed up to eat anything, but a tea would be good."

Mason got her a blueberry Danish with tea and coffee for himself. She eyed the pastry and eventually began to work on it.

"So, Mr. Program Manager, What's our first step?" she queried between bites, personal problems shoved to one side, which he accepted. Some things she talked about cut too deep on a personal level.

"What would you do?" he countered.

"Confirm everybody's schedule."

"That's it. Job one."

She cocked an eye at him. "I *do* know something about project management, you know."

"I'm sure you do, beautiful. Queensland and WA didn't send you an updated version. Give them a blast and start things moving with everybody else. South Australia already pulled two of their machines offline and are talking to Cannard Engineering about disposal. Make sure you're in the loop. This is something we're supposed to manage, not the letters centers. I'll call Cannard for a national quote and schedule, which I'll follow up with a formal email, and ask them to liaise with you for everything they do."

"Fair enough. Are you going to visit any letters center?"

"We'll see them all."

"We?"

"Every center should see both of us. Arrange flights and accommodation and let me know the itinerary. Separate rooms, of course."

"Of course," Leola replied with a straight face.

Mason wagged a finger at her. "Don't start. I'll call and tell them when we're coming. I don't care whether we go to Hobart first or Adelaide. We'll do Melbourne tomorrow and jet off on Wednesday."

She grinned and gave a mock salute. "Yes, sir." Her forehead furrowed. "We won't be able to visit every center by Friday."

"Not a problem. What we cannot do this week, we'll finish next week. After all the traveling, we'll be glad to have a free weekend. You'll also be able to move in then."

"What if things don't work out with my parents?"

"Call and come tonight."

"Sounds reasonable."

"No matter what, we must focus on our job. If we don't hit a major snag, we should wrap up the whole project by end of September. Another thing. On Sunday, we'll lunch at my parents' place. They're keen to see you."

"From what you told me about them, I don't mind seeing them either."

"It's settled, then. That reminds me. Do you want to join me on my Japan tour in October?"

"I think I'll be ready for a break by then," she said with feeling.

"Great! I'll confirm the booking."

"About the project. How do I report to you?"

"I'll create a program directory in Post's database to which you'll have access. I already set up everything and I'll walk you through it. Update each state's Issues Register and your Microsoft Project files as you go. I'll take a look at them every now and then. I don't want status emails. After all," he added with a grin, "you can give me verbal updates over dinner when you move in."

She cracked a grin. "Creep."

"We won't micromanage anybody. Post engineers know what they're doing."

"They do."

"Our top priority is to coordinate decommissioning cycles to ensure floor space is available for replacement inventory Siemens is bringing in."

"Agreed. What about the people, Mason?"

"Post HR will handle it."

"I'm glad I don't have that one," she put in and sipped her tea.

"Me too," he agreed wholeheartedly. It made sense for Post to manage their staff. That's why they had a Human Resources section. "Now, how about some lunch?"

* * *

Leola sat quietly beside him, fingers locked in her lap. Not much traffic along the tree-lined road. Most people were doing their own thing at home on a pleasant Sunday morning. Bright sunshine streamed between broken clouds. Very conscious of her presence, enveloped in her favorite fragrance, Mason shot her a quick look. She turned her head and a faint smile touched her lips. They had no need for superfluous words, synchronized as they were in thought. He felt relaxed and content, not wanting anything right then. He had it all, much more than he hoped would ever happen to him. If all this turned out to be a dream, he hoped not to wake.

The car whispered in the background.

Both had a busy week. After a quick visit to the Hobart letters center, they took a flight to Adelaide and glad-handed the site manager and some of the engineers who worked with Cannard. To Perth on Thursday and Darwin the next day. A PR exercise perhaps, but in Mason's mind, a necessary one. All site managers and senior staff were pleased to see them and showed their appreciation with group dinners at exclusive restaurants.

By the time the Uber driver dropped him off in front of his house late on Friday, he rushed his shower to get ready for his dinner appointment with friends, not in the mood for a long night out, but he had not seen the guys in a while and looked forward to swapping the latest gossip.

The tram stopped at Little Bourke Street, the entrance to Chinatown brightly lit with lots of pedestrians going in and out. With late-night shopping and available entertainment that ranged from intellectual to more earthy, Friday night always attracted large crowds dressed in all sorts of gear. Mason sported black corduroy pants and a light brown leather jacket, enough to keep out the descending chill.

He walked through the Oriental Pearl entrance to a welcoming smile from a petite Chinese girl, the place packed with locals and a variety of other faces. A pervasive odor of Chinese cooking filled the noisy room decorated with traditional wallpaper images and hanging paper sphere lights. Liam Anderson saw him, thin as always, pushed up his rimless glasses, and waved.

"Hey, Mason! We thought you wouldn't make it!"

"I'm not late," he countered. "You guys are early."

"A nice evade." Logan Bernard, still a little chubby, pinched his little goatee and lifted a glass of Chinese beer. "Pull up a rock, man. Nice to see you."

Mason shook hands with Arthur Landry and the other two and dragged back a chair that almost touched the corner wall. A welcoming smile still fixed on her face, he nodded to his receptionist.

"A beer for me as well."

"So, what's been happening?" Arthur demanded. "Started your job with Global Systems?"

"Giving them a hard time."

"That figures," Logan drawled. "Always the troublemaker."

"Untrue and unfair, but considering the source, I'll let it pass."

"Hah! Still no ring on the finger, I see."

"You mean, a ring through the nose," Mason replied and the others laughed.

"If it is, it's the most comfortable one I ever had. Seriously, my boy, you ought to—"

"I know. I should get married and settle down." His beer arrived and he poured himself a glass. After a hefty swallow, he leaned forward. "Actually, there *is* someone I met at Post."

Liam slapped him on the shoulder. "Way to go, man! About time."

"That's what my old man said."

"You should have brought her over so we could check her out," Arthur said.

"This is supposed to be a boys-only night, remember?" Mason countered.

"He's afraid one of us planned to steal her," Liam replied sotto voice, peered at Mason, and shook his head sorrowfully. "As I thought. Anchors." He glanced at the others. "He's had it."

"Okay, boy, spill it. We want to know everything," Arthur demanded.

The conversation never became more intellectual, not that Mason minded. The objective of the gathering meant to forget about work, weighty world issues, and family troubles, which none of them appeared to have. At least they did not say and he never dug for it. He cared about each of them, and would help instantly without question if needed, but without deliberately inserting himself where he might not be wanted.

It felt good to catch up with everybody, swap yarns and latest gossip, and renew a long bond. Logan Bernard, always wiry and fit, put on some weight—he blamed his wife for that—which caused inevitable ribbing from everybody else. Even Arthur dropped his normal reserve and exchanged friendly banter. As the evening wore on, his Singapore noodles dish comfortable in his stomach, Mason felt glad he came. There were not many opportunities in their busy lives, families to take care of, to forget everyday little things for a while and simply have fun.

They laughed in the crowded, noisy restaurant filled with appetizing scents and harried waiters where nobody gave a damn what the four were talking about. Mason felt enriched when he left. He should definitely invite everybody to Mr. Macedon for a weekend blowout.

Afterward, he walked to Collins Street and took a tram that dropped him off along Clarendon Street a short distance from his place.

Sleep came easily that night.

The next day, on a clear, sunny, mid-afternoon Saturday, he spied a red Honda slip into the empty spot in front of his house, the resident parking tag he gave her during the week prominent on the dash. His neighbor disliked losing the spot as he handed over the tag with a wry smile, but understood why Mason wanted it, grateful he had the spot for as long as he did.

Mason opened the front door as Leola walked up and beamed. "Welcome to your new abode."

She gave him a quick kiss and pulled back from his embrace. "It feels strange doing this, you know."

"Moving in with a confirmed bachelor or not jetting around everywhere?" he teased.

"You know what I mean. It's been a long time since I lived with another man."

"You'll get used to me," he replied softly, sympathetic to her emotions, his own not entirely ordered either. Excited to have her here, he also wanted to make sure he did not startle her or drive her away by becoming possessive. She can have all the time and space she wanted to become comfortable. He also needed time to adjust to her quirks and ways of doing things, never having lived with a woman before.

"You're not running away," he pointed out. "You're moving in. A big difference."

"I suppose. Mom is still not entirely happy with this, especially Dad, but they've accepted the inevitable. They didn't chill me out, which leaves room for reconciliation."

"They prefer a daughter to visit them, rather than alienate you completely," he said and guided her inside into welcoming warmth. Although not windy, the mild breeze made the air chilly.

"I'm glad we were away on business all week," Leola said and followed him into the kitchen. "I dreaded coming home last Monday—"

"So you said."

"—but it all worked out."

"Nice of your father to sell you the house without any strings."

"That part is not over yet, Mason."

"Let's not worry about it. You're here. That's all that matters. Care for some tea?"

"I don't mind."

Later, he carried her two suitcases and smaller bags into the guest bedroom. With a mischievous smile, she told him she needed at least one more trip home to bring up everything. By late afternoon, unpacked and more or less settled in, they became domestic and cooked dinner. Nothing fancy: salad and grilled sandwiches, neither in the mood for something elaborate, especially as his mom would undoubtedly go all out tomorrow.

As the evening wore on, Mason sensed her apprehension and unease. Would he turn into a wolf and demand payment for allowing her to stay with him? He refrained from making the usual jokes, sensitive to her feelings and need for reassurance.

Around 9:30, she begged to be excused and went upstairs. Halfway up, she stopped and looked at him.

"Thank you," she murmured.

He nodded and flashed her a smile.

His tumbler of bourbon empty, tired watching world events on YouTube, around ten, he decided to retire as well. A quick shower, he slipped into bed, his thoughts preoccupied with the woman on the other side of the wall.

Eyes closed, not yet asleep, he heard the bedroom door open. She slipped into bed beside him and lay quietly on her back, her soft negligee warm on his skin. Without saying anything, he pulled her close and rested his head on her shoulder, not wanting anything else.

After some endless time, she faced him, and her arm went across his side. Then she cried softly. He kissed her forehead and held her against him. Sleep eventually blanked out everything.

Over breakfast, Leola did not say anything about the previous night. Her radiant, happy eyes spoke for her.

Mason pushed back the memories as the car whispered to him.

He slowed and turned left onto Powell Street. "Almost there."

"It's very nice here," Leola observed. "It doesn't feel like we're in the middle of the city."

"That's part of the attraction living in the eastern suburbs. Everything is old and established with an almost country feel."

"Country feel…That's it exactly, now that you mention it. The new developments are modern and tidy, but they're all somewhat sterile."

"That's why people like to live in the east, if they can afford it."

He braked, pulled into his parents' driveway, and switched off the engine. "Here we are."

Leola regarded the brick veneer house, the double garage, tall trees, and neat lawn with interest.

"Nice."

He glanced at her. "Ready?"

She gave him a small smile. "I feel as though I'm going in front of a judge."

He could not help himself and snickered at the image her words created. "Relax. It won't be that bad. Come on."

Mason escorted her to the front entrance. About to press the bell button, the door opened and his father grinned at them. They were obviously expected.

"Welcome home, son. And this must be Leola."

"It's a pleasure to meet you, Mr. Adamov," she gushed with a smile and grasped his extended hand.

"It won't be after you get to know me. Not according to Mason, and it's only Nikola, okay?"

"Are you trying to drive her off already, Dad?" Mason retorted in mock protest.

"Merely a heads-up. Come on in, you two." Nikola stepped to one side and waited for his guests to enter the lounge.

A broad smile on her face, his mom opened her arms, walked to him, and embraced him. "Good to see you again." She turned, inspected Leola with a glance, apparently liking what she saw. Without hesitation, she hugged her and planted a peck on her cheek. "I hope you will regard this as your home too, my dear."

Somewhat taken aback by the greeting, Leola nodded. "I hope so too, thank you. I see now where Mason got his unique hairstyle."

Brianna brushed the blond streak along the right side of her head. "This? Runs in the family." She stepped back and swept a hand toward Nada. "This is Nicky's mom."

Leola gave another nod. "Pleased to meet you, ma'am. Mason told me a lot about you, and I feel I already know you."

"Thank you, my dear. I'd like it if you called me Nada."

Nikola clapped his hands and pointed at the lounge chairs and two sofas. "Make yourselves comfortable. Drinks? Bourbon for you, Mason? Leola?"

"Some white wine, please."

"Crisp or mellow?"

"A chardonnay, if you have it."

"Great. Mom?"

"Amaretto for me. A small sip won't kill me," she added with a cackle.

"Brianna?"

"A chardonnay for me too."

Everybody seated and apparently comfortable, Mason felt pleased. First impressions were always important, and his family seemed to give Leola a tick. He saw Grandma looked at her, a strange expression on her face.

"I cannot put my finger on it, but you seem familiar as though we met before. Impossible, of course. In my younger days, I worked at Olex Cables in Tottenham. Our group had a nice leading hand, Sonora Lanaro, a few years younger than me. You look exactly like her, my dear."

Leola gasped and her eyes went huge. "Sonora? That's my father's mother."

This time, Nada gaped. "You're Lanaro? Well! What do you know?"

"Small world," Nikola remarked as he handed out the drinks.

"Your grandmother and I were good friends," Nada said. "The resemblance is uncanny. How is the old girl?"

"Doing well. We see each other now and then."

"I'm not sure she'll remember me, but next time you see her, please extend her my warmest greetings."

"I'll do that."

"Mason tells me you live with your parents," Brianna queried.

"I used to, but I'm with Mason now."

Mom shot him a startled look. "You never said that."

"It only happened yesterday. Long story."

"And none of my business."

"Come on, Mom! You make everything your business!"

Behind her words, he sensed judgment and a hint of disapproval. Not that he gave a damn what she or anyone else thought. Not anymore.

Something totally unexpected happened then. He felt an uncountable sense of release and freedom. The guilt, pain, frustration, longing, and need for approval he carried all his life tumbled away in a rush of liberation.

He did not give a damn...

In a startling revelation, he knew it to be true. He did not need anyone's approval except his own. Distilled to its essence, no one else could judge his actions. A generalization, of course, as others did judge his work, but on a personal level, he was accountable only to himself. All those years, he tried to please his friends because he valued them and wanted their approval. Mostly, he sought his father's acceptance. Denied, he retreated into a private world where he found pretend acceptance. Despite what he told himself, during that time, he secretly still craved his family's approval. Now, he saw his parents as ordinary people—if parents can be ordinary—not someone he should feel obligated to. Thankful for what they did for him, certainly, but without the need to translate that gratitude into a lifetime's burden.

As though someone pulled back a veil, with Leola beside him, he found his completeness, free of the ghosts that used to haunt him. The feeling left him almost giddy.

His mom pouted. "Manny!"

He blinked. "What?"

"Are you with us?"

Nikola cleared his throat. "On a different astral plane. Anyway, it's nice to see him finally settling down. We all wondered—"

Nada slapped her forehead in a gesture of irritation. "*You* wondered, Nicky!"

"You did too, Mom…" Nikola started, then his face went blank. After several seconds that seemed like an eternity, he blinked. "…but never said so. Not directly, anyway." He noted their curious expressions and blanched. "I did it again, didn't I?"

Brianna reached out and patted his arm. "It's all right, dear."

Leola turned to Mason, clearly puzzled. "Later," he told her. He needed to talk to his mom about Dad's condition.

"No matter what, Leola, we're happy to have you part of the family," Nikola declared.

"Hear, hear," everybody echoed.

Brianna hit her thighs and stood. "Let's get into the dining room and feed our guests."

"I could use a bite myself," Nikola growled, which earned him a smack on the back of the head from Brianna.

"Can I help?" Leola offered.

"I'm good, dear," Brianna shot back and disappeared into the kitchen.

Mason helped Grandma to a chair and sat next to her, with Leola beside him. Dad sat opposite him and fiddled with his bourbon tumbler.

Brianna appeared carrying a white ceramic tureen. "Chicken soup with homemade noodles. The supermarket stuff never get it right."

"My mom makes her own as well," Leola added.

"Do you cook?"

"Mom taught me and my sister well."

"Good! Then you know the way to a man's heart," she replied with a merry cackle, and everyone joined in.

"Need help with the soup, Grandma?" Mason offered. In reply, she held up her bowl.

He filled it and offered the ladle to Leola.

"Did you always work for Post?" Brianna asked.

"My only job so far. It's a good working environment. In the IT department at least. It gets pretty hectic on mail center floors."

"Their stamp and shipping prices are atrocious," Nikola declared. "I don't understand why the government doesn't do something. Post is a public company."

"They're looking at that, Dad," Mason said quietly.

"Ripping off the public, that's what they're doing," Nikola grumbled and continued to eat his soup.

In part, Mason agreed with his father and wanted to say more, but he could not violate his nondisclosure confidentiality agreement.

"What does your father do, Leola?" Brianna asked to break up an uncomfortable moment of silence.

"Real estate. Property management mainly."

"This Covid thing must have hit the sector hard," Nikola added.

"Business isn't booming, but things are slowly picking up. That's what Dad said."

"Things *are* starting to ease a little," Nikola agreed. "At least we're not seeing dictator Dan on TV every day giving us death and hospital statistics, assuring us that all those draconian restrictions are there to save us. Dick!"

"I gather you don't have much time for him," Leola added and spooned some soup.

"While he and his government are busy saving us, in the process, they destroyed countless businesses, created massive unemployment, and broke up who knows how many families." Nikola pointed a finger at her. "I tell you, the man is an outright criminal."

"Let it rest, dear," Brianna said firmly to cool his temperature. "We're supposed to be enjoying ourselves, not get gloomy."

"You're right. Sorry. No more politics."

"At least you still have a job," Mason said. "And so does Mom."

"I'd go nuts stuck in this house every day," Nikola agreed.

Brianna arched her eyebrows. "You mean, stuck with me

every day?"

Nada laughed merrily, which pleased Mason, glad to see her enjoying herself. "You walked into that one, Nicky."

"The doghouse for me tonight for sure," Nikola growled, which caused a ripple of mild laughter around the table.

Soup done, his dad helped Mom clear the table and bring in sliced meatloaf accompanied by baked potatoes, roasted vegetables, and a mixed salad. A woven basket of small rolls completed the ensemble.

Leola took a bite of meatloaf and her eyes opened wide. "I'll must get your recipe, Brianna. This is delicious."

"I'm glad you like it. Actually, it's Nada's creation."

"Something I picked up from my own mom," the frail woman said. "It used to be one of Milan's favorites."

"Mason told me about his grandfather. He must have led an exciting life."

"A scoundrel, but we loved each other deeply."

"What about your parents, Brianna? Where are they?"

"Both are still alive and living in Melbourne. They came to Australia after the war on the assisted passage program. It cost them ten pounds each! Can you believe it? They went back to London regularly to visit the family, but not anymore. It's a long way to go and the old bodies can't take it anymore."

"So, settled into your new job, son?" Nikola asked.

"I like the people at GS, Dad," Mason said, happy to dispell the blanket of moody nostalgia that threatened to settle over them. "My Post project won't be too much of a challenge, seeing how Leola will be doing all the work."

"Creep. An overworked, underpaid slave. Is that all I am?"

"There's no justice." This earned him another punch.

"You'll be good for Mason, dear," Nada put in, receptive to the connection the two had. "He needs to settle down," she said and glared at him. "If you hurt her, though, I'll put you across my knee."

Mason raised both hands in surrender. "Peace!"

"Do you still paint, Manny?" Brianna asked.

"He did an unbelievable portrait of me in oils," Leola gushed. "I never believed he could do such work."

"A waste of time for a grown man to mess with such stuff," Nikola growled.

Stung a little, Mason put down his fork. "No, you never did, Dad, but then, you didn't understand many things about me. You still don't."

Nikola straightened his imposing frame and the atmosphere became tense. Brianna looked at him, concern all over her face.

"Nicky—"

"I didn't mean anything by it, son. Paint, play a piano, fly an airplane, do whatever you want. You're a very intelligent and capable man, and I'm proud of you. I guess it's something I should have said more often. You'll have to excuse me when my mouth doesn't catch up with my brain."

Touched by this unexpected confession, Mason felt his tension ooze away, admitting that he should not be so touchy. Only a moment ago, he told himself he did not care what his dad or anybody else thought.

Skits!

He lifted his wine glass and gazed into his father's eyes. "To you, Dad. I don't understand many things about you either. I may have been slow to say it, but I do appreciate what you and Mom did for me. Looking back, I didn't exactly make things easy for you."

"Well said, son," Nikola replied with a relieved smile, and they clicked glasses. He took a sip and glanced at Leola. "Is he always this difficult?"

"I'm yet to find out," she drawled and Nikola guffawed.

"That's part of the fun living together," Nada added with a grin.

Brianna jabbed Nikola in the side. "Help me with the dishes, you ruffian. What do you like, Leola? Tea or coffee?"

"Tea for me, please."

Soon afterward, Mason smelled freshly percolated coffee. His parents served everybody, and in a finale, Brianna brought a tray of sliced walnut roll lightly sprinkled with caster sugar. He rubbed his hands in appreciation.

"I did not forget, Manny."

"Thanks, Mom," he said and turned to Leola. "Now you know my weakness. Nobody makes these things better than her."

"I can see how you're salivating to get your hands on a slice," she said, picked one up and bit into it. "Wow. This is fantastic. Moist and the filling is really creamy."

"I'll give you the recipe, dear," Brianna promised. "It's the only way to keep Mason pacified."

Leola laughed. "Thanks. I'll remember that."

Nikola served another round of whiskey, a small one for Mason. Sunday night, the cops would be on the prowl.

All too soon, the evening finished and he said his goodbyes with a promise to Grandma he would visit next weekend.

Brianna hugged Leola and brushed her cheek. "It's been lovely to meet you, my dear. I hope you'll come again soon and we can talk."

Nikola grasped Mason's hand and squeezed hard. "You found a rare one, son. Don't lose her."

"I'll try not to, Dad."

The night cold and clear, the car hummed as the heater worked. He turned onto Toorak Road and merged into the traffic.

Leola gave him a quizzical look. "Manny? Where did that come from?"

"No idea. Mom's been calling me that forever. One of her quirks."

"I kind of like it."

Both were lost in their own thoughts for a while.

Mason squinted at particularly bright bluish oncoming LED headlights, hating the things. In his view, they ought to be banned as a safety hazard.

"Your parents are wonderful," Leola remarked at length, "but Nada is a doll, though."

"She's something special, all right, and helped me over some of the rough spots with my parents. Too bad Gramps isn't around. You'd have loved him. As for my parents, we had our ups and downs."

"Back there, you had a moment—"

"With Dad? A few weeks ago, we had a terrible fight and I thought I'd never see my parents again. Gramps sorted me out and I patched things up, but I guess the wounds are still a little tender."

"Gramps sorted you out?"

"His ghost. I went to Mt. Macedon to think things through and talked to him." He noted her bemused expression and smiled. "I talked to myself, obviously. I'm well adjusted, you know."

"Of course. I won't buy the straitjacket I planned to get you for Christmas."

"Nice of you. You saw how things look on the back veranda. I sat there sipping coffee, mulling over my spat with Dad, thinking what Gramps would say. He said I should apologize. They were my words, but he could have said them. The next day, I drove to my parents' place and apologized for being a jerk, not mentioning that I thought Dad was also a jerk. It came hard, as I had a lot of accumulated emotional baggage that colored my view of them. As always, Gramps hit it right on, and I turned a new page with my father. As you've seen, the healing process still has a way to go."

Leola bit her lip. "It's true what you said about not understanding our parents. It's something I can relate to. They didn't go out of their way to make my life easier either."

"From your perspective."

"I guess. About your father. What happened back there?"

"You mean the momentary lapse? Involuntary episodes of mild narcolepsy. So far, it doesn't require treatment, but as he gets older, it probably will."

"How often does he have these episodes?"

"Mom tells me about once or twice a week."

She shook her head in wonder. "He seems to fall asleep for a few seconds."

"That's how it works," he agreed.

They reached his place, the lonely street filled with pools of light from tall poles. The garage door rumbled shut and he switched off the engine.

"It's great to visit, but there is nothing like home," he declared.

Inside, nice and warm from the automatic heating system, he sprawled onto his favorite recliner and gave a contented sigh.

"Care for a nightcap or something?" he asked her.

"Thanks, but I'll grab a shower and call it a night. We're flying off to Sydney tomorrow, remember?"

"Do you need your back soaped?"

"Creep." She laughed and fluttered her fingers at him. "'Night…Manny."

"'Night."

It looked like he'd be stuck with 'Manny'. He'll live with it.

A balloon of cognac at his side, he put on Vivaldi's *Four Seasons* and allowed his mind to sort and shelve everything that happened over the last two days. Eventually, the music ended and he made his way upstairs. A relaxing shower put him in a mellow mood and he crawled into bed. Fingers locked behind his head, he stared into blackness where the ceiling hid. After a while, he rolled over and closed his eyes.

Chapter Nine

August faded into memories of frigid days, driving rain, and icy winds Mason swore came straight off Antarctica. Trees started to show green buds and foolhardy flowers braved the frost and ventured to bloom. Overall, bearable weather charged his spiritual wellbeing, but it played only a small part. Still cold on most days, especially at dawn, frequent sunshine gradually replaced the biting chill with spells of welcomed warmth. Predominantly, Leola's presence lit his days.

During his run through Domain Park this morning, the stars hard and bright, he jogged up the Shrine of Remembrance steps and gazed at the lit city mosaic spread before him as the eastern sky turned purple, then deep red. The crisp air made his face tingle and he inhaled deeply, relishing the sensation. A solemn peace enveloped the metropolis already awake as cars flowed along its arteries that brought life to offices and industry in a promise of a great spring day. The cold eventually prompted him into action and he descended the steps.

A few days after Leola moved in, he told her of his running routine and invited her to join him. She immediately rejected such an uncouth notion, rolled over, and went back to sleep. She did not mind a brisk jog on a pleasant weekend afternoon, but shuddered at the idea of hazarding herself in cold darkness. He figured she might change her mind once the days became longer and the nights warmer, not prepared to bet either way.

That set the pattern. He had his jog, a shower, made breakfast—sometimes finding it waiting when he returned—and enjoyed each other's company until time came to catch a tram to town. She did not diet, but watched what she ate, and generally approved of his food selections, introducing several items for him to try. Her body had the ability to burn off whatever went in, an inexplicable phenomena, he decided.

Both liked to take in their early news fix and debated heatedly some issues, also accepting the other's views without rancor, sometimes laughing at the silliness and tragedy of it all. Leola had firm ideas about many things and he accepted the depth of her ranging mind, enjoying their clash of wills. All part of getting to know each other's habits and learn what it took to live together in harmony. So far, it worked.

He turned into Cobden Street and slowed down as he approached his house.

Mondays…He never understood why people moaned about starting a new week. A new dawn, day, week…an opportunity to create, contribute, experience, and grow. It should not feel like some form of punishment or drudgery. It never made any sense to him, but then, he simply had to admit that people were different. Did he see himself as the only sane person in an incomprehensible crowd? The thought made him smile.

He did not mind Mondays at all, but drew a line working on a weekend, and hardly ever did so far. To him, life reflected a composite of activities, each contributing to what made him whole, even if others thought him odd. To turn himself into a work slave meant compromising his core beliefs and objectives. There must be time to fill the soul with music, reading, painting, sit on the balcony smoking a cigar, gaze at a blazing sunset, and a myriad of other gossamer things that bound everything together. That is how he looked at it. He had seen colleagues who made work and career core pillars of existence, and it turned them into shallow, two-dimensional caricatures. In so many ways, not real individuals at all. Experts in their field, but otherwise devoid of substance. A simplification, granted.

Cannard Engineering were on schedule and old inventory slowly made way for new equipment. Melbourne and Sydney were the only sites to be completed, with Brisbane done by Friday. A week ago, a Post technician at the Sydney facility received a severe electrical shock when he touched open leads with a standard screwdriver without first disconnecting power. The Communication Workers Union rep immediately stopped all work and put a boycott on the site, demanded a check of all electrical equipment and compensation for the injured technician. Processing of letters stopped and Operational Health and Safety stepped in to investigate the incident. It did not take long to sort out the mess. The technician received a reprimand for violating procedure and the Union rep a third HR warning for being a known troublemaker, and Post fired him. Surprisingly, the Union made only a token protest. It seemed they were not overly enamored with the guy either. The mail floor elected a new rep and everybody went back to work. Strike action meant no pay and nobody wanted that. No apology from the Union for shutting down the site for two days and setting back Mason's schedule. Par for the course.

He sent a diplomatic email to Cannard, with a CC to every letters center manager, requesting they remind everybody working on any machine to review safety procedures. Thankfully, nothing else soured his coffee. He should be pleased at the overall progress, and did derive a measure of satisfaction to have the project humming, with ample credit to Leola in his reports to Clarke. Positive feedback from Post to GS made Renolds smile at him during weekly status meetings.

On the same day the Post technician had his snafu, Mason received a general email announcing the appointment of Murray Lloyd, former Sydney West Letter Facility manager, as Head of National Letter Processing. Only mildly curious, Mason wondered why Raymond Clarke took this long to make the appointment. According to Leola and the Post rumor grinder, Lloyd surprised many senior managers who eyed the position for themselves. Always ferreting out the juicy stuff, Leola told him Lloyd divorced a year ago in an acrimonious settlement where his wife retained custody of two children—boy and a girl—and their house. A case of loving his job more than wife and family. Anxious to put the grim episode behind him, Lloyd welcomed a move to Melbourne headquarters. So they said.

Only a week on the job and still coming to speed with Post's national environment, decommission old equipment to usher in new Siemens Flats Sorter Machines, Lloyd left the Union fubar to his program manager. Mason kept him in the loop with email updates, but never received a response. He met the taciturn, reserved man when he visited the facility with Leola early in August, and liked his quiet, efficient approach to doing business. He expected to be summoned for a fireside chat quite soon for a verbal update on the decommissioning program. In all respects, Lloyd should have no complaints.

The Post job a professional success, Mason saw dark clouds massing on his personal horizon, which no amount of sunshine could disperse. They did not dump on him yet, but the portents looked grim. No mystery where they came from just when he thought life with Leola started to settle into some normalcy. Normal as could be living with a woman he still to fathom. Why the hell couldn't parents stop meddling!

She even shared his bed now, although not every encounter an intimate one. Both were happy simply to be close, talk quietly into the small hours, midnight coffee in bed, or simply enjoy each other's physical presence without wanting anything else. In some ways, Mason found this familiarity far more personal and satisfying. At times, weary from work, wanting some personal space, he did not begrudge her sleeping in her room. As the days unwound, he slowly learned more about this wondrous woman. Conversely, she learned about him, but he spared her the painful parts. She could read between the lines in the same way he inferred some unpleasant episodes in her life, neither prepared to bare their soul completely just yet. There were adjustments, such as not running into the bathroom naked, making sure he did not use her towel or toothbrush, prowl around the kitchen in underwear, not minding that she failed to wipe the washbasin or kitchen sink after use, something that initially irritated him…a list of many small things he guessed she also had to adjust to.

Last night around nine, his mom called.

Leola sat beside him, legs curled under her, supple and comfortable as only a woman can be in such a position. He figured they must have rubber bones. A glass bowl of freshly made popcorn at her side, they watched a colorized version of *Teacher's Pet* with Clark Gable and Doris Day, something she pulled out of his varied DVD collection. Not into modern action thrillers full of silly car chases, shootouts, and shallow dialogue—she did enjoy, as did he, Keanu Reeves' first *John Wick* movie, simply because it had a good story, although it did contain some overcooked action sequences. Leola held up the Gable DVD and made a sassy remark about his ancient tastes. His manhood challenged, he dared her to watch it. Eyebrows arched, challenge accepted, she slipped the DVD into the player. As the movie unfolded, her giggles validated his taste in old films—some of them—happy to see her totally absorbed.

His cell went off and he frowned when he saw the caller name. What could she want at this time of night?

"Hi, Mom, What's up?"

"I hope I'm not interrupting anything, dear."

"Not at all. Leola and I are watching a movie."

"Can we talk?"

"A moment," he said and glanced at Leola. "Be a minute."

She nodded without turning away from the screen. He got up, padded into the kitchen, and pulled back a breakfast stool.

"So, how are things with you and Dad?"

"We're fine. And you?"

"More or less settled in with Leola."

"You should bring her over again, Manny. She's a charming girl."

"We will. Work keeps us pretty busy and we cherish our weekends doing things together."

"Been to Mt. Macedon lately?"

"We planned an outing for yesterday, but something came up. We visited Grandma instead since she wasn't spending the weekend with you."

"She told me. It's nice of you to keep in touch with her, Manny."

"Next to you, she's my favorite girl."

His mom laughed, and he pictured her radiant face as she smoothed back the blond strip of hair.

"Even Leola?"

"That's different, Mom."

She sighed and he waited. "You like her a lot. I can tell."

"Mom, don't push. You did it to me with Aliana—"

"You were a silly young man who didn't recognize a good woman when you had her," she retorted sharply.

"She used me. I thought I loved her, and I admit to being a little silly, but not for the reasons you think."

"Manny—"

"Ever since we had that dinner at your place, you've been calling, forcing Leola on me. I love her and I like to think she loves me, but it's far too early to talk about an engagement or something. We only met."

"She's living with you. That must mean something. Love is not on a schedule, dear, and you're not getting younger either."

"She's living with me because her parents' nagging drove her away in the same way you and Dad drove me away."

"Manny!"

Mason bit his lip with chagrin and winced. "Look, Mom. I'm sorry. I didn't mean that, but I don't like your interference in my life."

"I only want what's best for you. There's no reason to be snotty about it."

"I said I was sorry! I know you mean well and you want a bunch of grandchildren running around your house—"

"That has nothing to do with it. It is simply time you settled down and had a family. Look at your friends. Each with kids and happy."

"And I'm pleased for them, but there is no note in my calendar that says it's the day I'm getting married. This needs to work out in its own good time, Mom."

"There's never a perfect time to get married, Manny. If I waited until I knew everything about Nikola, I'd still be a maid. Part of the magic of marriage is getting to know each other."

"I realize that, and I'm getting to know Leola, but I'm not a twenty-something driven by hormones and mere physical desire. I'm a grown man and she's a mature, complex woman. Getting married is an important step that requires serious deliberation before we commit ourselves to something else."

"Pfui! You're talking like marriage is one of your projects subject to analysis and planning. It isn't. Sometimes you must make a leap of faith. When you marry, you don't get a certificate that love is forever. It's a package you unwrap over time. You can be happy for a while, but love can fade and even disappear, and one day, you find you're living with a stranger."

"Is that what happened to you and Dad?" Mason blurted out. This time, he did not regret the words as a cascade of memories came flooding. Memories of silent evenings they spent with only the TV for company, Dad anxious to return to his frigate, and later, burying himself at Thompson Engineering, with Mom crying at night, and Mason making his own company in his room.

The silence dragged and he wondered if he overstepped the line.

"It did happen, Manny, and there were days I wanted to leave him, but we talked it through and remained together after we realized why we married. It worked out. There will be such days for you and Leola, but they should not be the reason not to marry."

"What we have now is good enough."

"You need to be responsible and do the right thing by her. If you don't commit, she'll see that you're only using her and she'll leave. You'll be alone again, embittered, and filled with regrets. I don't want to see you like that."

Mason sighed, not in the mood to launch into a personal counseling argument.

"Mom, I appreciate your concern and desire to see me happy. I'm happy now, and Leola made me happy. Let's see what happens. Just don't push. She's getting the same thing from her parents and I don't need all your extra baggage in our relationship."

"Her parents are urging her to marry? I didn't know that."

"No reason why you should. I don't want you or Dad or them in bed with us. When we decide to take the next step, you'll be the first to know."

"Okay, Manny. I won't belabor the point. It's only—"

"I know. Say hi to Dad. 'Night."

"Good night, dear."

He switched off, refilled his cognac balloon, and sat beside Leola. She saw his dark countenance and switched off the movie.

"I heard snippets of what went on. One-sided, of course. Care to talk about it?"

He did not care to talk about it, his feelings scraped a little raw, tempted to go straight to bed and put the whole thing into one of the 'open at own peril' drawers. He took a sip of cognac, faced her, and gave a small smile.

"It's Mom."

"I gathered that."

"She's trying to get us married off. I know she means well, but I resent manipulation, and she's very good at it. After all, she practiced it on me all my life."

Leola chewed some popcorn. "Dad's the same. He doesn't like me living in sin, as he calls it. What rankles is his hypocrisy. He'd be quite happy to see me live in sin if you gave him that 20K. When he calls, he doesn't let me forget that you're rich and can afford it. Mom is worse in a way, urging me not to let such a wealthy catch through my fingers."

Mason laughed. "Is that all they see? My muscular bank account?"

"I'm oversimplifying, but—"

"In a way, I can understand their attitude—"

"That's the boy genius talking…Manny."

He grinned. "I guess I'm making excuses for them. Parents want to see their children taken care of. However, along the way, they can be the causal factor why couples never get together."

"Like us?" she murmured, eye bright.

He took her hand and stroked it. "You made a courageous decision to move in with me. After all, we hardly knew each other. We still don't, but I like what I learned so far. It showed you trusted me and cared for me in the same way I care for you, my blossoming spring flower. I did not betray that trust and never will." He lifted her hand to his lips and kissed it. "Every day you're with me, in some impossible, inexplicable way, you are more beautiful, radiant, and mysterious. A package I want to open. I never want to let you go and I will love you forever."

She stroked his cheek. "Nothing is forever, my romantic prince."

"You will be for me," he said gruffly and reached for her. She slid into his arms and the kiss became hot and steamy. Eventually, she pulled back, her face firm with resolve.

"Show me a little bit of that forever."

Without a word, he led her upstairs, his mom the last thing on his mind.

That happened to be yesterday.

Pleasantly warm and a little sweaty from his run, Mason opened the front door and sighed with satisfaction at the wave of heat that came from inside.

"That you, Mason?" Leola called from the kitchen.

"Expecting someone else?" he demanded.

"You know how it is. A new man in bed every day, but don't worry. You won't bump into any of them. They're all on a tight schedule," she remarked offhandedly, nibbling a piece of toast. She reached for the TV remote to kill the ABC *Breakfast* feed.

He sat on a stool and looked at her. "There's room for only one man in this house, and I'm it. Got that?"

"The rest will be shattered."

A chuckle escaped him as he picked up a piece of toast. "Tough cookies. Anything interesting on the news on this gorgeous September 12 morning? Not as gorgeous as you, my ray of sunshine."

"Not much. They buried the Queen—"

Mason groaned. "Charles will be our king? Gods! We should definitely become a republic."

"Ukrainian forces regained control of the Kharkiv region—"

"Another ungodly mess of West's making. What else?"

Leola shrugged. "Nothing much. Unless you want your dose of Covid death stats for the day."

"Spare me! Slept well?"

Her eyes radiated inner fire. "Wonderfully well, especially after the workout you gave me last night. You were particularly energetic, not that I minded," she added hastily.

"You were a bit of a tiger yourself," he shot back, the memories bright in his mind.

"I know why we were both so energized. For me, it felt akin to catharsis purging my parents."

"Me too, but most of all, I couldn't get enough of you."

"Horny old goat. We better have breakfast before we start something we won't be able to finish."

"I'll finish it," he growled and made a grab for her hand. She squealed and pulled back.

"Creep!"

He stood, walked around the bench, and gathered her in his arms. His eyes bored into her fathomless black depths.

"I love you, Leola Lanaro, and that's all there is to it."

"I know. The toast—"

"Is that all I'm getting?"

She ran her fingers through his hair. "It's more than you deserve, you lecher. Groper too," she crooned.

He kissed her hard, then playfully slapped her firm behind. "I need a cold shower." Her merry laugh followed him up the stairs.

***

He hardly had time to sit down and power up the computer when the phone jangled.

"Mason Adamov."

"Hi, Mason. It's Van in Sydney," answered the seemingly always cheerful head of Cannard's engineering team. Except this time, he did not sound cheerful.

"You're going to unload something bad on me. I can tell."

"Sorry to sour your Monday this early—"

"Others are standing in line to do it to me."

"—but this is something where I need your input."

"Couldn't Leola Lanaro handle it?"

"Probably, but you'll catch shit if this bombs out."

"Talk to me, Van, while I still have a sense of humor."

"According to our schedule, Siemens were supposed to deliver three Flat Sorters on Wednesday."

"Don't tell me. The shipment is running late."

"I wish. The thing is, the machines are already here. Post has three semis in the parking lot and Siemens engineers are sipping coffee waiting for somebody—me—to tell them where to put them. I wanted to tell them where to put them, all right."

Mason laughed, picturing Van tearing out his hair in frustration. "Your problem is that the old sorters are still on the floor."

"You got it. They wouldn't be if it weren't for that Union rep snafu. It cost us two days. The thing is, Siemens informed Sanderson, the new site manager, of the early shipment three days ago, but the bastard forgot to tell me, and now, he's on my case asking me what I'm going to do about it. He knows Post cannot afford to let those Siemens engineers twiddle their thumbs. Strictly speaking, commissioning new sorters is his problem, including any flow-on with late or early deliveries. However—"

"Since Siemens cannot do anything until you clear away the old sorters, this makes it my problem," Mason finished for him.

"That's about the size of it, and Sanderson is looking for a scapegoat for an issue he created. If we worked two twelve-hour shifts, my boys can have the three old sorters in pieces by tomorrow afternoon, but not removed. It's not like picking up one of those things with a forklift. Sorry, Mason. It's the best I can do. There are no extra people to throw at this. Everybody else is either in Melbourne or Brisbane."

Mason visualized the decommissioning schedule for the two sites and saw a possible out. "There's a two-day slack window in Brisbane. Bring your gang to Sydney to expedite removal of the three sorters."

"Mmm. That should work. They won't like it much, though. Today and tomorrow are supposed to be their RDOs."

"Pay them double time. My authority. I'll send you an email to that effect. As you said, we cannot have Siemens sit on their hands. Leola Lanaro will arrange accommodation for your men."

"Don't worry about that, Mason. I'll take care of it. This still doesn't solve my problem, you know."

"Sure it does. You have four men in Brisbane? If they fly out within the next two hours, they'll be at your site by noon. With ten engineers all told, plus your regular Post people, you should be able to unplug two sorters by end of the day. There's no hurry with the third one. Better still, ask Sanderson to give you extra Post engineers. That way, you won't need your Brisbane gang."

"It won't work, Mason. We're already using everybody on site here. Keep in mind, while we're moving out the old sorters, the Siemens people will still be standing around doing nothing."

"They won't be. You said the new sorters are still in the trucks. Tell them to start unloading and unpacking. That'll take two or three hours per truck. In the meantime, you can unplug one old sorter and move it somewhere temporarily to clear a footprint for the new machine. It takes Siemens two days to plug in a new sorter and start testing. Once your new men arrive, you'll have enough resources to shift another sorter to some corner where you can disassemble them at your leisure. Siemens and Sanderson won't be able to complain that you held them back. If everything works out, your men can still have their RDO tomorrow. The priority is to clear floor space for Siemens."

"Sounds good, Mason. Leave it with me. I'll kick this around with Sanderson and Siemens engineers. This could have been a major fubar, you know."

"Keep me and Lanaro in the loop, Van," Mason said and hung up. He glanced at the empty mug on his desk with longing and touched a glowing preset button on his phone station.

"Hi, Mason. Lonely without me already?" Leola chirped.

"You know it. There is a small situation in Sydney," he said and quickly filled her in. "Keep an eye on things over there, okay?"

"And Lloyd? He's sure to hear about this."

"Leave him to me. See you at lunch."

"Bye," she replied and hung up.

He quickly composed an email to Van and sent it off, wrote another one to Lloyd, then reached for the mug to fuel, hoping for a dull day.

The list of emails alarming in its length, coffee beside the keyboard, Mason scanned the subject text to see which email to look at. Despite group calls and emails to all Post letters center managers to send routine stuff to Leola, he still received unwanted CCs and day-to-day stuff. Culling junk took up time he could otherwise spend on the national schedule and Issues Register. As each letters center decommissioned its sorters, his email list shrank, but too many still slipped through from Sydney and Melbourne, the largest. While at it, he updated his Issues Register with the latest event.

He sighed and kept plowing, deleting as he went. That's why they paid him the big bucks.

Without a knock, the door opened and Lloyd marched in.

"I got off the phone with Brisbane. They tell me you want to pull Cannard's men off the site. This will push back their decommissioning schedule, not something I want."

"I sent you an email that explains everything, Murray."

"Explain it now."

"Fine. Siemens delivered three new sorters early to the Sydney center. Cannard didn't have the men to decommission all the old machines to allow Siemens do their work, so I told Cannard to bring in their Brisbane engineers."

"What about the schedule?"

"There won't be any impact on Brisbane. Cannard isn't due to resume work there until Wednesday, which leaves plenty of time for his men to get back from Sydney."

"This wasn't a decision for you to make."

Mason gave Lloyd a hard stare, not looking for a confrontation. "As Program Manager, this fell within my area of responsibility. I couldn't have Cannard and Siemens wondering what to do while Post had a leisurely chat with everybody groping for a decision. The situation is contained with minimal impact on Post."

"This isn't over yet," Lloyd growled and stomped out.

"I'm sure it's not," Mason muttered to a closed door and sipped his coffee.

The new Head of National Letter Processing had to be kept in the loop, but he did not need to be involved with minor issues, which Mason considered this one to be. It could have turned into something more problematic, but the action steps he gave Van felt right. Anyway, if Lloyd wants to chew ass, he should do it to Sanderson who created the situation.

His cell went off and Mason's eyebrows climbed when he saw the caller name.

"Hi, Walt. What can I do for you?"

"If you got some time, come down to the office."

Mason quickly reviewed his to-do list and decided that Leola could handle everything.

"I'll be there in twenty minutes." Tempted to ask for details, he refrained and hung up. If Renolds wanted him to know something, he would have told him right away.

A hasty gulp of coffee, he dragged on his overcoat, powered down the computer, and walked out, the Sydney thing pushed into the background.

The Uber drive to Global Systems uneventful, he absently watched other cars, pedestrians, clattering trams, and shop windows. The sun shone from a clear sky and made everything cheerful.

Delora beamed when he walked in. "Hello stranger. I thought you left us."

"Still serving out my sentence," he told her as he strode toward Renolds' office, her laugh in his wake. He knocked and opened the door when he heard a muffled 'Come in'.

"Ah, Mason. Take a seat."

Karter Kending smiled and nodded. "Giving Post a hard time?"

"Every day," Mason replied, removed his overcoat, and sat down.

"We'll try not to keep you too long," the Director of Infrastructure Projects remarked with a grin.

"Not a problem, Walt. I'm not exactly overworked right now."

"So you said last Wednesday at our status meeting. That's what we want to talk to you about."

"You said that from this week, you'll be at Post on Mondays and Thursdays only," Kending put in.

"That's right. The Brisbane site will be finished by Friday or Monday at the latest, which leaves Melbourne and Sydney. Both will be wrapped up by end of month. Clarke knows about the change in my working days."

"Two weeks ahead of your original schedule," Kending remarked evenly. "Raymond had some nice things to say about how you handled the decommissioning program."

"Thanks, Karter. I appreciate that."

Kending raised a hand. "Thank Clarke, but then, Walt and I always thought you were an asset at GS. You have a background we wanted: systems design, project management, infrastructure implementation, and strategic planning. Your work in the United Arab Emirates and Bangkok amply demonstrated those skills. That's why we recruited you. However, your work at National Post established your attributes as a strategist, planner, and thinker.

"Walt here may not agree with me, although infrastructure projects are valuable revenue streams, our strategic planning work generates most of our earnings, and we face stiff competition from the likes of IBM, KPMG, Deloitte, and others. A broad generalization, I admit, and I'm not telling you anything new, but their business model is to ingratiate themselves into an organization's management structure with the objective to eventually dictate policy to garner future business. We differentiate ourselves by providing clients with clear-cut, unbiased analyses and recommendations. Not used to getting unvarnished reports, some of our past clients couldn't make us out since we didn't fall into the standard mold. They came around eventually, and word-of-mouth advertising allowed us to slowly expand our market footprint. That's what you did with Clarke and Deakin, and they liked it. Because of that, I want to steal you away from Walt."

Mason sat back. "Excuse me?"

"You heard me. You've hardly been with us two months, but your performance proves that your career path isn't in infrastructure. I want you in my department full time, and so does Terry Deakin. You know that Post appointed him to implement their Post26 Strategy program and he asked for you. You already possess good knowledge of that program, and the work will give you a leg up on how we handle strategic stuff. What do you say?"

Mason smiled. "Do I have a choice?"

"Not really."

"I appreciate your vote of confidence, Karter." Mason turned to Renolds. "I hope this won't be a source of conflict, Walt. After all, you brought me into Global Systems to run infrastructure projects."

"I brought you in to be an asset for GS," Renolds remarked evenly. "Don't worry, Mason. I'll find somebody else."

Kending glanced at Walters. "Lavinia will make a good principal consultant for you. It'll broaden her skillset by doing infrastructure work and she's almost done at BHP."

"Not a bad idea. Let's talk about it later."

"Murray Lloyd already knows that you'll be working for Deakin," Kending added with a glance at Mason. "Keep him in the loop with your decommissioning thing anyway."

"Although I don't report to him, I'm already giving him status summaries."

"Good! Don't worry about the budget side of your work, and you don't need to put in any timesheets. Deakin is funding everything. I expect to see you here tomorrow and I'll lay out what you'll be doing for the Post26 Strategy project."

About to tell him of his little spat with Lloyd, Mason restrained himself. Karter and Walt did not have a need to know or cared how he managed his work. All they cared about were results, which is as it should be. Anyway, he doubted that anything would come out of it even if Lloyd cried on Clarke's lap. The Head of Parcel, Post and Products also only cared about results. Still, Mason did not want to make Lloyd an enemy and planned to smooth things out with him.

"If there is any additional material I need to see—"

"I'll send you a directory link. By the way, Deakin said you can keep your current office."

On the way back to Post, he dragged out his cell. "Everything okay in Sydney?" he asked Leola.

"Since nobody called, I'm taking it that things are fine."

"We need to be on top of this," he told her. "Call Van and get an update. He needs to know we're in his corner. If you didn't already, call Sanderson. The site manager may also need his hand held."

"I'll do it right away."

He heard her sniff and immediately became concerned. "Are you all right?"

"Dad rang and got stuck into me again."

Skits!

"Look, I'll call you as soon as I'm in the office and we'll talk. Ten minutes tops."

"This is so awful, Mason," she moaned, barely in control of herself.

"Hang in there. We'll hash this out as soon as I get in."

Why now, when things looked good with Leola?

The Uber barely stopped and he scrambled out, raced up the entrance steps and through the lobby, and jabbed the elevator button. A sharp *ting* and the doors slid back with what appeared maddening slowness. He touched the ID card to the sensor, mashed his finger against the eleventh floor button, and bit his lip.

Kara waved, but he did not see her as he hurried to his office. He opened the door and froze. Leola looked up from the visitor chair, eyes raw from crying, jumped up, hugged him, and wept softly.

He kissed the top of her head and held her. "Let it out," he murmured. He hated to see a woman cry. It generated so many conflicting emotions: helplessness, an overwhelming desire to hold and protect her, take the pain she felt onto himself, anger at whatever reduced her to this state, and a desire to lash out.

It took a few minutes for her to settle down. She eventually pulled back from his embrace and dabbed at her eyes with a tissue. He steered her to a chair and sat beside her, one hand in his.

"I thought I had it covered with Dad," she murmured miserably. "Apparently not. When he called, it started off amicably enough. Then it started!" Her eyes flashed fire. "Did I sleep in my own room and called me an ungrateful slut. They brought me up right, and now, I brought shame on them. He said Mom shunned her friends, afraid to face the scandal I created, and accused me of being selfish. If I had any shred of decency, he said, I should come home and you would court me as proper gentlemen do. He unloaded lots more besides. Totally shattered, I hung up on him. He rang back, but I refused to pick up." Bright red spots colored her cheeks as she stood and paced. She stopped and looked at him. "I'm not bad, am I?" Tears rolled down her cheeks. "Oh, Mason, what am I going to do?"

"I'll take care of it," he told her firmly, picturing his fist smashing into Renzo's face.

"I'm so sorry for all this."

"Don't be. Go home—our home—and take a long, hot bath. A tumbler of bourbon will help you relax," he added.

She tried a brave little smile, but it did not quite come off. "Only if you share the bath with me."

"Glad to, but I need to sort this out with your dad first."

"What are you going to do?"

He stood, expression grim. "I'll go and see him right now and end this."

She gripped his forearm. "Don't provoke him. In his state, he's liable to do anything."

"So am I. If he doesn't lay off, I *will* provoke him. Your parents have no right to boss you, and it's time to draw the line."

"I shouldn't have moved in with you," she moaned in anguish.

Startled by her admission, he looked hard at her. "Do you regret it?"

Her black eyes regarded him without blinking. "Not for one minute. It's just—"

He patted her hand. "I know. You also want to keep your parents onside, but it must be on your terms, not theirs."

"What if they don't want to see me anymore?"

"Don't work yourself into a state over hypotheticals. We have to deal with the situation as it is now. Go home, okay?"

She nodded and exhaled loudly. "This isn't how I expected things to happen."

He squeezed her hand and walked out. Something else he must take care of first...

Mason knocked on the door, heard a sharp 'Come!' and walked in. Lloyd looked up in surprise.

"Got a minute, Murray?" He sensed the man's reserve, but this had to be done.

"What's on your mind?" the tone brusque and hostile.

Mason looked at the man, puzzled. Why should Lloyd bear a grudge? As an executive responsible for the entire Australian mail processing system, he should be above petty personal grudges.

"I want to apologize if I appeared to come on a little strong back there, and I hope we can make a fresh start."

Lloyd bit his lip and sat back. His desk neat and tidy, everything in place, he picked up a pen and fiddled with it, perhaps unconsciously.

"I appreciate this, Mason. On reflection, I should be the one to apologize. You were doing your job and I had no business muscling in. You contained the situation."

Mason relaxed a little, unable to read what went on behind those brown eyes. Glad, though, that Lloyd appeared to bear him no ill will.

"Damn it! Things piled up on me lately and I guess I took it out on you. You heard the rumors," Lloyd went on. "A mixture of exaggeration and misinformed gossip. No matter. Clarke's appointment caught me off-guard, never figuring I had a chance given the competition. However, now that I'm here, despite obvious commercial challenges, I intend to make letter processing efficient nationwide. In part, thanks to you. Post dragged its butt for years babysitting old equipment, which cost us millions in upkeep and parts procurement. You showed everybody what positive action can accomplish, which, by the way, earned you some enmity from a number of people who wanted to maintain the status quo. Ignore them. Keep doing what you're doing and I hope you'll be as successful working with Deakin on his Post26 Strategy program."

Mason raised an eyebrow, and Lloyd gave a mirthless smile.

"I'm also connected to the grapevine." He stood and extended a hand. "My door is always open if you need anything."

They shook hands and Mason nodded. "Thanks, Murray."

Downstairs, as he waited for his Uber, Mason wrestled with an unsettling thought. Something he did not want to dwell on, but the nagging little voice at the back of his head kept gnawing at him.

He understood and accepted that Leola may be upset after the first reactionary round with her father. A normal response from anyone, he told himself. Her behavior in his office bothered him, though. A grown woman, not some flighty teenager, he expected more resolve from her and a degree of ability to handle her parents. She had conflicts with them before and said as much. Her apparent helplessness to stand up for herself, reduced to an emotional wreck, not something he expected. A character flaw or him overanalyzing? Still, it bothered him.

To him, her conflict represented a simple scenario. Then again, to her, perhaps not so simple.

'If you're so smart, moj mali stroj, why didn't you resolve the situation with your dad?'

Gramp's voice echoed in his head and Mason sighed.

"Easy to be analytical and judgmental when it's someone else's problem, eh, Gramps?" Mason muttered as the Uber stopped at the curb.

Ti banac.

Mason gazed at the stately old brick veneer residence, not looking for a confrontation, but not prepared to let the situation fester. He told the driver to wait and climbed out, not expecting the coming encounter to last long. Then again…

Quick stride up the driveway brought him to the front door and he pressed the blue chime button. Hurried footsteps came from inside and Martina gaped.

"Mrs. Lanaro, I need to speak to you and your husband."

"Who is it?" Renzo's throaty bellow came from the lounge.

"It's Mason."

Renzo appeared and stopped in the doorway. "What do you want?" Dark eyes impenetrable, stance openly antagonistic.

Mason did not expect this to go down well. "It's about you and Leola. Both of you."

"It's none of your business how I handle my daughter," Renzo grated.

"It became my business when I fell in love with her."

"Forcing her to live with you so she can be your plaything is your version of love?"

Martina pulled at his arm, but he shrugged her off.

"She made her choice willingly, but you're too blinded by your prejudices to see that. You're now exacting revenge for her behavior by demeaning her. Apart from being your daughter, she's an individual who deserves respect."

"She lost my respect the moment she abandoned her family to live as a whore."

Mason realized his words meant nothing to Renzo. "Very well. I'll put it this way. If you call Leola again, I'll get an Apprehended Violence Order issued against you."

Renzo went pale and prodded Mason on the chest. "Get the fuck out of my sight, you scumbag! Next time I see you, I'll rearrange your teeth! You'll never have her! I'll see to it," he hissed and slammed the door.

"But you'll forget your indignation if I pay you twenty thousand, eh?" Mason shouted. Scratch everything he thought he liked about the man.

"Fuck you!" came a muffled reply.

Mason shook his head and walked down the path to the waiting Uber. The driver must have heard the exchange, but his face remained expressionless.

"Back to Post," Mason told him and buckled up.

That could have played out better at so many levels, he reflected as the car accelerated down the quiet street.

'Your diplomatic skills could use some adjustment, boy,' Gramps announced cheerfully.

Perhaps, but Mason did not crawl to anyone, especially an asshole like Renzo.

'Proves my point.'

Skits!

Time to take this up to the next level.

Perhaps Mom had it right when she said love had no schedule.

The driver pulled away and the car whispered down the street.

According to the weather guys, he should expect a balmy nineteen degrees with clear skies. So far, they were on track. Everything else in his life, personal and professional, should also be on track. It would be if it were not for two giant blowflies in his stew—his mom and Leola's father. They said opposites attract. Perhaps he should get Renzo and his mom in the same room and slug it out once and for all. It also saved time repeating himself.

He moved into his St. Kilda bedsitter as soon as he financially could to get away from his parents, thinking it solved everything. It did some things, but it also shelved others, as the encounter with his dad in July so poignantly demonstrated.

You cannot live with them, and you can't shoot them. At least, he wasn't supposed to. Polite society kind of frowned on that, but there were moments on some days…

He had it sorted out with Dad, to his vast relief—his fault in part. Mom's hints that he should get married were taken as inconsequential banter mothers indulged in. Now, her psychological war manual open in earnest, she started her filing down campaign. He had enough brains to see that. However, it did not take a high IQ to recognize the moves. Even if he wanted to punch her on the nose to vent frustration as he could with Renzo to get some peace of mind from her nagging, he might be forced to tell her bluntly to stay out of his life. It would hurt her, and he would get his peace, but at what price?

'What do you think, Gramps?'

'Talk to Nada, boy, and get a woman's perspective,' came the immediate reply.

Mason chewed his bottom lip and mulled over the words. Perhaps not such a bad idea at all. He had raw intelligence to spare, but his grandmother had worldly experience, a treasure beyond price.

'*Do it now,*' Gramps added, which answered Mason's unspoken question.

Decision made, he leaned forward. "Take me to the Terniary Aged Care facility in Hawthorn."

"You got it!"

The Uber rolled into the visitor's parking lot and Mason climbed out. At the reception desk, Evana looked up in surprise.

"Mason! This is unexpected. Is anything wrong?"

"Nothing's wrong. I just need to speak to Grandma." She could see he held something back, but she did not have to know.

"She's in her room."

"Thanks," he said with a nod and strode down the corridor.

He knocked, and a moment later, the door opened. Nada's eyes grew large and her face broke into an angelic smile of welcome.

"Mason! What brings you over here, dear? Not that I don't want to see you, of course. Has something happened?" She grabbed his arm and pulled him into the lounge. "I'm having some tea. Care for a cup?"

"Thanks, Grandma, but not now."

She sat down and waited for him to pull up a chair. "Tell me what's wrong."

"Why does something have to be wrong to see you?"

Her eyebrows arched. "A Monday, and in the middle of the day? I wasn't born under a rock, you know."

He gave a loud exhale. "I'm in a bit of a mess," he blurted, figuring his dejected expression said it all.

"I can see." She raised a hand. "You and Leola are doing fine, but her parents and Brianna started to work on both of you." She saw his bewildered gape and laughed.

"Easy enough to figure out, my boy. I know, because my parents did exactly the same thing to me. Too young to marry, they said. Only eighteen, what did I know of love? If you're determined to marry, pick a respectable Party member who'll provide for you and give you security. Milan is a nice enough young man, but he has nothing to offer you. What about love, I told them. *Love won't keep you warm on cold nights, my daughter*, Dad used to say, always practical."

Mason looked at this frail old creature in wonder. She could be reading his thoughts, never mind the details.

"Mom isn't that bad," he said, "but she never lets up, always grinding me down."

"That can be the worst kind of pain, and you know what to do," Nada said firmly. "Apply those smarts of yours."

He smiled. "Tell her to buzz off, is that it? Politely, of course."

"Of course. If you keep taking it in silence, it will only encourage her. Same with Leola's parents. Here, though, it is something she must resolve herself. Support her, but you must be careful not to overstep the line by interfering."

Mason winced. "Ouch. I just had a falling out with her father."

"What did you do?"

"I went to see him and told him to stop badgering Leola. It didn't end well."

Grandma patted his knee. "You shouldn't have gone there, but I understand why you did it."

"I alienated Leola's parents even further," he concluded remorsefully.

"You wanted to protect her, but you did yourself a disservice."

"You mean, she may be grateful for my help, but also resent me for butting in?"

"I'm afraid so."

"She asked me to help her, and I told her I would see her father."

"My dear Manny. When a woman asks for help, most of the time, she's only looking for emotional support and someone to lean on. We *do* know how to take care of ourselves…most of the time," Nada added with a chuckle.

"So, what do I do?"

"Tell Leola everything and leave the rest to her. She'll either kiss you or be angry."

"And if she's angry?"

His grandmother shrugged. "Then she's angry. Either way, you must not be masculine and take charge. Leave her space to handle this herself. What you *can* do is be there for her. We women are complicated creatures often driven by symbolism, emotion, and hormones. Fire and thunder at one moment, tenderness and warmth the next. Every man since time started had to learn this and live with it. Women, on the other hand, want support, not dominance or control. An occasional dose of both at the right time can do wonders, though. Any relationship, especially a marriage, must be a partnership. You and Leola have only begun, which makes the rules doubly important if yours is to last."

Mason sighed and shook his head. Some genius he turned out to be, not able to see the obvious despite all the books he read.

"You're very wise, Grandma, and I'm sorry to unload this on you."

"Bah! You kids live in a different world, and my attempt to give you what I think is sage advice may be hollow ramblings from an old woman."

"A woman with a lifetime of troubles behind her…and solutions," he added with a grin.

"There were some good times along the way as well, my boy. You want to stick around for lunch? We're having roasted chicken with all the trimmings."

He stood. "I must get back to Post. I'm in dereliction of duty as it is by coming here instead of sitting at my desk pretending to be doing something to earn my princely salary."

"Nonsense! You showed responsibility and a firm grasp of what is important to you and Leola."

"Thanks, Grandma. Gotta run." He kissed her cheek and headed for the door.

"Will you be at Nicky's place this weekend? I'll be visiting."

Mason stopped in his tracks and turned. "How about all of you come to Mt. Macedon? I'll bring Leola and we'll have the place to ourselves. It's been a while since you were there and the fresh air will do you good."

She looked wistful. "It *has* been a while and I confess to missing the place. It's a wonderful idea, dear. I'll talk it over with Nicky."

"Even if they can't bring you, I can come and pick you up."

"I'll let you know."

He grabbed the door handle and paused. "About Dad's narcolepsy—"

She waved him to silence. "Nothing to worry about."

"Has Mom mentioned anything to you about his prostate?"

"Everything appears all right for now, and thanks for asking." She motioned with her hand to go. "Bye, my boy."

"Bye, Grandma. Love you."

At the facility's entrance, he booked an Uber and waited for the sun to warm his smiling face. Grandma…Like Gramps, always knew the right thing to say.

He pulled out the cell and tapped a Contacts icon.

"Mason! Where are you?" Leola replied breathlessly.

"On my way back to Post. And you?"

"At work. Dad called—"

"I can imagine what he said," he growled and felt his face heat.

"When you said you'd take care of him, I didn't expect you to start a war. It only made things worse for me."

"I didn't start anything, and I'm sorry if I added to your bag of troubles, but I will not stand by and let him bully you. If you want me to keep my distance, tell me. I'll carry a towel on my shoulder you can cry on whenever you feel like it."

She laughed, and Mason cracked a grin.

"Creep. We need to talk."

"I figured as much. I'll be in the office in twenty minutes."

"This is better done tonight at home. I'd love to chat now, but I'm a working girl with responsibilities."

"Hah! Tonight, then. Talking about work—"

"I called Van and Sanderson, and the situation is under control. Sanderson managed to find two extra engineers and Van didn't have to bring down his men from Brisbane. Siemens are unloading their machines and everybody is happy."

"Good work, Leola."

"Somebody must run this project. Should I email Lloyd with an update?"

"No," Mason said immediately. "He doesn't need to be involved with details. If he wants a status check, he can talk to Sanderson."

"I guess. See you tonight."

"No lunch?"

"I'm in the middle of something with my AI thing. Lunch will be a sandwich on the run." She paused for a second. "I may be a little late getting home."

"Oh?"

"I need to talk to my parents to see if we can patch things up."

He did not like it, but understood, Grandma's words loud in his mind. He approved of her resolve to face her issues, but feared what the outcome might do to her emotionally if Renzo exploded. In adversity, the spirit grows, he reminded himself. She must fight her own battles if she is to grow.

"Don't take any crap off them, okay?"

"Bye."

The line went dead and he stared at the phone for a second, then shoved it into his pocket. His Uber slid to a stop and he climbed in.

Back in the office, he checked the email Inbox, culled several dead messages, and opened the Issues Register, now almost cleared, not so when the program started. Strictly speaking, many items the letters center considered critical enough to demand his attention, Leola could have handled them. With his help, it only took a week or so before she recognized what items sent to him and CC'd to her, belonged in her bag. After all, Cannard Engineering had done decommissioning and disposal for Post before and knew what they were doing. It took time to educate Post people what the project manager must see and what Mason should deal with.

A quick update of his timesheet and he had everything pretty much wrapped up for the day. A glance at the computer clock said 2:34 pm. He powered down and headed down to the cafeteria. A hot turkey sandwich and a bottle of apple juice to take away silenced inner growls of dissent.

Snack done, a mug of coffee warm between his hands, Mason gazed absently out the window, not actually seeing the stark city sprawl. He had some hard thinking to do. He did not charge this moment of introspection to Post, he reminded his conscience and got a snicker in return.

Talking to himself, talking to Gramps, a ghost, he wondered what a mind bender would make out of his pretzel psyche if he spilled everything. None of anybody's damn business anyway. He had not slipped any of his cams, yet.

In his high school chemistry classes, he saw how a supersaturated solution instantly turned into a web of spreading clear or colored crystals with addition of a single drop. It never ceased to amaze him, although the process not complicated at all. Perhaps not, but still visually stunning.

That is where he found himself now—in a supersaturated state. One little push and he would have his magic crystal—Leola. To his chagrin, he found himself unable to make that final step, and it bothered him. Could he be genuinely irresponsible as Mom suggested? Happy enough to enjoy living with Leola and all the pleasant side benefits the relationship produced, but unwilling to commit?

Skits!

He committed to her every day.

His inner self tittered.

Mason sat there and his eyes roamed the skyline. He turned that gaze inward, spread everything, and had a hard, brutal look at himself, and what he wanted in life. Particularly, what he wanted with Leola in his life.

At the end of his self-examination, the drop fell and the supersaturated solution crystalized. The plunge into the unknown a little daunting, he also experienced a thrill of anticipation. This would cut the floor from under everybody and shut them up for good, he reflected comfortably.

Decision made, suffused with a warm feeling, he grabbed his overcoat and strode toward the elevators with a wave to Evana. Downstairs, he flagged an Uber at the rank and asked to be driven to the Bourke Street Mall. As with the other strictly personal trips today, he did not use his Global Systems credit card.

The precious item safely in his pocket, he took a tram home and prepared things for her return.

The casserole on a gentle simmer, garlic bread kept warm in the oven, dishes laid out, blue candles ready to be lit—he intended the evening to be special—Mason sat in his favorite recliner, a glass of heavy Shiraz in hand. Meyerbeer's *Les Patineurs* filled the lounge with a medley of short pieces. The wall clock said 7:16 pm.

Tonight, nothing would divert him from his objective regardless of what transpired between Leola and her father. He smiled as he pictured the look on her face when he confronted her. Pow, right in the kisser.

Another glance at the clock and he frowned. What kept her anyway?

The front door opened and his heart beat a little faster. Control, he told himself firmly. It worked, up to a point. He quickly turned off the CD player.

Leola walked in, threw her handbag on the couch, and flashed him a small smile. Mason stood and beamed.

"You took the scenic route home?"

"I went to see my parents as I told you—"

He lifted a finger. "Let's have dinner first and dissect your visit later. There's a casserole on the burner. One of my specialties. Unless you already had dinner?"

"Just soup Mom laid out."

"Great. You want anything to drink?"

She glanced at his glass. "Whatever you're having. It's the night for it."

"Your visit that good, eh? Wash up and we'll tackle the world later."

She nodded, picked up her handbag, and made her way up the stairs. She did not look agitated or emotional, but whatever took place with her parents left a visible toll.

He upped the oven to heat up the garlic bread, laid out the casserole, and lit the candles in time for her to come down and take a seat. He poured her a glass and she immediately took two deep gulps.

"Wow," he remarked with raised eyebrows.

She shrugged. "Rebuilding my defenses," she said and glanced at the candles. "What's this?"

"Something to put you in the mood."

"In the mood for what?" She immediately raised a hand. "Never mind." She sniffed the casserole and filled her plate.

He brought out the garlic bread and pried open the foil. A pleasant aroma wafted up with the steam, He took a slice, filled his plate, and nodded to her.

"Bon appetite."

She took a spoonful of casserole and pursed her mouth in appreciation. "Mmm, tasty. It looks like you've been paying attention to your mother."

"Afraid not. It's all self-taught. When I moved out, I learned to cook or starved, not much into pizza and fast-food stuff. Although I did indulge once in a while."

The meal done, coffee served for him and tea for her, a tiramisu for dessert bought at a cake shop on Clarendon Street, Mason filled himself a tumbler of bourbon. He took a sip.

"So…"

She understood what he meant.

"When I showed up, I thought Dad would slam the door in my face. That's when Mom surprised me. She ignored him and pulled me in. My heart raced fast enough to burst. I could have lost it all then and there, tempted to throw myself at their mercy in contrition for being a bad girl. Something held me back. I wasn't mean or bad, my inner voice insisted, and I should not knuckle under. I'm twenty-eight and I know what I want."

Mason sat and listened, glad to see this side of her character. He always suspected she possessed this inner strength. Her emotional outbursts? Perhaps she felt she could unburden herself to him without judgment. The fact that he did judge made him a little ashamed. He should not have doubted her, but he too had his all too human frailties.

"Mom brought out the soup to ease the tension and I could have hugged her for understanding. Next came the gnocchi and meatballs, and they looked yummy, but I couldn't eat anything else. Too keyed up." A puzzled expression crossed her face.

"Then she said something strange. Something I never heard before. She told me how her parents reacted when she wanted to marry. Fresh out of university, still living with his parents, he had nothing to give her, they said. Mom didn't listen, of course. Mom twenty at the time, carefree, quick to make a decision, love in her eyes, she didn't listen to a word they said. The practical side of getting married the farthest thing from her mind. Oh, she and Dad discussed it in passing, but Mom would not be swayed.

Leola looked hard at Mason. "She said her parents tried everything to dissuade her from a rash marriage. At least take time to think about it. Mom looked at me and a tear slid down her cheek. Now, she said, we're doing the same thing to you. That's when I too became teary. Dad sat there in silence, a heavy scowl on his face, but judging by his look, Mom's words hit him hard. I couldn't make him out. Finally, I asked him to say something, anything.

"He focused on me and called me a fool for throwing myself at you. Apparently, how they raised me meant nothing. Mom countered by saying he was unfair, but he silenced her. He didn't approve that I lived with you like a common slut, but if that's how I wanted to be, he wouldn't stand in my way." Leola's eyes misted. "Then he said he won't sell me the house.

"He also kept bugging me about that 20K he wants from you. I told him it wouldn't happen, but he kept chipping away. He does the same thing to his prospective clients. Grinds them down until he wears out their resistance. It makes him a good real estate salesman, but I hated it when he did it to us kids. That's how he got Mum to go out with him," she added with a smile. "Anyway, that pretty much ended it for me and I left. This is such a total disaster," she moaned.

Mason recalled Grandma's words and marveled. It seemed that every parent's objective in life revolved around controlling their children. He grabbed her hands and smiled.

"Look at it this way. At least they didn't kick you out. You left willingly. The house? Forget it. You already have a house here with me."

"As your kept woman," she snapped, then winced. "I'm so sorry. I didn't mean it."

The time ripe, he reached into his pocket, opened the small red velvet box, and held it to her. She gasped and color drained from her face.

"Not kept, but a partner, companion, lover, and friend forever…as my wife. Will you marry me, Leola, the only sunshine in my life?"

"My goodness." Color suffused her cheeks. She stood, walked around the table, and kissed him hard.

"Is that a 'Yes'?" he mumbled against her lips.

She gurgled happily and ruffled his hair. "Yes."

"In that case…" He took her left hand and slid the ring onto her finger. "It's official."

She splayed her fingers and held the ring to the light. "Probably only ten bucks, but it's the thought that counts, so they say," she teased, a mischievous look in her eyes.

"I'm not a rich guy, you know," he cautioned her, "regardless of the scurrilous rumors your parents are spreading."

"I'll settle for what you have," she whispered into his ear and kissed him again. After a timeless moment, she returned to her seat, reached for the glass, and drained the wine.

He held up the bottle. "More?"

She shook her head, her fathomless eyes bright. "It'll spoil the surprise package I have for you."

"A package I cannot wait to open."

"Creep."

He sipped his bourbon, face serious. "You know, this solves everything, for us and our parents. Nobody can complain now that we're living in sin."

"I hope so. Dad—"

"Forget him. Forget everything, my sweet. We have each other and there is only the now."

She examined the ring. "What brought this on? Not that I mind," she added in haste.

"I boiled everything down and looked at the fundamentals. Your dad's opposition, house, my mom's whining, you unhappy, which made me unhappy, and I realized that none of those things mattered. I'm not saying we should alienate our parents, but what matters is that we love each other. Not as juveniles driven by hormones, but as two serious people who had life throw us some curves. Wait for some illusory perfect moment to marry? That moment might never come, or we may not recognize it when it does. I don't know about you, but I wanted more from our relationship than mutual cohabitation, pleasant as it is."

She smiled. "Ah, you're such a romantic, but I'm glad you took the plunge. I started to wonder if you would, tired of my parents and everything. We'll make this work…Manny. You made me so happy, I could cry. One thing. What do you think about having an engagement party?"

"An engagement party? I'm glad you mentioned that, my sweet, because I don't want one. We can have one if you mind is set on it."

She seemed to hesitate, then nodded. "I can do without it."

"We can have a night out with your friends if you like, and I'll show you off to mine."

"I do have two friends, but not really close ones anymore. We were all in high school, but kind of drifted apart when I went to RMIT. We meet every now and then to keep in touch, and there's no one at Post enough I want to invite."

"In that case, we'll settle for an evening with my three friends. They're all nuts, but you'll like them. We met when I started at RMIT and managed to stay together."

"Married?"

"With kids."

Leola chewed her bottom lip. "You know, my parents will probably raise a fuss over the party."

"So could mine, but it's our decision."

Not sure he should bring this up, mindful of Grandma's words about instant death of his relationship if he deceived Leola in any way, he took the plunge. He had not deceived her exactly, the decision made before he proposed, but he had proposed, and she should know.

"I need to tell you something. Two weeks ago, I took out a loan for a hundred thousand and bought some shares."

Her eyebrows climbed. "Does that mean you *are* rich?"

He shrugged. "Not hurting."

"A little money in the bank is always nice to have. Thanks for telling me." She stood and reached for his hand. "Time to open my present."

Her hand in his, serenely happy, Mason walked with her up the stairs.

The doorbell rang and he exchanged a glance with Leola.

"Beats me."

"Leola!" came a throaty bellow.

She gasped and placed both palms against her mouth. "Oh no!"

"Come out or I'll smash this door!"

Mason's sense of wellbeing and peace shattered, the prospect of a ruined evening cast a bleak cloud over his countenance.

"Wait here," he told her and made his way down the stairs.

Loud bangs came from the door. Mason unlocked and looked calmly at Renzo.

"Mr. Lanaro—"

"Where is she?" Renzo demanded and tried to push past. Mason held him back with an open hand, the reek of alcohol strong on the man's breath.

A gray Camry, lights on, engine running, stood parked beside Leola's red Honda.

"Daddy…" Leola stopped beside Mason, stricken with grief.

Renzo tried to grab her hand. "You're coming with me right now, young lady. Enough is enough."

Mason took a step forward, which forced Renzo to back off. "She *is* home."

"You'll never have her, you devil's spawn!" Renzo screeched and threw a punch.

Mason blocked the clumsy attempt and stood face to face with him. "You're drunk! Get out of here before I call the cops."

Renzo shook his fist and retreated down the path. "This is not the end of it. If you want cops, I'll bring 'em!"

"Dad! We're engaged!" Leola shouted in desperation.

In his drunken stupor, Renzo did not hear her, or the words failed to penetrate. He stumbled around the car, got in, and the Camry tore down the street.

The porch light opposite came on and Mason's neighbor came out. "Is everything all right there?"

Mason waved and closed the door after him. A nice guy, his neighbor did not have to know everything that went on. Leola fought to control her emotions, and her tragic look ripped his soul. The battle lost, she clung to him and sobbed. He held her tight and gently stroked her back, not saying anything. What could he say in such a moment anyway?

She pulled back after a time, sniffed, and wiped her glistening cheeks with an impatient flick of a finger.

"Damn the man!" she hissed.

Anger had replaced anguish and he approved. She had a lot to be angry about, but she could do herself a lot of harm if she sank into a depressive state.

"That's my girl," he told her gently and kissed her forehead.

"He didn't hear anything I said!" she replied in wonder, eyes large in surprise.

"He's obviously carrying a large chip from my visit and wanted to lash out. Half drunk, it didn't help things. He'll calm down eventually and we'll sort things out tomorrow." He tugged at her hand. "Let's go upstairs."

"I don't feel—"

He smiled tenderly and brushed her cheek. "You, here, now, is the best possible present I could hope to have. All I want is you beside me."

Her eyes turned deep black. "I cannot believe we found each other," she murmured huskily. "You're such a wonderful man. Nuts at times, but wonderful," she added and her cheek dimpled.

Mason heard a car pull up and a door banged. A moment later, the doorbell went off.

"It looks like the fates are determined to sour our night," he groused and walked to the door.

Renzo stood there, hair disheveled, but he held himself straight. He saw Leola and blinked hard. Whatever feelings raged inside him, he kept them under control.

"You're engaged?" he remarked, voice hoarse and deep, and cleared his throat.

Leola took a step toward him and extended her arm. He seemed to gaze at the ring for an eternity. He cleared his throat again and opened his arms. Leola let out a cry and embraced him.

"Oh, Daddy…"

"My daughter. I've been such a fool," he mumbled into her hair. "Can you ever forgive me?"

She kissed his cheek and hugged him. "You can be such a dick sometimes, you know."

"I know," Renzo said and held her at arm's length. "You're engaged," he repeated, not quite believing it. He turned to Mason. "Mr. Adamov, I said some terrible things—"

Mason raised his hand. "There's no need to apologize. I understand it all."

"I wish I did, but I must say this. I've been selfish, pigheaded, and judgmental. I'm sorry for that," he said gruffly and held out his hand.

Mason took it and they shook. "Care to come in?"

"No, no, thank you. Some other time." Renzo turned to Leola and his mouth twitched. "Your mother will be so pleased." He walked quickly to his car and drove off, trailing white vapor in his wake.

Looking ecstatically happy, Leola pulled Mason inside and jumped up and down with glee. Happy to see her happy, he swung her around, then squeezed her against him.

"Oh, Mason. This is so good!" Breathing a little hard, she gazed into his eyes. "He must have heard what I said after all."

"But in his agitated condition, it didn't register."

"He came back," she said and shook her head, unable to believe it, then gave a little squeal and hugged him again. "Maybe we could open my present after all," she cooed suggestively.

Tempted to call his parents and tell them the news, he decided it would keep.

Chapter Ten

The next morning in the kitchenette, Mason bumped into Lavinia Stroud. Her blonde hair cascaded down her back and swayed as she moved. A navy blue sweater and pants replaced her usual black attire. Violet eyes cut into him and she slowly tilted her head.

"My, my. You move fast, Mason."

"How's that?" he asked, coffee carafe in hand.

"The poisonous Post study done in two weeks and you're still alive, the decommissioning thing almost mopped up, and you had me transferred to Walt." She winced and looked sorrowful. "What did I ever do to you?"

He placed his mug on the bench and raised a hand. "I had nothing to do with it!"

"Camel poop. How did you do it?"

"Honestly, Lavinia—"

She laughed, which made her face shine. "Don't be so literal-minded. Actually, I don't mind a change. BHP wore me out. Besides, Karter doesn't need two principal consultants—yet. With the Post26 Strategy, though, he will if Post gives us more business."

"I'm glad you're taking it so well," Mason said vastly relieved. It worried him a little yesterday how she felt about the move, considering it a demotion perhaps.

"How are you and Leola Lanaro getting on?" she remarked casually and sipped her tea.

He goggled at her, and she chortled at his incredulous expression. "My dear man, everybody at National Post knows you've been hitting on her, and so does everyone here. You can thank Turner for that."

"I'll clip his ears!" he growled, then guffawed at the humor of it all. "It shows?"

"Your tongue must be worn raw dragging it on the floor whenever she's around."

He admitted the remark had a lot of truth. "For your information, snoopy nose, Leola and I are doing fine. As a matter of fact, I proposed to her last night." He saw no harm saying it, as everything would come out soon enough.

Lavinia beamed. "Way to go! Congratulations."

"Thanks."

"She must be very special to trap someone like you."

His eyebrows rose. "Someone like me?"

"A geek. A very nice geek, mind you."

"Considering the source, I'm not offended. But, yes, she's very special."

"I'm glad for you, Mason. Don't forget me when you send out the wedding invitations." She fluttered her fingers and undulated her perfumed body toward her office.

Wedding invitations? The engagement just happened, for crying out loud! Then again, he and Leola should talk about it. He pictured his parents and her parents taking charge and winced. He hoped the reception would not turn into one of those Italian functions with hundreds of guests he never met. Traditionally, the bride's parents paid for everything, and he would need to look into that.

Stop this crap! He and Leola haven't even set a date. Should they? He bit his lower lip. No rush, he decided. They both needed to get used to the idea first.

Skits!

Mug in hand, he walked to Kending's office and knocked.

"Come!"

The Director smiled and waved at a chair. "Relax."

"I spoke to Lavinia—"

"She'll give Walt a few more gray hairs," Kending said comfortably, his blue eyes friendly. "She gave me enough of them," he added and leaned forward. "Did you read the notes I sent you?" A high achiever, he expected everybody else around him to keep pace.

"This morning," Mason replied and took a sip of coffee. "I'm surprised Deakin wants me to do this."

"Why should you be surprised?"

"Post has enough senior people—"

"You know the ins and outs, and your decommissioning study report reflects that. You proposed sale of redundant Post buildings, creating shopping center outlets, and stamp price reduction, among other things. What he wants from GS is a tactical plan to implement our recommendations, with cost and revenue breakdowns he can show the Board. They think he's nuts he ever entertained doing this, but since they allowed him to push the idea, they're willing to see what we come up with. They're not dumb, Mason. The Post Board knows that mail service is a profit bleeder and they want hard options to minimize the drain. I can't do everything. I'll have my hands full with other aspects of the Post26 Strategy program." Kending gave him a hard look.

"One thing. Your report to Clarke had a missing section. I didn't mention it before and neither did Walt. Given what you'll be doing for Deakin, I want to know your reasons for leaving it out."

"A judgment call, Karter. My original suggestions were controversial enough. The idea that National Post should provide customers with a free email service to replace physical letters may have caused Deakin to question my sanity."

"I questioned your sanity! That's why I'm glad you left it out."

"I could not risk getting Terry distracted by the idea, which would jeopardize acceptance of my report, potentially compromising our chances to get the account."

"You could have discussed it with me first," Kending pointed out.

"Should I have?"

Kending snorted and shook his head. "No, you didn't, because I reached he same conclusion you did. However, now that you're in it, do you seriously want to consider this option?"

"Definitely, but not right away. Most people have a computer at home and probably an email system. All businesses certainly do. The only reason Post sends out physical mail is that some customers don't own a computer."

"Or they simply like getting a letter."

"Perhaps. Because many people do use email, that accounts for the bleed in physical letter volumes. However, there are probably hundreds of thousands out there who don't have a computer. Their kids likely own one as most schools now insist students have some kind of laptop, or the customer doesn't have any kids. Lots of reasons why someone may not own a computer. However, parents may not be too keen to use their kid's computer as an email platform. There are things they don't want them to see. Besides, a kid at school limits access during the day."

"Don't tell me. You want Post to buy people computers and give them email access?"

"That's it. Look at some ballpark figures. You can get a cheap laptop for $600. Let's say half a million customers, that's $300 million. For such a large order, Post would get a hefty discount. Maybe even fifty percent."

"Anything is possible. What about connection and modem costs?"

"Say, eighty dollars for a modem, less discount, gives you an additional twenty million once-off investment. For around $170 million, National Post could be saving themselves a truckload in annual labor costs, letter sorting machines—"

"They just invested six hundred million in new sorters!"

"Which should last them twenty years. By then, I'll bet you anything, physical letters will no longer exist. Apart from equipment, letters processing is a direct cost that cannot be depreciated. What income they get from postage stamps is a token drop in the bucket. The future, Karter, is in electronic mail, not in more efficient letter sorters or distributed postal outlets. The savings Post will generate by going electronic can be invested into more effective and competitive parcel handling processes. Deakin will kiss your feet."

Kending laughed. "If he doesn't throw you out of his office first when he reads your proposals."

"Look, even though this is not in the Post26 Strategy paper, someone at Post must have thought about it."

"Agreed, and tossed it out!"

"I'll crunch the numbers and give Terry a presentation he won't be able to refute."

"If one exists, why not ask him for a report on the idea?"

"I will, but after he reads my draft. I want a fresh look at the concept myself."

Kending sighed. "You know, of course, even if he buys it, this could be political dynamite internally. Lots of letters center managers will fight to keep their empires, as will the Union."

Mason shrugged. "Nobody likes change. Remember what you told me yesterday? 'We differentiate ourselves by providing clients with clear-cut, unbiased analyses and recommendations.'"

"What if this invites putting our heads on the chopping block? Like it or not, Global Systems is a business and we need paying clients to survive." Kending raised a hand. "I'm not saying we compromise our business practices for the dollar. There are enough outfits out there already doing it. Make sure you present both sides of the equation equally without injecting personal bias toward a preferred solution you happen to like."

"You can trust me to do that, Karter."

"Fine, run with it. Turner can data mine for you if you want. Deakin wants to see you at two this afternoon. For God's sake, don't mention this email thing! Not now anyway."

Mason grinned. "I don't want my head chopped off either."

Kending waved a hand. "Go away. You've already given me extra gray hairs, and it's only day one. Jesus!"

In his office, Karter's comments sharp in his mind, he thought his ideas were sound, but would Post's business model support them? Just because something made sense and ought to be implemented did not mean it would be. Any business, especially a huge corporation such as Post, was not a logical or rational entity. Fallible, biased, career driven people ran the business who worked to primarily benefit themselves. Job tenure, climbing the corporate power ladder, and everything the doors of ambition opened constituted behavioral drivers. Anything that threatened those objectives, they destroyed ruthlessly. Along the way, all those things also helped a business to grow. A kind of perpetual treadmill.

What were Terry Deakin's buttons? He manipulated the system to get the Post26 Strategy program. Now that he had it, what drove him?

When he presented his decommissioning study to him and Clarke, they were receptive to change. Or merely humoring him, knowing his ideas would never get traction? They *had* some traction or Deakin would not waste time looking at them.

At his desk, he reached for the phone and pressed a glowing preset number button.

"Terry Deakin."

"Morning, Terry. It's Mason."

"Ah, the prodigy. You rang to thank me for dragging you into my new empire?"

"Not exactly. However, the job does give me an opportunity to cause more waves of consternation."

"That'll be right. What can I do for you?" Deakin asked briskly, a busy executive giving an external consultant a generous amount of his time.

"I need information on the part you're having me do, Terry. A data miner is doing the heavy lifting for me, but if you could give me a name of one of your database experts who knows where things are stashed, I'd greatly appreciate it."

"I'll text you."

"Thanks. See you at two," Mason said and the line went dead. He pressed another button.

"Scott Turner."

"It's Mason. My office if you have a minute."

"Your wish is my command."

Within seconds, a knock, and Turner walked in. He exhaled and plopped his lanky frame onto a visitor's chair.

"I'm working on the Post26 program with Karter," Mason said.

"I heard."

"Is there anything you don't know what's going on around here?"

Turner shrugged. "I keep my eyes open and ears to the floor."

"Figures. I want you to dig out my Post decommissioning study report and read the sections that deal with reduction of stamp prices, selloff of underutilized postal offices, and relocating services to shopping centers and malls." His cell gave a beep and Mason frowned. Message from Deakin.

"Once you're familiar with what I'm doing, I need you to do some serious data harvesting. I want stats on letter volumes processed by outer suburban and country offices. Number of employees, salary costs, number of post offices, everything. Find out how many people Australia-wide don't have an email or Internet service. Major telcos and the National Broadband Network Co can give you the numbers. Everything for the last ten years."

"A lot of this stuff could be confidential," Turner pointed out.

"You signed the non-disclosure confidentiality agreement, then it shouldn't be a problem. You do a good job on this and I'll give you a red star in your report book."

"Wow. Definitely something to fight for," Turner replied with a skeletal grin.

Mason opened Deakin's message and held up the screen to Turner. "Take a shot of this. It's your contact at Post who'll help you get the data I want."

Turner dug out his phone and snapped a picture. "What's my timeframe?" he asked and immediately raised a hand. "Silly question. Will yesterday do?"

"Out," Mason told him with a grin.

Alone again, he looked at his cellphone, made a decision, and tapped an icon in his Contacts list. It took three rings.

"Manny, nice to hear from you, dear," his mom answered cheerfully. "You caught me between classes. Why the call? Not that I mind hearing from you."

No use dragging this… "Last night, I proposed to Leola."

His mom gave a squeal. "That's wonderful, dear. I couldn't be happier for you. Did you set the date?"

"Not yet."

"Well, there's no rush. Your father will be over the Moon. Can you give me Leola's number? I want to congratulate and welcome her to the family."

Mason saw no harm in it. "I'll text it to you."

"You *must* bring her over this Sunday for lunch."

"Actually, I thought we should all get together at Mt. Macedon. Grandma likes the idea."

"Does she know about the engagement?"

"Not yet."

"I'll fill her in, including the outing. We haven't been there in a while and Nada will enjoy he trip. When did you plan to go up?"

"This Saturday. You guys can bring Grandma, or I can pick her up, and we'll spend the weekend. If you want to leave early, I can take Grandma home on Sunday."

"Let me talk it over with Nicky and Nada."

"Got to go back to work, Mom. Say hi to Dad for me."

"Will do. Bye, dear. You made me so happy."

Mason smiled, hung up, then shot her a quick text.

Another call to make…

"Mason! I was about to ring you," Leola gushed. "You'll never guess what happened."

"My curiosity is aroused."

"Dad called this morning and apologized again for last night. Then get this. He asked me to come to the Dominion office and bring my check for that fifty thousand you gave me. That house in Keilor I mentioned? I own it now!"

"That's fast. How did you do it?"

"When I came to his office, he laid out papers and asked me to sign. One a contract of sale, and the other a loan agreement with the Dominion Group. No bank loan! The Group paid Dad two hundred thousand and I would pay them 150—at no interest! Can you believe it?"

"I'm thrilled for you, Leola. Your father turned out to be very generous."

"The really good part, the Dominion Group will help me rent the place, keep an eye on the tenants, and the rent will cover my repayments. This is the best, Mason! Just when I think I have my parents figured out, they go and do the damnedest thing."

"Yeah, I know. You can tell me all about it over lunch."

"No lunch, I'm afraid. I'm a working girl."

"We'll celebrate tonight, then. I spoke to Mom about our engagement and gave her your number. I hope you don't mind. She wants to congratulate you personally."

"No reason why she shouldn't have my number."

"Another thing. I'm arranging an outing to Mt. Macedon for this weekend. My parents and Grandma are coming. With everything that happened last night, I forgot to mention it to you."

"Sounds nice and I could use a break. They're running me ragged with this AI project. It's all exciting stuff, mind you, but it gets intense."

"Pace yourself. Trust your people to do their job and don't micromanage. You're a manager, not one of them."

"I know, and I keep telling myself that."

"Not to worry. Love you."

"I thought of something, Mason. If we're going out, I could invite my parents. Let everybody get to know each other. What do you think?"

"Not a bad idea."

"By the way. I spoke to my grandparents about the engagement. They're all happy for me."

"So am I."

"Creep."

"Did you tell them there'll be no party?"

"I did. They don't mind as long as we invite them to the wedding. I wish my parents were that reasonable."

"See you tonight."

He placed the cell on the desk, leaned back, and smiled.

Ti banac.

Leola had a house…

When Renzo wants to get something done, it appeared he wasted no time doing it.

Genuinely happy for her, he sat back deep in thought. Different elements in his life had come together, piled up in a mound he had to make sure did not bury him, personal and professional. The decommissioning program near completion, he must not allow himself to become slack or distracted. When the last sorter left Sydney and the final report handed to Clarke, only then could he totally focus on the new Post study. Along the way, he would gather information, slot everything into an appropriate memory drawer, and let his mind slowly start the analysis process, identify risks, threats, market competition factors, advantages and disadvantages, and potential public reaction to his proposals. Equally important, he must interpret and gauge National Post's reaction and receptiveness. Who would lose the most career-wise? What resistance could he expect? Some people would help, others hinder, and others would fight him once everybody figured out what his study meant for them. Each must be identified and the tactics defined how to handle them.

Should he even care about the internal machinations, or leave that to Deakin who probably had that under his wing? He knew what Post wanted. The Post26 Strategy paper told him, albeit in vague, general terms. They sought to rationalize letter pricing and delivery and update their retail network. Every one of those objectives fell within the sphere of his study. He'll wade in, hash out every component with Deakin, and see what happens. That's what they paid him for.

His eidetic memory gave him a tremendous advantage—and he used it—by giving him the ability to recall anything and everything by wishing for it. However, it did not provide answers. Those, he had to hammer out himself with the use of standard strategic planning methodologies, procedures, and analysis tools. He might be a genius, but he could easily falter if he did not know the mechanics of his job.

At their first meeting, Lavinia Stroud said, 'Always satisfy the client.'

He may not like the political aspects of his study, but at the level he now played, he would be remiss if he failed to be cognizant of them. Anyway, once he had a draft, he would run it past Kending and get his input. He liked to dish it out in a way that left no room for misunderstanding and abhorred obfuscation in any form. However, he also recognized the need for occasional delicacy in order to satisfy the customer. Kending would know how to sugar it for Post, because in a way, Mason had two customers. He could not risk Global Systems' chances keeping the Post account by upsetting their sensibilities.

He finished the last of the coffee, went to the kitchenette to wash up, waved to Delora in passing, and headed for the elevators. He had a lot of work to do at Post to set up his project. He could stay at GS and do everything on his computer, but he wanted to be close to Deakin, certain they would have some interesting discussions.

A wry smile tugged the corner of his mouth as he waited.

Something else he had to keep in mind. Deakin appeared to be a nice enough person on the outside, but he could still be a back-stabbing bastard on the inside. He had to be tough to reach his current position, and that invariably meant he climbed over more than one body. Mason did not want to be one of them.

The meek may inherit the earth, but it would be in small cemetery plots, he reminded himself.

Could he step over some bodies to achieve his objectives? The tricky bit he faced, what did 'stepping over' mean? Could he be a bastard if required? He figured that over the course of his career, he would likely find out. However, he had no desire to inherit that small plot, physically or professionally.

Leola, the other major element in his life, also a multidimensional diamond that sparkled and glittered. She cast a light on his life, but shadows lurked in the background. With the engagement announced, his mom would stop her nagging about being a bachelor and Leola's father appeared appeased. On the other hand, he had no doubts she would start her filing down campaign about the engagement party. He wondered if Leola's parents would do the same thing to her. He wanted harmony, not ongoing warfare.

Wait until the weekend when everybody got together and let them show their underlying natures, real or a facade.

One more thing to do...

He dug out his cell, tapped the Nuts group icon in his Contacts list, and began to type.

Hi, guys,

A bit of trivia for your amusement. That girl I met at Post? We're engaged.

Mason

A broad grin on his face, he waited. The responses came almost immediately.

Liam Anderson: *Anchors! They'll get you every time. Let's have a stag night out and you can tell us all about it.*

Arthur Landry: *Way to go, buddy! I'll arrange a venue.*

Logan Bernard: *You'll never regret it, you old fart. If you do, it'll be your fault. It's always the guy's fault. That's what my wife says.*

Mason typed quickly, *Thanks, everybody. Looking forward to the luau.*

Downstairs, he walked through the broad plaza that fronted the twin Rialto Towers toward the Uber rank, having pre-booked a ride. Patchy clouds smeared the sky, but the sun took out the chill. Pedestrians on both sides of Collins Street flowed in steady lines going who knows where. Cars crawled from one set of lights to another. Two trams exchanged clangs as they passed each other.

Mason climbed into the comfortable, clean car, and showed the driver his booking reference. With a screen that displayed the way to the National Post headquarters, the driver pulled into the street. At the taxicabs line, bored owners waited to pick up a fare, resenting the fact that he picked a competitor. When Uber first emerged on the Australian scene in 2002, customers flocked to them. Far cheaper than cabs, a fixed trip price, always on time, the cars new and clean, drivers did not use roundabout maneuvers to reach a destination to get a larger fare as some cabs did. He'd been in dirty, smelly things with a surly driver who considered serving a customer an imposition. Taxi companies fought

Uber's rise, but Mason had little sympathy for them. The loss of customers? They did it to themselves.

They forgot the rule to satisfy the client.

Golden hair done up in a bun, Kara smiled as he walked toward his office.

He powered up the computer, snagged a mug of fresh coffee, and went to work. A quick glance at his list of emails—nothing he needed to worry about—he created a new directory on the PC and set up several sub-directories. He retrieved a USB stick from his pocket and copied a feasibility study template. After the basics were filled in, he added the terms of reference in an appendix and appended the Post26 Strategy paper as another appendix. All he needed now were volumes of data from Turner. Of course, nothing stopped him from doing his own research.

A sip of coffee, he cracked his knuckles, and opened Google.

Two hours later, the slush directory full of articles and graphs, his stomach declared it might be time for a refill. He glanced at the computer clock and blanched, almost one pm! On the way to the elevators, he wished Leola could join him.

As he made his way through the crowded cafeteria in search of a table, he suppressed a grin. Everybody at Post knew about his affair? Not that he made an effort to hide it, and why should he? Still, he did not realize his advances were that obvious. If his relationship generated idle gossip and some cheer for somebody, the rumor grinder can hum as much as it liked.

At 1:40, a knock, and Deakin stood in the doorway.

"Something came up and I can't keep our appointment. We'll chat another time. Bang on my door when you have something I can chew on."

Mason looked at the closed door and shrugged. If the Director wanted something to chew on, he would give him a bucketful.

* * *

Mason wiped his hands on the small towel. "How's the salad coming along?"

"Almost done," Leola replied briskly, plucked a piece of lettuce out of a large steel bowl, and popped it into her mouth. "A touch more vinegar."

"Don't forget the cashews," he reminded her.

"Or the apple cubes. I got it, Mason. You done with the potato salad?"

"The onions and bacon bits are fried," he replied as he opened the fridge to retrieve a pot of boiled, cubed potatoes. He mixed everything, added condiments to make it tasty, covered the glass bowl with cling wrap, and back into the fridge.

"Looks like we're ready," Leola declared with satisfaction. "All we need are the freeloaders."

The barbeque arranged for one pm, one last look at the large wooden table on the back veranda to check the setup, he nodded. A glance at the wall clock showed 11:24 am, and Leola grinned.

"Aren't you glad we came early?"

"I must admit it took longer to get it all done than I expected," he confessed.

One thing he did not have to worry about—his electric Weber barbeque. Purists declared that a charcoal grille delivered the best results. He admitted the smoke added a distinct flavor, but he refused to fuss over a charcoal burner with all the cleaning up it required.

After an initial discussion what to prepare for lunch, everybody eventually settled on a simple barbeque. Mason and Leola provided the salads, and the others organized meats and dessert. He knew what Mom would bring—walnut roll. His favorite. When he asked Leola what Martina had in mind, she shrugged. "No idea."

He watched Leola finish the salad, radiant and happy, and his heart sang, equally happy. She positively glowed. With a house all her own, she had reason to be happy, and did not stop talking about it.

She never said she loved him, not in words, but in many small ways, she expressed it in the way she looked at him when she thought he would not notice, the way she smiled, laughed, touched him, and how her eyes sparkled when they glanced at each other. He did not need the words to see she loved him.

The interior pleasantly warm after the morning chill, the last dying embers faded in the wood heater. Through the kitchen window, he saw a gray Camry pull into the driveway. "Your parents are here."

"And so are yours," she added with a tilt of her head.

Sure enough, a blue Audi trailed the Camry.

"I hope Dad doesn't start harping about that 20K again," she hissed.

"He's still bugging you about it?" he asked, his voice sharp.

"Indirectly. It's becoming a real pain."

"Enough is enough. I'll talk to him."

She grabbed his arm. "Don't! It'll only make things worse."

He pursed his lips and gave her a hard look. "What do you want me to do? Let it slide?" he said and walked to the front door.

"Just leave it."

He greeted Leola's parents, somewhat cool when he shook Renzo's hand, then helped Grandma in. Everybody had a bottle in hand or a basket of something. He wondered if they weren't overdoing it.

"Thank you, dear," Nada said and paused. "It's been such a long time and I miss it. I miss Cricket." She took a long look at the backyard and the flowering plums and apples. "What a sight," she murmured.

"Here, sit down. Tea?"

"Yes."

Mason shook hands with Dad and gave Mom a quick hug. No need to introduce Leola's parents, as Dad said they all met on

Thursday evening at a nice Italian restaurant on Lygon Street and everybody had hit it off.

"Renzo, Martina, I want you to meet my mother, Nada," Nikola announced.

Formalities out of the way, Mason invited everybody to the lounge table. Drinks served, the atmosphere became congenial.

"Nice place, Mason," Renzo remarked, playing with his tumbler of scotch.

"I spent a lot of time here."

"Let me know if you decide to sell. I'll get you a good deal."

"Dad!" Leola protested. "Stop it! No business, okay?"

"Just saying." He took a sip and focused on Mason. "Leola told us you don't want an engagement party. Is that right?"

Mason suppressed a groan. The filing down had started in earnest. On Wednesday, his mom called, pointing out how disappointed all her friends and his would be if we didn't have a celebration, not to mention Leola's family. He allowed her to rant for a while, then cut her off firmly. No party. Subject closed.

Last night, huddled in bed, Leola confided how her father worked on her to change their mind. Tradition, he said.

"Consider our gathering here as the next best thing," he replied evenly. He had no desire to enter into an argument and spoil the day for everybody.

"If you're worried about cost, your father and I will take care of it. Cost shouldn't be a problem, though, seeing how you can splurge a hundred thousand on shares."

He shot Leola a glance and wondered how much what went on between them she blurted to her parents. Her dejected look told him she regretted her *faux pas*. He would sort it out with her later.

Nikola raised his eyebrows. "You bought 100K of shares?"

"Nothing you needed to know, Dad."

His father raised a hand. "You're right. It's none of my business."

Renzo cleared his throat. "It's my business when—"

"Enough already," Nada interjected softly in a voice that nonetheless held vibrant force. "If Mason and Leola don't want an engagement party, we should respect their wishes and give them our blessing."

"That's what I've been telling this oaf here," Martina declared vehemently. "As usual, he doesn't pay any attention to me. Stubborn like his father." She winked at Mason. "Runs in the family."

"Now, my dear—"

Nikola stood. "Renzo, why don't you and I take a walk, get some fresh air, and let the ladies have some girl time."

"I'll start the barbeque," Mason said, glad for the temporary truce of hostilities, certain the war would resume later.

Leola also stood. "Mom, Brianna, more coffee or tea?"

"Thank you, dear," they echoed.

"More tea for you, Grandma?"

Nada flashed her a warm smile. "Grandma…I like how that sounds, my child."

"And I like saying it," Leola said and walked into the kitchen.

"Don't mind the others, Manny," Nada told him firmly. "You know what you want and nobody else has a say. Tradition doesn't mean blind adherence."

Mason patted her arm. "Thanks for saying that."

'Hear, hear,' Milan's throaty voice echoed in his head. *'Your grandmother always had a practical, down-to-earth head on her shoulders.'*

'As did you, Gramps,' Mason replied as he made his way to the fridge to get the meats and stuff.

"Hold the coffee, Leola!" Brianna declared and stepped behind Nada's chair. "It might be a good idea for us girls to also take a walk."

Nada nodded and stood. "I'd like that."

When everybody left, Leola poured herself a fresh cup of tea and waited. Mason looked at her.

"What?"

"Say it. I have it coming."

He understood what she meant. "Some things are better left between us," he remarked after a moment.

"I know, and I'm sorry. It slipped out. Dad called me yesterday about the engagement party, telling me why we should have one."

"Yeah, my mom handed me a litany as well."

"He then said he'll pay for everything, especially since you're too stingy to give him a lousy twenty thousand for the reno. I told him you were not stingy. I don't know how it happened, I somehow let out about the hundred thousand. I think he resents how well you've done for yourself at half his age."

"Skits! I don't give a plugged toss what he thinks or what anybody thinks about the damned party. I want all of us to get along. After all, we'll be one big, happy family soon, but I won't be bullied or managed by them."

"I don't want that either," she confided. "I wonder, though, for the sake of peace, maybe we could have the party. A small one, mind you."

Cracks in the wall already, he mused.

"Do you want one?"

"No, not really."

"Neither do I. Our parents will have to accept that we run our lives, not them. They're family and all that, but they don't make decisions for us."

Leola winced. "It's just…"

He brushed her arm. "To keep the peace, I know, but if we give in this time, what about the next time, and the next? Appeasement never works, Leola."

She walked up to him and brushed her lips against his. "How did you get to be so wise?" she murmured huskily.

"Gramps keeps me in check," he told her with a grin, then gathered her in his arms. The kiss he gave her far from a casual peck.

Eventually, she pulled back and exhaled. "The barbeque…"

"What barbeque?" he said and kissed her hard.

The rest of the day turned out to be fun, filled with casual conversation, some reminiscing, exchange of family histories, and occasional laughter. Everybody had their fill of food, sassing Mason for burning the sausages, overdoing the stakes, and serving raw chicken. He did not mind and threw back an occasional barb.

When dessert time came, Brianna served her walnut roll. Mason added a jar of compote cherries he bought from Gabby. Everyone loved the combination and Martina demanded the recipe.

Renzo surprised Mason with his wit, charm, and engaging conversation. Outlandish opinions and one-liner world-savers were tossed around with abandon. The bastard seemed to possess an endless supply of jokes, and many of them poked fun at religion, which left them all in stitches. Regretfully, by late afternoon, he called it a day to head back to Melbourne. His parents declared pressing matters and took Grandma with them. She told him how she enjoyed visiting her old home and hoped to come back soon. Mason promised to bring her up anytime she wanted.

Leola's hand in his, they watched the two cars pull out of the driveway. A wave and they were alone, the house filled with echoing memories against the backdrop of a setting sun.

"That turned out well," she remarked and closed the door.

"I'm happy that our parents clicked," he told her.

She cocked her head and an impish smile dimpled her cheek. "Wait till your father gets to know my dad better."

He laughed. "Their problem, not ours." He topped up his tumbler and sipped, then rubbed his hands. "Time to get the burner going. It gets nippy here at night."

"It won't be nippy if we're in bed with a comforter over us," she suggested demurely.

He looked at her in mock surprise. "And all this time you kept telling me I'm the randy one here."

"That's before we became engaged," she replied with unbeat-able feminine logic.

"The dishes…"

"What dishes?" she whispered and flowed into his arms.

* * *

Terry Deakin tapped the folder on his desk with a stiff finger, gave a long sigh, and looked up.

"Has Karter Kending read this?"

"He read it," Mason replied evenly.

"And?"

"He thinks I'm nuts."

"He's right, but he let you give me the draft. Why?"

Totally at ease, Mason did not break eye contact with the portly, balding Post director. The piercing brown eyes looked back with an intensity he knew demanded straight answers. Anything else and he could kiss his career with GS, and probably the IT industry as a whole. It won't come to that, though, or Kending would not have approved the draft after amending several sections to make them more politically acceptable to Post. The entire report, however, contained a cluster of bombs ready to explode in Deakin's face…unless the Director defused them, and the report gave him ammunition to do it.

"Because it fulfills a number of important Post26 Strategy objectives."

"A noble piece of paper aimed to placate the government in Canberra and tell the public that National Post cares for them," Deakin growled.

Mason grinned. "Which it doesn't. I know. Although not advertised, Post is a profit center like any other corporation. The only difference, you're not listed on the stock exchange. You're a government entity."

"Which some of our Board members wish we were not, but since we are—"

"In today's cutthroat environment, Post needs to be better than the next guy."

Deakin sat back and laughed. "Damn me, Mason. Your cynicism never ceases to amaze me. I would dismiss it if it were not right on the mark. As you know, Post is constrained by legislation, which severely limits what we can do."

"That's why you pushed the Post26 Strategy study. To raise awareness that Post better get off the dime," Mason added quietly.

"Oh, we've known that for a while. Organizational inertia, my boy, and disposition to change kept you back. That Yankee bastard Clarke said you had a holistic approach and your work to date showed it. That's why I pulled you into my project. By the way, how's the decommissioning going?"

"I should have it wrapped up by Wednesday."

"Good work. Is Murray Lloyd giving you a hard time?"

Mason grinned. "We're getting along fine."

"Good man, that. Back to the subject at hand…" Deakin tapped the folder again. "This stuff builds on elements you included in the decommissioning study, but in ways I did not anticipate. Clarke will go ballistic when he reads this."

"Why should he? If Post26 is implemented, it will grow his department and influence. He can't resent that."

"That's it exactly…if implemented. Oh, we tinkered around the edges, but we never did anything…until forced into action by our competition. Then you dumped this on me. I can argue the merits of Post policy, but I cannot refute the volume of charts, graphs, and statistics in your report. Something I'll crosscheck with our people. You look confident about the contents, which means everything is solid. Is there anything in there I can pick apart?" Deakin mused with a touch of pique.

"Despite the research that supports my findings, I am not plugged into the Post network, Terry, or its rumor mill, a valuable source of institutional information. Because of that, I may have missed something."

Deakin sighed. "You didn't miss anything of importance. Despite being an outsider, you captured Post culture nuances and our internal political framework remarkably well. Is somebody on the inside an informer?"

Mason cracked a smile. "Research, Terry."

"Okay, wiseguy. I'll run your report past some of my people and get back to you with changes and any additional information I feel needs to be in the final version. If Clarke happens to knock on your door and wants a chat, fishing is your best bet."

"I am aware of my obligations—"

"I'm sure you are, and I didn't mean it that way. He likes you and will want to play that card. Remember this, though. He is also ambitious and a ruthless achiever, or Post would never have hired him. He'll use anyone to further his goals, and premature disclosure of your report would give him a lot of playing chips with the Board."

"Because you want to use those chips yourself?" Mason ventured, mindful not to presume too much on their friendly relationship, realizing that Deakin also had ambitions.

"You like to cut it plain, don't you, but you're right. I don't mind what is said in this office, but right now, you work for me and no one else, and that includes Global Systems. Are we on the same page?"

"My loyalty has always been to National Post as a GS client, Terry."

"A nice evade, seeing how GS pays your salary." Deakin tilted his head. "I could use a good 2IC, you know, and I would make it very attractive for you."

"If I accepted, I fear my feet would rust. Right now in my career, I need diversity."

"Of course," Deakin said briskly, stood, and stuck out a hand. "I'll be in touch with Kending about your report."

Mason grasped the proffered hand and they shook.

He closed the door after him, paused, and smiled.

Kending warned him that his report put him on a fragile political limb with Post. Would Deakin saw it off to grease his agenda, whatever that might be? Mason liked to think not. Anyway, he would likely find out soon enough.

Back in his office, he made calls. The first one to Cannard Engineering, thanking them for their outstanding effort. He then called every letters center manager and expressed his appreciation for their cooperation and support. All were glad to see the old sorters out the door. Some centers had new Siemens machines to break in, but that wasn't Mason's problem. Done, he sent official emails to everybody that said the same thing, with a CC to Clarke and Lloyd.

A separate email to Raymond praised Leola's unstinting efforts during the sometimes frustrating times should help her career. He hoped the Head of Parcel took the email objectively, undoubtedly aware of the engagement, and not something Mason sent because of any personal consideration.

Done, he swiveled the chair to gaze out the window and slowly drained the last of the coffee. A knock and Clarke opened the door.

"Got a minute?"

"Of course, Raymond. Just finishing up."

"I did a quick scan through the emails you sent. Great work, Mason, but that's what I expected from you. Murray Lloyd already started the post-mortem with the letters centers. Between the two of us, Post won't be doing another decommissioning project like this for a couple of decades."

"Don't expect me to handle it," Mason quipped, and Clarke laughed.

"How do you like working on the Post26 Strategy program?"

"Post needs it implemented if it's to contain the competition."

"A nice evade, but I won't press you. We'll catch up once Murray is done with the post-mortem to get your personal feedback," Clarke said and closed the door.

Mason dug out his cell and glanced at the time display: 11:52 am. He scrolled down the Contacts list and pressed an icon.

"Hi, Mason. How did you go with Deakin?" Leola's bubbly voice made his day brighter.

"He hasn't thrown me under the bus, but the day is young."

"He wouldn't do that."

"He would if he had to, and you know it."

A sigh. "I suppose. I hate office politics."

"You must learn to play if you want to stay in the game, and it only gets harder the farther up the ladder you go. For some, playing the game becomes the job, and that's the part I don't like."

"Were you born this cynical or did you take a course on it?"

"The school of hard knocks, my sweet."

"You want to grab a sandwich or something?"

"It'll have to be a quick one as I must get back to GS."

"I can come to your office if you want a quickie."

He pretended astonishment. "You are totally shameless and without morals, Leola Lanaro."

"That's what Dad always tells me. See you downstairs."

This time, he beat her out the elevator. The one opposite gave a sharp *ting* and she appeared. Without saying anything, she planted a kiss on his mouth, grabbed his arm, and pulled him toward the cafeteria entrance. Pleasantly full without being crowded, they headed toward the serving counter. She snagged a hot chicken salad and a bottle of apple juice, while he helped himself to a tuna salad and orange juice. At a window table, both sipped their drink.

"After yesterday, coming back to work seemed somewhat surreal," she remarked.

"I know what you mean. Mt. Macedon does that to you," he agreed.

"I love it there. The peace and quiet and the relaxed atmosphere, but I cannot see myself living there. I'd go batty. There's nothing to do."

"That's why you never see many young people during the week. They come flocking on weekends to escape the city rat race."

"Your grandmother is unreal. An angel."

"One of my favorite people, all right, and a fountain of wisdom," he remarked and munched his salad.

"Like your grandfather the ghost?" she added with a grin.

"You'd have loved him. He could be crabby and cantankerous at times, but I adored him. What about your grandparents?"

"Oh, they're all right. I always liked my maternal grandma. Brian and Despina gravitated more to my dad's parents. They all made us feel welcome and protected, but I never had a deep relationship with any of them. I guess the three of us enjoyed our own company more. When we turned teenagers, the visits sort of faded. Oh, we got together for birthdays and holidays, but fewer spur-of-the-moment visits. You?"

"An only child, I have always been kind of alone, even at school. Dad in the Navy and Mom busy lecturing at RMIT. When she got home, she didn't want me crawling all over her. At school, I found kids to be cruel to someone who doesn't fit in."

"And you didn't fit in."

"Much smarter than the others, I found their interests and boisterous games somewhat silly. Gramps understood me perfectly and I pestered my parents to take me to Mt. Macedon for weekends. When I got my driver's license, I borrowed Dad's car and went up on my own."

"Which undoubtedly added to your father's collection of gray hairs," Leola quipped.

"No argument, but I'm a careful driver. Never a speeding ticket or anything."

She arched her eyebrows. "My, a sterling character."

"Let me put it this way," he replied sotto voice. "They never caught me."

Her laugh turned heads their way.

"From some of the reminiscing on Saturday, your dad's parents lived a colorful life."

"Believe it. When I had a problem, Gramps was there to sort me out."

She searched his face. "You miss him a lot, I can tell. Is that why you talk to his ghost?"

"If I told that to a mind bender, he'd commit me."

"Is there anyone else you talk to?"

"Apart from you? Grandma is the only one left."

"You don't confide in your parents much?"

"It's complicated, as you know yourself."

She gave a long sigh. "Unfortunately, I do. If only they treated me as a responsible adult. It became worse when I moved back with them. I didn't want to, but stark economics forced my hand. You don't know how grateful I was when you told me I could come and live with you."

Instead of making a flippant remark she might misunderstand, he reached for her hand and stroked the ring finger. "And I couldn't be happier that you did."

The snacks done, they departed with a hug and a kiss, knowing they would be in each other's arms later tonight.

Back at GS, Delora greeted him with a cheerful smile. "Mr. Kending wants to see you."

"So does the whole world," he muttered and strode toward the Director's office. He knocked, heard a 'Come', and opened the door.

"Ah, Mason. The man I want to see. Grab a chair. Terry Deakin called."

"I'm not surprised," Mason said and crossed his legs.

Kending grinned. "He's not sure whether to hug you or burn your report. I told you what might happen. Never mind, he's not going to do either thing. He hired us to do a feasibility study and you gave him your findings. Our findings. The draft you gave Deakin had the GS name and logo on it. By the way, did he offer you a job with Post?"

Mason grinned. "Actually, he did. How did you know?"

"Hard experience, my boy. We lost several good people to our clients with that gambit. We do a great infrastructure program or strategic study and they reward us by stealing our consultants. You weren't tempted, were you?"

"Not for one moment. I know why Deakin did it. I take the job and he controls me. If I step out of line, I'm out on the street."

"I'm glad you saw through his ploy." Kending folded his arms. "I could use you on other aspects of the Post26 Strategy program, but Joe is handling that part well enough. Do you want to go back to Walt and do more infrastructure work?"

"If you don't mind, Karter, I'd like to stick with strategic studies."

"I thought you might. Anyway, Lavinia is settled in her new role and doesn't mind the change. By the way, good job wrapping up the decommissioning program. Walt tells me you're almost done."

Mason smiled. "It should be by Wednesday. It has been an experience, but I'm glad to see the back of it."

"I'm sure. It appears Clarke called him to congratulate GS. This will spread through the industry and give us more brownie points."

"I guess it all counts," Mason conceded.

"Damn right it does. This is how we attract new clients. Anyway, with your feasibility report on the back burner until Deakin gets off the pot, I have something else that may interest you. A government study."

"Federal?"

"The Department of Infrastructure, Transport, Regional Development, Communications and the Arts wants a detailed look at proposed infrastructure requirements that must be met to satisfy expected population growth over the next thirty years, whether through births or immigration. Over the years, governments from both Parties commissioned studies on this. Finally, they want to do something about it and the Minister wants an update on a White Paper done four years ago. Frankly, it's a bucket of goo. Anything the government plans must be coordinated with the states, who have their own objectives and timeframes, and resent any moves by Canberra to muscle in on their turf. However, as we both know, some things are legitimately within the federal government's purview, and they have the money to do them. I know the Minister and GS got the job without having to tender. You'll be 2IC to an Executive Level 2 manager with a team of four. They are all subject matter experts. Keep one thing in mind. In the public service hierarchy, an EL2 is a god."

Mason frowned. "I don't get it. If the Minister already has subject matter experts, why do they need us?"

"Ah, the man doesn't know everything," Kending said. "He wants us to tell him what he already knows, of course."

"Like the Post decommissioning study."

"The federal government wastes millions every year on external consultants. Since it does, I have no qualms seeing that GS gets a slice of the pie."

"I get it. What are our terms of reference?"

"Review the White Paper and its recommendations and prepare an evaluation report by end of November. The EL2 knows you'll be taking leave in October."

"You were very sure I'd take the job." Mason made it a statement.

"You'll be spending some of your time in Canberra. I'll send you links to all the information I have, including how to log into the Canberra system. When you're ready, call the EL2 and arrange a meeting."

"Can I quit now or after the meeting?"

"Get out."

Out in the bullpen area, Mason broke into a broad grin. On impulse, he made his way to Turner's cubicle, and Scott looked up in surprise.

"Anything I can do for you, Mason?"

"You already did. I want to express my thanks for the great job you did researching my Post thing."

"I appreciate it," Turner remarked casually, not overwhelmed by the thanks.

Some people simply cannot be managed, Mason mused.

"At our next senior staff meeting, I will propose that you be advanced to senior consultant."

Turner's skeletal face registered genuine astonishment. "I...I don't know what to say. I never expected—"

"This to come from me?"

"Frankly, I always believed you didn't like me much."

"You can do great work when you put your mind to it, Scott. What you need is polish your people skills."

Turner grinned. "I know. Joe has that one in hand." He stood and stuck out a thin hand. "Thank you, Mason. I won't forget this."

They shook hands and Mason slowly walked toward his office, not sure he did the right thing. Turner had proved his skill as a superb data harvester and analyst time and again. Everybody in the office said so. He simply rubbed people the wrong way. A little recognition may prod him to step up a few notches. The man had potential and Mason noted how Turner secretly fretted as a consultant while others around him got promoted. Anyway, if it did not work out, GS could always fire him.

Whether it worked out or not, he made Turner's day.

He powered up the computer, snagged a mug of coffee from the kitchenette, and checked his emails. Sure enough, Kending sent him one with all the links he needed. The first order of business, read everything GS had about the job, then log into the government site and see what the god-like EL2 had.

As the afternoon wore on, the subject and its national scope fascinated him. An ambitious program of work woefully neglected by successive governments. They produced a White Paper four years ago and only decided to look at it seriously *now?* Look at it only, not necessarily do anything about it, he reminded himself. The Minister could be dusting off his resume with an eye on a cushier Cabinet post. Mason did not care.

Stick to the terms of reference, he told himself. After all, he would not be running for election. Let the EL2 handle the internal politics angle.

Around 5:20, he had enough and closed shop. Most bullpens were already empty. He waved to Delora and waited for the elevator. Didn't the girl ever go home?

Downstairs, the afternoon crush in full mode, cars clogged Collins Street both ways. Pedestrians created ant lines toward the Southern Cross railway complex, or headed uptown for shopping, entertainment, whatever. Mason squeezed himself into a tram going his way, grabbed a stanchion, and hung on for dear life as the steel monster hissed along the tracks.

September had almost shut its doors to make way for spring, which made the evening clear and mild. He relished the brisk walk from Clarendon Street to his place. The lounge window lit, it looked like Leola beat him home. He opened the front door and slid the slim black Vuitton briefcase under the row of coat hooks.

"Leola!"

Still not completely used to living with someone else, he figured they were settling in well without the awkward self-consciousness that hung over them during the first two weeks. Even though they lived together, he went out of his way to respect moments when she sought privacy. The other little things were adjustments to established habits, and both made allowances.

Married life, he told himself, could be pleasant. Anyway, he had figurative umbrellas for those days when it rained. He also knew it would rain sometime, but when it happened, they would deal with it. Rain cleared the air, someone said. Provided it did not come with hail, he amended. If such a day did come? One of life's turns, that's all.

Leola sat on the couch, legs curled under her, a crumpled tissue in hand. Eyes puffed from crying, it looked like her day had more than a little rain. Immediately concerned, he sat beside her and took her hand.

"What happened?" Somehow, he knew what happened.

"It's Dad. He called me this afternoon about the engagement party. He didn't shout or rant, but he made it clear I owed it to the family to have one. I didn't need to do anything, he said. He would take care of everything. It's such a small thing, he said, but important. Why were we so stubborn? He didn't give me a chance to say my peace, telling me I should talk to you, and hung up."

Mason gave a long exhale. One of those life's turns had come early. "Shit! This has gone far enough." He made to stand, but she grabbed his arm.

"There's more. About an hour later, your mother called and gave me the same treatment. I'm so sick of this, Mason! I wish we were off to Japan right now."

Mouth tight, he dug out his cell and pressed a Contacts icon.

"Hi, Mason," Nikola replied. "I want to say again what a great time we had at Mt. Macedon. Grandma loved it."

"Is Mom there?"

His father immediately sensed the tension. "What's going on?"

"Put her on."

"Just a moment."

"Manny! It's so nice to hear from you."

"Mom, I'm sorry I gave you Leola's number, although you would have got it sooner or later."

"What's wrong, dear?"

"You are what's wrong. I don't want you calling her or me about the engagement party! We're not having one and that's that. If you think calling her or me will change our minds, or Renzo will change hers, stop it! It's our business how we handle things, not yours. Is that clear?"

"Well! There is no need to be snotty about it."

"Put Dad on."

"Mason? I heard part of that. I'll sort out your mother."

"Do *you* want us to have an engagement party?"

"It's nice to have one, but it's your decision."

"Good night, Dad." Mason let his arm hang, phone in hand, and looked at Leola. "Call Renzo."

"Mason!"

"Don't worry. I won't jump down his throat, but we need to settle this."

She bit her lip, dug out her cell, made the connection, and held the phone to him.

"Renzo, it's Mason."

"I know why you're calling."

"I'll say this once. Stop pressuring Leola! Got that?"

"She has a right to know how her mother and I feel."

"You don't have the right to badger her to do what you want. It's not your decision!"

"Why are you so bloody hung up about the fucking party? I'll organize everything. All you need to do is show up. It will mean so much to her mother. I know it will mean a lot to your parents, especially Brianna."

"Did she call you?" Mason demanded in a dangerously soft voice.

"We had a chat this morning."

Mason squeezed the phone, then let go, afraid to break it. "For the last time, Renzo. Stop bugging Leola!" He hung up and tossed the phone onto the couch. He could say lots more, but the way he felt, it would have gone downhill and possibly ruined everything permanently.

Leola dabbed her nose with a tissue and sniffed. "I'm so sorry, Mason."

"There is nothing for you to be sorry about," he said wearily and sat beside her. The whole messy thing affected him more than he thought it would.

"This won't stop my father, you know. He'll keep grinding away until we give up in frustration. That's how he works."

"Well, I'm not one of his sales clients," he said and searched her face. "What about you? Are you with me?"

Her eyes widened. "Of course, I'm with you. What a silly thing to ask."

"In that case, stop sniffling and brace up!"

She sat up and glared. "Well, excuse me if I feel a little down because my dad's an asshole."

"Look, I didn't mean it that way."

"How exactly did you mean it?"

"Stand up for what you want! Don't get depressed every time he calls. I don't like what's happening either, but right now, it's you and me together that's important. You told me you're with me. Then be with me. Next time your dad or my mom call, give them the finger and hang up."

Despite the tension, she chuckled. "You're such a creep, Mason."

"So you keep telling me."

She let out a long exhale. "If it were only that easy. It's just…"

"I know. Peace. You said that already."

"For the sake of both our families—"

"We've been over that, Leola," he told her sharply.

"I know. Still…"

About to lose it, tired of everything, he grasped her arms. "Say it and we'll have the damned party and your peace."

"No, I don't want an engagement party."

"Then put it behind you, for Chrissake! Don't let your father get under your skin."

"You're right, but I'm torn between what I want and keeping my parents happy."

"And it's tearing you up, but we can't let them run our lives."

She grabbed his hand. "Let's get married now! We'll get a civil celebrant—"

"We can't. We need to lodge a Notice of Intended Marriage at least one month before the wedding date."

"Shit!"

"We'll weather this if we stand our ground." His eyes turned to the liquor cabinet. "I could use a stiff drink. You?"

"I don't mind a bourbon either."

Tumbler in hand, her glass on the coffee table coaster, he wrapped an arm around her.

"Parents! Christ!"

Color back in her cheeks, she laughed. "They're certainly bucking for it."

He liked to see her bright and bubbly much better than cloaked in gloom. Her readiness to descend into an emotional response worried him a little. He did not want to dwell on it, but this apparent character weakness kept churning his mind. A woman's thing perhaps? He never had a sister and did not know about such things.

'Ask Grandma,' Gramps' voice came clearly.

Not a bad idea, he mused.

'Keep one thing in mind, moj mali stroj. Women are driven by symbolism and feelings, and they express emotion more readily than men do. Don't mistake such a display as weakness.'

Definitely something to chew on, he acknowledged.

Another more disturbing thought popped into his head.

Did he resist having an engagement party out of stubbornness and ongoing resentment because his parents still wanted to manipulate and control him? Candidly, he admitted the possibility. Did he fear wounding his pride if he gave in? Something else occurred to him, which amused him in a way. Leola might be resisting for exactly the same reasons.

"A penny for your thoughts," she promoted.

"They're not worth that much," he said and took a sip of whiskey.

"Then give them away for free."

"I'm thinking that you may be right. About keeping the peace, I mean. A party would make everybody happy."

"Remember what you said about appeasement?" she replied softly.

"Skits! Why do things have to be so damn complicated? If we give in to them, it will make us unhappy. If we don't, we still end up unhappy."

"A no-win scenario for both of us," she agreed, picked up her glass, and played with it.

"Why can't they just wish us all the best and be satisfied with that?" he groused moodily.

Leola took a long pull of whiskey and held out her glass for a refill.

Both got a little tight, which made getting up the stairs somewhat challenging.

Chapter Eleven

Over breakfast the next morning, subdued and downcast, Leola hardly said ten words. Last night, she went to her room without a word. Mason disliked seeing her morose and attempted to lighten the atmosphere by being jovial and doing things for her. It did not help. In the end, he gave up, not wanting an argument. Saying she needed to get to Post early, she walked out to catch a tram and left him to clean up.

Mug of coffee warm between his hands, he sat back in his favorite recliner deep in thought. He did not need a PhD to understand Leola's behavior and gloomy mood. Women experienced emotional swings for many reasons, but he could scratch most off the list. He knew the reason why she dragged herself around the house—the damned engagement party.

That single factor had put her under considerable stress, anxiety, and uncertainty. Torn between her love for him and her parents, her emotional compass refused to settle down and naturally created internal havoc. Her teary outbursts last night? Perhaps not a sign of weakness as he thought, but an inability to reach a workable settlement acceptable to everybody. The problem, something he admitted readily, they had no such elegant solution. Someone must blink first, but all would still lose because it promoted underlying resentment. Her apparent acceptance last night may have been a desire to placate him more than anything else.

He tossed it around looking for angles until forced to face the inevitable.

Pride soured everything for everyone.

'The art of living in harmony is compromise, moj mail stroj,' Gramps' words burned like a flare in Mason's mind.

Provided both parties were willing, he amended. Compromise could also be interpreted as appeasement, he reminded himself. Without the strength of character to make a stand and defend his beliefs and principles, compromise meant allowing himself to be pushed around in the illusory thought that it made everyone happy. It may make others happy, but deep down, he would harbor bitterness for allowing himself to be manipulated.

If not pride, what then?

'Selfishness,' Gramps retorted immediately.

Perhaps a more insidious cancer that ruined relationships, and parents were experts at selfishness handling.

His mom wanted an engagement party because of tradition. Renzo wanted one because it brought shame on the family if they did not have one. Mason considered both selfish reasons.

He sighed, finished coffee, set the alarm, and walked out into a clear day. He too needed to get to work. With the sun still low, sharp shadows ruled the streets. On the downtown tram, his mind freewheeled despite the noise and crush of people around him.

Delora greeted him with a smile, chipper and apparently carefree as always. She could not be that happy all the time, he mused. A front she put on every morning?

"Something wrong, Mason?"

He stopped to look at her. "Why do you ask?"

"When you've been married as long as I have, you can read the signs."

"It's Leola. She's in one of her mood phases," he explained, unwilling to lay bare his problems that would only serve to create inevitable gossip.

"We all get the blues sometime, and it can hit us for no apparent reason. Give her space to sort it out for herself and be there for her." She tilted her head. "A bunch of roses can do wonders."

That tugged a smile from him and he strode quickly to his office. Nothing urgent in his email list, he dug out his cell, deciding to take Gramps' advice. It took four rings to connect.

"Mason! This is an unexpected surprise."

"Sorry to bother you this early, Grandma—"

"Nonsense! Just finishing my porridge."

He winced with distaste. As a kid, Mom tried to get him onto the stuff. Even smothered with honey or maple syrup, he refused to eat the revolting mixture. Feed it to horses, he told her.

No use putting it off, he took a deep breath and made the plunge. "I'm in trouble, Grandma, and I could use your advice."

"It's Renzo and Brianna, right?"

"They're both badgering her and it's making Leola miserable. No matter what we do, someone will feel hurt, and I don't want it to be us."

"It's always complicated, dear, but you knew that already."

"I want to be strong for Leola—"

"At the same time, you don't want her to accept something she may resent."

"What do I do?"

"Try honesty. Get everybody together and talk it over. Tell them why you and Leola feel the way you do and ask them to be open themselves. Everybody must be honest without maneuvering to gain some sort of advantage, or this will not work."

"I thought we made it clear on Saturday that we didn't want an engagement party."

"But you didn't say why. You and Leola must be honest with each other before you can ask others to be honest with you. You two need to come to an understanding first."

"We have an understanding. No party."

"Do you?"

Mason recalled Leola's behavior this morning. "What happens if we cannot reach an agreement with the others?"

"Don't waste energy worrying about something that hasn't happened, Mason. Be clear with Leola first."

"You're a treasure, Grandma."

Nada gave a merry chuckle. "It's easy for me to pontificate. I don't have your problem."

"True, but you witnessed others in a similar situation."

"One of the benefits of old age, dear."

"Love you."

"Love you too. Bye."

Mason pocketed his cell and exhaled loudly.

Honesty?

Skits!

All this time, he thought he had been honest, but perhaps not.

If it took honesty, he would start with Leola tonight and settle what *she* wanted. No lunch at Post, she said in a brittle voice over toast. He had to settle this quickly before it became gangrenous.

Time to do some paid work.

About to open the federal government project directory, his cellphone twittered. His eyebrows climbed when he saw the caller ID.

"Mom…" he responded coolly, still sore at her from yesterday.

"I won't keep you long, Mason," she replied with equal restraint.

Mason, not Manny, eh?

"Your father's prostate problem flared up and he needs a prostatectomy. They booked him at The Alfred for October 4th. They say he should make a full recovery without the need for follow-up treatment."

"Thanks for telling me, Mom. About last night—"

"You made yourself clear. Do what you want. You always have." she said and hung up.

He stared at the phone for a while, then slid it into his pocket. Well, he got honesty of sorts. He would try a different gambit at another time.

His dad had prostate problems for some time, and Mason hoped this operation would be the end of it, provided Dad had not left it too late. Getting him to see a doctor was asking to pull teeth without an anesthetic. His mom often said if Nikola looked after himself the way he cared for his car, he'd be in perfect shape. She abandoned trying to change that aspect of his character long ago.

Around ten, Mason called Elvin Stoner, the EL2, and arranged to see the god tomorrow at 10:00 to go over the study's terms of reference and get input not included in material GS already had. Sounding very friendly, Mason looked forward to the meeting.

He then called Cannard's team leader at the Dandenong Letters Center. The last sorter should be out and gone by day's end, the man said, sounding relieved. He also said that Leola had checked up on him about a half hour ago. Mason thanked him, added congratulations for a job well done, hung up, and pumped his fist.

"Yes!"

No more sorters, and he did not want to see another ever. The whole program of work went fairly smoothly, he admitted. Thanks to Cannard's expertise, but also due to Leola's careful management. She had proven herself an excellent infrastructure and systems application manager. Definitely an asset for Post. Mason planned to applaud her in a substantive way tonight.

Roses, eh?

The rest of the day proved uneventful, if cramming his head full of information could be called uneventful. Around five, he called it a day, dismayed at different levels of bureaucracy that ruled Canberra. Did their wheels need all those wasteful reviews, procedures, and steps a report must go through before a minister sees anything? If a business ran like that, they would go broke. He had to talk to Kending—after he saw the EL2. Operational reality may be different to what written procedures demanded. He hoped so, or he faced a daunting challenge.

Well, that's what they paid him for.

Already home when he arrived, Leola received his peck on the cheek with indifference. He did not want to read more into her cool reaction than may be there, and held out a bouquet of red roses framed by white carnations.

"Congratulations, my sweet."

"For what?" She held the flowers without sniffing them, something he knew women did instinctively.

"For closing the decommissioning project, that's for what," he replied, somewhat exasperated.

She deigned to take a sniff. "Thanks. Sweet of you."

"What's going on, Leola? You've been cold this morning, and you're acting as though I'm a burglar."

"It's not you. I simply have some things on my mind."

"Care to share? Maybe I can help."

"This is something I must work out for myself."

"Is this about the engagement party? If it is—"

"I don't want to talk about it."

"Okay, then. How about we celebrate the end of your project with an evening out? I know a great Turkish restaurant in South Yarra."

"Not tonight. I'm rather beat."

"Fine. Then let's make something we can rescue out of the fridge."

"I already had a grilled sandwich. I think I'll take one of your books upstairs and call it a night."

"In your room?" Her eyes deep black and unreachable, he gave a sigh. "I have an 8:05 flight to Canberra tomorrow, which means I'll be off around seven."

"I'll see you tomorrow night, then." She turned and he made to grab her arm, then stopped himself.

"We must talk, Leola."

"Not tonight." She walked to the bookshelf, paused, and pulled out a green cover hardback. Without a backward glance, she disappeared up the stairs.

So much for honesty, Grandma.

For once, Gramps' ghost remained silent. Better that way, he figured, not in the mood for philosophy.

A grilled sandwich, eh? If good enough for her…

He got a long roll from the bread container, cut it into halves, and added cheese and hot Hungarian salami slices. He needed something to spice up his day. Two minutes in the microwave, he added cold pickles to the plate, poured himself a glass of Shiraz, and carried everything to the breakfast table. Out of habit, he switched on the TV for the ABC news, then switched off. He already had all the bad news he could take. Instead, he slipped Beethoven's 7th Symphony into the CD player and started on the tasty sandwich.

Finished, he cleaned up and stood in the middle of the lounge, his breathing loud in his ears. At least it felt like it.

Hello silence my old friend…

A while since he last listened to silence. Since August 20, to be exact. The day Leola moved in with him. Almost six weeks they spent together. It seemed like a lifetime. An exciting, wondrous lifetime.

Why the hell didn't she want to talk to him instead of bottling it up? If he tried to snap her out of it, he feared she might explode like a shaken can of Coke. Perhaps she needed some alone time to sort out whatever bugged her as Delora suggested, and would eventually open up.

It churned his insides to see her in this state, though.

The symphony done, silence returned. He went to the bookshelf, dragged out Mary Stewart's *The Hollow Hills*, and trudged upstairs to his empty room. A quick shower, he crawled into bed, opened the book halfway through, began to read, and quickly lost himself in Merlin's magical world. That's how Stewart painted it.

Not much magic in his life right now.

* * *

The Boeing 737 tilted its wings and lined up on final approach to Canberra Airport. The wings rocked a little, became steady, and the runway became a rush. The pilot landed with a crunch and immediately engaged reverse thrust, which pressed Mason against the business class seat. Apart from better service, drinks, and food, it allowed him to exit the aircraft quickly. One thing he hated about air travel with a passion—the waiting to board and get off. The government paid for this flight, so he may as well enjoy it.

A parade of questions his mind served spoiled his enjoyment, demanding answers he did not have. He must have a long talk with Leola to clear the air between them, for sure as hell something bugged her big time. It wasn't him, she said, but he did not believe her. What creep thing did he do to make her so unhappy? It could not be only her father. If she yelled and raged at him to let it all out, he could handle it, but her uncompromising silence ate at his insides. Yesterday, he even thought to cancel his Canberra flight and confront her. In her dark mood, he suspected the gambit would have failed.

Tonight...

Briefcase in hand, he cleared the domestic terminal, booked an Uber, and emerged into a crisp morning. Canberra enjoyed mostly great weather, but its higher altitude made for some very cold nights. Bright sunshine turned the sky deep blue, which compensated a little for the chill as he hurried to the Uber rank.

The driver headed downtown without any attempt to strike a conversation. Something Mason appreciated, not in a mood to chat.

He liked Canberra's planned layout, broad avenues, and relaxed atmosphere. He told himself more than once to take a weekend and have a good look around. A federal and Capital Territory government city, most of its inhabitants were civil servants or supported the government with various services. The town also hosted untold consultancy companies eager to tap into the federal money well. He would ask Kending why Global Systems did not have a local office. Not enough business to keep one open? With modern telecommunication, emails, and online teleconferencing, a permanent Canberra office may be a redundancy and an unnecessary expense.

The Uber rolled to a stop at the imposing Phillip Law Street building and Mason climbed out. Through the sliding glass doors, he strode quickly to the security counter ten minutes short of ten o'clock.

"Mason Adamov to see Mr. Elvin Stoner."

The gray uniform guard rummaged through the counter and offered him a pass. "Keep it pinned on you at all times. I'll page Mr. Stoner."

Three minutes later, a somewhat portly, dark-skinned man of average height dressed in a conservative black suit, walked through the security portal, beamed a smile, and held out a hand.

"Mr. Adamov, a pleasure. Welcome to Canberra."

As they shook hands, Stoner did not look like a god to Mason. Then again, what should a bureaucratic god look like?

"Nice to be here."

"Not if you work and live here," Stoner quipped. "Let's get you upstairs where we can talk. The flight over okay?"

"I'm here in one piece," Mason said, and Stoner laughed.

"Live to die another day."

Mason touched his pass to the red pad at the entrance portal. It turned green and two plastic barriers slid back.

"From *The Bucket List*. You saw the film?"

"One of my favorites. Call me Elvin."

"Mason."

The elevator took them to the second floor and Stoner guided him along a gray-carpeted space that hugged the wall toward his office. The open-plan floor had the same bullpen layout of modern workplaces everywhere. People walked around, chatted, or hid themselves at their workstations.

Stoner's corner office, lit with floor-to-ceiling windows, a long bookshelf that occupied a whole wall, a small meeting table and chairs tucked into a corner, guarded a large solid wood executive desk shoved before the window. Stoner sat down and waved to Mason to drag up a chair. A few seconds later, the door opened, and an attractive young Asian lady peered in.

"The usual for me, Kelsy. And you, Mason?"

"Black coffee with one sugar, please."

She nodded and withdrew.

"I'm glad you told me where to go, Elvin. I didn't know the ministry had two buildings."

"It fooled a lot of people. Blame it on the previous Coalition government. In a mistaken belief to increase efficiency and eliminate redundancy, they merged three separate ministries into a single monster. Between the two of us, the move created more inefficiency and bureaucratic overhead. However, far be it for me to criticize my employer. I'm only a humble public servant."

Mason looked around the office and smiled. "Humble appears to be doing well."

"Tilting at windmills pisses people off, and that's not my MO."

"Is that why you asked Global Systems to review and update the White Paper?"

"If what you say pisses people off, or the Minister, you'll wear the blame. You don't look surprised."

"Should I be?"

"I guess not. You're young to be a principal consultant, but Renolds would not have given you to me if you didn't know your way around the traps."

The drinkables arrived and Mason took several sips. "Excellent," he observed.

"The usual government issue Nescafe isn't fit to drink. When I took over, I insisted on their Gold Blend. What we're drinking is my special roast Kelsy keeps percolated for me 24/7. Privilege of rank."

Open, friendly, Stoner represented an iceberg, most of it underwater, and Mason did not intend to underestimate him. An EL2 executive, Stoner wielded real power. Power that could blast Global Systems out of future government work if Mason pissed him off.

He noted the man's speculative gaze without looking away.

"I heard about your work at Post," Stoner said. "Impressive. They should have scrapped those ancient sorters years ago. They still would not if competition had not forced their hand. Terry Deakin will drag Post's butt into the twenty-first century with his Post26 Strategy program, though," he added comfortably. "Don't look surprised, Mason. I always do my homework with people who work for me." He pushed away his cup and became serious. "I take it you read the White Paper?"

"And all the material you sent Renolds," Mason replied evenly.

"Any initial thoughts?"

"Like National Post, the Coalition dragged their butt and did not implement any of the Paper's recommendations. In May this year, Labor came into office and promised to do something. Today is September 28. I can only interpret that for the federal bureaucracy, four months can be considered fast work. As for my thoughts, I'd like yours first. You've been at it for much longer."

Stoner shook his head. "No can do. My team of experts is gathering current data needed to update the White Paper, from which you'll prepare changes and recommendations. Four years of inactivity is a long time and the environment has shifted considerably. Everything is more expensive and urgent, and the Covid-19 pandemic didn't help. Our population is booming, largely due to expanded immigration, which invariably created a lot of pressure on national infrastructure and services required to accommodate this increase. The Minister and the Cabinet want to show the public they're doing something about it. I'm restating your brief, but I want to make sure you have my take. It will be your job to tell me my options. In turn, I'll tell the Minister what he can do."

"Not what the government *should* do?"

"Ministers set policy, Mason, which ultimately comes from the Prime Minister and the Treasury who'll be paying for it. Everything we do has a political dimension. The government is not a business profit center. Efficiency and effectiveness are theoretical concepts inside the public service. Remember that and you'll do fine."

"Don't piss you off, is that it?" Mason said with a grin, appreciating the frank overview.

"Oh, I won't jump down your throat if you rub my nose in reality. However, I cannot afford to rub the Minister's nose raw. Ministers and governments come and go, but the bureaucracy is there for keeps."

Mason laughed. He could not help it. "Fine with me. I'll be the bad cop to your good cop."

"I knew you'd understand. How about I introduce you to your team? Tell them what you want-done and they'll deliver."

"Do you want me here in Canberra?"

"That will not be necessary. We both own a phone and WhatsApp. Once you have your draft report, I may ask you to come up to discuss the findings. If you need anything, call."

Mason nodded and stood. "Where's the closet? I need to change into my Superman outfit."

Stoner cracked up. "Damn me, Mason, that was good. Superman outfit. I'll have to remember that."

Grouped together in adjoining bullpens, Stoner introduced Mason to four permanent staffers—two youngish men and two women. All four had a relaxed, unhurried attitude about them. It looked like the public service paced its people.

After the introductions, they all went to the downstairs cafeteria for coffee and snacks where Mason got to know his team better. Stoner left him to it, begging pressing business. They took him to a conference room and told him what each of them did and how it fitted into the White Paper review. He did not know what Stoner told them about their temporary new boss, but they were all initially very deferential toward him. He quickly put them at ease. Managers succeeded if their staff performed. Bluster and intimidation rarely worked. Those who forgot those basic facts were never good managers and usually did not last long.

Around three, he shook hands with everyone and caught an Uber for his 3:45 return flight, head full of new information and insights.

At the airport, the gate packed with passengers, he did not wait long before an attractive attendant announced boarding of flight QF439, and would all passengers have their boarding passes ready for inspection. This is where his business class ticket came in handy. He walked through the checkpoint, certain that some in economy class watching in the queue gave him resentful looks.

Tough chips, he mused.

Seated, buckled up, he gazed absently at the parked aircraft on the apron. A Virgin Air A320 pushed back, those on board undoubtedly relieved to be on their way. A Star Trek transporter would be handy right now, he thought. Such a device would not operate on the silly notion of disassembling a person into a 'matter stream' and reassembly at the other end. Like putting together an IKEA kit, things would always go wrong. The thing to do, of course—a very large 'of course'—would be to use one of the so-called curled dimensions as a doorway. No disassembly required.

Everyone on board, an attendant handed him a warm towelette and a glass of wine while the safety spiel droned in the background. He asked for a red. No such service for those in coach.

In the air, Mason reclined his leather seat a little and watched the pretty clouds, his mind operating on multiple channels: his Canberra visit, the White Paper review, analysis of accumulated data he already had, what his team would swamp him with, the engagement party mess, and most importantly, Leola. This in no particular order, and he skipped from one topic to another seemingly at random, but he gave each item serious attention and slotted his views and findings into an appropriate memory drawer.

Priority one, Leola. Always his first consideration. Parents, friends, and relatives were important in life. They provided an anchor to his past and a stable platform from which he could consider his future, but Leola *was* his future. Without her, life would be empty, a shell full of echoing silence no amount of books, films, music, or activities could fill.

He had no plan how to confront her, or the words to use. Simply stand before her and have it out?

His inner self gave a snicker as he pictured those IKEA assembly instructions.

The aircraft landed smoothly at Melbourne Airport, and Mason eagerly exited with a polite nod to the smiling attendant at the door. As usual, streams of people jostled along the corridor toward boarding gates or were coming out like him. Each probably had only one thing on their mind—get out of here!

Mason booked an Uber on the run and stepped out of the Qantas domestic terminal to be greeted by a sight of cabs queuing to take on fares, individuals waiting for one, car horns blaring, airport attendants waving at cabs to clear the way, and the prevailing stink of petrol and avgas. Thunder shook the air as a heavy jet took off. The sun low in the sky, it slowly shut down the day.

Finally on the Tullamarine Freeway, the driver put on some speed. Mason watched the heavy flow of cars going out of the city and felt a little sorry for everyone who had to endure such a crush twice a day. It took some twenty minutes to reach South Melbourne. The driver slowed and stopped beside Leola's red Honda. Mason got out and slammed the back door, and the Uber immediately pulled away.

He glanced at the Honda and frowned. Packed full with her stuff, he wondered if she made a visit to her parents' place to pick up more things. Women never had enough of anything, his friends told him. A shrug, he walked to the front door.

"Leola! It's me!"

Dressed in dark green slacks and white turtleneck, she rose from the couch and stood there, features impassive, eyes cold. A heavy blanket of dread descended on him and he let go of the briefcase. It made a loud thud as it hit the floor.

"I'm leaving, Mason. I wanted to tell you in person rather than slink off while you were gone, although sorely tempted." She took a step toward him, stopped, slowly pulled the ring off her finger, and held it up. "I can't do this anymore. I never expected everything to be so difficult. The constant hackling, pressure, you…"

He stared at the ring and blanched. "Me?"

"You're a driven man, Mason. Strong and full of purpose. You know what you want and you don't let anyone get in your way. Not even me. This purpose swept me along like a tide and

I felt helpless to resist, thinking I wanted the same things you did. Perhaps I should have spoken up earlier and told you what I wanted and how I felt. Then everything suddenly piled up on me and it became too late. It tore me and pulled me apart from several directions. Something had to snap, and it did. I cannot hide it any longer, Mason. What we have won't work, not the way things stand. I need time to reflect, and I cannot do it here. I'm sorry to hurt you like this. I never meant to, but I must do this." The last words came out in a rush and her eyes glistened, ready to spill.

He wanted to take her in his arms, crush her against him, and whisper soothing words. To his chagrin, he found himself frozen, unable to move or say anything. The pressure in his chest eased and he took a deep breath.

"Don't do this, Leola. Please! Let's talk. If I've been a creep, tell me and I'll fix it, but don't leave. I need you!"

"And I need you," she whispered, "but not like this. Here." She held the ring closer to him.

Indescribable pain sliced through him. He never thought it possible to feel such anguish. The hard look on her face told him that nothing he could say would sway her. He took the ring and a ray of light touched one of its faces. It glittered for one brief moment, then faded. Faded as she prepared to fade from his life.

"Where are you going?" he managed in a heavy voice filled with love, anger, resentment, and all the things he wanted to say, but could not. Too late for everything.

"My house in Keilor. Don't say a word or I'll lose it all. Goodbye."

She rushed to the front door and he heard a strangled sob. The door slammed shut behind her and he stood rooted, her ring in his hand. He heard her car start and the sound faded as she drove away.

His body bled inside. He could feel it. Hot, burning knives of pain scoured every part of his being and he felt the ashes fall. He thought…

What did he think? That he had it made? With her at his side, he wished for nothing else. She made him complete. He slowly looked at the ring. How could everything crumble so fast? The fates can indeed be terrible and cruel.

Inevitably, he lashed out, and he lashed at Leola. A coward, she refused to face him and talk it through. Instead, she took the easy way out to escape their problems.

'Fool!' Gramps' voice thundered. *Do you realize the courage it took to say the things she said and take the only course open to her? You're the coward for not protecting her from Renzo and Brianna. Nada told you what to do and you didn't do it.'*

"Ah, shove it, Gramps," Mason muttered and put the ring on the coffee table.

Bloody hell! He must be so screwed up to talk to a ghost. *Skits!*

His grandfather's ghost or the calm, rational part of himself that watched over him? He used his grandfather as a convenient label for his thoughts, that's all. A conscience can be a fucking pain in the butt sometimes, he decided.

Okay, they were his own words. Should he act on them, or were they personality flaw markers? Damn it, he did confront Renzo and Mom! What else could he have done? 'You must be honest with each other before you can ask others to be honest with you.' That's what Grandma said, but he *had* been honest with Leola, and she said she did not want an engagement party. Honest or domineering, unconsciously pressuring her to accept his position to maintain harmony in their relationship? Did she secretly want one and feared his rejection? She should have said so! He would not have jumped down her throat.

He slowly dragged himself up the stairs and looked into the en suite and guest bathroom. Nothing of her left. He saw her used towel in the hamper and reached for it. It smelled of her. Her room equally empty as though she had never been there.

The time for discussion and reconciliation gone, his mind made up, he hurried down the stairs and walked into the garage. The roller door slowly wound up as he started the Forester. Mouth tight, he backed onto the street and jammed down the accelerator. The tires screamed in protest.

It did not take long.

He pulled into the driveway calm and collected. He had no intention to rave or rant. It would not accomplish anything, but his parents needed to hear what he had to say.

The doorbell chimed. A few seconds later, his father opened the door and his eyebrows climbed in surprise.

"Mason! This is unexpected."

Without a word, Mason walked into the lounge. Brianna saw his grim expression and immediately got up off the couch.

"Manny…"

"Leola left me and you helped drive her away. You and Renzo. I hope you're satisfied, Mom." He turned and walked out without a glance at his father. He could have said a lot more, but to what purpose?

"Manny!" his mother cried out and he heard hurried foot-steps.

He climbed into the Forester, backed, and took off down the street. Several seconds later, his cell trilled and he read the caller ID on the screen—Mom. He let it ring. When she started to leave a voicemail message, he switched off, all bridges burnt.

Not quite. One more thing to do.

Deeply troubled as he drove to North Melbourne, he allowed his feelings to simmer. He parked in their driveway, strode quickly to the front door, and pressed the doorbell. Renzo opened and frowned.

"What brings you here, Mason? Is something wrong?"

"Everything is wrong, Renzo, and you made it that way."

"What the hell are you talking about?"

"Leola left me, thanks to you. I should slam you around for what you did to her, but I won't soil my hands. I hope your nightmares are worse than I can imagine them," he said and turned.

Renzo grabbed his arm and spun him around. "What happened?"

Mason shook him off and climbed into the car. The engine purred as he drove off, leaving Renzo staring after him.

The airconditioner whispered to keep the interior warm. Dusk slowly settled and the city stood in panoramic glory, the skyscrapers lit from within. Traffic steady, not heavy, he hit Clarendon Street.

Mason parked and slowly walked into the lounge. He stepped to the liquor cabinet and grasped a bottle of bourbon. Prepared to pour himself a stiff one, he stopped. Getting stoned would not solve anything. He gave a heavy sigh, replaced the bottle, and slumped into his recliner.

All he could look forward to now were empty days and empty nights filled with memories. He knew he could not hope to find another woman like her and promised himself not to even try. If the reward for love meant the kind of pain he endured now, he did not want it. The bitterest of all fruits.

Leola!

Not in the mood to eat, he percolated fresh coffee and slid a CD of popular 70s music into the player. Mug in hand, he allowed the haunting tune of *Music Box Dancer* to wash over him. It finished and Demis Roussos sang *My Friend the Wind*. Mason liked the oldies. They had melody, good lyrics, and powerful vocals.

Suddenly, he sat up. He should drive to Keilor, confront her, and patch things up! Then he remembered he did not have her address. Damn! He would see her tomorrow at work, he told himself, and they would talk. He must not let her leave him. Must not!

He had no idea how long he sat there. Still in his travel suit, he felt grubby in more ways than one. He washed the cup and dragged himself up the stairs. A refreshing shower, he crawled into bed utterly weary, physically and mentally.

Fingers locked behind his head, he stared into the ceiling's dark depths.

Men were not supposed to cry, he told himself, and blinked hard to clear the sting in his eyes.

* * *

He did not sleep much, tossing and turning, his mind too disturbed to relax into slumber. Consequently, morning found him weary and dejected. He even forgot to turn on the TV for his usual dose of news. He had his bad news dished out to him last night.

His phone said to call 321 for voicemail messages. They could be from anybody, but he sort of already knew who called. Two were from Mom, and he deleted both without listening, then did the same with Renzo's call.

Screw them all!

Coffee for breakfast, he booked an Uber to Post. Work can wait. Right now, he had a more pressing thing to do. Tempted to call her, he refrained. Some things were better handled face-to-face. Anyway, if he called, it only gave her time to run somewhere.

Traffic heavy going both ways, the driver eventually stopped beside the National Post headquarters. His Post ID clipped on, he headed for the East Tower elevators. On the ninth floor, he walked to a bullpen and leaned over the divider. A youngster, no tie, looked up from his computer.

"Yes?"

"Where is Leola Lanaro's desk?"

The youngster turned and pointed. "Far corner."

Mason nodded and waded between the bullpens, only to find her workstation empty. A young brunette, cup in hand, ambled toward him.

"Can I help you?"

"I'm looking for Leola."

"Not in. She's been away since yesterday. Back on Monday."

Dejected, he sighed. "Thanks."

That explained the car last night, he told himself as he slowly walked toward the elevators. She must have made more than one trip to her Keilor house to clear away her stuff and chose to wait for him with a final load.

On the drive to GS, he felt drained and empty, as though someone had scooped out all his insides.

His phone rang. Reluctant to make the connection, he did it anyway. "Dad."

"Mason, you left last night without giving anybody a chance to talk."

"What is there to talk about? Mom did all the talking already."

"Don't be a jerk, son. I know you're upset—"

"Upset? You have no idea. We must sort this out sometime, but not now. It's all too raw and I'm not in the mood for it."

"Brianna is beside herself, you know. What you said hurt her deeply."

Mason gave a bitter laugh. "She's hurt? Consequences, Dad. She manipulated Leola and me and it blew up in her face."

"I'm not excusing her—"

"Look, another time, okay?"

"Did you try to talk to Leola?"

"She's gone to her house in Keilor and I don't know where it is. She's not at work either."

"Call her, you idiot!"

"Bye, Dad."

"Wait! Come over tonight."

"You could have stopped Mom, you know," Mason added bitterly and hung up. He stared at the phone, then swore in disgust. He scrolled down the Contacts list and pressed Leola's icon image. After six rings with no answer, he hung up without leaving a message.

Renzo called a few minutes later, but he switched off.

The phone pinged, which meant another message. Certainly the day for it.

Skits!

He flipped open the cover, tapped the icon, and gave a wry smile. Arthur Landry…

You and your girl are cordially invited to attend a gathering on October 8 at The Olive Tree, 19 Park Street, at 7 pm. Apologies for the short notice, but it took time to organize a date acceptable to everyone.

Liam had the bad taste to break his left arm lifting a pencil, and you will be required to sign the cast.

See you there, buddy.

Mason grinned. That's Liam, all right. Always a little awkward. The Olive Tree? A stone's throw from his place. Good timing, because on the twelfth, he and Leola were off to Japan. Then again, perhaps not.

About to reply with a cancel, he decided to wait until he found out where he stood with Leola.

For the rest of the day, he tried to bury himself in the federal study, but his mind refused to focus. He retained everything he read and could recall it later at will, but compared to his personal troubles, the study seemed kind of pointless and silly. Politicians playing games, and Stoner playing his own game with everybody, ready to unload all the blame on Mason and GS if things went south.

His conscience sneered. Feeling sorry for himself, was he? Life no longer a rosy carnival he imagined? Too tough out there, right?

He gazed out the window and reluctantly accepted that he allowed himself to sink into morbid self-pity. Life did not care for his wounded sensibilities. It kept going as it ground him up.

"Suck it up," he muttered.

Fine. He would be a professional until five, then start to feel sorry for himself again. Why shouldn't he? All the manly, unemotional macho crap? Save it for the corny movies.

Ti banac.

Wrapped up for the day, he took his usual tram to Clarendon Street and walked home. He needed a brisk jog around Albert Park Lake, having missed yesterday, and not feeling very bouncy this morning.

Close to his house, he stopped abruptly when he saw the Camry in the spot Leola used. His parents must have seen him walk up and got out of the car. His mom looked absolutely shattered, Dad somber beside her.

"If you came to apologize, it's far too late."

"Son—"

"Go away. I think you've done enough for me already."

"Mason! It's Nada!" his mother cried out.

"What about her?"

"Not out here," his father grated, teeth clenched.

Mason unlocked the front door and disabled the alarm. About to slam it in their face, he sighed and turned. "Come in."

Inside the lounge, he invited them to sit, but both chose to stand. "What about Grandma?"

Nikola's face contorted with emotion he fought to control. "Son, she's gone."

Mason stared at him, not wanting to believe the worst. "What do you mean, gone?"

"She's dead. They found her in bed this afternoon. She took a nap…"

No wonder his father looked distraught.

"Skits!"

As though he did not have enough troubles! Not fair! Now, he had nobody to confide in. Apart from endless days and nights of loneliness, what did life have for him? He had his friends, but some things he could not discuss even with a closest friend.

"I'm sorry, Dad." Shallow, even trite, but what else could he say? He did mean it, though.

Nikola nodded. Brianna did not bother to wipe the tears from her cheeks.

"Where is she?"

"Terniary Aged Care had one of their attending physicians do an examination and issued a death certificate. Natural causes, they said. Old age basically. The body's at Century Funerals around the corner from the care facility."

Somewhat appropriate, Mason thought.

"I want to see her," he declared, still dazed by the news. Nothing appeared real anymore. He spoke to her the other day!

"In the morning. There is nothing you can do now," his father said harshly. Something went out of him then. "These things happen. Death, I mean, but I never thought it would happen to her. She seemed so permanent and indestructible."

Mason knew that mere words meant nothing now. Poets and writers tried, but when reality showed its hard face, the words became pale, insignificant things. He stepped to his father and embraced him.

"I know, Dad."

Nikola clung to him, gave a heavy sigh, cleared his throat, and the Navy commander mask slipped back into place. He glanced at Mom. "There's another reason, perhaps more pressing, why we're here."

His mother took a step toward him. "Mason…Albeit a little late to change how things turned out between you and Leola—"

He waved her to silence. "Not now, Mom!"

"Shut your mouth!" his father commanded. "This must be said, and maybe the only time it can be said. For once in your life, listen!"

"Your father and I had a long talk last night, and he forced me to face up to some hard truths about myself. I did manipulate you and Leola because I thought you were making a mistake about the engagement party. All along, it wasn't about the party, but controlling you two. I did not consider what both of you wanted." She pressed her lips to hold back the spill of emotions that threatened to add to her grief. Mason did not go out of his way to ease things.

"All I can say…Manny, is that I'm sorry. Too little and too late, especially if Leola is gone for good. I don't know what else I can tell you."

"I don't know what else you can say either," Mason said, his voice cold and detached. "You already told Leola and me enough. Great job, Mom."

His mother winced as the words hit her.

"Renzo knows where Leola lives," his father pointed out gently.

Renzo *did* know, Mason acknowledged. He should have thought of that himself.

"You know what to do," Nikola added firmly. "He and I had a long heart-to-heart this morning. He said he called you…Never mind. I think you'll find him equally contrite."

Mason snorted. "That's really great! You guys drove away the only woman I ever loved and all you can say is that you're sorry? Wow. That makes up for everything."

"Do you want her back, or do you want to stew in your misery like a petulant child?" his father snapped.

Mason bit his lip, not sure he wanted to confront Renzo, a man he loathed and who contributed to his anguish. Did pride hold him back?

'*Sort out what you want, moj mali stroj. Leola or revenge,*' the calm voice reverberated in his mind. Would he start to chat with Grandma's ghost now? He would commit himself if that happened.

Deep down, he knew Leola was lost if he waited until Monday, unless she chose to return willingly. Her look last night told him she never would. If he waited, her feelings may set in concrete and both would lose, dooming themselves to a lifetime of regrets and lost chances.

Why did everything have to happen now? Torn with indecision, wanting to see Grandma, he knew he must first resolve things with Leola.

What cost pride?

Brianna touched his arm. "Go to her, my son. Whatever you decide, engagement party or not, I will not say one word. It's always nice to have one, but this will be up to you and Leola. I only want to see you two happy. You waited such a long time to find someone like her. Don't let her get away now. Grandma can wait."

Mason exhaled. "Mom, you're a pain."

She cried with relief and clung to him.

"I'm sorry, sorry," she kept whispering.

"Son, I can drive us to Renzo's place if you like," his father promoted.

"Let's do it," Mason said, relieved to be doing something he felt right.

His mother leaned back and searched his face. "If she doesn't come back, I want you to know that I will never forgive myself."

Sure, that would make up for everything.

Nothing he wanted to add to that, he followed his father to the car and took the back seat with Mom. She reached for his hand and held it firmly. Not totally reconciled or in a particularly friendly frame of mind, he accepted what it cost her to come and bare herself to him. Strong, willful, prideful—it appeared to run in the family—she swallowed all that to admit a serious mistake. Could he do less?

Renzo was equally contrite, eh?

Fucker!

Mason did not care for his contrition as long as he told him where Leola lived.

'Don't be a churlish ass,' Gramps admonished.

Perhaps Gramps had it right.

Honesty, Grandma said. Yeah.

'I'll miss you so much, Grandma.'

As they made their way down Kings Way, Mason had to give his parents credit for coming to see him, grudgingly given. With Grandma gone, they overcame personal grief to try and patch things up with Mason and Leola to secure his future, and perhaps theirs as well.

With Mason's navigation, Dad got there easily enough and parked in the driveway. Everybody got out. Renzo must have heard the car pull in and opened the front door, Martina at his side. He walked briskly toward Mason and held out his hand.

"I'm glad you came. All I can say is that I'm sorry. In the light of what happened, my words may not mean much, but that's all I have to give."

Everybody so sorry suddenly. Mason wanted to punch him in the nose.

Aw, hell!

He swallowed his pique and took the proffered hand. They would not be buddies anytime soon, perhaps never, but he did not seek to marry the guy.

"Tell me where she is, Renzo, and save your apologies."

"I guess I deserve that. I'll take you to her. Follow my car. I called her a few times, but she didn't answer. I even rang Post, but they told me she's on leave. I went to the house then. She may have been there, but she refused to come out, and I couldn't use my passkey. She changed the lock. I don't blame her for being mad at me."

"Let's go," Nikola prompted.

Mason agreed, in no mood to hear Renzo's litany.

An easy drive down Tullamarine Freeway, Renzo took the Keilor exit off-ramp, turned right at the Old Melton Road, and almost immediately took a left onto the parallel slip road. A turn into a court and they were there. The nice brick veneer house and the elegantly landscaped front yard, a contrast of colors in the descending dusk. A light shone from the lounge window, which gave Mason hope. This could still turn into a disaster, but he would face her, no matter what.

He walked quickly to the front door and pressed a red-lit button as the porch light automatically came on. The chime sounded unnaturally loud. For a long time, nothing. Then came the footsteps. She opened the door a crack and peered at him.

"I have nothing to say, Mason," she declared in a brittle, distant voice, and made to shut the door. He pushed it open and stood before her.

"Then I'll do the talking. If it's the engagement party, I don't give a damn. I had a lot of time to think about it, but I won't bore you with psychological claptrap and my desire to spite my parents by not having the party. I'm here to own up, as are my parents and yours. They don't give a crap either. The only thing that's important to me is what you want and what will make you happy. You mean everything to me, Leola. You're my whole life. Without you, I don't want to live. I'm begging you to come back. If you need time to decide, I'll understand, but tell me you're not gone forever."

"You will accept whatever I want?" she asked in a small voice.

"Just say it."

"I fought against Dad too. He always had to be right!" she added with venom. "I simply couldn't take it anymore from anyone. I also hated your dogmatic attitude. I only went along with your decision because in a way it made sense. Inside, I resented it, and I resented you.

"When I married Sandy, we had a simple civil ceremony and a small reception. Young, foolish, I thought I didn't mind, but somewhere inside me, I did. The whole thing felt empty and sterile. With you, I wanted to do it right. You don't know how it is for a woman, but for a girl, a wedding is a dream come true, and you were a dream come true for me. Or so I thought. I know it's tradition and all that, but I did want an engagement party, if only a small one. Then everybody started to work on me and I couldn't take it anymore."

"You should have told me!"

"You had your mind made up."

Mason swallowed and it went down hard. He *had* been dogmatic. "I'm sorry for not understanding, but I want to make it up to you. Please tell me there's still a chance for us."

Her eyes turned misty and her mouth curved down. With a cry, she walked into his arms. "You don't know how hard it's been for me these last few days. Creep," she murmured, head against his chest.

He pulled back, cupped her face between his hands, and kissed the tip of her nose. "Creep and jerk," he agreed, and her cheek dimpled.

"I love you," she murmured, and his heart leaped. The first time she ever said it.

She looked over his shoulder and slowly stepped to her father. He embraced her and held her tight.

"My sweet daughter," he mumbled, voice thick with emotion. Martina smiled and embraced both of them.

Mason heard a sniff and turned to see Mom dab at her eyes. Nikola gave him a solemn nod of approval.

"I'm proud of you, son."

"Thanks, Dad. I'll be around at ten tomorrow."

Leola brushed her eyes, face serene. "Care to come in every-one and celebrate?"

Nikola shook his head. "My satisfaction is seeing you two to-gether again, and you won't get any guff from Brianna anymore." He gave a terse nod and climbed into the car.

"Come here," Brianna murmured and embraced Leola in a hug.

"We'll be going as well," Renzo announced. "You and Mason can celebrate for all of us. I'll arrange a van to come tomorrow morning to take all your stuff back to Mason's place."

"Thanks, Daddy."

Mason took Leola's hand and took her inside, content as he could be under the circumstances.

Chapter Twelve

"Good morning, my sunshine," he whispered tenderly and kissed the top of her head.

"Morning, my shining prince," she murmured and rolled onto her back. "What time is it?"

"Going somewhere?"

"You need to go to work."

"I'll call in sick because I'm sick in love with you. The nice part, there is no cure."

She propped herself on one elbow, eyes unfathomable. "Does that mean you'll be sick for the rest of your life?"

"Delirious. The cure I had on Wednesday night almost proved fatal."

She gurgled. "In that case—"

"In that case, don't cure me."

"Deal," she said and snuggled closer. "I want us to be like this forever."

"Suits me."

"You surprised the hell out of me last night when you showed up at my door. I know how you found out where I lived—Dad—but I never expected you to show up. I thought you hated me for walking out on you."

"When you left, I must admit I had mixed feelings. It took some serious soul-searching before I came to my senses."

"Did you go to Post to look me up?"

"I did. Imagine my chagrin when they told me you took the week off. A dirty trick if you asked me."

"A test of character. You hated my father, but you still went to him to find out where I lived. I always knew you would come after me," she purred.

"Between my love for you and my hate for him, he counted for nothing. I'm glad, though, that everybody discarded playing mind games and finally accepted that what we wanted is the only thing that mattered."

"We had to kick heads to do it, but it worked out in the end," she added with a contented sigh.

A startling and, in many ways, amusing thought popped into his mind. What if Leola deliberately engineered everything? She decided to leave him in order to precipitate a crisis and get everybody together in a desperate effort to resolve a toxic situation. He disliked the implication, but his analytical side could not discount the possibility. What if she did? If she did manipulate everybody, it showed a remarkable level of skill he did not think she had. The depths of a woman's guile should never be underestimated, he reflected wryly—if that is what she indeed did.

Mason steeled himself, forced to face another hard reality. "There's something I must tell you. My grandmother died yesterday."

Leola looked at him and color drained from her face. "Nada? How did it happen?"

"The sands of time ran out for her. I must go."

"I'll go with you!"

"You heard what your father said. He's sending a van to collect your stuff."

"Forget that! I'll call him and arrange a better time. I can always move once we're finished with your grandmother."

"I'd like that," he told her simply. "I know my parents will appreciate seeing you."

"Let's grab breakfast and get going. I can pack some necessities into my car and leave them at your place. When do you want to go and see your parents?"

"I told Dad I'll come over at ten."

She immediately threw back the bed cover. "In that case, let's hustle."

He cracked a smile. "I like it when you take charge."

As Leola threaded her way through congested traffic, he made two calls.

"I'm glad you rang, Mason. Mr. Clarke asked if you could see him at your earliest convenience."

Probably a congratulatory chat for closing the decommissioning project, he mused. "Perhaps on Monday. I'll let you know, Kara. Death in the family."

"Oh, I'm sorry to hear that. I'll let Mr. Clarke know."

Next, Delora.

"Not sure if I'll be in on Monday. Things are fluid right now. Please tell Karter he can still call me if he needs anything."

"Of course. Sorry to hear about your loss."

"Me too."

Leola parked in her spot, the permit tag prominent on the dash. His neighbors get agitated when someone parks illegally and are quick to call a tow truck.

Mason helped carry her things inside. The essentials, she said: toiletries, cosmetics—*how much makeup things does a woman need*, he wondered as she laid everything in the en suite and guest bathroom. Shoes, of course. Enough to open a store. He understood now why Renzo organized a van.

A shower, change of clothing, nothing formal, and they clambered into his Forester.

"I still can't believe she's gone," Leola remarked for the third time. "She seemed so vibrant when I saw her at Mt. Macedon."

"You never know when it will hit," he agreed.

He stopped in the driveway and his mom opened the front door. The shock more or less worn off, his father looked better, but Mason knew the pain lingered for months. It did for him when Gramps died.

Brianna served coffee and tea, and they all seated themselves in the lounge.

"A civil celebrant at Century Funerals will hold the service on Monday at 10:30," Nikola announced. "No crowds, just us. I understand a few people from Terniary will be there." He glanced at Leola. "Your parents said they'll come."

Leola nodded, face grave.

"From there, they'll transport the casket to Altona Memorial Park for cremation," Nikola added.

"I still think it's wrong," Brianna interjected.

"We've been over this countless times," Nikola said wearily. "That's what Dad and Mom wanted. End of argument."

Brianna sniffed loudly to show her displeasure.

Mason did not care one way or another. When his time came, they could put him in a large trash bag and the garbage truck can haul him away with the rest of the rubbish. Not a devout Catholic or anything, Mom nevertheless had her preferences. Tradition again.

"Once done, we'll take the urn to Mt. Macedon," Nikola concluded and gave Mason a probing look. "I know it's your property and everything, and your business what you do with it, but do you intend to sell?"

"I thought about it, Dad, but I like the place, and not only because of all the memories. I don't know about tomorrow, but right now, I have no intention to sell."

His father nodded and that ended the discussion. "Do you want to invite anybody?"

"My friends if they can come. They spent some wonderful days up there even when Gramps lived."

He added a note to his memory machine to call Gabby. The woman had known his grandparents forever and may want to attend the ceremony.

Nikola slapped his thighs and stood. "Right. Let's do this."

At the funeral home, an elderly man ushered them into a cool, austere little chapel where Grandma's casket lay in state. Everyone hung back while Dad paid his respects. Tall, rigid, at parade rest, he gazed at his mother for some time, then stepped back.

When Mason looked at his grandmother's face, a curious sensation rippled through him. A sensation akin to warmth, and his grief washed away. She looked serene, head on a white satin pillow, wearing what he interpreted as a faint smile. Only his imagination perhaps.

She had a hard life in Yugoslavia, maybe even a harder one when she and Milan came to Australia. Not understanding the language, although Milan did, or the system, alone without friends at first, a trained operating theater nurse, it must have been hard to labor in a factory. Hard at first, but they had a good life later.

Mason turned and faced his father. "Dad…"

"She's with Milan, content at last. I couldn't wish more for her."

That summed it up nicely, Mason decided. He would miss her forever, and his father certainly would, the last link with his past severed, but Dad did not want his mother living out dreary days merely to satisfy him with her presence. Mason liked to think she knew he and Leola made up and went to her last rest content. That's what he preferred to think.

Lunch at Mom's place—she insisted—and Mason drove home in peace, Leola beside him, quiet and supportive.

Century Funerals spared Dad a lot of running around by issuing notices to the government for her pension, concession, and health cards. They also squared away things with Terniary Aged Care, lawyers from everyone at their elbow. Dad's lawyer took care of probate proceedings. Not much to be done there as Dad held his mother's power of attorney. Still, it all had to be done. Gods! It took more paperwork to die than get a bank loan.

The rest of Saturday uneventful after Leola sorted everything out to her satisfaction and they became domestic. Brianna invited them to dinner, but Mason declined, figuring Dad needed some quiet time. He accepted a Sunday lunch, a simple affair without Mom's usual trimmings. For dessert, she served something different—cheese and jam *palačinke* crepes. Leola went nuts over them, insisting that Brianna give her the recipe. Not sure whether to cry or groan, Mason expected to eat *palačinke* without end from now on, unless Leola made a walnut roll. He consoled himself with the notion that she would eventually get tired of it and prove to him her culinary skills she bragged about.

On Monday morning, formal and serious, Mason picked up his parents and drove to the funeral home. Evana and some of Grandma's inmates attended, looking solemn. They probably had reason to be solemn, thinking it could be them next. Gabby came and offered her condolences to his parents. His friends came and he introduced them to Leola, assuring them that the dinner outing at The Olive Tree was still on.

Dad gave a simple, brief eulogy, and they all retired to the adjoining reception room for snacks and drinks, while Century Funerals transported the casket to the crematorium. By the time Mason got there, they had the brass urn ready. Dad took it and cradled it in his arms.

No one said much on the way to Mt. Macedon. Mason got the cypress sapling out of the trunk, grabbed a shovel, and followed Dad to the back of the property. Two holes done, they buried the urn and planted the sapling next to its larger companion. Dad again took a moment to confer silently with his departed parents. Back in South Yarra, Mom served a light dinner. Mason went home to close an important chapter in his life and open another.

He woke to a pleasantly mild October morning, his body coursing with energy demanding an outlet. Leola rolled over as he slid out of the bed, fully asleep. He grabbed his running pants and T-shirt and dressed in the bathroom.

Still dark outside, hardier stars glared with brittle indifference. He limbered up to stretch the muscles and began his run. An occasional car whispered along Clarendon Street as he headed toward Albert Park Lake. The city ablaze with lights made for a postcard picture. Only two other joggers ventured on the track ahead of him and they did not meet.

Refreshed, he slowed as he neared his place. The lounge light meant Leola had stirred. He walked into the warm interior to the sound of a bubbling percolator and hissing tea kettle. Dressed in a purple nightgown, she looked up from the kitchen bench.

"Morning. Had a nice run?"

"Great. You should try it sometimes."

"I'll wait until the movie comes out. Bacon and eggs for breakfast?"

"Let me grab a quick shower first."

No TV to disturb their thoughts, they conversed quietly, Mason profoundly happy the two of them were back in normal routine.

"How is your AI thing going?" he asked.

"The last two weeks were a little difficult. A technical problem, but we have it sorted out. You must come down to where we humble slaves work and I'll give you a demo."

He arched his eyebrows. "Humble? You? If what I've seen in the last few days is humble, look out world when you get riled."

Leola laughed. "Creep."

He reached for her hand and kissed it. "Keep saying that. It reminds me to step down and be humble."

She rolled her eyes. "That'll be the day."

Washing up done, hand in hand, they strolled up the narrow street to catch a tram. He left her at the Southern Cross station where she caught a train to Post, and he continued down Collins Street.

Delora, happy mask in place, waved when he walked in. "Such a lovely day, and I'm stuck here," she moaned.

"No justice, and all that," he replied airily.

Her face turned serious. "Sorry to hear about the family death."

He shrugged. "Time ran out for my grandmother. For what it's worth, it came suddenly and she did not suffer."

"That's always good."

"Is Katter in?"

"He asked for you actually."

A knock, a 'Come', and Mason opened the door.

"My condolences for your loss, Mason," Kending said and waved at a chair. "I won't keep you long. Stoner called me on Friday, wondering where GS dug you up. It seems you have a habit of leaving positive impressions with our clients."

Mason smiled. "That's got to be good, no?"

"It is. Do you need some time off with the family?"

"Thanks for asking, Karter, but I'm all right, and I want to keep my mind busy. Mopping around the house won't bring her back."

"Her?"

"My paternal grandmother."

"How old was she?"

"Ninety-four."

Kending nodded. "A long life. Terry Deakin also called on Friday. He wanted to see you. I told him about your family thing and he sent both of us an email with changes and additions to your draft report. I went over it and everything looks good. I also sent you some amendments. Wrap it up and shoot it to him."

"No problem. I need to go to Post to see Raymond Clarke."

"Have you started to pack for your holiday yet?" he added with a grin.

 Mason chuckled. "This weekend. Looking forward to it."

"I could use a holiday myself."

A mug of fresh coffee, Mason powered up the computer and quickly scanned Deakin's PDF attachment and Kending's notes. Nothing urgent that won't keep until later. Too bad no lunch with Leola, but after an absence of several days, he understood she probably had a raft of things on her plate.

He checked for new files from his Canberra team. So far, nothing. A little fire under their public service butts to get them in the groove may get some results. It is not as though they started the project yesterday! He wanted to have something for Stoner before jetting off to Japan.

Done, he dug out his cell. "Hi, Kara. It's Mason."

"Good morning, Mason. A terrific day to be outside."

"I know, and we're punished for being good."

She giggled. "Somebody has to work. What can I do for you?"

"Please check if Mr. Clarke is available."

"A moment…He's free all morning. I mean, he'll be in his office."

"Right. Tell him I'll be around in twenty minutes."

The Uber drive to National Post a crush as always. He climbed out of the car and ambled up the main steps.

Kara waved when he walked toward Clarke's office. All smiles, Head of Parcel pointed at a chair.

"It sucks when someone dies in the family."

"These things happen."

"I understand you and Leola Lanaro are engaged."

"That's right."

"Any grief from parents at either end?"

Mason gave a sour chuckle. "Let me put it this way. Sometimes it would be better if they lived on another continent."

Clarke had a good belly laugh. "Been there. Anyway, I wanted to congratulate you for completing the decommissioning project. Murray Lloyd had nothing but positive feedback from the letters centers about you and Lanaro."

"You should tell her that."

"Lloyd has already done so. How are things with Deakin's program?"

"I'll have a completed draft ready for him this afternoon."

Clarke smiled. "But you can't talk about it. It's all right, Mason. I'll get to see it soon anyway." He stood and offered his hand. "If you get tired of GS, I can use you at Post."

"Thank you for your support and cooperation, Raymond."

"That's what I'm here for."

Back at GS, it did not take Mason long to finish Deakin's report.

Around five, he called it a day.

He stepped off the tram on Clarendon Street and made for the local flower shop. This time, he bought a bunch of white roses surrounded by red blooms. The last time he gave roses to Leola, it did not go down well. He hoped she would be more receptive this time.

He actually whistled as he walked casually toward his—their—house.

Epilog

Mason leaned back, took a sip of cognac—he could still enjoy wine and spirits—and puffed on his King Edward cigar. After all the decades, they still made them. He tried other brands, but always returned to his favorite smoke. Opposite him, Leola, vibrant and seemingly everlasting somehow managed to retain a fine figure, hair considerably grayer with strands of white—his too—concentrated on her book. Every now and then, she pushed up her reading glasses that slipped down her nose. She could have had corrective surgery, but refused. He had given up years ago to change her mind. Stubborn like her dad.

His gaze wandered past the small vegetable garden he and Leola tended out of sheer habit—it did produce an almost endless supply of various lettuce, tomatoes, and herbs—past mature fruit trees whose branches almost overlapped, providing great shade, to the four cypress at the back. In 2053, at eighty-one, his father succumbed to a recurring prostate cancer even modern treatment could no longer check. Mason planted his cypress next to Nada. Two years later, he planted another one for Mom. She could not live without Nikola and welcomed death's embrace.

Leola's parents also passed away years back, they only had each other now.

Life went on.

Sometimes when he felt nostalgic and the memories crowded each other, he would walk to the bottom of the plot, sit on the small, weathered, wooden bench, stare absently at the four cypress, and fix faces to each of them. He hardly ever talked to Gramps anymore, preferring to remember the real man, not something he conjured in his mind. When in such a mood, Leola left him alone most of the time. Sometimes, she chose to sit beside him and they would hold hands and remember together, not saying anything. They had no need for words, completely in tune with each other.

At ninety-three, he did not long for death—geriatric medicine in 2084 had advanced remarkably—but did not fear it either. Still able to do everything he did at seventy, although not with the same energy and stamina, he considered himself ahead of the curve. He and Leola had their two sons and a daughter, nephews and nieces, and great-grandchildren. His Dad passed away satisfied, knowing the Adamov family line remained secure. They all visited, thankfully not too often, and remembered birthdays most of the time. He did not hold it against them when one forgot. At Christmas and Easter or a birthday, it made for quite a crowd at a restaurant able to hold them all.

His youngest son and daughter inherited an eidetic memory, as did some of the grandchildren. In a way, everybody these days had access to unlimited data. Twenty-five years ago, every child at five had a chip implanted that opened a world web of interactive communication. Despite the safeguards, some people resisted, citing conspiracy theories about government manipulation and control. Everything in life had its dark side, he admitted. Successive generations would simply have to deal with it.

He and Leola waited almost eight years until the technology stabilized before they took the implant. If the government did manipulate them, they did it at a level Mason could not detect.

All his three lifetime friends were gone. Four years ago, Arthur Landry the last to go. Lots of years between them, and lots of warm recollections.

Over the last twenty-six years, professional work behind him, financially doing very well from his investments portfolio—he immediately shared out his parents' inheritance, as did Leola— he turned his hand to writing fiction. To his surprise, and the surprise of his agent and publisher, Harper Collins, his books were not blockbusters, they were nevertheless popular. Between projects now, he waited for inspiration, with an occasional dram of something to help lubricate the old brain cells. His mind still sharp as ever, he relied a lot on his eidetic memory and brain chip when creating a new book.

He recalled fondly how he sat in the same chair Gramps used, puff on his cigar—Mason never took to a pipe, although he did give it a go—and regale his youngest son with some of Gramps' stories. The other two were never much into that stuff. Something the kid once said lodged in his mind.

"You should write a book about these stories, Dad."

A few decades later when he ventured to write, the words surfaced, and he went over every story Gramps told him. 'Why not,' he eventually decided. The dark fantasy book turned out to be one of his best sellers.

Two magpies fluttered into the garden and began to peck at the ground. One generation died and another took its place in a never-ending cycle to create progeny. When in one of his philosophical moods, he sometimes questioned the purpose of it all. These days, he spent a lot of time questioning everything. Then again, everybody did, but age gave him a deeper perspective on things.

Overhead, a flying car, a Toyota Empira by the look of it, cast a moving shadow, then disappeared.

Mason still followed local and world politics, but ongoing antics that had not changed in hundreds of years, had long ceased to have any relevance for him. Many things had changed and yet remained the same. Politicians vied for power and schemed how to hold onto it. That is how the world ran. NATO gone and Russia now part of the European Union for the last thirty years. Who could have thought it? China ceased to threaten a Taiwan invasion years ago, the regime turned into a quasi-parliamentary republic. Climate doomsayers still prophesized a global catastrophe yet to eventuate and governments everywhere had grown weary pouring trillions into an effort to green everything. Consistency in change, he mused.

Leola put down her book and peered at him. "Want to go for a walk to Gabby's?"

Dead some eleven years, they, as many others around the neighborhood, still called the place Gabby's. Right up to the end, she hit on him and cackled. Although greatly changed, new dwellings everywhere, Mt. Macedon somehow managed to retain the old, relaxed atmosphere of a country town, which, he supposed, made it so attractive as a retirement destination.

Mason drained his cognac, stubbed out the cigar, and stood. "Why not? While we're still young."

Ti banac.

About the Author

Stefan Vučak has written twenty-one novels, which include eight SF books in the Shadow Gods Saga. His *Cry of Eagles* won the coveted Readers' Favorite silver medal award, and his *All the Evils* was the prestigious Eric Hoffer contest finalist and Readers' Favorite silver medal winner. *Strike for Honor* won the gold medal.

Stefan leveraged a successful career in the Information Technology industry, which took him to the Middle East working on cellphone systems. Writing has been a road of discovery, helping him broaden his horizons. He also spends time as an editor and book reviewer. Stefan lives in Melbourne, Australia.

To learn more about Stefan, visit his:
Website: www.stefanvucak.com
Facebook: www.facebook.com/StefanVucakAuthor

More Books by Stefan Vučak

https://www.stefanvucak.com/Books/

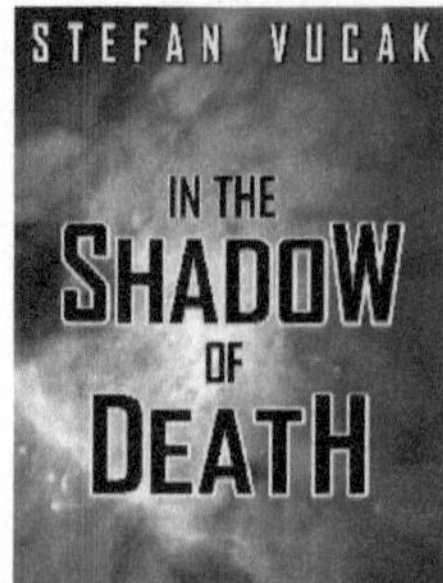

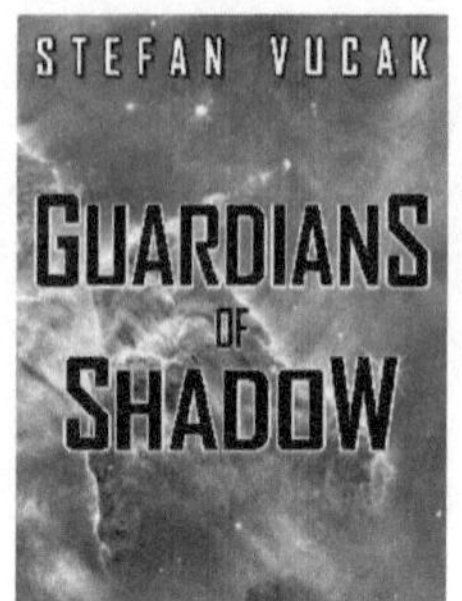

9 780645 116397